CHILL OF BLAME

Genre: Historical Fiction /Action-Adventure

Book Cover Picture design by Nick @ PCPlace

Book Cover insert Michael Whitehead on 'Winifred'

Australian Light Horse Assoc.

i

CHILL of BLAME

Published at Ingram Spark
by Elizabeth Rimmington. 2024.
Queensland. Australia

National Library of Australia
State Library of Queensland

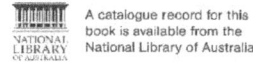 A catalogue record for this book is available from the National Library of Australia

978-0-6454944-1-9 (Print)

978-0-6454944-2-6 (Epub)

≈

Dedication

To the memory of the men of The Australian Light Horse

And their magnificent Waler horses.

And to those who keep their memory alive.

APPRECIATION

To Caroline and Margaret for your invaluable input and support.

To Carol and Nicholas R, your assistance is treasured.

To Michael Whitehead - Australian Light Horse Assoc.

for sharing your formidable knowledge.

To the fellowship and support of good friends within the local writing groups and local library.

Blame and Guilt – two sides of a coin – currency for Tragedy and Heartache.

Chill of Blame

Review by Margaret Bevege Ph D, author and historian.

Elizabeth Rimmington's latest novel 'Chill of Blame' has caught the spirit of rural Australia in World War I convincingly. The two contrasting settings depict the home front and the war front. Basically it is the story of a family coping with anxiety and depression at home while their young men face the demands of desert warfare. There is tragedy and joy and long years of just keeping going.

I found the description of the Light Horse Brigade's activities from basic training, travelling to Egypt and fighting in Palestine engrossing. The detailed descriptions of army life and the famous charge at Beersheba blended history into the novel seamlessly. The wonderful waler horses became characters as the trooper and his mount bonded as one.

Station life on a cattle property in North Queensland rang true. I did struggle at first with a mother's obsession but more than a century ago depressive illness, including post-natal depression, were little understood. Congratulations to Rimmington for focusing on the effects on both the sufferer and those trying to support her.

The characters in 'Chill of Blame' show so many different kinds of strengths and the reader will empathise with them right up to a satisfying conclusion.

CHILL OF BLAME

Written by Elizabeth Rimmington.

CHAPTER ONE

Billy and Joe

Charters Towers January 1917

Held steady with his teeth, Joe Daley's tongue curled at the corner of his lips. The frown of concentration drew his eyebrows together to almost meet the brown wavy forelock fallen over his forehead. His left hand held the writing paper steady. His eyes focussed on the pen and paper in front of him. Even in the dull glow of the hurricane light, his tidy penmanship was displayed clearly to any reader. Billy's chuckle drew Joe's gaze from the note.

"What?" He looked up to see his brother, older by only eleven months, waving their paternal grandfather's old water canteen above his head.

"I knew at Christmas time; Gran would never throw Pops' old canteen out." The musical tone of the water from the sink tap deepened as the water level in the container rose.

"So that's why you were so keen on gifting Pops a new water canteen for Christmas. How long have you been planning this mad escapade?"

"Joe, I told you a few months back, on my birthday, I planned to join the Light Horse to fight in the Middle East. You don't have to come with me if you don't want to." Billy turned off the tap and corked the canteen. He moved over to the pantry cupboard where he pushed aside the stool his grandmother used to access her higher shelves. Billy stretched his long lean frame to drag down the tin of biscuits from the top shelf.

1

"Yeah, but I didn't really think you'd go through with it. Mum will have conniptions. Remember, we're supposed to be eighteen before we join up. You know she has her heart set on your taking over Grandpapa's bank in Townsville."

A wicked grin filled Billy's face. "Mum's got to learn to listen to what she's told. I won't spend my life sitting behind a desk like Grandpapa Dawson. Anyway, that's why we've got those permission notes you've written."

"Running off to join the war is a bit extreme don't you think?"

Billy's long fingers ingrained with stubborn dirt began to transfer biscuits into a smaller tin on the table.

"That's okay, she'll blame you."

"Ain't that a fact. I may have a few pounds weight on you, but you've shot up these past twelve months and I don't tower over you anymore. You're the eldest, shouldn't you be looking after me? Why has she always demanded I look after you?" Joe removed the excess ink from the pen nib by scraping it on the neck of the ink bottle before he laid the pen gently on the table. He screwed the lid back onto the ink bottle, then took up the piece of blotting paper and padded his work.

"It's my sweet charm, brother." As he spoke, Billy lifted the two signed letters lying on the table in front of Joe. He read slowly searching for any mistakes they may have missed during their composition.

"Cunning rat is more like it." Joe looked up to watch Billy as he inspected the two forged letters; one was from William Daley permitting his eighteen-year-old son William (Billy), to join the army. The second letter was from a fictional father William Dawson, permitting his eighteen-year-old son Joseph Daley Dawson, to join the army. "Have I missed anything?"

2

"Nah, looks okay. That was a good idea making out we're not brothers – just in case." Billy reached out and touched Joe's shoulder. "Remember what I'm always telling you. I will do what I think is right for me; not what my mother thinks I should be doing. The guilt is all mine; it has nothing to do with you. Promise me you understand what I'm saying. I don't want to be responsible for your feeling guilty."

Joe stood. He nodded his head and wrapped his arm around Billy's shoulder. He then reached down and took up the forgeries, folded them neatly and slipped them into envelopes before handing them to Billy. He began to read the last note on the table aloud.

Dear Pops and Gran,

Sorry to spring this surprise on you but Joe and I are heading off to join the Australian Light Horse. If we wait to ask our parents the war will be over before we even get there to do our bit.

With love from Billy and Joe.

A frown marred Billy's forehead for a moment. "Why put my name first?"

"Because this is all your idea."

Billy's grin flashed again. "Well, put it on the table beside your bed then." Billy shoved the canteen and tin of biscuits into a small sugar bag. He tied one end of a lanyard around the neck of the bag and the other end at a bottom corner to make a sling to go over his shoulder. The clock in the lounge room chimed 9 p.m. "And don't dawdle. Gran and Pops will be home from the church meeting shortly." Billy laughed as he tidied the kitchen, removing evidence of their skulduggery. "Joe, don't forget to bring the other bag with our things."

In the small bedroom, Joe slipped sideways between the twin beds to place the note at the head of Billy's bed where he hoped it would not be discovered until morning. He fussed over the two arrangements the brothers had built with pillows and blankets covered with a sheet to give the impression of two innocent boys sound asleep. He hung the sling of the second sugar bag over his shoulder and left the door partially open on his way out.

With a fond look about the kitchen, Billy dowsed the light before the brothers jammed their dark felt hats upon their heads and slipped out through the back doorway, shutting the door behind them. They crossed the garden to the side gate leading into the wild shrubbery on the vacant block next door, making their way towards the rising moon.

No sooner had the boys sat themselves down in the shadows at the end of the railway station platform than the mosquitoes arrived in droves. They each rolled down the long sleeves of their shirts and pulled their socks over the leg-ends of their trousers leaving only their face, neck and hands to defend.

"I hope we put the tickets in that bag, Joe. This is not the time to discover we've forgotten the train passes." Billy slapped both sides of his face simultaneously. "Got you, you beggars." Both his hands came away bloodied. "How long is the train going to take? It will be sun-up soon. The thing should have been here hours ago."

Joe smiled in the darkness. Billy's impatience had been a family joke ever since he could remember.

"Billy, it's only a few minutes since the town clock struck midnight. Since when has a train ever been on time anyway?"

At that moment, the rumble of the approaching train brought the brothers to their feet. A strong light in the distance moved closer.

Chill of Blame

Joe opened one eye. Morning sunlight streamed in through the open window along with the occasional embers from the train's engine fire. He shut his eye and repositioned his body to place his back into the sunlight.

"Don't go back to sleep, Joe. We're just coming into Townsville. Don't you want to see the big smoke?"

"I've seen it all before. I'd rather catch a bit of shut-eye."

"How can you sleep? Aren't you excited? Do you want a biscuit? Do you want a drink?"

"I'd prefer a sleep," Joe mumbled.

"No point going back to sleep, we'll be at the station shortly. We'll have to step smartly to catch the southern train once we get there."

Joe groaned. Experience, over nearly sixteen and a half years, had taught Joe when Billy was in a pother about something there would be no placating him.

"Tell me again, Billy, why we are catching the southern train? Can't we just sign up here in Townsville?"

Billy sighed. His fingers combed the thick black curls on his head.

"Think about it, Joe. This will be the first place they'll look for us. Even though Dad won't mind, he'll probably be proud, but you can bet our Mum will be on his back wanting him to contact her family to find us and drag us back home." Billy uncorked the canteen. "Here, drink." He passed it over to his brother. Billy untied the lanyard and reached inside the sugar bag "Want a biscuit? That's why I plan to sign up in Sydney. Even if she telegraphs her uncle in Brisbane, she won't find us."

Joe groaned again as he hauled himself upright. He lifted the canteen and drank.

"I suppose that sounds right."

An assortment of soldiers filled the railway carriage heading south. Most wore uniforms that showed little wear and tear. A group in one corner sang popular songs to the accompaniment of music from a fellow with a mouth organ. Intermittent shouts rose from the other end of the carriage where a two-up game was in full swing. Dotted throughout the seats, men sat upright with their heads drooping as they vainly hoped for a bit of shut-eye. Joe planned to join this lot.

When the train slowed to a stop near the banks of a swollen Burdekin River, nearly everyone swarmed the windows like blowflies around boiling cabbage. The front door of their carriage slammed open and a railway guard entered. Heads turned. Joe and the few still dozing stirred in their seats. They sat up higher to listen.

"Attention everyone! This is as far as this train can go. Flood waters have damaged the rail bridge. A barge has been provided to take everyone across to the Home Hill side where you will be met by another train going south."

The army man with shiny new corporal stripes on his sleeve quipped, "What, the army making sure us blokes don't get extra leave here in the tropical north, then?"

The passengers scrambled to collect their belongings and rushed outside to take in the sight of the swirling floodwaters. Billy and Joe, each with a sugar bag holding their possessions, did not waste time making their way out onto the river bank. The narrow strip of timber pylons holding the railway lines was just visible above the raging waters of the Burdekin River.

A voice rose above the roar of the waters and the gasping comments from the passengers.

"It's on the way down, now. You should have been here yesterday."

Chill of Blame

The shout of a tall slim man with his arm outstretched lifted heads towards the far river bank. Twisted twin ribbons of steel had been snapped and bent by the flow of powerful waters. The heavy timber pylons over there were either missing completely or crushed like splinters.

Joe slipped and slid through the mud to assist a woman holding a heavy basket on one arm while keeping control of the two young children clinging to her skirts with the other. He called for Billy to help.

What appeared to the onlookers to be a very small open vessel struggled to make headway through the strong current as it approached the bank where the passengers stood watching and waiting. Doubt, and not a little apprehension, filled every person within the crowd.

Under the guidance of the vessel captain, the family groups were loaded onto the barge first.

"You blokes and the mail and supplies can wait for the next trip." He called up to where Billy, Joe and the other men from their carriage stood.

Everyone on the bank watched the vessel and its precious cargo as it ploughed through the dirty brown churning waters. Only occasional gasps of horror or relief broke the silence as the vessel slowly fought its way to the other side. A cheer broke out when they saw the passengers climb the distant bank.

Silence returned to the group on the north side of the river while their gazes followed the boat back on its torturous journey to collect them.

Joe and Billy were squashed against the rail at the bow of the vessel as they made the journey over the flooded Burdekin River. Brown waters swirled only inches below their feet. They watched in awe at the sight of tree trunks, broken branches, dislodged dunny houses and other fragile structures that rolled and roiled within the torrent of flood waters. Debris appeared and disappeared at the whim of the raging current. Some collected in huge clumps in the timber pylons of the bridge. A yell and pointing fingers drew everyone's attention to the sight of a weakening beast as it struggled to keep its head above the unforgiving waters.

By the second day of the journey to Brisbane, only a few noisy passengers remained. Snores, grunts and groans from many others replaced the music of the mouth organ. Billy moved on to listen to advice from a soldier in uniform. Joe snuggled his head into a corner, even though not asleep. He pulled his hat down over his eyes. Worry, at the trouble they might have brought upon their Gran and Pops from their mother, weighed heavily on his mind. He knew full well how spiteful she could be when thwarted in her plans – especially when they included the apple of her eye, Billy. Twenty-four hours had passed since their absence would have been discovered. He presumed Pops made the trip out to Billabong Downs to deliver the message. Joe felt sure Pops would not take Gran with him. Pops always tried to shield her from the worst of his Mum's tantrums.

Joe watched the animation on his brother's face. Throughout their lives, Billy's mad escapades tested Joe's patience, loyalty and survival skills. Joe's reflections on childhood memories wandered off unsupervised.

Most of our boyhood adventures weren't serious but one or two were life-threatening – like the time we almost blew ourselves up experimenting with the dynamite sticks Dad used for blowing the stumps in the paddock. For once Billy listened to the voice of reason and restrained from fixing the detonator. Joe's eyes shone at another memory. *I've lost count of the times one or the other of us should have drowned swimming in forbidden waterways. At least the*

8

experiences ensured we both became strong swimmers. A smile twitched Joe's lip. A frown marched across his brow. *This jaunt doesn't appear to present any escape route. I don't really mind going off to war. I planned on doing so anyway when I turned eighteen.* Joe shook his head. He sat up quelling a groan deep inside his throat. He admitted to himself. *It's the cloak-and-dagger way of doing things that sticks in my craw.* The thought of Pops suffering the harsh tongue of their mother burnt inside his belly. *And what about our father? He always treated us fairly and honestly and now we've betrayed him also. He should have been told of our plans. Mum will be sure to make Dad's life a misery.*

Joe directed his mind to the future for Billy and himself. Being a trooper in the Australian Light Horse held an appeal. Pictures of the heroic troopers printed in the daily newspapers sprang to mind. After working on horseback since small children, he knew there was little chance they would be rejected in qualifying – as long as their forged notes passed scrutiny. Based on information obtained from their cadet instructor at college, they had agreed not to let on about their relationship in case officialdom decided, being brothers, they should be separated – hence the altered surname for himself.

As their train carved its route along the coastal flats between the Great Dividing Range and the sparkling Pacific Ocean of Queensland, the flood waters were replaced with drier country around Rockhampton. Several hundred miles further on, market gardens and dairies providing food for the citizens of the towns and city, dotted the countryside.

At Brisbane, the pair almost missed the change-over to the train going to Sydney. Holding their sugar bags close to their bodies and with long strides, their racing feet thudded in unison along the platform in the direction indicated. Heads turned. People looked up to smile at the two young men dressed in crumpled long trousers and blue shirts as they flew by. The train began to shuffle forward just as Billy jumped on board pulling Joe in behind him. Their laughter of relief rang through the half-filled carriage gaining the attention of the other travellers who looked up and grinned in reply. The countryside of New South Wales passed unobserved as both boys slept away their exhaustion and tension of the past few days.

The evening of the following day found Joe and Billy on the outskirts of the army's Holsworthy training camp. They ate the sandwiches purchased before leaving the train station and drank water from their canteen. Sleeping rough in the bushland was not new to the pair but sleep eluded them. Excitement at their success so far and the thrill and anxiety of the unknown ahead kept the brothers talking most of the night.

In the dawn light, Billy and Joe presented themselves at the gate indicated. They were not the only fellows seeking acceptance into the Light Horse ranks. A string of hopeful soldiers-to-be like themselves, some leading their own mounts, ambled their way towards where they were instructed.

A voice roared out over their heads, not unlike the sound of the train on which Billy and Joe had arrived.

"Attention! What a motley crew of riff-raff. Stand up straight! My name is Sergeant Sibley – believe me, you'll remember it. Now snap to it! Get yourselves into two straight lines, if you can count that far." All heads turned towards the voice which erupted from a shortish man who strutted back and forth along the verandah of the Administration building. A slight limp of the right leg did nothing to slow his progress. Not a crease crinkled the man's uniform. Not a smudge marred the brassware on his buttons, buckles or boots. Not a speck of dust tainted the slouch hat with its emu feather oddly tattered against the perfectly brushed fur. He let out a pronounced sigh as the new arrivals, in mismatched clothing and odd head gear shuffled and scuttled into some semblance of order.

"Step forward, those who have worked horses before." His voice rose a fraction. "And I don't mean pony rides at the local show grounds." Sergeant Sibley's voice travelled through the lines of volunteers with little apparent effort.

Billy and Joe stepped out to the front with at least thirty other fellows spanning a wide range of ages, leaving a similar number behind. Like carving up a Christmas turkey, the sergeant separated the proclaimed riders into three groups: very young, mature and those rather past fighting battles. He re-formed these three groups into orderly lines before turning to address those left behind.

"Corporal Linton will now sort the remainder of you." The sergeant pointed to a tall man standing at attention behind him. "Between us, we will see what you're all made of." He nodded to the corporal before instructing his three lines of potential recruits. "Okay, you lot, quick march to the horse yards."

Sergeant Sibley lined the men up outside the fence of a strong set of yards in which several horses chewed on the few blades of grass remaining. A water obstacle had been set up at one end of the yards and a sod-wall jump, about four feet high and nine feet wide, at the other.

Billy turned to Joe and pointed at the horses inside the yards.

"An evil bunch of dog meat, I'd say. Whatever you do, keep away from that piebald with the thin ears. Remember what Dad always said about piebalds, 'Steer clear'."

Joe joined his brother in assessing the horse flesh on display.

"Keep away from that one with the long lower jaw too. He's had plenty of practice pulling on bridle bits, I'd say."

"Quiet in the ranks!" The sergeant's voice roared out over the yards. Even the horses inside the fence lifted their heads with interest.

11

"Each man will have their turn at catching a mount using a bridle. They'll then ride their catch bare-back over the water jump before they go around and over the sod wall." Heads turned towards the men at their sides. Some with anticipation and some with insecurity flagged in the glance of their eyes. Sergeant Sibley took a deep breath as he analysed the group of men in front of him.

After about an hour and a half watching and waiting, Joe lined up for his turn. They had witnessed some successes, some maybes, and some dismal failures.

"Try for the grey at the back," Billy's whisper fell upon Joe's ears as he stepped up to take his turn. Joe felt pleased to hear his brother agree with his own choice. Joe took the bridle handed to him by the sergeant. He gave a strong pull on each of the leather straps and checked all the buckles before gathering the bridle up into his left hand. With a soft footstep and a gentle voice, Joe walked between the restless animals making his way towards the grey horse. The grey made a token gesture of avoidance, but Joe's quick hands soon had the bridle bit in its mouth, the leather strap over the animal's ears, and the chin strap tied, before the gesture became anything more. He grabbed a handful of mane hair at the withers and vaulted up onto the horse's back. Joe stroked the animal's neck and soothed away any further nervousness. The horse and rider moved off at a slow trot to the water jump. Joe halted the horse in front of the jump and sat for a moment sensing the animal's feelings on the obstacle. He turned the horse and walked back to make his approach. It seemed the horse held no fears at the water jump.

Joe approached the sod-wall jump in a similar manner. This time the grey snorted displeasure at the wall at close quarters. Joe walked him back around before making his approach. He felt a slight hesitancy as the grey came closer to the wall. Joe spoke quietly and stroked its neck. At the final moment, sensing the horse's pause, Joe dug in his heels and hissed loudly between the animal's ears. The pair sailed over the jump without any further trouble. Joe felt his body threaten to fall forward as they came in to land. He clamped his legs around the horse and took his bodyweight on his hands against the withers. After releasing the horse and returning the bridle to the Sergeant, Joe felt the man's gaze on his back.

The Sergeant's stare was one of respect and surprise to see such a skill in one so young. He smiled and gestured to the assistant at his side.

"Bring up the Devil next."

When Billy approached the Sergeant, he was surprised when the man handed over the reins of a bridled horse at his side. Billy eyed up the brown horse with a fork-like white blaze down the length of its nose. This would have been the last horse he would have picked if given a choice. Restless feet, three white and one brown, stomped the ground. Whites of the eyes flashed out upon the world. Like an angry cat, the horse's ears lay almost flat against its head.

Only Billy heard the Sergeant's words. "I've been watching you today, Daley. Cocky little rooster ain't yer? This is your ride."

Billy raised his eyebrows. His grin flashed. Billy always liked a challenge. He felt the pull of the reins as he walked the horse away several yards. He stopped and ran his hands down the animal's coat speaking softly. One hand ran down a front leg and lifted the hoof with little objection. He repeated this process on a back leg with no problems.

"Get a move on there, Daley. Yer supposed to be riding the damn horse not making love to the thing."

Billy ignored the man and spent a few more seconds calming the animal before he gathered up the reins and moved to mount. The blaze on the equine nose reached towards the sky as the horse threw its head up. Billy tightened his hold on the shortened reins. Without

13

any further hesitation, Billy vaulted lightly onto the horse's back. He pulled the reins in even tighter as he did so and snapped his legs around the horse's ribs. The horse shuddered and stood still. After several gentle words, Billy moved the horse off to examine the water jump.

Sweat gathered on the horse's coat. Billy felt the tremble run through the large body. He began his approach at a slow canter waiting for the horse to protest but it took the jump – if not cleanly. Billy felt himself scrambling a little to remain seated as the Devil floundered out of the water on the far side. Unfazed, he guided the animal towards the sod-wall jump. Devil's head strained against the bridle. Billy kept him on a short leash before they made a jerky slow trot back to begin the approach. He knew beyond a shadow of doubt the horse had no intention of making the jump over the wall. It became a battle of wills. Billy tucked his toes in behind the front legs. He felt a slight hesitation and responded immediately. Holding the reins tightly in one hand, he slapped his thigh loudly with the other. At the same time, he whistled – a piercing whistle that threatened to burst an eardrum while he heeled his boots into the horse's ribs. Any thought of further hesitation disappeared. Devil flew over the jump smoothly. Billy held his position with every one of his leg muscles clenched tight against the animal's hide.

Billy turned the horse's head and rode back to where the Sergeant stood speechless. Pleasure and disbelief showed in his expression.

"Son, not too many men have been able to ride that horse over the jumps. Congratulations."

Billy's grin flashed as he saluted. "Thanks, Sarge … er Sergeant Sibley."

After a simple lunch of tea and corn beef sandwiches in the Mess Tent, the chosen men lined up outside the Administration building where they were to have their medical examinations. From here, those who passed entered another office to be sworn in as men of the Light Horse.

As he signed the papers with his incorrect age and altered name, Joe felt an uneasiness wash over him. The pen slipped within his sweaty grasp. He felt the guilt written all over his face. Surely someone here would pull him up and question him further, but no one seemed too worried. In minutes, the brothers but not brothers, walked out into the sunshine each holding a carbon copy of their contract and the number of the horse they had been allocated.

Billy nudged Joe's side. "I hope that bloody sarge hasn't given me the horse number of that Devil I rode this morning."

Sergeant Sibley's voice drowned the noise of the chattering newcomers.

"Back into formation. We're off to get you sheep shorn and some decent clothes to put on your backs."

The tables in the Mess Tent now held multiple heaps of uniforms when the recruits, with hair clipped short, ambled in. Once they had been measured and told their size, they moved forward to receive their Australian Imperial Force jacket, trousers, and leather leggings. Each man received an Australian slouch hat and a nine-pouch bandolier.

"Don't go looking at the bandolier like that, Daley. Let's see if you know how to handle a rifle before you get any ammo."

Billy's grin flashed. "She'll be right, Sarge … Sergeant Sibley."

The men all received a canvas haversack to hang over one shoulder. This haversack was to hold their clothing, rations and personal gear. They each received a quart water canteen with a leather strap to be slung from the other shoulder.

What was to become their most treasured possession lay in the brown paper bag inside their hat; a small piece of emu leather hide with its brown-tipped, white feather attached.

Like sheep behind the shepherd, the men followed the sergeant outside to where several stacks of tin tubs reached as high as the roof of a tent.

Sergeant Sibley explained, "Each one of you will collect and keep one of these tin tubs. These tubs have several purposes. Firstly, it will be your cupboard in which to store all your belongings. Hopefully, it will go some way to keeping your tent tidy. Secondly, the tub will be for you to wash your rancid bodies in – assuming you do wash occasionally. I don't want the horses spooked by the stink of you. Thirdly, the tub will be used to wash your clothes in – believe me, you will be washing your clothes regularly."

Each trooper took a tub and loaded their newly acquired possessions inside.

Acres of tents set out in formation over grass nipped short by lines of horses filled Joe's vision as he and several others followed behind the sergeant. Even in the late afternoon, the January heat and humidity pressed down upon the men. Sweat ran down their faces, their arms and their backs. All sides of each tent were rolled up out of the way to enable any breeze within the vicinity to pass over the occupants. Joe caught Billy's eye. Excitement danced in his brother's smile and flashing eyes. So far so good. Tonight, they were to sleep under a Light Horse tent.

"Four men to each fighting section. Each tent holds eight men – two sections. Eight sections will make a troop. Each man will look after his horse tied up on the ground line outside the tent. I'd suggest you make friends with the horse allocated to each of you. You'll find the number you were given branded into the animal's hoof." A sly grin turned on his audience. "You'll find these horses only recently broken in, so don't think you're going to get a lot of sleep tonight."

At a glance, Billy noticed the restlessness of newly broken horses attached to the picket lines.

Joe and Billy found two other men already set up in the tent they were allocated – B532. Both had short-shaven heads and wore singlets and shorts.

A blond giant looked up from the cards in his hand. "G'day. Pick any of the spare swags." He pointed to six thin rolled groundsheets each with a blanket. "These two are our swags." He pointed to the two rolls nearest to himself. "Feet to the middle and heads to the outside. My name's Carter and this bloke who's got the joker in his hand, is Martin."

Martin swore a litany of curses before asking. "How do you know what I got here?"

"Joe," Joe pointed to his chest and then to his sibling. "That's Billy."

Over the evening meal of thin stew and mashed spuds, Joe and Billy met the other four occupants of their tent. Bluey, whose thick mat of ginger hair still covered his scalp despite its earlier trim sat next to Sullivan, a quiet chap with hazel eyes who made Joe think of still waters running deep. Mouse, who equalled the blond giant in size, had a receding hairline. The last man said everyone called him Streak. He claimed to have a pair of very fast legs.

Joe did not miss the glint in his brother's eyes. Billy was never known to be slow to line up for a foot race. Joe envisaged some great entertainment for their new friends in the not-too-distant future.

Later, after their evening meal, as they walked back to their tent through the shadows cast by a half-moon above the gum trees on the ridge, Billy turned to Joe.

"I'm going to talk to our horses before we turn in. You coming?"

17

Each animal stood tethered with head and heel ropes to long picket lines between the rows of tents. In the feeble light of a match, Billy and Joe identified the government broad arrow brand and the initials of the purchasing officer. The pair found the recently reapplied horse's army number tattooed on one of the newly shod hooves.

Billy's fine hands stroked his horse smoothing its bay-coloured coat, its mane and its nervousness. He outlined the white pattern not unlike the shape of a buckle in the middle of its nose.

"I'm going to call this fellow, Buckles. What about you, Joe, have you got a name for your horse yet?"

Joe's horse had a streak of white running down its face from the off-side ear to the middle of its top lip.

"Straps, that's what I'll call him. Just like the first pony I had as a kid. Do you remember him, Billy? He had a brown coat and a strip of white almost identical to this one." A wave of nostalgia broke over Joe. It quickly ebbed away into an acceptance of the choice he had made – after all, there was no other choice.

Joe and Billy gathered up their saddles, saddle blankets, bridles and grooming brushes lying out on the ground in front of their horses and stashed them in the tent beside their swags.

CHAPTER TWO

Billabong Downs

January 1917

The cattle bellowed their protests. They complained at having been pushed from their familiar paddocks to be penned within the confines of the cattle yards. Dust rose into the air along with the wall of noise that followed the riders over the flats. They travelled towards the homestead compound where the late afternoon sun reflected off the iron roofs. A lather of sweat and dust blended into mud on the skins of both the horsemen and their mounts after a day of hard riding.

In the lead rode the three older men. William Daley sat tall on a brown horse in the middle. The road map of lines covering his face echoed the clamouring worries hidden inside. On his right, rode his brother and partner in Billabong Downs, Miles Daley. Both the black horse and its rider hinted at a touch of grey in their manes. The man and horse moved as one. On William's left rode Geoff Bardon. Ever since William and Miles first moved onto the property in 1902, Geoff worked as Head Stockman. Geoff rode with the reins hooked over the knee pad of the saddle. His hands cradled the mouth organ at his lips. His brown horse with the white half-moon between its eyes, flicked its ears in time with the tinny music flowing over its head.

A short distance behind the men, weariness lay heavy upon the faces of Miles's two sons – Doug, at fifteen years of age and Mick, nearly two years younger. Both boys were home from school in Charters Towers for the school holidays.

A screeching wail rose into the air to hang like a cloud over the homestead. The piercing notes drifted out dampening the bellowing of the stock behind them. It instilled fear into the souls of the approaching riders. Geoff slipped the mouth organ into his shirt pocket and took up his reins. The men spurred their mounts into a canter. The boys behind lifted their heads and did the same.

"That's Mabel's scream," William called. The men relaxed and the horses fell back to a trot. "One day that woman will call wolf once too often," William grumbled as they reined in at the stable.

"Leave the horse, William. I'll sort it. Go and see what has Mabel in such a pother." Miles nodded at his older brother.

Geoff Bardon dismounted. He and Miles shared a knowing glance as they watched William making his way towards the ruckus. William's wife was never short on ideas for grabbing attention.

"I'll leave you to it, Miles." Geoff unsaddled, rubbed his horse down and led it to the night paddock.

Miles turned to his offspring. "You lads must be beat. Unsaddle and rub down your horses before letting them out, then head home and clean up. Your mother will have our dinner on the table right about now."

The sound of the boys' voices talking to someone on the path outside the stable lifted Miles's head. His father approached. An involuntary smile flashed at the sight of the old man wearing his hat shoved down tight to cover the bald pate. Only a few straggly snow-white curls showed at the back of his neck.

"Hello, son," the old man smiled a wan smile as he reached through the rails and stroked the nose of Miles's mount.

"Are you the cause of Mabel's hysterics, Pop?"

"I'm afraid so, son. She'll never speak to me again, no doubt."

"What the hell did you say to her?"

"I delivered a message from William's boys. They left us a note sometime during the night."

"Billy and Joe? I thought they were working a few days cleaning up your yard at Charters Towers."

"That's as may be but the rogues have run off to join the army."

"Bloody hell, no wonder Mabel's throwing tantrums." Miles stood with his hand resting on the top of the bridle he was about to remove. "Even though the powers-that-be give out little information to the public, the word doing the rounds is that the war is almost over, why would the lads want to join up now?" Before his father got to offer any comment, Miles's head snapped up again. "Hang on a minute, Billy might be nearly eighteen, but young Joe is not yet seventeen." He removed the bridle, but the horse remained unmoving. Miles wiped the animal's coat with the saddle blanket. He turned to lean against the top rail from where he could better see his father on the other side of the fence.

"You haven't seen the latest papers then, son. I've brought them with me." Mr. Daley senior raised his thick white eyebrows above his fading brown eyes. "Germany looks like it might be winning against the Russians. If that happens, they'll regroup and throw everything at us. We don't have much steam left."

"Thanks, I'll read them after tea tonight." Miles hitched the saddle over his shoulder and delivered it into the shelter of the shed. He called back to his father.

"You slip up to my place, Fran will have tea waiting. I'm sure it'll be only hot tongue and cold shoulder at William's house tonight. Tell Fran I'll be along as soon as I unsaddle William's horse."

As he unsaddled the brown horse, Miles's thoughts were on his two nephews. It had not surprised him to hear Billy had joined up; he'd been threatening to do so since his seventeenth birthday. Joe on the other hand had always been the quieter of the two. He stood every bit as tall as his brother and more solid in his build. No doubt they could both pass themselves off as eighteen at a pinch. Miles knew it was not unknown for lads to fib a bit about their ages to join up. All their lives, Joe seldom left Billy's side. The odd thing about the pair was Joe always seemed to be the one protecting his older brother Billy.

Having heard it all before, Miles did not even glance upwards at the raised voices coming from the house on the west side of the compound. Once at his residence, he rinsed the grime from his face and hands at the hand-operated pump near the back steps. Dust scattered across the landing when he stamped his boots before removing them. As he entered the kitchen, Miles closed the door behind himself choosing to shut out the noise and accepting the heat.

He was pleased to see Fran had the forethought to invite William's two girls over to share the evening meal. At their young ages, Cissy and Maud did not need to hear their mother's rants against their father. Wide brown eyes stared out from the two pale faces sitting near their Aunty Fran. Miles's only daughter, eight-year-old Mavis, clung to the table corner near where he was to sit. She waited to draw security from his solid frame. Pop entertained Doug and Mick at the middle of the table with stories of his younger years. Miles sighed. These meetings were becoming a regular occurrence. He walked over to lay a gentle hand on his Fran's soft hair with the grey streaks glinting in the light of the kerosene lamp at the centre of the table. Love and warmth filled the glance between his brown and her hazel eyes.

"It's all your fault, William Daley. You and that damn father of yours. No doubt he's been romanticizing the war to the boys and now they've left to join the army. I knew it was going to come back and haunt me, letting them stay with your parents."

Chill of Blame

William stood on the opposite side of the kitchen table. His mind refused to absorb the words of this harridan in front of him. He felt confused, yet fascinated, in the change nearly twenty years of married life had wrought upon this woman who once reigned as the belle of the Townsville debutantes. No doubt she was right. It was his fault. How many times as he lay in his lonely bed in the dark of the night had he asked himself if he ever loved the young Mabel or just lusted after her? He should never have married her and dragged her into the loneliness and hardships of cattle station life. William pondered why some women never coped with the isolation while others – just take Miles's wife, Fran, and Geoff's Maggie – they thrived on the challenges faced every day. He raised his head as his own wife's voice threatened to remove the paint from the kitchen walls.

"And that wastrel son of yours, Joe, what on earth did he think he was doing? I bet it was his idea leading my son astray."

William's mouth opened and shut. He sighed. He watched her with a wary eye. The once shiny well-brushed raven locks hung dull about Mabel's face and shoulders. The effects of life's hardships had ploughed deep gouges into her forehead. The dancing eyes, once the colour of precious black opal now filled with hatred and accusations, stared out from the depths of her eye sockets. William's sigh slipped across the table. He doubted very much his father would have romanticized the war to the boys – not after his own experiences during the Boer War. Never once had Mabel accepted any part of the blame for her own choices. He pondered on the disappearance of the smooth rosy cheeks now sagged with lines far beyond what her forty years warranted.

"Don't forget, Joe is your son too. Doesn't it bother you – him going to war also?"

"The government can accept him as my contribution to the war effort." Mabel slapped her hands onto the tabletop.

Hunger and weariness drew William back into the here and now. He shook himself into action and moved over to the bread bin. Gratitude for the thoughtfulness of Fran and Maggie rushed through him like a morning breeze when he found a fresh loaf baked by one or the other's hands – not his wife's, he knew. Seldom did Mabel manage to complete any household chores these days. He lifted the lid on the pot sitting on the edge of the warm stove. Again, he thanked his friends as the appetizing aroma of meat stew greeted him.

"Can I serve you up a plate of stew?" He asked in a quiet voice. This woman, now a stranger in their home, turned and walked out of the kitchen. William sat and began to satisfy the hunger of a hard-working man.

CHAPTER THREE

Holsworthy Training Camp

January 1917

The penetrating notes of reveille dissipated on the already muggy pre-dawn air when Sergeant Sibley appeared like an angry bee buzzing around the lines of tents accommodating the most recent intake of volunteers. His voice whipped the laggards into action. Men stumbled out of the tents, most wearing no more than their shorts. Not one among them had washed their faces, shaved or combed what little hair remained on top of their heads.

Carter, the blond giant, groused long and loud.

"What's biting his bum? Did he wet the bed or something?" His mate, Martin, rubbed sleep from his eyes but quickened his pace to find Billy and Joe standing outside their tent beside Carter. Early starts to the day had been a part of life at Billabong Downs since ever Billy and Joe could remember.

"If you fellows want to be fed this morning, you'll each have to see to your horse first. Can I presume you've had the nous to locate and identify your mount last night? Each horse is to be fed, watered and groomed. All manure is to be removed and carted to the manure heaps over to the west." The sergeant pointed in the general direction for those who may not know their compass points. "Once you have accomplished these chores, you are to become familiar with the ablutions block and make yourselves as human as possible and I mean clean and shaved humans in uniforms. Breakfast is in the Mess

25

Tent between 07.00 hours and 08.00 hours. A minute later and you'll go hungry so I'd suggest you get a move on."

"The beggar doesn't even stop to take a breath." Billy's whisper fell upon Joe's ear but he managed to contain the smile tugging at his lips.

The brothers, but not brothers in this army, made their way over to their horses only a few yards from the tent in which they slept.

"Billy if you get the feed and water for these nags, I'll clean away the shit and give them a brush."

"Suits me, Joe. I'm starving and I don't want to miss out on breakfast."

While Joe found the manure shovels and one of several wheelbarrows stacked neatly two tents along, he noticed Martin and Carter were also working together as a team.

Joe laughed when Carter mumbled quietly after checking about him to ensure Sergeant Sibley wasn't going to jump out from anywhere.

"We've cleared the shit, now what are we going to do with it?" Carter cast another glance around him before he asked, "I wonder where that overworked jack-rabbit sleeps? We could dump the lot in his tent."

"He'd have you slung up before lunchtime." Joe offered his opinion through an amused chuckle.

A corrugated iron-roofed shed with two walls stood beside the Mess Tent. Smoke billowed from a sunken fireplace over which hung a large cauldron, filled with simmering porridge. Steam rose from another large cauldron of cooked porridge set on a stump at the front of the shed. The line of hungry uniformed men stretched out through the dappled shade of a few scant trees nearby. Discomfort at the feel of the rough material of their jackets on their hot skin and pride in their new status shone in equal measure on all faces. A bench at the front of the shed held several stacks of rectangular metal containers for their food and tin pannikins for their drink. In wooden trays on the same table were knives, forks and large spoons. Every man selected one of each as they passed.

Thick porridge served up by one man in khaki landed with a thud into the metal food dish held out by each man in the line. A second man in khaki slopped a dollop of watered-down milk on top of the cereal. Occasionally a dipper of water was emptied into the cauldron as the porridge began to catch on the bottom. Each man required both hands and steady concentration to carry the two rounds of unbuttered bread, the container of porridge, along with a pannikin of weak tea – no milk nor sugar. A knife, fork and spoon stuck out of the men's top shirt pockets.

The men moved into the mess tent to find space on the wooden forms on either side of the long trestle tables. Voices quietened as the hungry men ate. Plates, pannikins and cutlery clattered. The sound of the voices rose as the level in the food plates lowered. Sergeant Sibley banged on a table to demand attention.

"Cut the noise! You sound like a mob of ladies at a church sewing group. When you've finished eating, you each get to wash your plates and cutlery in the tub of hot soapy water on this table. Those eating tools will remain with you throughout your sojourn with the Light Horse Division. Take good care of them. Bring them with you to every meal. No plate, no food – no pannikin, no tea." Sibley strode down the length of the tent before issuing another message. "Before you collect your horses you can line up at the side tables to collect some more of your gear." He pointed to another trestle table loaded high with equipment.

"We've been given a knife and fork. Does this mean we'll get a feed of steak and eggs?" Billy leant over to speak in Joe's ear.

Joe made no reply when he looked up to see the sergeant appear at Billy's shoulder. He frowned a warning to his brother. It was Sibley who answered Billy's question.

"Never seen steak and eggs on the menu, Trooper. It's just as well too. You'll find the knives as blunt as a peeping-tom's nose."

Once more the sergeant lifted his voice to remind the recruits, "Be grateful to our cooks here in the Mess Tent. Once you reach the war zone, you'll each take turns cooking for the other three men in your section. It ain't too hard to heat a can of bully beef and boil a billy of tea to go with the dry biscuits. Of course, while the cook's doing that, the other three blokes will be caring for the cook's horse along with their own."

Each man left the building with their eating gear and a heavy greatcoat which left them shaking their heads as the sweat ran down their backs.

The men grumbled, "Sarge, what use will these be in the desert? I thought it was supposed to be hotter even than here, out there in the desert?"

Sergeant smiled an enigmatic smile. He'd experienced the cold of the desert at night in the wintertime.

Every horseman present recognized the canvas water bucket and nose bag for the horse's drink and grain which was added to the load to carry. They all knew what to do with the spare two horseshoes and nails contained within the leather pouch. Not all were familiar with the heel ropes and the length of picket line but that shortcoming would be short-lived.

As the men hurried across to their tents with Sibley's voice ringing in their ears, Billy asked, "I've heard our dad talking about this Waler breed of horse. They're going to have to be pretty special to carry all this gear we've been given. I hope they'll be able to carry the rider too."

"That's why the saddles are built differently from our usual mustering saddles." It was Sullivan who explained.

Martin coming up on the inside of the group told of his experience with the Waler breed of horses.

"Billy, believe me, these horses are something special. I worked with them for a couple of years out west. They have a strength and stamina you'll be lucky to find in any other horse."

"How did they come about, then?" Joe interrupted.

"They took an English thoroughbred stallion and placed it over a brumby mare. The result has been the best of both worlds. Now they can't breed them fast enough. The Light Horse will take all they can get."

The men wasted little time in tossing all the new equipment into their tin tubs at their individual sleeping spaces in their tents. They hurried outside again to release and saddle their mounts. Sergeant Sibley expected them to be at the parade ground in double quick time.

Within the hour, Sergeant Sibley's mounted amateur troopers, if not amateur equestrians, gathered in disarray in the open field where they were to be introduced to their first day of parade-ground drilling – the Light Horse way. Except for those men who arrived with their own mounts, which the army had since bought for thirty pounds and reallocated back to the original owner, the horses and riders faced a long journey towards bonding. All men and most of the horses were ignorant of the army's way of life.

"Silence in the ranks! You sound like a gaggle of geese! Give me four straight lines behind these men." With Corporal Linton's help, the sergeant lined Billy, Joe, Carter and Martin across in front of him.

Joe grinned when he heard the loud sigh and saw the sergeant's eyes roll in his head as the men and horses tried to generate some organization in their gathering.

With order established, Sergeant Sibley began their first lesson on how to teach their horses to stand still. Within fifteen minutes, his roar, at the sight of wide yawns of some within the troop, stirred those horses already compliant with the new instructions. Those non-compliant horses threw up their heads and made it clear they wished to retreat. In an attempt to calm their mounts, the dismounted riders clung tightly to the reins and saddles. When peace returned, Sergeant Sibley spoke in a moderated tone.

"For the smart alecks who think they know it all. Remember, when the squadron has dismounted to enter armed combat and it's your turn to hold the four horses of your section, you'll be pissed off if your mates haven't trained their horses to stand still when ordered." He cast his glance around the parade ground. "There'll be more than a loud voice going on in any battle. I want to be able to walk up behind your horse and fire a shot over its rump without starting a stampede." Sibley stood staring over the gathering for five minutes. Silence from the men deepened. Even the snorts of horses and hooves stamping or scraping lessened. "These steeds need a bit of exercise more than you fellows need to know how to drill the army way." A murmur of agreement settled rapidly along with the dust. "We're going to hold a three-mile relay race between the sections." Sergeant Sibley's facial expression dampened the cheer threatening to erupt.

"All troopers will remain dismounted unless running their heat in the race. The lesson here is to rest your horse when and where possible."

Billy's eyes lit up. He loved a race – on foot or horse. Either challenge stirred his blood.

Joe chuckled in anticipation. He also craved the chance to test the limits of his mount's capabilities.

Each heat consisted of six sections competing. The four men of each section were placed at marked intervals around the track circling the parade ground. Each of the first six riders held in one hand, a bayonet secured in its leather scabbard, to pass on to the second rider who would pass it on to the third and then onto the fourth rider.

With no warning, the starting whistle echoed across the flat. After a scrambling start, the horses and riders settled into their run. Taunts and yells of encouragement stalked the noise of the whistle. The ground trembled. It thundered with pounding hooves.

As the third rider of his section, in the first heat, Joe took the bayonet clean and set his body, mind and horse towards the fourth rider, Billy. He chanced a glance around to find there was only one rider ahead of him and his horse.

Joe's memory of relay races at college filled him with dread at the thought of being the one to drop the relay baton. He held his breath holding the bayonet scabbard by the blade end, giving Billy every chance of taking the handle with little trouble.

Billy kicked up his horse and reached out for the bayonet. Both animals ran side by side for several feet before Billy's confidence in his hold satisfied him. He inspired his mount to fly.

"Go, Billy," Joe shouted with glee.

It took all Joe's strength to haul his horse in. The animal wanted so much to keep racing with the riders ahead. After the completion of their run, the other competitors in the heat joined him at a canter as they took a shortcut through to the finishing line. Birds burst through the canopy of leaves to escape this intrusion.

Two riders in the race were neck and neck as they approached the finish line. From the distance, Joe recognized Billy's figure stretched out along the horse's neck. He did not need to see his brother's face to know determination hung on every feature. Billy never liked to lose.

The two riders passed the finish line with not a hair to separate them but the lanky lad on Billy's left had dropped his bayonet back along the track and was disqualified.

Sibley lost interest in the relay races once all sections had competed even though the winners of the heats did not get the opportunity to test their mettle against each other.

"Will you schoolgirls stop the whining, these animals need more work. Now fall in, we're going on a twenty-mile horse ride." Mumbles of discontent shuffled along with the horses' feet as they again formed four lines behind Billy, Joe, Carter and Martin. "You might like to remember if you waste too much time here, we may be late for your next meal and the kitchen won't wait for you." The threat to their stomachs' future stirred the troops into action. Horses and men led off behind Corporal Linton, heading southwest.

One day blended into another of parade drills, weapons practice, sentry duties, signals, tactical reconnaissance, survival, horse work and daily chores. Each man and his horse developed an enduring bond based on trust and respect. For the first time in two months, Sergeant Sibley announced a few hours of relaxation. The men were not required to report to the parade ground until it was time to give the horses their afternoon workout. Dressed in shorts and singlets, Billy, Carter and Martin sat in the shade at the edge of their tent playing a game of cards. They had a few pennies riding on the outcome.

Joe watched them for ten minutes before he retrieved his notebook and pencil from his jacket pocket and slipped away. As he disappeared along the line of tents, he heard Carter's voice egging a slower player on.

"Come on, will you?"

Chill of Blame

Joe made his way through the trees to a peaceful part of the small creek where the cool shade and musical waters soothed his soul. He dragged the pencil and notebook from the pocket of his pants before he sat with his back against a tree trunk and began to write. The sandflies were few and far between at this time but an abundance of flies kept his left hand busy while his right hand worked the pencil.

Dear Pops and Gran,

Billy and I want to tell you how sorry we are to leave you and the Towers in such a cloak-and-dagger manner. I'm afraid we were only thinking of ourselves and how to avoid trouble with our Mum and did not really consider the position we were putting you into.

We have joined the Australian Light Horse and if our Sergeant is correct should be on a troop ship heading to Cairo within another month or two. As you know, Billy has been saying for months he planned to join up and it seemed easier for me to go with him. Our Mum would never have let Billy leave, since he is under eighteen. This seemed the only option.

"Just what do you think you're doing, Joe? I knew you were up to no good when I saw you sneaking out of the tent."

At the sound of Billy's angry hiss, Joe's hold on the pencil sent it streaking across the page.

"I'm writing to let Pops know we're all right and what we're up to."

"How bloody smart is that? Once Mum gets word of that letter, how long do you think it will be before she'll have someone in her family dragging us out of here and home by the scruff of our necks?" He poked his forefinger into his brother's shoulder.

"Billy, Pops won't tell her, if I ask him not to."

"Don't be so naïve brother. He might not tell her, but he will tell our dad and you know how Mum can sniff out Dad's secrets before he even knows he has a secret. Pops and Dad don't stand a chance."

"Well, I'm not leaving the Australian shore before we apologize to Pops."

"Bloody hell – well, send it if you must, but NOT until we're on the ship. They collect all the last mail home before we set sail. Will you agree to that?"

Joe sat in silence for a moment as he contemplated all that Billy said. He did have a point.

"Okay Billy, it goes in the last mail home."

Joe watched Billy's back as he strode off. After some moments, he bent and added some words to the bottom of his letter.

Billy asked me not to post this until we are leaving Australia.
From Joe and Billy.

Joe folded the page and slipped it into an envelope which he placed inside the notebook.

CHAPTER FOUR

Billabong Downs

January 1917

During the night, there was little sleep for William. He lay upon his bed on the verandah listening to Mabel inside as she shuffled about banging cupboard doors. Several times she stomped over to the joining doorway near his bed with various demands and rantings.

"Are you awake, William? I want you to take me into town tomorrow. I'll send a wire to my father. He'll find my son and bring him home again, even if you won't. If you and your father and that wastrel son of yours, Joe, had not filled my Billy's head with all this nonsense, he would never have left his mother and run away to fight some silly war."

William refused to answer although the words cut him to the quick. His heart lay heavy in his chest with the knowledge his sons did not trust him with their plans. He drew the feather pillow over his head and attempted in vain to muffle her spiteful words. William acknowledged the boys knew Mabel could weasel any information out of him. They often teased him on that very subject. He presumed this was their reason for not telling him until the deed was done. Towards morning, silence settled upon the house.

As the fresh day lightened in the east, William's head ached – his mind dull. He dragged his legs over the side of the bed and sat considering his options. Miles and Geoff expected him to help with the overdue fence repairs today but the thought of lying back and closing his eyes tempted him. The knowledge that within a few hours Mabel would be at it all again stirred him into action.

He stoked the fire in the woodstove and cooked porridge for his breakfast. William added extra oats for his wife knowing full well by the end of the day it was going to be a solid glug untouched in the bottom of her plate.

At the stables, he found his brown stallion waiting for him in the small yard. With the bridle in one hand and the weight of the saddle on his left shoulder, he strode outside and prepared to mount up. Even the histrionics of his deluded wife could not be allowed to hold back the work of the property. He whistled up the young blue dog.

William swung up into the saddle and moved off past his brother's house. Fran stood in the backyard hanging newly washed sheets on the clothesline.

"Morning, William. I'll drop over shortly to see Mabel's alright." She waved.

William nodded his head and threw a salute. It had been a fortuitous day when his brother broke his leg and ended up as a patient in the Charters Towers Hospital where he met this nurse who became his wife – a caring woman with a patient nature.

Two hundred yards further on, he passed Geoff's home. The former school teacher, Maggie Bardon, waved down to him from the verandah where the younger children on the property sat around a long wooden table, heads bowed over the lessons on their slates. His own two girls, Cissy, thirteen, and Maud eleven-year-old, waved furiously. The girls spent most of the year at their maternal grandparents and went to school in Townsville but they were not expected back there for another two weeks.

The brown curls of Miles's daughter Mavis, bounced on her shoulders as she concentrated on her work. Her two elder brothers, Doug and Mick, now attended school in Charters Towers where they stayed with their paternal grandparents during the school terms. No doubt Miles had them on the sharp end of the fencing wire this morning as they also had two weeks left of the Christmas school holidays.

Maggie's own two boys, Stewie aged eight years and the one named Splinter aged five years, glanced up at the rider passing by. It was doubtful if the hairbrush had disturbed their tousled brown heads this morning. Maggie and Geoff's second born, six-year-old Evie, folded a long blond plait around her small hand as she stared out over the paddocks. Boredom hung like a rain cloud above her head. Evie's considerable intelligence centered on Mother Nature and her animals. Things like reading, writing and arithmetic came a long way down on her list of priorities. William felt a smile struggling to emerge at the sight of the hope in her blue eyes. Hope that her father's boss might invite her along to wherever he was going.

Gradually, as his horse cantered towards the eastern paddock, he felt the tension within him subside. A smile tugged at his lips at the sight of his young blue dog, Nips, backing up when a kangaroo it had been chasing turned for a confrontation. His brown eyes brightened. Even the prickly job of fencing was preferable to spending time in Mabel's company on a day like this one promised to be if he remained at the house. The companionship of Miles and Geoff usually filled his day with humour.

The faint aroma of smoke led William to the banks of the waterhole where the willow trees draped over the cool water. Geoff used a thick twig to stir the billy of tea brewing at the edge of the small campfire when William approached. Miles and his two boys called out a greeting as they tossed sticks of wood onto the timber supply kept at the campsite.

"Hello, William, come to lend a hand, I hope," Miles greeted his brother. "I've barely any skin left on my hands from the barbed spikes of this wire."

"What about us, Dad?" Doug laughed. "Mick and I have no blood left."

"Well, I had hoped you'd have this fence all done when I arrived, and here I find the four of you lazing the day away having a picnic." William smiled, a wan smile, as he removed his pannikin from his saddlebag and tossed it to the head stockman to be filled. He swung his right leg over the horse's rump, removed his left foot from its stirrup and dropped lightly to the ground on both feet. "Do you think we'll knock the work over with five pairs of hands this afternoon?"

"Maybe," Geoff offered the black tea to William. "Here get this into you, it looks like you need it."

"Thanks, Geoff. I see Maggie has the kids lined up doing their lessons this morning. As usual, young Evie looked about as interested as Miles looked when he was dragged off to the opera in Sydney on his honeymoon."

Geoff's laughter was reflected in his sky-blue eyes as he handed over two oatmeal biscuits.

"The lassie hardly remains awake in class but as soon as the missus releases them for the day, she's outside with her dog and horse faster than a rat up a drainpipe."

Miles picked up a biscuit from the tin plate near the fire and settled back with his tea.

"It's a treat to watch her work both her dog and her horse. She'll be a chip off the old block, Geoff."

"Maggie says she's been tailing around after Doug and Mick here making a nuisance of herself. She'll miss them when they go into the town school." Geoff dragged the felt hat from his head and rubbed his fingers through the blond hair encrusted with sweat and dirt.

"Maggie never has any complaints of Evie hanging around the kitchen making a mess trying to help with the cooking, then?" Miles laughed.

"In her dreams – she envies Fran for having your Mavis a willing helper in the kitchen."

Miles downed the last of his tea and spat out stray tea leaves that had filtered through his lips. "We've got enough wire here to finish this last length of the fence. Someone will have to take a trip to town soon to order some more. We just need another electric storm like last week and we'll have the cattle stampeding in all directions."

"Maggie was saying she and Fran plan to deliver Doug and Mick to your Mum's place in town ready for school next week. No doubt they'll place any orders we need." Geoff followed suit with his tea. "Come on then, this ain't getting the baby fed."

"You're right, Geoff. Doug, Mick," Miles called his sons, "can you check the fence along the length of the creek and take note of what needs to be done in that area?"

Yells of glee raced ahead of them across the paddock as the pair galloped off before someone thought to bring them back to help handle the barbed wire.

As William rode beside his two friends towards the work ahead, a flush of gratitude warmed his heart for their tact in not having mentioned Mabel's ruckus last night. The volcano may have subsided but he knew full well it simmered deep down in his gut.

Silence lay over the timber house standing on its stilt posts. The once blue and white painted building held scars where the harsh sunlight and strong dust storms had stripped patches of paintwork. Any signs of previous flower beds were long since buried under weeds trimmed with a sharpened scythe by the roustabout on the property – an elderly man named Gazza who camped in the men's quarters on the edge of the homestead compound.

In the main bedroom upstairs, her dark eyes snapped open. The curtains billowed in the morning breeze. Mabel's gaze took in the sunbeams stumbling across the bedroom floor. How long had it been since her Billy left to go to war without a word: one day, one week, one month? Her eyes fell shut. She pulled the pillow over her head and struggled to gather her thoughts. The high-pitched whine of the nesting hornet inside her skull bored into every corner of her brain. Its muddy nest suffocated much of her memory. The remainder appeared at intervals through a shadowy haze.

Mabel struggled to retrieve her recollections but only brief glimpses appeared before they slipped away like the tide through her fingers. A busy Friday morning in the streets of Townsville – her mother's usual shopping day. An occasional motorcar engine growled within the clatter of horses' hooves. The wheels of spring carts, family carriages and heavy drays rumbled along the street. Drivers geed-up or called, 'Whoa,' to the horses hauling people and produce to their destination. Mabel felt again the swish of the ladies' long skirts close to her young ears as she clung tightly to her mother's hand. She recalled the street smells filling her nostrils: manure, urine, leather, dust, perfumes, unwashed bodies and flowers at flower stalls. Most of all, she smelt again the perfume of lilacs on the small handkerchief held to her nose. On quieter streets, she relived the glow of admiration from her mother's friends when they greeted each other.

"Oh, Mrs. Dawson, young Mabel is a picture to behold."

"Have you ever seen such a perfect skin? It has the glow of a pearl shell."

"Wondrous eyes, the colour of a black opal."

Chill of Blame

"Oh, I have never seen such glorious hair."

How could she ever forget her father's loving smile of surrender when he capitulated on everything she ever wanted – his repetitive but empty warnings?

"Now, young lady, you cannot have everything you want, you know. You have three brothers with whom you must share, remember."

In Mabel's mind, a quietness descended as the scene transformed. The gasps throughout the ballroom as the debutante in white stood on the threshold. The professionally cut gown highlighted her hourglass figure. Lustrous hair pinned high on the back of her head framed the perfection of a face enhanced with little makeup.

Mabel threw the pillow aside. She sat up. A muffled screech filled the bedroom in the here and now when she caught the vision within the dressing table mirror. A haggard face peered back, the hair askew and skin texture lost in the lines of a sun-hardened face and rippled lips turned down at the corners.

Swirling shadows swallowed her memories. The hornet's drone increased. Rough and aging hands pressed over her ears to stifle the noise. Darkness washed over Mabel. She fell back and lay prostrate in an untidy heap amongst the sheets.

"Damn, what's that woman up to now?"

Miles and Geoff looked up on hearing William's curse. A stream of rising dust ahead drew their gaze. They recognized Maggie riding fast towards them on her chestnut horse. Geoff spurred his mount into a gallop to meet his wife. William and Miles kept pace with him. Thick dust billowed out behind them.

Geoff held his arms about Maggie's shoulders where she sat leaning in the saddle to receive the comfort.

"It's Mabel, Mister Daley," She swallowed. Tears threatened to fall. "She wandered off. Fran and I found her down past Lorikeet Creek. She refuses to come back home. Fran is still with her. I must get back because I have left Cissy in charge of the children."

William shook his head. "I'm so sorry, Maggie. I'll go and sort Mabel out."

Doug and Mick joined their father. "Can we help, Dad?"

"No, boys, this is something your Uncle William needs to look after."

As he approached Lorikeet Creek, William felt the tears spring to his eyes when he saw Fran leading her horse, plodding along through the thick dust. Mabel sat drooped in the saddle. She might make him as mad as a tormented wasp, but his love for Mabel remained deep down. The idea of her being lost in the bush was not something he wanted to think about. He swallowed several times before he felt he could speak.

"Thank you, Fran. I'm sorry you have been put to all this trouble."

Fran smiled but before she could speak, Mabel made her presence felt.

"William, I am not going back to the homestead. I am going to my father's place in Townsville. He will bring my Billy home where he belongs."

Fran caught William's gaze. She rolled her eyes.

"I'm sorry, William, that is all I have been able to get out of her."

CHAPTER FIVE

Last Weeks in Training

February – March 1917

Sergeant Sibley strutted up and down behind the line of soldiers stretched out face down on the ground with their .303 Lee Enfield rifles aimed towards the targets at the other end of the field. He did not seem to interrupt the litany of instructions in the care and safety of the weapons they held, to take a breath.

Billy's grin lifted over the stock of his rifle to look at his brother.

He whispered, "The jack-rabbit ain't game to walk across the front of our line of weapons."

Joe dropped his gaze to the rifle barrel under his nose at the sight of Sergeant Sibley's appearance above Billy's left hip.

"You're damn right I'm not foolish enough to walk in front of you lot with loaded weapons in your hands. I've taken all the weapon fire I want from the Turks. I don't relish the thought of having men on my own side shooting holes in me."

Billy rolled over in disbelief. "How'd you get here so quick?"

"Always observe the opposition, lad, if you want to keep ahead of him."

Barely had the sergeant moved out of hearing when Billy cursed.

"He creeps around like a bloody dingo."

Standing one hundred yards at the back of the riflemen and on the other side of a fence, several soldiers each held a group of four horses. When the call to "Fire" reverberated across the flats along with the immediate gunfire following, most of the horses threw up their heads, pawed at the ground, snorted, and dragged back on the reins. Curses came loud and fast as each holder fought to maintain order. Two mounts escaped – galloping off, away from the racket.

Sibley called to the riflemen. "Whoever owns those two horses better go fetch them and work a bit more on their tolerance of noise. You'd be walking back to camp wounded or not, if stuck out in the Sinai Desert."

A new lineup of riflemen and horse holders took up their positions. By the time all the troops had proved themselves with a rifle, horses were scattered throughout the large paddock. Men trekked through the long grass shaded by a few grey gum trees. They clambered over rocky ridges and dry gutters, searching for their mounts.

In the Mess Tent that evening, Sergeant Sibley's sparkling blue eyes and frequent smiles gave the impression he was rather pleased with his troopers' outing on the firing range. He was heard to comment to Corporal Linton.

"These blokes might look like refugees from a hobo's camp, but they mostly know how to fire a rifle. They might show the enemy a thing or two. They'll want to quieten their horses down a bit though or they'll be taking lots of long dry hikes."

"So, Sarge, you'll be issuing them their ammo then?"

"Yeah, Corporal, the usual: ten rounds of ammo with the rifle and fifty rounds in their pouches."

Linton nodded before he asked. "Do you plan on having them shooting while mounted tomorrow?"

"May as well. Get the worst over in one hit. Let's see what issues we need to deal with."

Later, with light rain falling on the canvas of their tents and running in small waterfalls over the edges, every man cleaned, polished and oiled his rifle. With equal energy and detail, they cleaned and sharpened the bayonet too. Each man attended his mount, weapons and ammunition in a way that appeared contradictory to the lack of attention they gave to things like official orders and their code of dress.

As the trumpeter heralded time for lights out, Billy lay with his eyes wide open. Excitement charged every nerve in his body. The heart pounded in his chest. The blood roared in his ears. He listened to the soft snuffles of Joe's breathing from the groundsheet nearby. The temptation to wake his brother nearly won out, but for once he gave a thought to Joe's weariness and need for sleep. When the rain ceased and the clouds thinned, he turned over to stare out into the moonlight casting shadows along the line of horses, some with restless feet.

His thoughts drifted to the challenge of a footrace presented to him by Streak at the evening meal table. Billy grinned at the thought of the fellow's attempt to bluff him by standing over him as he sat at the table. The man's advantage of height did nothing to shake Billy's confidence. Many runners taller than himself had eaten his dust. There were times he surprised himself with his speed.

The time was set for the day after tomorrow at first light. They were to run the seven hundred yards from one end of the parade ground to the other. Streak offered a bet of ten pounds. At this thought, Billy reached up and scratched his thickening scalp of hair. That could be a problem.

When told of the challenge while they settled their horses for the night, Joe had brought him crashing down to earth.

"Billy, what on earth induced you to make a ten-pound bet with Streak? You don't have ten pounds. Even if we both dobbed in what we owned, we'd never reach ten pounds."

Billy just shrugged his shoulders. "Well, I'd better make sure I damn well win." The smile that accompanied this remark had long since died. Reality kept him awake.

In the office at the back of the administration building, it took some moments for their eyes to adjust to the moonlight, as it replaced the quashed lights. Sergeant Sibley and Corporal Linton were in deep discussion about planning for the arrival of their superiors in three days' time.

"Tomorrow, I want you to inspect the troopers and their tents. The Major will be accompanied by a veterinarian and a couple of farriers so make sure the horses and surrounds are up to scratch."

Linton grinned. "I have little doubt the horses and their weapons will be in top condition, but those blokes and their tents will be another matter."

"Do your best." The sergeant laughed as pushed his chair under a desk now cleared and cleaned. "Oh, before we call it a night, I wanted to ask if you've heard the gossip of a foot race planned between the Rooster and the tall fellow in the same tent. The one they call Streak?"

"You mean that Daley chap? I'd be deaf and blind if I hadn't, Sarge. They've got a ten-pound bet on it. Everyone's talking."

Sibley tapped his fingers along the top of the chair back.

"I'd doubt if the Rooster has ten pence to his name let alone ten pounds. No doubt the little beggar will have a good chance of winning, but we don't want bad feelings in the camp if he is outdone." He turned and walked through the open doorway. "I have an idea I'll sleep on tonight. I'll let you know in the morning what I'm going to do about that."

Chill of Blame

At daylight, the noise level in the Mess Tent settled to a dull murmur of voices and scraping of spoons when the sergeant's voice lifted everyone's head.

"Listen up, troopers." Sibley banged the table with a clean soup ladle four times. "I hear we have a foot race in the planning. I also hear there is a sizeable purse for the winner. Well, you can forget it. We cannot be seen to encourage gambling here in the camp."

All eyes swung to the speaker. Jaws dropped. Groans filled the tent and moved outside on the light morning breeze. So dismayed were some of the men that their porridge went down the wrong way. Harsh coughing followed the groans across the tables.

The sergeant continued, "We do however encourage our men to push themselves to the limits of their physical capabilities. Competitive running and similar events build character and stamina. There will be an official footrace. It will be the day after tomorrow. The original runners will take part AND any others who feel they'd like to test their speed may also compete. Give your names to Corporal Linton if you wish to try." An explosion of voices responded. The ladle sounded again. "Oh, and did I mention there'll be an army prize on offer."

A smart aleck from the tables called, "What'll that be, Sarge, extra parade drills all round?" Laughter erupted from all corners.

Sibley let the laughter wash over him before he spoke again.

"No, lad, that will be your prize for interrupting me." More laughter followed. The sergeant took a deep breath. "The prize for the fleetest of foot here will be a dozen of our own Tooth Company Brewers Draft Malt Ale. Of course, he will be expected to share with all other contestants."

Feet thumped on the ground. Spoons drum-rolled on the wooden trestle tables.

Once more Sergeant Sibley stood quietly letting the enthusiasm settle.

"Now for the bad news." Moans came long and loud. They were ignored. "Today, Corporal Linton has been charged with conducting an inspection of all living conditions – humans and horses. When he has finished you will all know what standards we expect every day of the week." Soft grumbles rose in the hot air. These were ignored. "Did I mention we are expecting visitors the day after tomorrow? The top brass will be witness to the foot race and you will also have the pleasure of their company through your tents and picket lines." Eyes widened and jaws dropped but a hushed silence remained. "Your skills and those of your mounts on the parade ground and firing range will be part of their entertainment." This time the rumbling voices of complaint and horror came hesitantly at first, before it rose in a crescendo restrained by the canvas above, but the sergeant had slipped away. Corporal Linton remained to direct traffic.

"Come on, you blokes. Get that tucker down your necks and get back to your tents. I'll be over to inspect everything at 08.30." Spoons worked quick time. The scrape of boots as the men climbed over the wooden forms followed by the rattle of their eating gear in the tubs of soapy water overtook the voices of question and complaint.

The sun hung low in the sky when Sergeant Sibley and Corporal Linton had the chance to catch up on the outcome of the inspections earlier in the day.

"It was bad, Sarge, but not as bad as I feared. It was as expected. The horses and weapons could pass any inspection but tidiness and cleanliness are sadly lacking in their living conditions. I'd like to take another run at them tomorrow."

"Thanks, Corporal, go for it. And push cleanliness. Explain to them when they're fighting overseas it will be personal cleanliness that may keep them free from disease, just as much as knowing how to handle their horses and weapons."

"Yes, Sarge."

"There was something else I want you to think about too. The latest news on the arrival of our transport to Alexandria is set at about three weeks. Before that date, I must complete a report on my recommendations for those men who may be promotional material. Can we talk about that after the brass leave on Thursday?"

"Of course."

"Come on then, Corporal, it's time we wet our whistles and the canteen will close in half an hour."

Clouds hung heavy in the sky above. Troopers sat tall in the saddles. They marched quick time, slow time, forwards, sideways and diagonal. They turned, they wheeled on a fixed pivot, they wheeled on a moving pivot. They changed direction and reformed into different groupings. Mounted on well-groomed horses at the front sat Sergeant Sibley's superiors whom he called The Brass – although never to their faces – a Major Dickson and a Captain Shaw. Their bland, almost bored expressions, never revealed if they noticed the bumbling within the ranks but Sibley knew full well these men never missed a trick. His heart drooped.

When the drill exercises ceased and the dust settled, the sergeant led the guests to where the foot races were to be held. The Major and the Captain were settled in at the finish line talking in desultory tones between themselves. They threw an occasional comment to Sibley like one might throw a dog a bone. Sergeant Sibley's stomach churned. He suffered this home-bound service knowing his wounded body could not return to the battlefront. He usually accepted his lot but this chore of nursing the brass gave him the shits – literally. He clenched his gut hard. At this moment, he envied Corporal Linton who had the duty of starting the runners, seven hundred yards away at the other end of the track.

Billy's grin and sparkling eyes lit up his face. He held out his right hand to his main rival. Streak shook hands but the man's face remained impassive. Four other men lined up at the starting line with Billy and Streak. Billy noticed they all stood at least a head above himself. Two of the runners, Jack and Neville, must have been in their mid to late twenties. The last two, Squiz and Curley, were young fellows not much older than himself.

"Line up!" Corporal Linton called. With little fuss, the six men moved over to stand with a toe on the line drawn in the dirt. "On your marks." BANG. The shot from the corporal's revolver surprised Billy and young Squiz for a second. Billy was last off the line but had passed Squiz within ten yards. He settled into a steady pace just behind Curley, Neville and Jack who were closing up together. His eyes barely left the back of Streak's head who ran about eight yards ahead of these three. At the one-hundred-yard mark, Streak pulled away. Billy increased his pace to overtake Neville and Jack. Curley maintained his distance of about five yards behind Streak, which suited Billy fine. He ran just behind Curley's right shoulder.

The positions of the men remained unchanged until the five-hundred-yard mark. Streak increased his speed pulling away from Curley whom Billy could hear struggling a little for breath. Billy slipped past the heavy breather and closed the gap to a few yards between Streak and himself. The leader must have heard the running feet behind his right ear. The tall skinny man could not help but look behind losing a precious split second. A split second which Billy took advantage of.

At the six-hundred-yard mark, Billy ran two feet away from Streak. He was pleased to hear the man struggling to contain his breathing rhythm, yet Billy was not fool enough to think his rival was done. Someone with the confidence of Streak did not bet ten pounds on a race he thought he could not win. Billy concentrated on his own race. He breathed easily and his legs felt good under him. His balance and tempo remained smooth. He let his mind drift off to Billabong Downs where he frequently ran the two miles from the swimming hole to the house when he was late returning for afternoon chores.

At the six-hundred-and-fifty-yard mark, Streak made his move, but Billy was prepared. He pushed down the pain and lifted his efforts to a new level. Streak once again could not help but sneak a peek at the competition. It was the split-second Billy required to pass his opponent and move to the front by a foot – twelve inches; not far, but it was all he needed to win the race.

As the virgin picket-line rope hit his chest, Billy felt the satisfaction wash over him like cool water on burnt skin. He heard the oft-repeated words of his Pops.

"Billy, it's not only strong legs and deep lungs that win a race, lad. Using your mind to analyse the race and competitors helps too. Never forget that boy."

A random thought surprised him. He was glad Joe had not chosen to join the competition. He knew full well Joe might be the one person who could beat him in a serious race.

Snappy salutes bid the senior officers and the accompanying three farriers farewell as they cantered down the front driveway into the late afternoon sun. Sibley felt the tension fall away from himself in a rush like rainwater down a drain pipe. He snorted a big breath before he turned to the corporal at his side.

"Come on, Corporal, this deserves a stiff snifter before we talk about those promotional recommendations."

Linton smiled. He knew about the bottle of whiskey hidden in the back of the sergeant's desk drawer. At least he had good news to report from the farriers who had inspected the men's horses during the day.

Sergeant Sibley poured generous nips of whiskey into the two tin mugs on his desk. He handed one over to the Corporal.

"Thank goodness that's over for the day. Hopefully, we won't see The Brass back over our way before we're ready to load this lot onto the ship."

Corporal Linton sipped at his mug as he stood at the window staring out into the falling dusk. He smiled.

"Did I tell you I received word from the weapon's training ground today? They want our lot over there for training with their machine-guns in the morning. They've now got a Vickers, a Lewis and one of the new Hotchkiss machine-guns to play with. I said I'd bring them over right after breakfast."

"Make sure they ride their horses over there. It'll give the animals a first-hand experience with the noise of the weaponry. The men can also get into the habit of taking turns of one man in each section holding the four mounts while the other three of the section work the guns." Sibley put his empty mug on the desk. "Will you have time to take them over there?"

"Yeah, I offered to pick them up and bring them back, but the Lieutenant said he'd send a corporal from there back with our men." Linton sipped slowly and swallowed. "Do you ever feel like a nursemaid, Sarge?" Linton ran his fingers through his thinning grey hair and dragged his hand down the lines of his face. "I curse every day this damn bullet they say lies next to my spine. I just wish it had been a direct hit into my heart."

Sergeant Sibley sighed. "I curse my damaged body often; I can tell you, Corporal. But, when I load a mob of these fellas onto a ship bound for the battlefront, I feel some satisfaction knowing they'll heap revenge onto the enemy for myself and my mates. I make sure I've done the best job I can to enable them to do just that." Sibley shook himself. "Well, come on, fetch the lists of our latest secret weapons and we'll talk about who we think may be potential promotional material."

Within an hour, pencil marks graffitied Sibley's copy of the list. Linton wrote their final comments against the names on his copy of the list. They had reached the names of the men in tent B532. Pencil marks slashed through six of the names leaving only two, William Daley and Joseph Dawson unscathed.

"Daley's the one I call Rooster, isn't he?"

"Yes, Sarge, and Dawson is his mate."

"They're the youngest of the lot of them in that tent, aren't they?"

"Yes, Sarge, but both of them run rings around nearly everyone within the camp with their horse and rifle skills. As far as I know, they're off stations up north and went to the same boarding school."

"I wonder why they came all the way down here to join up and not somewhere in the north?"

"Who knows, and I don't ever ask." Linton looked up from his paper. "You know, Sarge, the Rooster's a popular chap amongst the men. There's not a man in camp who wouldn't follow him to hell and back. He might make a good leader one day."

"I know what you mean. He's as brave as they come." Sibley chewed on the end of his pencil. "There's something about the Rooster that concerns me. I feel he tends to go off half-cocked at times." Sibley stood and stretched his legs and his back before sitting down again. "That mate of his, Joe Dawson, has the same skillset and a steady nature to go with it all. I like that in an officer."

"As you know full well, sometimes in battle we need someone who can make snap decisions and not overthink things too much, Sarge."

"Okay, you're right. There's always that. How about we give them both a recommendation with those additional comments?"

"A done deal." Corporal Linton sighed as the trumpeter signalled lights out.

"Let's leave it at that for the night. We'll get back to it in the morning while the men are off learning about the machine-guns."

CHAPTER SIX

Billabong Downs

February 1917

The halo of white hair and beard caught one's eye before the dust ingrained lines on the sun-tanned face of Gazza, the roustabout on Billabong Downs. In fact, the title may have been very much an exaggeration given the man's age and remaining abilities. Gazza milked two cows each morning supplying the fruits of his labour to the three housewives on the property. Using a scythe, honed to an edge that could split a hair, Gazza kept the grass under some sort of control around the houses. Occasionally he took his treasured rifle and shot food for the dogs. William, Miles and Geoff often pondered on how he never seemed to miss a shot considering his rheumy eyes defied any possibility of accurate vision.

Fran ensured Gazza received a cooked meal every day, slept in a clean bed and wore reasonably clean clothes. He lived in the men's quarters on the edge of the homestead compound.

Today Gazza joined the small group heading into town. He and Geoff prepared the horses and dray. Fran and Maggie gathered the children together. Doug and Mick were to return to Charters Towers for the new term of school. They roughhoused each other vying for who was going to drive the horses. Their mother quickly solved the problem.

"Gazza will take the reins this morning."

Moans of complaint were forthcoming, but very softly.

"Can I hear you grumbling?" Fran asked. Her eyes smiled.

"No, Mum," the pair replied in unison.

Mick took the chance to argue. "Augh, Mum, you do realize this will be the last time we get to drive the dray until the end of this next term."

"If you continue to argue with me, it might be the last time for much longer."

Mick bit his lip but not for long when he looked up to see their father leading their saddled horses.

"Come on, you two. You'll never fit in there. Here, you can be the outriders for this lot."

William was there to see Mabel settled on the wooden seat on one side of the dray. He tucked the cushion under her bottom. A fleeting frown of worry appeared across his forehead.

"Now you behave, Mabel. Fran and Maggie will need a hand with everything that has to be done."

Mabel swung her head in the opposite direction.

William turned to his sister-in-law. "Fran, are sure you'll manage with Mabel along? You have a lot to do in town. Mum and Dad will give you ladies the spare beds in the house to sleep in tonight. The boys can camp outside with Gazza."

Maggie settled Maud and Cissy with their two suitcases behind the driver's seat. They were to meet their maternal grandparents at the railway station before travelling with them back to Townsville where they attended school.

The three smallest children, Stewie, Evie and Splinter, were placed on the seat beside their mother, Maggie.

Fran with Mavis tucked in by her side, settled on the seat beside Mabel.

Gazza cracked the whip and stirred the horses into a brisk walk.

Shouted wishes for a good journey and a safe return filled the air. Everyone waved their farewells except Mabel who sat with her perfumed handkerchief held against her nose while the other hand secured her hat upon her head.

Pain lay upon William's face when his wife refused to look back at him.

Miles called to his two boys now mounted on their fractious horses.

"After that rain we had last night, you'd better ride ahead and check Lorikeet Creek isn't running too deep. Then ride back and let Gazza know." He waved them off.

William looked up at his brother. "Did I miss something? There wasn't enough rain last night to deepen the creek, Miles."

"No, William, there wasn't, but those two are chewing at the bit and their horses are just as flighty. Hopefully, the gallop will settle them all down."

After a stop for lunch at Half-way Creek, it was nudging three o'clock when they arrived at Charters Towers. To avoid the February heat nestled between the buildings of the main street, Gazza guided the horses around the back streets to park in front of the railway station. He placed the whip handle in its holder and secured the brake tie before climbing down from the driver's seat.

Fran reached over and took Mabel's hand gently in her own.

"Mabel, your parents should be at the station now. Will you walk the girls in to meet them or would you like me to come with you?"

Mabel looked up as if surprised to find them in the township. She snatched her hand back and spoke in the haughty voice only Mabel could master.

"I will take my girls to the station myself, thank you." Trembling hands smoothed the hair back under her hat. Mabel stood a little unsteady on her feet. She shuffled her way to the back of the dray where Gazza stood in silence waiting to help her to the ground.

"We'll come right back to pick you up after I finish with the orders," Fran spoke to Mabel's stiff straight back.

Fran hugged the two girls in turn.

"Bye, Cissy. Bye, Maud. Say hello to your grandparents for me, will you? I'll have to go now to the produce agents and order the wire your father wants for those fences before the shops shut."

"Yes, Aunt Fran. Bye, Aunt Fran," they replied in unison as they jumped to the ground behind their mother. Gazza reached in and lifted down the suitcases. The pair went to follow in the direction their mother had taken. Mabel was seen disappearing through the front doors of the station.

Fran and Maggie exchanged glances.

"Do you think I should go after them, Fran? Mabel does not seem to even know the girls are there."

Fran chewed her bottom lip. She turned to her older son.

"Doug, let Mick hold the reins of your horse while you run in and check Mr. and Mrs. Dawson are inside and make sure the girls and Aunt Mabel meet up with them, please?" As Doug dismounted, she added, "Try not to let them see you are watching."

"Yes, Ma," he replied as he handed over his reins to his brother then turned and left at a trot to follow his cousins.

Fran turned to her friend and spoke quietly.

"I do hope I have done the right thing letting Mabel go in there on her own."

"Fran, surely there is nothing to worry about. As you said, Mr. and Mrs. Dawson should be there by now. They will see she is alright."

At that moment, Doug came back at a run.

"Everything is okay. The Dawsons are there and Cissy and Maud are with them."

"Where's your Auntie Mabel?"

"Oh, she's there too. She ran straight into Grandpapa's arms and won't let him go." Doug retrieved his horse's reins and jumped nimbly onto the animal's back. "Mick and I will go round to let Gran and Pops know you're in town."

Fran nodded distractedly – her mind on the picture of Mabel and her father. It was Gazza who focussed her attention.

"Will we go down to the produce merchant's now, Mrs. Daley?"

"Yes please, Gazza."

Mabel's dark eyes lit up at the sight of her father. A small frown appeared briefly when she noticed the attention her parents were paying her daughters.

"Papa," Mabel called.

"Mabel, my sweet daughter." Mr. Dawson straightened up. Cissy and Maud were enfolded into the arms of their grandmother. "It's good to see you. Where's William?"

"He's busy. He is always busy." Mabel pouted.

It was Mr. Dawson's turn to frown. "Mabel, it's a good thing William is a hard worker. You never have to be worried about his providing for you and your children." He reached out and drew his daughter in for a kiss on the cheek.

"Yes, yes, Papa, of course. I came to town with the girls today to speak with you. I want you to do something for me."

"Have I ever refused to help you, Kitten?" Mr. Dawson fell back into his old habit of addressing his daughter when she was a young girl.

Mabel's smile, which was meant to be coy, became a macabre thing amongst the deep wrinkles of her face.

Mr. Dawson stepped back; one eyebrow raised in question.

"How can I help you? Is it something William can't do for you?"

"Billy has run away to join the army. I want you to find out where he is. Make them send him back home where he belongs. He's not yet eighteen, you know."

Mr. Dawson looked down at the petite Mabel looking up at him with her lips drawn into a tight line.

"Yes, Mabel, but he's not too far off it."

"Well, I want him home. He is not to go off to war. They can take Joe if they want but Billy is mine."

The bushy eyebrows of her father lifted to nearly touch the brim of the grey hat on his head.

"Mabel, what are you saying? Have both boys gone off to join up?"

"Yes, and it's all William's fault and his father's. They've put the idea into Billy's head no doubt. Joe is supposed to look out for his brother. He should have stopped Billy, not encouraged him further."

Mr. Dawson stood silently while he absorbed all he had been told. Having heard more than she wanted to hear, Mrs. Dawson ushered the two young girls towards the tea-room further down the platform.

"Come, let us sit and you can explain further." Mr. Dawson led his daughter to a wooden form towards the back of the platform area. His gaze returned to her face several times as they moved forward. The frown on his forehead deepened. He felt the tension rising in his daughter, always a precursor to a tantrum in the young Mabel. His anxious gaze turned to seek his wife for support but the bright red silk scarf attached to her wide-brimmed hat disappeared through the tea-room doors.

Mabel's father helped her onto the seat before sitting by her side. He looked about them relieved to notice few people in the area.

"Now, Mabel, tell me all that has happened."

"Oh, Papa, I knew you would help me." Mabel smiled. Her obsidian eyes glowed.

"I have not said that, Mabel. I want to hear about everything that has happened."

"Yes, Papa, but that is alright. I know you always do whatever I ask." She laughed with a girlish excitement.

"Hmmm, we'll see," Mr. Dawson mumbled as the frown deepened further.

It was a rambling tale Mabel told, full of diversions, blame passing, demands and tears. Quite some time had passed before she came to a stuttering end.

"And that is why Billy must be brought back to his senses and return home."

Mr. Dawson remained silent for long moments. He looked down upon this woman, almost a stranger, at his side. Like a movie matinee presenting the news headlines, his facial expressions revealed shock, sorrow, disappointment, delusion and even disgust – not just at his only daughter, but at the failures of his wife and himself in her upbringing.

Mabel's impatience exploded. "Papa, William never takes me anywhere. I want to visit the city more often. I want to wear fashionable dresses and meet friends from my own class. I feel suffocated."

Mr. Dawson's eyes opened wide. His voice tightened. "Mabel it was your choice to leave the city and live on a cattle station. No one pressured you. You must remember, William's time is not his own. There is a lot of work in caring for the land and for the stock it carries."

Once again Mabel interrupted her father, triggering the return of his deep frown.

"That is all William can talk about, the land, and the stock. It is all cattle sales, cattle prices, cattle breeding, fattening cattle, fencing cattle. When it is not cattle, it is horses and the effort needed to train them – or his dogs. What about me? William cares for the wretched stock more than he does his wife. I want some attention. I am sick to death of them all. I want to mix with people who can at least string together a sentence filled with interesting subjects suitable for polite conversation."

Mr. Dawson bit his tongue before he next spoke.

"Mabel, what about Fran and Maggie? I thought you enjoyed their company."

"The pair of them are no better, only their subjects are cooking, housekeeping and childrearing. I want to meet intelligent and civilized people. Billy was the only person who made me laugh. And now he has gone away to the war."

Mr. Dawson glanced at the fob watch drawn from the waistcoat underneath his suit coat. If the train was on time, it should be ready to leave this station for the coast within half an hour. He pondered the options if he decided to take his daughter's complaints seriously. He struggled with the probable backlash if he did not.

Uncomfortable in the silence, Mabel jumped up and stomped away a few steps then turned and returned to her seat. Patience had never been one of her virtues. She looked askance at her father. The thought of him refusing her request had never entered Mabel's mind. She looked up at him when he took her hand in his own and began to speak.

"Mabel, my dear, I have never refused you anything in your life but this time will be different." Mr. Dawson watched his daughter's eyes open wide and saw her attempt to speak. "Hush, Mabel." He held tightly to Mabel's hand when she attempted to pull it away. "Mabel, for once, listen. Billy and Joe have obviously decided this is what they want to do and they are now young men with intelligent minds. If this is what they want, I do not think it is for us to deny them this chance to serve their country. In fact, I admit a great admiration for their determination and courage. We, as a family, should feel pride in their decision. No, I will not be chasing them around the country to shame them in front of their peers and drag them home again. I congratulate them and wish them the very best. Another thing you need to consider is what do you think it would do for the business if we refused them permission to fight for their country and commonwealth. Our family bank would be treated as pariahs." Mr. Dawson took a deep breath. "I think we have to accept their choice and pray to God to bring them home safe."

Mabel ripped her hand out of her father's grip.

"God, what God? When has he ever done anything, I wanted? Accept their choice? That is not going to happen. I am Billy's mother and I say he is to come home." Her voice rose in decibels with each word uttered.

"Quiet, Mabel. This is not a place to raise your voice. People do not need to know our business. Remember, Joe is your son also. You seem to have forgotten that."

Mabel jumped to her feet and opened her mouth to yell abuse at her father. Her shriek blended in with the train whistle's high pitch of warning. Five minutes to departure.

"Enough," Mr. Dawson demanded in a quiet but strong whisper. "Whatever has got into you?" He glanced along the platform, pleased to see his wife herding Cissy and Maud onto the train. He raised his finger in acknowledgment.

Mabel threw herself back onto the wooden form and burst into noisy tears.

"You never do anything for me," she burbled.

"It seems to me that I have done too much for you over your lifetime. Pull yourself together, Mabel. Our country is at war. You are not a child anymore. You are a grown woman with four children. I suggest you behave like it. Firstly, you can start seeing things from another person's point of view." Relief washed over Mr. Dawson like a cool shower on a hot day at the sight of Fran Daley and Maggie Bardon from Billabong Station striding down the platform towards them.

"We'll look after Mabel, Mr. Dawson," Fran smiled. "You don't want to miss your train."

"Thank you, Fran. Thank you, Mrs. Bardon. When Mabel settles down, will you tell her I am sorry but it is not my place to help her."

"Goodbye, Mr. Dawson," Maggie smiled.

Fran and Maggie waved to the Dawsons, Cissy and Maud as the train whistle's screech echoed along the platform again. Steam spurted out from the engine as the wheels engaged on the track and the train pulled out slowly heading east.

When they turned back to Mabel, she was seen stomping out the front doors of the station.

Back at the property, mud caked the three men's bodies from top to bottom as they worked with spades and shovels to remove a cow from the bog. From the edge of the partly dried waterhole, a young calf bawled out its distress. William spat the mud from his mouth before he spoke.

"I do hope Mabel doesn't play up in town, although I have to admit Fran and Maggie seem to handle her very well. If she starts picking on my mum and dad tonight, I'll be really angry. They don't need that at their age."

Geoff went to say something but thought better of it. He closed his mouth and scraped the mud from under the belly of the beast allowing Miles to push the folded heavy-duty tarpaulin sling underneath. William struggled to hold the animal's head steady as he dug around the front legs of the cow at the same time.

Chill of Blame

"What was you gonna say, Geoff – spit it out?" William sought a small clean area on his shirt collar in the hope of wiping mud from his lips.

Geoff dragged his legs through the mud up to his thighs around to the other side of the cow. He bent to search for the large metal ring attached to the end of the tarpaulin now halfway under the belly.

He shrugged. "Maggie says Mabel's unwell – has been for a while. She's not coping very well. We need to give her a bit of slack, is what Maggie says."

Miles threw his brother an anxious look. His gaze flicked back to Geoff. Eventually, he found his voice to add his own comment.

"That's about what Fran's been saying, too. She reckons that Billy, being so like his mother in looks and character, even as a baby, drew her to the lad so much. When Joe was born such a short time later with few similarities to herself, Mabel found it hard to nurture the child."

"Do you think she's losing her mind?" William directed his question to Miles.

"Fran says she's delicate. Billy and Joe's running off to the war just now has been too much."

"It's not their fault. They didn't know there was anything wrong with their mother. I've always tried to protect them and the girls from Mabel's worst moods."

"I don't think anyone is saying it's anybody's fault, William," Miles attempted to reassure his brother.

"I've got the ring," Geoff called with relief at having felt his fingers grasp the metal as well as at William's acceptance of their opinions. He hauled on the ring to drag the tarpaulin sling halfway under the body. Miles held firmly to the matching ring on his side of the beast.

"William if you want to bring up the draught horse and the hauling chains, we'll finish clearing what we can away from the legs and neck. Hopefully, we'll have this old girl out of here before dark."

The cow lay exhausted on dry ground while the men removed the sling and ropes. She lifted her head as the young calf ran over ignoring the presence of the workers. It nuzzled around looking for its mother's teats and milk. Geoff returned from the water trough not far away with a bucket of water to clean the udder before the calf took a mouthful of mud. At the calf's persistence, the mother brought herself to her feet and shook her body vigorously. Mud, dried and moist, flew off in all directions. The cow drank from the second bucket of water Geoff presented.

As the three men watched the mother with her calf, grins stretched across their faces.

"I thought for a minute there, we were all going to join the old girl in a mud burial." Miles's grin turned to a relieved laughter.

CHAPTER SEVEN

Farewell Australia

March 1917

Dawn broke in a golden shiver across the water like an omen of goodwill. Joe felt his shoulders lift and straighten. He reached down to pat the neck of his horse.

"Troop – Halt!"

At the roar from Sergeant Sibley, the four long lines of recruits and their mounts shuffled to a halt at the entrance to the docks. Leaving Corporal Linton in charge, the sergeant rode off to ascertain where the ship carrying his charges to Egypt was docked.

"Well, Straps, here we are – our first sea voyage." Joe glanced at his horse and the load the animal carried. He unhooked the water canteen hanging over his left shoulder, removed the cork and lifted it to his lips to sip. They had endured an hour's lecture the previous evening on the how and why to preserve water where they were going.

He shrugged his left shoulder to settle the canteen into place beside his .303 rifle with its ten rounds of ammunition slung diagonally across his back. He re-settled the rifle butt behind his right hip. The next item to be realigned was the haversack over his opposite shoulder. His few clothes, daily rations and personal possessions including his notebook and two pencils proved to be more awkward than heavy.

Proud fingers hitched up the bandolier with the neat leather pouches, five across the front of his body and four across the back.

The weight of ninety rounds of ammunition had made a sunken track in the skin of his shoulder. He then hooked his fingers under the leather to relieve the pressure.

Joe wriggled his bum deeper into the saddle. His fingers ran lightly over the mess tin, billy can, pannikin and enamel plate attached to the back of the right-hand side of the saddle. He made a quick inventory of those items at the back of the saddle starting with the horse's canvas water bag and nose bag with its one-day supply of grain for his mount; his mate. While there, he patted the bundle made up of the heel rope, removable length of picket line, and the leather case with its two horseshoes and nails.

Joe pushed at the bundle in front of his saddle giving his thighs a bit of clearance. He heard Billy's whisper from his right.

"With our greatcoat and waterproof groundsheet tied up to the front of the saddle, I'm damn glad they let us put our blanket under the saddle over the saddle blanket. There's hardly any room left for me in the saddle. Why we want a blanket in the middle of the desert, I can't understand. I thought the desert was supposed to be as hot as hell."

Joe looked across to Billy who rode the bay horse he had named Buckles.

"Silence, in the rank you two." Corporal Linton's voice turned both their heads. The man called in a voice almost as piercing as the sergeant's voice. "Troops – dismount!"

As the corporal moved off down the line of men, Billy whispered once more.

"That beggar's getting more like Sibley every day."

As he stood on the near side of his horse's head, Joe felt pride hiss through his veins, filling his self-esteem to overflowing. He could almost hear inside his head the sound of Pops pumping up the inflated tyres on his new bicycle.

Chill of Blame

This was followed by Gran Daley's oft-spoken warning in Joe's ears.

"Pride comes before a fall, young man, don't you forget it now."

His wandering mind pictured the abrupt conversion of his mother's once beautiful face into that of a vixen when she criticized Joe's shortcomings – an increasingly frequent occurrence it seemed of late. Furrows distorted her forehead, the skin tightened around her nose and mouth and her eyes became black stones. Joe had no doubt, that if his mother knew her second-born was having a moment of pride, she'd be livid. Only Billy was encouraged to take pride in his achievements. With these thoughts, Joe felt today's pride dissipate into the humid air of what promised to be a hot day.

After what seemed like hours, Sergeant Sibley rode back to his recruits and swung to the ground. He and Corporal Linton had a short discussion until the sergeant, on foot, led the men and their horses off towards their ship. Joe's eyes roamed everywhere at once. He could not remember having seen so much action on either of his two trips to the Townsville wharves as a child. Here, in New South Wales, large machines hauled crates and army machinery up and onto the many ships with heavy ropes attached to the bollards on the wharves. Men's voices yelled from all angles and whistles blew repeatedly. Innumerable trucks, loaded to the limit, rumbled and growled along to their destination. Joe reached up to pat Strap's chin. He was very pleased to see his horse unflummoxed by the commotion going on around them. He noticed in front of him, Carter's strong arms and shoulders bulge as he strived to control his horse's swinging head. Martin used his body to stop his horse from breaking away. A glance over Strap's withers assured him Billy had Buckles under control.

Corporal Linton stood on the wharf holding the reins of his and the sergeant's horse. Pride beamed in his eyes as he watched the recruits board the ship.

All the recruits experienced some trouble or other with their horses as they followed Sibley up the railed loading ramp hanging precariously over the water from the wharf to the deck. The sergeant then directed the men in guiding their animals into the lines of stalls covering much of the top deck. The men were left to settle their animals while Sergeant Sibley went to hand over his duties to the officers who would be responsible for seeing the recruits arrive in Egypt. Later, when Joe saw the sergeant and Corporal Linton leading their horses along the wharf, heading back to the training centre, a sense of sorrow surprised him. He felt some disappointment in not having had the opportunity to say goodbye. They were good blokes.

The grey skies and darkening sea matched Joe's mood as he stood sheltered in the narrow space near the lifeboat davit. Hardly a stalk of hay could fit between the troopers crowded in the small area under the canvas awning shading the fo'c's'le of the vessel. Other than the nautical necessities of the ship, the remainder of the top deck was taken over by the single stalls for the troopers' mounts. A canvas shelter ran the length of the port and starboard sides of the ship to provide some relief from the weather. The area where the crowd of men now stood seeking the last glimpse of the coast, was to be used three times a day to exercise their horses. Somewhere on his right, he heard the peal of his brother's laughter along with shouts and ribald comments from others. Around them, the horizon had long since shrunken to a couple of hundred yards distance. Behind the ship's wake, the coastal shoreline had disappeared some time past. Joe jumped at the sound of a voice, thick with an Irish brogue, near his shoulder.

"Five times I've waved away our Australian homeland and each time it has brought a tear to the eye."

Chill of Blame

Joe looked up into the blue eyes of one of the farriers from the remount unit. The officers of this unit were charged with seeing the reinforcements and their mounts, as well as the one hundred replacement mounts, arrived safely in Egypt. The farriers groomed, exercised and fed the remounts as well as supervised the recruits' care of their horses. The man was a shade shorter than Joe and it seemed the thick tight black curls on his head had escaped the barber's shears in recent times.

"It does have that effect, doesn't it? The miserable sky does nothing to improve matters." Joe reached out his right hand. "Joe Dawson's the name." Joe realized there was barely a pause as he introduced himself. The new surname was growing on him.

"G'day, Mick McCready." The men shook hands. "I'm just going down to the deck below to see how the remount horses there are managing, now we're into the swell of the ocean waves. Want to join me?"

Joe smiled and nodded. "Sure."

The two men pushed their way through the crowds to the top of the horse ramp leading down to the second deck. Except for the small exercise area at the bow end of the ship, this deck too was taken over by horse stalls.

"I suppose you've found your accommodation on the next deck down. The supplies and equipment are in the bowels of the ship below that."

Joe nodded his head in the affirmative. He did not want to talk or breathe lest he risked sucking in too much air when a thick blanket of odours threatened to suffocate him. From even further below where the men were housed, the acrid smell of vomit and unwashed bodies seeped up the companion ladder to assail his nostrils and stir his gut. He swallowed. The clatter of restless horses' hooves provided a background noise to the snorts of their complaints from within their narrow stalls. A hotchpotch of aromas rose on stale air. These included the sweat of the animals' fear mixed with the smells of manure and urine. Like a wispy wraith, fumes from the ship's engine weaved through all other smells. Joe gasped and again swallowed hard. He squinted his eyes to see better in the dim light.

When they loaded their horses into the long lines of stalls on the top deck late yesterday, and when they fed, watered and groomed them in the glow of hurricane lanterns this morning in the shelter of the wharf, he had not appreciated the extent of the cramped conditions in which the horses, down here on the deck below, were to travel. At the other end of the horse stalls on this deck, several minders were caring for the remount horses. These were the replacement horses for the troopers fighting in Egypt.

Mick McCready caught Joe's attention once more.

"Old Berryman will be along soon with what volunteers he can stir up to get the pumps working. He'll show you boys how to hose out these stalls and clear the scuppers. Old Berry...."

Joe interrupted, "Berry?"

"Yes, Sergeant Berryman – he's a bit tart when you first meet him, but once you get to know him, he's a great bloke really. He'll have a duty roster on the bulletin board for all the routine chores like this. You can tell your friends this ain't no fancy holiday. They'll have to work their fare." Mick's chuckle brought a rueful and short-lived smile to Joe's lips.

Joe's stomach rolled over with each roll of the waves outside. He tasted bile in the back of his throat. He did not like the idea of spending too long down here below deck.

"Come on then, Joe, you check those on the left and I'll do these on the right."

Joe felt the vomit rising in his gullet. He swallowed hard. Mick's voice sounded as if from far away.

"Are you alright? Even in this gloom, I can see you've turned as white as a sheet. If it's sick you're feeling, try to concentrate on a specific chore. Ignore everything else around you."

Joe nodded his reply and with each inhalation, he sipped warily at the stale air. Mick led the way to the first line of stalls. His melodious voice began talking to the horses without a pause as he climbed through the rails of the first narrow pen into the limited space with its four-legged occupant. His rough hand reached up and lightly massaged the forehead of the first animal. Initially, the head pulled away and the whites of its eyes stared out blindly.

"These beggars are barely even broken." McCready lifted his voice for Joe to hear. "That will be the job of us remount chaps – to quieten them down as we travel over the desert to wherever we are to deliver them."

The drone resumed – like a parent comforting a child – as he spoke to the horse. The smooth strokes over the white blaze on the equine face moved around the head and ears and under the chin. As the animal settled, both Mick's hands worked on the muscles of its neck, back, sides and legs. A tremble ran through the gelding's body and it finally calmed.

"We were told we had to exercise our horses three times a day as it will be a six-week trip or more." Joe moved to the next animal and imitated Mick's behaviour.

"Yes, they must be walked regularly. The poor blighters will get very little exercise, I'm afraid. The troopers' horses will have one-on-one attention from their riders but these remounts will only have the few of us farriers to attend to them most of the time. That's why Old Berry will roster you fellas to help out. Sometimes the horses can hardly walk by the time we get there." Mick stood up straight to stretch his back muscles. "The mules and draught horses down the line there are the ones I feel sorry for. They always seem to end up in the worst corner of the ship."

"Do you lose many on the journey?"

"More than I'd like. I hate to lose any horse."

Joe opened his mouth to ask what happened to the dead animals but shut it again when he realized he did not want to think about that right now. Not when he was already trying to quell the revolt in his belly.

The farrier's stroke moved down the accessible legs of his animal. He did not force the horse to lift a foot, striving to maintain balance as it already was.

"Like us, they'll get their sea legs in a few days," Mick explained. He chuckled his infectious mirth. "And like us, they'll wobble about when they step out onto firm land once more."

Mick and Joe glanced up when the voices of several men were heard descending the ramp.

"Whatcha doing there, Joe?" Billy's voice called.

Joe explained and asked for the new arrivals to join them in making their way along the lines of horses, massaging and inspecting as they went. He introduced them to Mick McCready the farrier.

The men settled down to the chore of soothing each horse they came to until the ship's bell called them for their mid-day meal.

"I'm starving. I could eat a horse and chase the rider," Billy called.

"A few of these ship's meals might cure you of that desire, lad," Mick chuckled. "Sometimes I have to toss up between starvation or eating the food. It's a hard decision."

Joe drew in a noisy breath and swallowed hard. His stomach kicked and bucked like an unbroken colt.

When the evening skies cleared, Joe and Billy were two of the many troopers who chose to bring their hammocks up onto the deck to sleep in the fresh night air. They hung like horizontal bats from every jutting steel hook or other attachment available. Their conversation was short-lived as snores overtook their words.

A week later and Joe still struggled not to gag as he ran the last few yards up the ramp and onto the top deck. He stood with both hands clenched on the bulwark, sucking in the clean air. Today, the atmosphere in the lower decks seemed even worse than usual – if that was possible. Once his breathing returned to normal, he cocked his head at the sound of rifle fire coming from the stern of the ship. Loud shouting from the men accompanied every gunshot. Joe's first thought was for the horses. His gaze swung across the deck to where Buckles and Straps stood in their stalls unmoved as they chewed on their morning feed. He smiled at this success in their training. His boots clattered on the deck as he ran between the horse stalls, towards the gunfire.

Men from his training group were squeezed into every space available. Sergeant Berryman from the remount unit had them practicing their accuracy with a rifle. Joe looked up to where Billy's voice drifted down from the top of a water tank secured to the deck.

"Here, Joe, I'll give you a heave-ho." Billy knelt holding his hand out to Joe.

Once standing on the precarious lookout post, Joe's gaze focused on two large barrels alternatively bouncing on and ploughing through the water about two hundred yards behind the ship. A cargo net enfolded each barrel. Threaded through each of these roped nets, separate cables fed back to the vessel securing one barrel to the port side of the ship's stern and the other to the starboard side. As each drum danced on the crest of a wave in the wash of the ship, a large white circle with a smaller yellow circle inside, painted on both sides of each drum, became visible. A flag of canvas about eighteen inches square hung from a wooden stake clamped to the raised ridge on both ends of each barrel. These four flags, sodden in seawater, danced a wild polka as the drums bounced and tossed on rough waters.

The sergeant kept a record, written with a pencil in his small notebook, of the men's success or failure. Calls for bets rose above the shouts of glee or disappointment.

"How'd you go, Billy?" Joe leant close to Billy's ear.

The familiar grin brightened the day. "Bluey owes me two bob."

A voice came from below where they stood.

"The greatest win will be in staying alive when you get to the desert, Daley." Sergeant Berryman looked over at Joe. "Come on then, young'un. Let's see how your aim is."

Joe and Billy stared at each other in surprise. Before Joe jumped down, Billy whispered in his ear, "Bloody hell, he reminds me of Sibley back in the training camp."

Joe laughed, "It must be a part of the sergeant's training course – how to move fast and silent and hear things they shouldn't be able to hear." He jumped down to follow the man's lead.

Joe took up the rifle and checked it was loaded. His eyes examined the gunsights with a suspicious glance.

"You get three shots. The first will allow you to get some idea of the sighting on the rifle. The second bullet allows you to see if you've overcompensated and then you have one left to see what you can hit." Sergeant Berryman's quiet voice drifted in on his ear.

Some shouts of encouragement rose from the audience but Joe took no notice. He held the rifle steady – sighting down the barrel. Joe grunted and shifted his arm a little. With his feet steady on the moving deck, he concentrated on the targets floating out in the sea. None of the four flags appeared to have taken a hit as far as he could tell from this distance. He took some moments to assess the rise and fall of the waves in relation to his own rise and fall on the ship's deck. Joe heard Billy's voice behind him, but he remained unmoved.

"Geez, Joe – get off the pot."

The gunfire echoed across the waters. A shout rang out from the men behind Joe.

"He's hit the white target on the right, Sarge."

Out of the corner of his eye, Joe noticed the sergeant peering through a pair of field glasses. Joe brought the rifle down from his shoulder and with steady hands gently touched the sight adjustment. Once more he steadied his stance as he placed the butt of the rifle to his right shoulder. Without haste, he aimed and eased the trigger backwards. The second shot rang out. Material torn from the flag on the left end of the barrel attached to the port side of the ship sagged down in the water.

Sergeant Berryman held the field glasses to his eyes. Pleasure swelled up in Joe's throat but he did not waste time savouring the sensation. Mentally he stamped down on the old familiar serpent of jealousy and competitiveness which stirred deeper down in his core. The need to beat his brother slithered up his gullet with the taste of vomit. How many times had he hoped for a good word from his mother for any successful achievement, but on those occasions when he beat Billy at anything he took a scolding instead. The comfort of his father's words smoothed the hurt but never healed the wound.

Joe took a deep breath and gritted his teeth. He let his body relax as he challenged himself to a more difficult target. Behind him, a heavy silence hung over the crowd. Joe eased out his breath as gently as his finger eased on the trigger. Again, the gunfire echoed off the ocean. At first, it seemed as if he had missed his target. After what seemed like a lifetime, the flag on the right end of the port side barrel folded downwards on itself. The stick on which it was attached snapped where the bullet had hit it six inches from the top.

The spectators yelled and shouted their delight. Many were collecting their bets or digging deep in their pockets for change to cover their losses. Billy's grin covered his face as his hands filled with his winnings.

Joe lowered the rifle slowly. He struggled to quell the rush of pride threatening to explode in wild laughter. His face remained bland as he returned the rifle to Sergeant Berryman. The man stood open-mouthed staring at this young trooper who had achieved something he had not seen done before – three hits. The sergeant kept a tight grip on his smile. Admiration, part disbelief, and part envy reflected in his grey eyes.

"You have the makings of a sniper, Trooper."

"Nah, Sergeant, it was only a fluke – a lucky shot – that's all."

Joe clenched his mouth and cheeks to contain the smile threatening to blow his modesty to smithereens.

Behind him, Billy led the cheer.

"That's my boyo."

The sergeant changed the cheers to groans with his next instruction.

"Okay, you fellas, it's time those horses were given their massage and exercise. Jump to it."

The Australian Light Horse senior officer on board, Major Forbes, strode out onto the fo'c's'le where the men gathered to devour whatever food they had been issued from the galley. He stood straight and unmoving for a moment waiting for the grumblings to cease and for the men to notice his presence. Another officer, one seldom seen out on the deck, Lieutenant Burke, stood on the Major's left with a clipboard in his hand. The pale brown eyes without expression, set close together in his narrow face, stared out to sea.

The men made a token gesture of rising but the Major waved them back to their haunches.

"Right, you sorry lot, I'm Major Forbes and I'm the senior Light Horse Officer on board this tub. Don't bother complaining about the food. Please be advised it is ten times better than what you'll be eating most days in the desert." He paused before continuing and took a deep breath. "Don't bother complaining about the beer restrictions. I'll do my best to see you are otherwise occupied and do not have time to experience any withdrawal symptoms." The groans of horror dragged on for longer and louder.

"Now, I have a complaint. Your body odours are fouling up the air in my cabin. It far out-matches that of the horses. Lieutenant Baldwin and Sergeant Berryman, along with a couple of the sailors, will organize a canvas pool to be hung over the ship's side. Everyone is to take a bath in this pool every day. I trust this all meets with your approval." The Major's grin softened the sarcasm. He did not wait for the shocked troopers to collect their voices. He strode off accompanied by Lieutenant Burke towards the lines of horses.

The canvas pool became a favourite with the men, particularly after grooming and exercising the horses three times a day.

Joe watched the card game going on in the lane behind the horse stalls where he was working. It suddenly came to him that he felt great – back to normal. Nausea, headaches and wobbly legs did not torture him at all this morning. He spoke to Straps, his horse.

"That Mick McCready told me the sea-sickness would be over in two or three days. It's taken more like three weeks."

Straps took little notice as he savoured the small sample of syrup Joe had rescued for him from the galley. The animal rolled his tongue around his mouth and lips spreading the flavour in the hope of a longer period of enjoyment. Straps reached his lips over to inspect Joe's hands to see if any sticky liquid remained. For the third time, Joe held up his palms to be licked again by the rough tongue.

79

The sound of a ruckus rose from the card players when one demanded the cards be reshuffled.

A voice from the group called, "You want to be dealt in, Dawson?"

"No thanks, fellas, I'm going to join the boys throwing the horseshoes up at the bow when I finish here."

When Joe reached the area where a group of troopers had produced two old horseshoes, he stood back and watched. Even though it did not seem too far to the plate holding the spike on which to hook the steel shoe, the choppy ocean ensured very few men were successful. Steel rattled on steel on those occasions when the horseshoe connected with the spike but fate seemed to twist the ship at the delicate moment and the shoe fell away.

"I reckon we should get a point even if the damn shoe only hits the spike." Bluey's disappointment coloured his face red.

"That's alright, Bluey," Billy was heard to call back, "I've hit the spike more times than you anyway."

Joe smiled to himself. *That's our Billy, he's never flush with modesty,* he thought.

Martin and Carter, with whom he had shared the tent back in training camp, were there in the crowd. Joe looked over when he heard Martin, the peacemaker of their tent, comment.

"Give Bluey a chance, Billy, or let someone else have a go. You can't win all the time, you know."

Joe's head lifted. Such talk to Billy at their school inevitably stirred the hackles on his brother's neck. He hoped Billy would not choose this moment to cause an argument. He watched Billy's face darken and then in seconds his features cleared. Like the sun appearing from behind a cloud, a wide grin filled Billy's face.

"Okay, you blokes, I've gotta go take a leak anyway."

Joe followed Billy to where they often peed down the nearest scuppers.

He called, "Hey, Billy, I'm going down to see if Mick wants a hand with the remounts. Are you coming?"

"Yeah, mate, just hang on a bit."

Another day with little change in the routine, Joe paced the deck.

"Hey, Carter, have you seen Billy this morning?"

"Nah, last I saw of him he was taking a bath."

Joe wanted to scream his news to all and sundry but first he wanted to tell his brother. As he made his way to the port side of the ship to where the canvas pool had been designed to hang over the side of the vessel and into the seawater, he again savoured the absence of the seasickness which had dogged him for so long. A smile dislodged the frown from his brow. He jumped at the sound of the familiar voice.

"Hey, Joe, you look like you have something on your mind."

Water poured from Billy's body and shorts as he leapt from the Jacob's ladder and onto the ship's deck. Billy shook his fingers in Joe's direction sending a spray of cooling water over his head.

Joe grabbed Billy's wet arm and pulled him into the shelter of a storage crate on deck.

"I just overheard Lieutenant Baldwin and Major Forbes talking with the ship's captain. The captain's saying we'll be in Alexandria early tomorrow morning."

"Keep that under your hat for a bit, Joe. I'll make a couple of bob off some poor mug who hasn't heard that yet."

"I've only just got my sea-legs and now we're going to be back on dry land. Still, it can't come soon enough for me."

Their evening meal of curry and dried fruit still struggled to settle in their guts when Lieutenant Baldwin arrived on the deck where the troopers ate their meals.

"Remain seated," he called despite the fact not too many troopers made any genuine attempt to stand. "We'll be docking at Alexandria at first light tomorrow. Reveille will be an hour earlier than usual to give you time to groom the horses and have some chow before we lead the animals off the ship and into the yards on shore. The recruits will take their own mounts out first and then return to help with the remounts. Sergeant Berryman will supervise the activity on board ship here and I'll be at the stockyards on the shore to direct the traffic out there."

"Any questions?"

Joe felt Billy lean in close to his ear and whisper, "I made five bob off poor old Martin."

CHAPTER EIGHT

Billabong Downs

April 2017

Mabel watched the dust cloud stirring behind the approaching horse and buggy and recognized the new arrivals immediately. As her in-laws drove into the homestead compound, Mabel slipped out of her seat on the verandah and moved into the bedroom. Tears filled her eyes when she peeped around the edge of the curtain to watch the visitors drive directly towards Fran's house. Mabel pulled the drapes across the windows and slammed the door shut. She swiped at her eyes and mumbled.

"Of course, they're going to her place. No one ever comes here to see me." She brushed her eyes once again and dragged her fingers through the uncombed tresses. "They're probably all talking about me. Laughing at me because my Billy has run away from his mother. See if I care, the whole lot of them are beneath my contempt." Mabel threw herself across the unmade bed, pulled the pillow over her head and sobbed herself to sleep.

She did not stir when William left a cup of steaming tea and a saucer with two jam tarts on the bedside table later.

"Whoa, Ned, whoa, boy." Mr. Daley senior pulled on the reins bringing the horse to a stop at the front of Miles Daley's house. The dust settled around the feet of the grey horse pulling the buggy. The glances and rueful smiles of Pop Daley and his wife Mary met.

"Oh, Pop, I'm still not sure we're doing the right thing in sharing this letter with Billy and Joe's parents knowing Mabel's frame of mind lately."

Pop Daley reached his wrinkled hand across to wrap Mary's arthritic fingers within the nest of fading scars and callouses.

"Well, Ma, William will deal with this. We must let Mabel's words flow like water off a duck's back. Anyway, we'll let William decide whether she should be shown the letter or not."

At that moment, Fran appeared at the front door releasing her apron from around her neck and tossing it aside. She came down the steps and to her front garden gate where she greeted her in-laws with a wide smile.

"Hello, Pop. Hello, Mary. This is a lovely surprise. We didn't expect you out until Miles's birthday next month. Come on in, I was just making afternoon tea. You must be parched. The kettle's on the stove. I must have known you were coming, Pop, I've just finished cooking your favourite jam tarts." Fran stretched up to kiss her father-in-law on the cheek. She skipped around to the other side of the vehicle and kissed her mother-in-law too.

"Hello, Fran dear, it's lovely to see you again." Mary Daley held Fran's warm hand firmly as the younger woman helped her to the ground.

"Now, don't you ladies go eating all those tarts while I take Ned over and unharness him and settle him into a bit of hay and fresh water." Pop laughed.

As the two women climbed the stairs and entered the kitchen, Fran was not oblivious to Mary's reduced pace. She felt a sadness weigh upon her spirit at the thought of this wonderful woman slowing down.

"Now sit here, Mary, and tell me all the news from town until Pop returns. In the meantime, I'll pour you a cup of tea … or would you prefer a drink of cool water?"

"Tea will be lovely thanks, Fran." A cheeky grin lifted her lips. "I won't have any tarts yet or Pop will be saying we ate them all."

Both women laughed.

Mary Daley was onto her second cup of tea when Pop's heavy footsteps were heard coming up the stairs.

No sooner had Pop settled into a large pannikin of tea and three of the jam tarts, when the sound of William's and Miles's heavy footsteps raced up the backstairs along with the squeals of young Mavis.

"Hurry up, Dad. Come on, Uncle William, you are a pair of old tortoises."

"That's enough of the 'old' out of you, young lady. Aren't you supposed to be in class?" Her father asked.

"Mrs. Bardon said I can come and say hello to Gran and Pops for five minutes, Dad." Mavis laughed as she slipped in through the open kitchen doorway. The child rushed over to crush her Pops into a tight hug before repeating the process on Gran Daley.

"Not too rough now, Mavis," Fran warned, "it's not your brothers you're wrestling there."

Mavis grinned and kissed them both again on the cheeks before repeating this process with her father and Uncle William. She went to rush off again when she turned back to her grandparents.

"How long will you be here?"

"At least one night, child," Gran Daley answered with a smile.

Fran finished pouring the extra pannikins of tea just as William pulled out a chair to sit down.

"I'm dying for a good pannikin of tea. A man needs a decent drink of tea after a hard day's work outside," he said as he blew the steam from the black tea in front of him.

"Hear, hear," Miles and his father said in unison. The three men raised their pannikins to each other with a grin.

It was Mary who took up the men's usual chorus rolling her eyes as she did so.

"Don't give me one of those piddling little china cups when I come in for a tea break."

Laughter filled the kitchen. The smile remained in Fran's bright eyes as she turned to her daughter.

"Off you go now and thank Mrs. Bardon for allowing you to leave class to say hello to our visitors." Fran handed her a small tart with the proviso, "Eat that before you get back into the class."

"Yes, Mum," floated back up the stairs.

Fran offered the plate of jam tarts around the table once again. It was Pop who answered William's unasked question seen in the warm brown eyes and the tilt of his son's head.

"We received a letter from Joe and Billy yesterday." Pop Daley began searching through the folded notes in his top pockets. He dragged one out. "They posted this the day they left the harbour, it would seem," Pop commented as he squinted at the front of the dirt-stained envelope. He handed it over to William. "I'll leave it up to you to decide whether to share it with Mabel or not. I didn't want to upset her more than she already is."

William reached over and took the envelope.

"Thanks, Pop." He leant back in his chair, the tea and tart on the table in front of him forgotten. His dirt-ingrained finger traced the familiar handwriting of his younger son.

Dear Pops and Gran,

Billy and I want to tell you how sorry we are to leave you and the Towers in such a cloak-and-dagger manner. I'm afraid we were only thinking of ourselves and how to avoid trouble with our Mum and did not really consider the position we were putting you into.

Chill of Blame

We have joined the Australian Light Horse and if our Sergeant is correct should be on a troop ship heading to Cairo within another month or two. As you know, Billy has been saying for months he planned to join up and it seemed easier for me to go with him. Our Mum would never have let Billy leave, since he is under eighteen. This seemed the only option.

Billy asked me not to post this until we are leaving Australia.

From Joe and Billy

After a short time, he rested the paper on the table. His gaze threatened to burn a hole in the wall of the kitchen above the bench. William lifted the page and read again. Not for the first time in the past three months the hurt tore at his insides. The hurt that his sons had not confided in him. Rational thought dictated the reason. It was a known family joke, a painful one, for him at least. His wife Mabel had the ability to discover any secret he may have no matter how hard he tried to keep it to himself. William's thoughts reconciled the pain. *No, the boys were right. They had no choice but to do things the way they did.* He prayed silently. *God, look after my boys.*

As William came to peace with himself, he passed the letter over to Fran and Miles to read before he turned back to his father.

"I think in this instant it would be a mistake to show this letter to Mabel. It could only hurt her more and maybe send her into a further downward spiral. She is already in such a delicate state these days. The smallest thing could set her off and if she discovered it was Billy who wanted the letter held back until they left Australia it would break her." William drank deeply from his pannikin. He replaced it with a thud on the table. His lips curled as he spoke again. "Then, on the other hand, she would never believe it could be his fault – nothing is ever Billy's fault. Poor Joe would take the rap."

Mary reached over to pat the hand of her eldest son.

"William, I am so sorry things have turned out like this for you."

"That's alright, Ma, I'm a big boy. You and Pop built us tough." William smiled a wry grin at his mother before turning to his father. "Thanks for taking the trouble to bring the letter all the way out here for me to see, but I think it might be best if you take it home with you, Pop. If the boys send you any more letters, I really would like to read them. We will have to see how Mabel is coping at the time and decide if she should see the boys' letters."

Walking across the compound towards the sheds, Miles, William and Pop Daley were swamped by the children released from their classes. Mavis took up a prime position by her grandfather's side taking his hand into her own. The three Bardon children, all talking at once, skimmed around the perimeter of the three men.

Young Stewie Bardon strode along leading the parade turning back to speak to the adults.

"Are you going to help my dad finish shoeing the horses, Mr. Daley?" He directed his question to the senior of the three gentlemen by that name.

"I think my back might be past holding the weight of a full-grown horse, lad. Yes, I believe we are on our way to help your father with that chore."

Splinter, the youngest of the children gave a spurt of laughter.

"You don't have to hold the horse up when you're shoeing it, sir. My dad says it's all in the training. He says you mustn't let the blighters get away with leaning on your back."

The lines on Pop Daley's face scattered as he grinned.

"Is that so, young man? Well, I stand corrected."

Evie, the middle child of the Bardon family, edged her way in to command the second hand of Mr. Daley senior.

"My dad is going to teach me how to shoe my own horse on my next birthday."

The grey head turned down to look into the clear blue eyes at his side.

"And how old will you be then, Evie?"

"I'll be seven then and my dad says I'll be a big girl."

From her elevated position of two years older, Mavis moved in closer to her grandfather.

"She won't be grown up then, will she, Pops?"

Pops Daley was spared the sensitive task of refereeing the girls as they arrived at the horse stables where Geoff Bardon was hunched over with the front hoof of a brown horse resting on the left knee of his bent leg. Geoff attempted to use his right shoulder and upper arm to wipe some of the sweat running down his face. He let the horse's foot back down onto the ground and stood up. Geoff replaced the hoof knife into its slot in the leather apron at his waist.

"Hello, Mr. Daley. It's good to see you again. How have you been keeping?" The head stockman reached over to shake the hand of the father of his two bosses. It took a few minutes for Pop Daley senior to release the hold of the girls' hands at his sides.

"Punter seems to be calm enough today?" William asked the question as he leant over the rail to rub the white mark on the horse's face.

Geoff smiled. "We had a few words earlier before we began."

William and Miles took down their tool aprons hanging on the shed wall.

"Miles and I have come to lend a hand. I see you've already finished the troublemakers." William looked at the six horses resting in the shade of the gum trees in the paddock outside the railed yards.

"You know me, William, I'd rather get the most difficult ones done while I have a bit of steam left in me."

Stewie and Splinter watched the farrier work until they left at the sound of their mother's voice calling them to feed the chooks. Mavis remained with her Grandpops. Evie hung in close to the railings offering verbal advice to her father as he worked.

Fran and Mary Daley climbed the back stairs of William and Mabel's house. Fran knocked on the wall beside the open back doorway.

"Are you there, Mabel? Can we come in?"

"Go away, I'm sleeping. You'd better get back to your visitors."

It was Mary who called out in her tremulous voice. "Mabel dear, it is Mary. Can we come in?"

"Mabel, I've come over to invite you and William to join us for tea tonight," Fran called when there had been no response for several minutes.

"No thank you, I'm busy with important business letters."

On the verandah outside the back doorway, Fran and Mary exchanged questioning glances.

"Is that likely?" Mary whispered.

"I don't think so. William does all the business dealings for the property. Obviously, we are not wanted. Come, we'll go and get tea organized. I'll send something over with William later."

CHAPTER NINE

Alexandria to Ismailia

May 1917

The heat made itself felt before the sun lifted above the horizon. The recruits saddled their mounts prior to leading them down the railed ramp, in single file. Men and horses stumbled when they touched solid earth again. The horses in particular showed evidence of weakness in their legs after six and a half weeks, on board the ship, with little exercise.

A rutted dirt track led them past storehouses on the wharf and through a maze of colourful Egyptian trader's stalls where loud voices bartered their wares. In contrast, sober grey and green tarpaulins covered the weird shapes of equipment on the back of a line of Army vehicles. Half a dozen soldiers with eyes half closed against the morning glare stood on guard. Tired and weak though humans and horses may have been after their long sea journey, they began to fret as noise, crowds and colour pushed in upon them. With an unexpected suddenness, the world opened out ahead. The masses cleared. A dusty track led through a row of palm trees to a sea of army tents. A set of stockyards beside a narrow-gauge railway track enclosed the tents on the south side, while sheds, some strong-walled and securely locked and others with their posts holding roofs of corrugated iron or thatch, made up the north side. A group of men in partial uniforms worked around what appeared to be a cookhouse standing at the east end of the tent city. A stream of smoke drifted on the stale air. It became apparent to the newcomers that the canvasedwalled structures on the west end of the complex provided ablution facilities.

At the stockyards, the men removed their saddles and gear which they stashed tidily at the back wall of a shed adjacent to the yards.

Lieutenant Baldwin's voice hurried things along. "Don't dawdle about. Once those horses are settled, get back on the ship and report to Sergeant Berryman. He'll be needing help with the remounts."

Hands swished left and right in front of every man's face.

"Bloody hell, these flies are thicker than fleas on a mongrel dog," Carter muttered.

"Don't open your mouth or you'll swallow half a dozen in one go," Martin piped up.

"Maybe that's what the army wants you to do – a bit less tucker they have to provide." Billy joined in, as he gave Buckles a last lick at his fingers sticky with syrup commandeered from the discarded tins in the galley garbage, before turning back towards the ship.

Joe smiled but refrained from making a comment as he rubbed down his horse, Straps. He was busy trying to analyse the mixed bag of sensations twitching inside his body. Excitement puffed up his chest and churned his stomach. Anxiety, even fear of the unknown, attempted to dampen the enthusiasm. When he made his way back onto the ship he paused at the top of the ramp. The visible land was like nothing he had seen before. The dusty, sand-coloured buildings of Alexandria restricted the horizon. He briefly wondered where this unending desert they had been told about was hidden. He tried to capture it all within his mind. He wanted to report everything in his next letter to Pops Daley. The humid heat pressed down upon him. It felt like a heavy weight threatening to compress his body and steal his breath away. Joe slapped at the flies which had taken the opportunity of his distraction to settle on his face. Silently he cursed the irritating tickle of these pests on his bare skin already running with sweat.

One by one the remounts, supply mules and draft horses were bridled and led out to be secured into the pens of the stockyards where they had a little more room to move about. Many of the horses did not take kindly to the return of the bridle restraint. The two dozen mules gave little trouble. They stumbled along behind whoever was holding the lead rein. The fifteen draught horses also were happy to trudge along behind as if they could not wait to be done with the gloomy stalls and a world that rocked both day and night. When the last of the animals were settled into the stockyards, Mick McCready and another man from the Remount Unit appeared near the shed wobbling under the weight of two thick cardboard cartons which landed with a thud in the dirt. Dust sprayed up covering all those nearby. Mick removed his bayonet from the scabbard on his belt and sliced the boxes open. The two Remount Unit men began issuing horse fly-veils to the recruits.

"Put one of these on your horse then come back here and help us fix the remounts," Mick instructed the gathering crowd of men. "These flies will have them blind with blight before you can say Jack Robinson."

It was Billy who piped up with a quip, "You got any of those for us too, Mick, lad?"

"When you find enough corks, you can string them around the brim of your hat," Mick returned with a grin.

At that moment, two more Remount Unit troopers arrived with more containers.

Mick's grin spread like sunshine over his face.

"You'll be pleased to hear we do have gifts for you recruits. Everyone serving in the desert, and that will be you lot of suckers, has been issued with a second water canteen. Make sure you all get your extra canteen. It may save your miserable life."

With the last horse veil secured, the men thought they might investigate their surroundings, but Lieutenant Baldwin's voice once again called them to order. By his side stood Major Forbes and Lieutenant Burke, a man rarely seen by the troopers since leaving Australia.

The Major directed several of the recruits along with a group of his own men to begin guard duty to protect their horses, the camp and supplies.

"Everyone is to make himself familiar with the guard roster and ensure he turns up, in full uniform, at the time he is rostered. Pilfering is a way of life just to survive in this country. Make sure it's not our horses, our stores or our lives that are stolen."

Major Forbes handed the duty roster to Lieutenant Baldwin before he saluted and spun on his heel moving off in the direction of the ship. Lieutenant Burke followed the Major.

Lieutenant Baldwin took up the instructions where the Major had left off.

Barked orders soon had men dispersing in all directions. A troop returned to the ship to hose down the decks. Another troop helped where needed in unloading further supplies. A third troop worked with Sergeant Berryman setting up the officers' tents near the locked sheds.

"The remainder of you can gather your saddle and gear and settle into a tent. As usual eight men per tent. The recruits are to return to those sections you were with at the training camp in Australia beginning with the tents on the west side. This will be our home for a couple of days until the train arrives to take us all down to Cairo. You can thank the local squadron for our amenities. Don't worry, you'll get plenty of practice setting up your tents when you arrive in Cairo."

Before the day was out, the troopers learnt they were to enjoy their days of the relative comfort of tents and a cook house while working the remount horses for more than the previously expected couple of days. On the other hand, they were going to experience true bivouac camping (without their tents) with rations of bully beef, onions, dry army biscuits and weak tea sooner than expected.

As the sun dipped below the horizon, Lieutenant Baldwin called the men to order. The troopers lined up dressed in their shorts and boots and while only some wore singlets, they all wore their hats. The Lieutenant nailed another list of instructions to the notice board in the shelter of the entrance to the shed. When the shuffling feet and murmuring voices quietened, he spun around.

"I do hope your recent luxury cruise has not dulled your brains and you've forgotten how to fall into line." He turned to Sergeant Berryman, "Is that everyone, Sergeant?"

To the accompaniment of a sharp salute, the Sergeant answered in the affirmative.

"All but those on guard duty, Lieutenant. I'll meet with them when they come in later, sir."

"I have some good news for you all." The Lieutenant looked out across the gathering and lifted his voice. "Within two days, once our horses regain their land -legs, we'll be moving on." He paused. If he hoped the men might cheer in response, he was disappointed. The heat had drained them all. Lieutenant Baldwin continued, "The bad news is, the railway has been derailed en route to collect us and our orders have been changed. The Remount Unit is to drive the remount horses directly to the pontoon bridge at Ismailia, to cross the Suez Canal. We'll then travel to Kantara where we will pick up a train to take us along the coastline to the Light Horse camp near El Arish. If a train is not available there, we'll all wear a bit more skin off our butts as we continue our overland trip. The recruits will be assisting the Remount Unit in moving these horses." Baldwin swallowed a few times, struggling to stir up saliva within his dry mouth. "You are to read these orders and learn what your responsibilities will be during this horse drive. Some of you recruits have been chosen to join the scouts, and some have been chosen to ride these remounts in the hope of finishing their breaking-in process. Others have been chosen as guards to protect us all. Some of you recruits will join the remount troopers in charge of the supply mules and draught horses." The Lieutenant coughed and tried to clear his throat. Sergeant Berryman handed over his canteen to his superior who sipped at the warm water. The Lieutenant nodded his thanks and continued, "Each and every one of you is to make sure you read and understand these orders." He pointed to the papers he had nailed on the noticeboard. Just as he was about to salute the troops, he held his hand up with his finger pointing to the sky. "No doubt you will look forward to the improved diet we can enjoy here in the Nile Delta – the local food bowl. I believe Lieutenant Burke has lined up fresh meat, vegetables and even some fruit." Lieutenant Baldwin snapped a salute and spun on his heel heading back to his tent.

Later, when Baldwin walked into the Major's tent, the senior officer looked up from his writing at the small folding table. He sighed.

"One thing I've learned in the forces is all plans must be deemed flexible."

Baldwin sat on a camp chair and glanced through his notes again.

"I presume the powers-that-be feel it best to keep our current load of remounts away from those areas where the Glander's disease has been discovered."

"Yes, they're furiously doing as many Mallein tests as they can. The vet hospital is full up. They believe the ailment has come in through Salonika in Greece."

"Does this mean it may not be a foregone conclusion that we catch the train at Kantara? We may be overland all the way to El Arish?"

"I'm guessing that is a distinct possibility."

"Let's just hope the disease doesn't turn up in any of our lot."

"Our vet, Major Beams, is happy with this mob at the moment."

With the following day's sun at its zenith, the men sought shade wherever they could find it. All the tent walls had been rolled up in the hope of a passing breeze.

Sergeant Berryman and another remount unit sergeant, a man named Pete Dingle, walked through the campsites rounding up idle troopers, seeking help in the training of the remount horses in their care.

"Oh, Sarge, it's as hot as blazes out there, can't we do that when the sun cools off?" Carter had been one of the fifteen men selected to volunteer.

"Now don't go soft on me, Carter. What are you going to do when summer really sets in? We're just coming out of winter at the moment. If you're lucky you might catch a shower of rain this week. Give it a month or so – about July and August – and then you'll know what heat and dry is all about. This area …," he swung his arm indicating the East, "…is what the locals call the Nile Delta and it has the mildest weather you will find along your travels through Egypt and the Sinai Desert."

It was three days later before Major Beams, the veterinarian, proclaimed the horses fit for travel. Billy's excitement added to Joe's hesitant anticipation. Billy was one of the many recruits selected to ride those remount horses that the veterinarian felt needed work. Joe had been chosen to ride with the two teams of scouts based on Sergeant Berryman's recommendation after witnessing Joe's sharp vision and accuracy with a rifle. Carter and Martin along with twenty other recruits, were rostered with experienced men from the Remount Unit on regular picket and guard duties. Most nights, men from other duties helped with relief shifts on guard. The remainder of the troopers were to keep the horses under control as they travelled south-southeast through the Nile Delta then over to the Ismailia Crossing.

Joe rode close to Sergeant Berryman whose field glasses were almost a fixture in his right hand. With the signalman Rankin, from the Remount Unit, they made one scout team. While travelling in the more open areas where another presence could not be hidden in the landscape of the occasional groves of palm trees and shrubs, Rankin spent time teaching Joe the basics of sending and reading a signal. In return, Joe passed on a few of the tips from his grandfather on long-range shooting. The other scout team moving almost parallel and west of them became visible occasionally when both groups appeared on a crest simultaneously before they quickly disappeared into the shallow gullies. Sometimes, when something caught his eye, the sergeant called a halt below a crest. The man crept up the rise where he lay flat with just the top of his head above the horizon. Using a neckerchief stiff with dirt to throw a shadow on his field glasses and prevent their reflection in the unforgiving sun, he lay still and silent examining the area ahead.

Joe frowned as he tried to take in the country about him. He turned as the signalman spoke.

"You're looking troubled, Dawson, what's wrong?"

Joe paused to gather his thoughts before answering.

"This country is not what I expected. I imagined everywhere to be nothing but desert. This Nile Delta is rich farming land. I'm amazed at the fruit trees, the crops, and how many waterways have we crossed so far. The red lotus grows like carpets on the water and the number of different birds you couldn't count if you stopped a week. Most of the birds are similar to those we see in Australia – ibises, cormorants and egrets. We have them on the farm back home." Joe swung his arm about, "Yet out there, not a stone's throw away, the desert, with nothing but sand and little water, hovers in the mirages like a poisonous snake waiting to strike."

Rankin laughed. "Let's just hope we don't run into their crocodiles – maybe not as big as our salt-water crocs in the Australian north but big enough if you run into one face to face." He paused to take a breath, "Even worse can be those damn hippos, but then they're further south of here. I'd suggest you enjoy this luxury while you can. We'll be in the desert soon enough."

Later when they stopped in the shade of a small clump of trees, Sergeant Berryman reminded Joe and Rankin that it was only twelve months since the Turks prowled the area east of here. He explained how the Egyptian Expeditionary Forces, including the Australian Light Horse, pushed them off the Suez Canal and sent them on their way north into the Sinai.

"The Turks are a crafty enemy never to be taken for granted, so keep your eyes open," he warned them.

When Berryman called a halt, the three men sipped from their canteens and crunched on the army biscuits. Joe slipped his notebook and pencil from his shoulder bag and began to write.

Day One - Droving horses in the Nile Delta: Left Alexandria late this morning after a bit of confusion. Sergeant Dingle recorded which trooper rode which of the remount horses. Horses and men, a bit soft after the long sea trip. Major Forbes did not push us. Travelling south-southeast about 25 miles - Nile Delta a rich fertile country with orchards and crops.

At the beginning of the trek, the horses rushed, baulked and crowded each other again and again. Those riding the remounts attempted to keep to the outer edges, away from the unpredictable crush and gaps. Billy sat deep in his saddle with his weight on his feet. The horse that he rode on the first day desperately wanted to hide within the mob, but Billy kept him out on the edge of the other horses. Billy clamped his thighs when the equine devil tried to buck him off onto the ground. After only an hour, the muscles of Billy's thighs and calves felt as if they had been pummelled with a road roller. His arms, somewhat weakened after their six weeks at sea, trembled with exhaustion as he battled the animal. On occasions, the beast planted its front legs with little warning. Billy had to prevent himself from being tossed over the lowered head.

Shouts of laughter and encouragement from the other men accompanied any rider's ignominious descent into the dirt. Billy bit his lip with a determination of his own. He did not intend to be ridiculed if he could help it.

As the day wore on, the attitudes of the remount horses improved. The heat and exercise drained their will for opposition. Dust rose in clouds thrown up from the hundreds of hooves shambling through ruts and holes in the well-used terrain as they travelled parallel to the Nile River. The riders wore neckerchiefs over their noses to allow them to breathe more easily. Even under the brim of their slouch hats, they squinted their eyes against the unforgiving sun.

As the heat intensified and the sweating horses began to lose their desire for freedom and disobedience, they became more amenable. Major Forbes called a break during which time the riders transferred their saddles from their current mounts to each man's second horse. The men quenched their thirst on the hot and not-so-pleasant water from their canteens. Billy spat the first mouthful into the dirt.

" 'Struth, that tastes like the piss of a mule."

"You've tasted the piss of a mule have you, Billy?" The man they called Clappers, limped towards him into the deeper shade. "I've been told, the water only gets worse and less from here on in. I wouldn't be so quick to waste it if I were you."

Billy pulled up his legs to let the man pass by.

During the day of travel, the men stashed away any bits of wood they came across within the numerous articles hanging off their shoulders and saddles. At the end of the day, it took everyone an age to get into a routine of watering, picketing, grooming and feeding the animals in an unfamiliar environment. While this was being done, the chosen commissariat of each section, selected by picking the shortest straw, had a small fire going in his section's bivouac and the quart pots heating water for the tea. Tinned bully beef, onions and dry army biscuits went down the gullet more easily on a swallow of tea. When darkness closed in, the glow of numerous small fires across the large campsite lit the night.

"Geez, I hope you blokes don't take too many more days to get yourselves organized," Mick McCready shook his head and grinned when he turned up for a chat with Billy and Joe.

On the afternoon of the second day of the journey, any traces of high spirits in man or horse soon dissipated within the steaming heat rising off the land. Billy was pleased with the two mounts he had been given to ride today even though the second did surprise him once with a sidestep and a pigroot. Billy hauled in the horse and swore. The grey horse then wandered on peacefully as if nothing had happened.

"Bloody cunning grey ghost, you nearly done for me," he mumbled with a smile of victory and admiration on his face.

As the sun slipped away in the west, Billy watched Joe scribbling in his notebook by the feeble light of their fire. He reached over and poured water into the billy and shoved it further into the coals. He stirred the few black leaves remaining in the hope of another drink of tea.

"Don't you get sick of writing in that book, Joe? It must be like being back at school."

Except for a grunt, Joe ignored his brother as he wrote.

Day Two - Nile Delta: We travelled a bit further today - southeast – following the Alexandria to Cairo railway line. Sergeant Berryman reckons we've come nearly thirty miles today. He said tomorrow we'll meet the famous Nile River.

The sun tipped the horizon as the cavalcade of horses and riders moved on. By mid-morning the two scout teams met at a causeway stretched across the Nile River with a grass-covered island in the middle.

"I'm just going to hang back to talk to Major Forbes for a bit," Sergeant Berryman informed the scout teams. "I'll catch you up."

As he travelled with the scouts across the causeway and through the rich farmlands, Joe tried to take everything in. The male farm workers each wore a long dark cloak and a turban on their head. Most were on their haunches digging root vegetables from the rich soil. The women wore long dresses with hoods pulled up over their heads. Some were clothed in dark colours while others wore robes of brighter hues. The women supported heavy baskets full of vegetables on their heads. They moved to and from a rough shelter on the edge of the field where they emptied their loads. Young children guided a small herd of goats through the grassy edges of the cropland. Tall palm trees cast scant shadows over groups of older men watching the workers. The mounts of the men of the Light Horse were quick to nibble at any green pickings they passed.

The sun stood high in the sky when they emerged from a thick green forest to where the track wound its way through a plain of shallow lagoons. The scouts dismounted and proceeded to transfer their saddles onto their second horse. Sergeant Berryman arrived just as they were settling down to a drink of water and dry biscuits.

"The mob of horses is still a-ways back so I'll take a break too." He jumped to the ground and retrieved his canteen.

While Berryman and the Remount Troop leader of the second scout team discussed their latest orders from the Major, Joe took out his pencil and notebook and began to write.

Day Three – Mid-day: Crossed the Nile River. Still travelling south-east. Through farming land. Rankin told me we'll cross another Nile River again tomorrow.

Far behind the scouting team, Billy vented his disgust at having been allocated a horse that did not like water.

"Play up merry hell, would you?" He mumbled as they sloshed their way over a causeway built across the Nile River. When most other horses in the mob took the opportunity to slake their thirsts, his mount stamped its feet, threw its head about and attempted to pigroot. Billy was pleased to note his second horse for the day, on the lead behind, never flinched.

At Billy's best guess, they had covered about thirty-odd miles so far today when the sun began its descent and the Major called a stop at a bare plain near another river crossing. Settling the horses and men for the night went smoothly. Most bivouac fires were snuffed out early. Instead of the murmurs of gossip amongst the men lying on their groundsheets in the camp, it was snoring, snorts and farts, compliments of the tin bully beef and onions rations, which flavoured the night air. Every man had a blanket at arm's length in preparation for the anticipated cold night.

Billy's second Nile River crossing on the morning of the fourth day went much better for him than yesterday's crossing. He got a laugh at the expense of another trooper who had scored water-fearful mounts.

Joe waited patiently for Sergeant Berryman to rejoin him and Rankin and for the Major to call the "Remounts – Forward" order. He slipped his notebook from inside his shirt and the pencil from his pocket and wrote.

Day Four – early: The Sarge says we made nearly 40 miles yesterday. He said we'll turn more easterly today after we cross this second causeway and then follow the railway line that goes from Cairo to Ismailia. We'll camp on the edge of the desert tonight – not too far from a training camp at Moascar – where the Remounts' new Depot is in the process of being built.

"You taking notes again, Dawson?" Sergeant Berryman smiled as he rode up. "Well, come on then, at this rate, we'll have the mob passing us by."

Joe stuffed his book back inside his shirt and pencil in his pocket before taking up his reins and setting off at a trot.

Joe noticed the change in direction as soon as they began to travel almost directly east. The green countryside thinned out. Like long narrow tentacles, the strips of desert sand stretched across the green grasses. As the day heated up, the sun reflected off the pale sand and burnt any uncovered skin of the riders. The men shoved their hats more firmly upon their heads. The horses' pace decreased as the deepening loose sands dragged at their feet.

Chill of Blame

The sun sank on the evening of the fourth day's travel, while the men and horses slaked their thirsts at the waterway running beside the railway line.

Before each man settled for the night, his waterproof groundsheet was drawn up to cover his saddle, his rifle and himself. Light clouds of sand swept over the sleeping men in their cocoons to trickle in grainy rivulets down the hump of each body. In the morning the men quickly learnt to transfer the desert sand gently back into the ground so as not to fill everyone's eyes with the fine grit.

The dawn of the fifth day glared back at them from the pale sands. The fine grains lifted on the hot desert breezes making vision and comfort in breathing more difficult. Neckerchiefs covered the men's noses and mouths. Hats rested on the men's eyebrows in an attempt to protect reddened eyes.

Joe wrote: *Day five- Early: Another 40 + miles yesterday according to the Sarge. Today we should divert around Moascar and reach Ismailia this evening. Glander's Disease was reported in Moascar horses.*

On the fifth day, the column did indeed bypass Moascar. Joe reached down to stroke the animal's neck and murmur to his horse for the day. His gaze took in the buildings and rows of innumerable tents in the distance floating in a mirage on the hot desert vista. Joe looked more closely and saw the lines of horses between the tents. When he squinted and shaded his eyes, men the size of ants became visible. It occurred to him that he preferred to receive his training like this – on the go – rather than be stuck in a training camp performing endless drills like kids at school practising the steps to the old-fashioned waltzes. He snatched back a grin that almost escaped. The memory of his arm around Tilly Grayson's waist was never to be sneezed at.

Once they passed Moascar, it was only a stone's throw to Ismailia, according to Sergeant Berryman.

Billy and Mick began the fifth day riding side by side. Mick pointed to the distance on their left.

"That's the new Remount Depot they're building at Moascar," Mick spoke from the near-side of Billy's mount with a voice hoarse with dust and thirst. "Major Forbes has been ordered to avoid the usual camps to prevent contamination of the horses with this infection that's gone rampant recently." He stretched up in his stirrups and pointed to the east-southeast. "You'll see Ismailia out there soon."

"That's where you said we'd cross the Suez Canal, isn't it?" Billy lifted his canteen and filled his mouth with the tepid water. He swirled the fluid into every corner of his mouth before swallowing. His face curled in disgust at the musty taste.

It was mid-afternoon when Ismailia lay spread out in front of them surrounded by an ocean of sand. The newcomers paused to take it all in. In the distance, soldiers moved about on the far side of a narrow channel over which spanned a not-too-solid-looking pontoon bridge. On the opposite bank, some way back from the waterline, a line of small shrubby trees followed the canal. A trumpeter signalled halt, much to the surprise of several of the remount horses. They squealed and snorted. They threw up their heads. The majority of their number were too tired to respond. The riders of the more recalcitrant mounts snapped themselves out of their somnolent state. They gripped tight with their legs and retook control of the reins. Horses stamped in the hot sand as order gradually claimed men and horses alike.

Once more, it was Mick who filled Billy in on what procedure the major was likely to follow.

"He'll want to take this lot across tonight while they're feeling tired after a day's march in the sun. At sun-up, they'll be fresh and full of trouble. We'll water the animals and camp on the other side of the canal."

Billy's gaze followed the straight back of Major Forbes as he and the black horse he called Satan peeled off from his mob of volatile charges. The major made his way to the end of the pontoon on the near side of the Canal. He approached a soldier in khaki pants and singlet who waved his hands in the air while yelling instructions to the drivers of three loaded wagons hauled by teams of mules.

The soldier in pants and singlet removed the wide-brimmed slouch hat from his head and slapped it against his leg. He executed a lazy salute before lifting a hand to shade his eyes. The other hand pointed to the large group of men and horses waiting on the bank above him. The hand swung back and forth and sideways and up and down. From where he waited with the overlanders, Billy smiled. He hoped the words from the man's mouth might be a little easier to understand. He mumbled more to himself than to Mick.

"Chop that fellow's hands off, he won't be able to talk; as my dad would say." A wave of home-sickness washed over him.

Billy eased his horse to the edge of the mob and dismounted.

"You feeling the weight, Clunker?" He rubbed the animal's neck and spoke in its ear. Billy called each of the remounts he rode, Clunker. His grubby hand ran down the horse's front leg. Billy was surprised when he felt the heat of the sand. "No wonder you're restless. This must be burning your feet." It did not take too long before the heat penetrated his boots. He stamped the ground. Desire filled his gaze as he looked down to the damp sand near the water. "No doubt the Major will know where to get us all a drink before it's dark." He reassured his mount as his hands ran over the saddle, the girths, and the load. He smoothed what he could of the saddle blanket.

He felt the stirring in the horses around him and glanced up to see the Major returning. Smoothly Billy lifted into the saddle.

For the next thirty minutes, Major Forbes with the aid of Lieutenant Baldwin and Sergeant Berryman along with the experienced members of the Remount Unit showed the recruits how to place themselves on their mounts and lead the second horse they each had charge of, into a line on either side of the remaining unridden horses. The horses on lead reins were held on the side of the rider closest to the enclosed unridden horses to act as a quietening influence.

Billy looked down at Clunker as they shuffled forward towards the pontoon bridge. He patted the horse's neck.

"She'll be right, mate – they tell us this fragile crossing is as safe as houses but I'll not be putting any money on it." On Billy's left, the restless unridden remounts tended to push and shove forwards. Ahead of him, Mick's horse did not appear to appreciate having the animal on a lead rein at his near-side hind leg. It threatened to lift its hind legs and kick. Billy eased back a little further.

"Keep in close," Mick called. "I won't let him kick. Don't leave too much gap for those loose horses to take advantage of. The silly beggars will take it into their heads to dive over the side of this bridge most likely."

With one hand on the reins of his mount and one on the lead to his second horse, Billy nodded acknowledgment. He began to sing a song of the Australian Bush just like his father used to sing to quieten the stock on droving trips back home. The melody and the sense of home calmed his own apprehension.

The Major and lead horses strode out onto the first pontoon. The change of tone underfoot from the soft swish of the sand, the splash of water and then the echo of the timber planks on hollow floats, set a few of the horses into a panic which did little to calm those coming behind. As some of the frightened horses shoved forward and others either shied or planted their front feet in refusal, the procedure began to concertina. The men of the Light Horse clenched their saddles with their thighs and held short reins on their mounts. Gradually the procession moved forward as peace began to settle. With few exceptions, the animals further down the line exhibited little more than a raised head and a nervous shuffle when they felt the bridge beneath their hooves. The momentum of the mounts behind them and those with riders on their wings kept the herd on track to the other end of the crossing.

Horses were led to the freshwater canal running parallel to the waterway over which they had travelled. They were allowed to drink in small numbers at a time.

"Ever seen a thirsty horse drink itself until it couldn't walk, Daley?" Mick asked as the pair of men separated the next group of horses from the herd.

Billy swung his horse to his left drafting several brazen mounts back into the group waiting to drink.

"Not really, Dad was pretty careful about that. His dad, my grandfather, used to talk of the troubles they had with horses and water when he was in the Boer War." Billy walked his horse nearer to Mick. "What about you, Mick?"

"Most of us remount fellows have seen the result of gripe in the thirsty animals over-drinking at one time or another."

As had become their practice on this journey, Sergeant Berryman had the regular remount unit troops organized into several groups with allocated specific chores. Each of these units took recruits into their number to introduce them to the routine process of watering the remount horses as well as their own mounts. Only ten horses were led to water at a time. The others were held back in a herd to wait their turn. Most of the recruits were born to the bush and knew the strategy of this process to prevent horses, desperate for a drink, shoving and pushing in their haste and determination which often led to injury. Chances were, some might miss out on a drink altogether while others guzzled on the water giving themselves a dose of the gripe.

While the watering went on, the clang of steel on steel rang out across the campsite as a third team began to secure the picket lines. Water dripped from the muzzles of those horses now in the care of a fourth team who attached them to these picket lines. The men brushed out the sweat and sand from the horses' coats and attached their nosebags with their ration of grain. The nominated commissariat of each section began to prepare his section's bivouac but not before he went and drank deeply from the freshwater canal himself.

Weariness tempted Joe to forget his notebook entry after he had eaten his tin of bully beef. He sucked on the blister rising on his thumb where the hot fluid had spurted out when he stabbed the can with his bayonet. Half-heartedly he nibbled the dry tasteless army biscuit and sipped his tea. Slowly he retrieved the notebook and pencil and began to write.

Day five: End of day - have crossed the Suez Canal over the pontoon bridge and camped outside Ismailia.

CHAPTER TEN

Billabong Downs

May 1917

The early morning chill crept into his bones as William dragged his feet over the side of his bed. Even Nips the blue dog made a tardy exit from underneath; his nails scratched on the timber floorboards.

"Time to throw some blankets on the bed tonight, Nips," William advised as he threw on a flannel singlet and shirt. He drew a pair of thick trousers up his legs and retrieved the socks from inside his boots. Nip's tail thudded an impatient beat on the floor. The dog's dark eyes sparkled. If a dog could smile; he smiled. The old white dog Snowy, lifted an eyelid to watch the process from the mat near the bed.

With his boots and padded jacket in his hand, William made his way to the kitchen where he found Mabel at the stove with the billy boiling and a pot of simmering oats waiting.

He froze in the doorway and stared in surprise. Even on her best days, he was not likely to find Mabel up before him. To find her up and preparing the porridge was too much to absorb. Nips did not stay to learn the answer to the mystery. He scarpered down the stairs. Snowy ambled along behind.

"Good morning, William." Mabel's hair shone with brushing and lay tidy in a ribbon on the nape of her neck. A fresh set of clothes hung loosely from her shoulders, gathered into her waist with a gold-coloured buckled belt.

With his power of speech almost stolen, William stuttered a reply, "Morning, Mabel."

"Sit down, I'll serve up your porridge. Will you have jam or sugar on it today?"

"Sugar, thanks."

"Will you have your pannikin of tea with that too?"

"Er … please." William's mind struggled with what his eyes were seeing and his ears were hearing. *What's Mabel up to now? I've never known her to get up early on a cold morning, let alone cook my breakfast as well.* The chair scraped as he pulled it out from under the table. Wariness settled in his eyes as he went to sit down.

Mabel lay a small cloth in front of William before she gently set down the full plate of porridge with a large spoon beside it. He watched her closely while she poured his tea and placed it beside the oats. He lifted his spoon and paused. A dreadful thought slithered into his head. *Is this poisoned? How many times has Mabel threatened to kill me?*

"Eat up, William, it's nice and hot just as you always have it."

Does that mean the porridge is poisoned? William watched as Mabel served a small bowl of porridge for herself. His suspicion faded as she sat and began to eat.

Tentatively, William began to eat his oats. His gaze rested upon his wife more than on his plate. *She hasn't got a cup of tea.*

"Are you not having tea this morning?" He asked. "If I remember you love your first cup of the day."

"I've already had a cup of tea but I'll have another when I finish my porridge."

"Oh …," William sipped another spoonful of oats. "Can I pour your tea and let it cool for you?"

"Why thank you, William, that would be lovely."

Chill of Blame

William rested his spoon in the plate of oats. He rose to make his way to the kettle on the stove. Her cup with a few left-over tea leaves sat on the side of the sink. He rinsed it out and filled it up with the fresh brew. His hand shook as he placed the cup on the table beside Mabel – just as she liked it, black and no sugar.

Once back at the table, his mind continued to torment him. *If there is poison here in the kitchen it is unlikely to be in the tea then. Struth, I'm getting paranoid. She's going to send me around the bend just like herself, at this rate.*

When he stood to clear his dishes from the table, Mabel jumped up too.

"Leave them, William, I'll tidy up." She walked around the table and stretched up to kiss William on the cheek. His mouth dropped open. His hand reached up slowly to touch the spot in disbelief.

"Have a nice day, William."

"Er … you too, Mabel." William made to go down the stairs.

"Oh, William, when will you be going to town next? I really need to buy a few more dresses. I seem to have lost quite a bit of weight." She tugged at the bodice of her dress.

"Er … yes, of course, I'll talk to Miles and see what we need from the produce store. I know there's a cattle sale in a few weeks. We'll be going in then, no doubt."

If William had turned back once more, he may have heard Mabel's quiet reply as he stepped through the garden gateway.

"Of course, you'll be going to the cattle sale. What about what I want?"

In the shed, William found Geoff, Miles and Gazza in deep discussions about the fencing wire delivered by the mail truck the previous day.

"They only had twenty rolls – at least that's what Barnsey, the driver of the mail truck said," Gazza offered. He shifted the weight of the two buckets of fresh milk in his hands. "Shortage with supplies due to the war, I guess."

"Yes, that's what's marked on the paperwork I was looking at last night," William commented as he walked over to inspect the wire rolls.

"Fran and Maggie will be over this morning to divide the household stuff." Miles turned his head to ask his brother, "Do you think Mabel will join them?"

William smiled. "Lately, I wouldn't have bet on it but this morning she is almost back to her old self. Mabel may like to help with that."

Geoff led his brown horse with the white half-moon between the eyes out from the shed, a swag and billy tied to the saddle. Maggie had packed his saddle bag with supplies for several days.

"Come on, Serpent, we've got a few miles to travel."

At the hitching post outside stood the piebald pack-horse loaded with a roll of plain wire on one side and the shovel, pickets and tool bag on the other. Geoff mounted his horse and bent down to take up the lead rein on the piebald.

He called back to the others, "I'm off to check the boundary fences. I'll be back in a couple of days if all is in order."

"We'll have a drink waiting for you, Geoff," Miles laughed.

"I'll be needing it," Geoff smiled.

Mabel sat at her escritoire in her bedroom re-reading the letter from her two daughters who, while at school in Townsville, lived most of the year at her parents' place. She smiled a selfish smile knowing William had not seen this letter. She had slipped it out of the pile of mail delivered by Fran yesterday.

Chill of Blame

Dear Mother and Papa,

This school term has been unbelievable. Maud won all of her swimming races and I came top of the class again. Grandmama has promised a trip on the boat over to Magnetic Island these holidays as a reward. Hope you are both feeling well. Your sweet Cissy.

P.S. This is Maud's letter underneath mine.

Mother and Papa

The home science teacher has shown us how to bake Madeira cakes just like Mrs. Bardon can cook. I like the cooking class. I wish you were a better cook Mother.

Have you heard from Billy and Joe? When you write to them tell them to write to me and Cissy too. Everyone says our brothers must be brave heroes to be in the Australian Light Horse Army. They keep asking us what our brothers are doing.

Love from Maud.

Mabel read the last two sentences again and again. They stoked the furnace of her resentment. *Why hasn't Billy written to me, his mother? What's wrong with that hopeless Joe? He can write, can't he?*

Mabel reached into the drawer and retrieved the photo of her eldest son when he was three years old. Her slim finger traced his face. *No matter what they say, Billy is my son. Just look at him he is the spitting image of myself at that age.* Mabel stood up and took the photo over to slip it under her pillow. *If neither William nor my father will do anything, it is up to me to get my Billy home. I need to catch the train to Townsville and visit the army recruiting station myself.*

At the sound of the call from the back door, Mabel's head lifted. She folded the letter roughly, shoved it into her escritoire and pushed the desk drawer shut.

Fran's voice called again. "Mabel, are you there? Do you want to join Maggie and me? We're going to the shed to see if there is anything for us in the load the mailman delivered yesterday."

Mabel sat in silence. A scowl swamped some of the lines on her face at the sound of Fran's footsteps on the verandah. Mabel knew she had to get up and go outside or the nosey woman would come right into her bedroom. She forced a tight smile onto her face.

"Oh, I thought I heard someone calling. I've been busy."

"Hello, Mabel, it's good to see you up and about today. Will you join us?"

"No, I'm sorry, I'm just planning my winter wardrobe."

Fran's jaw dropped open. She took several seconds to answer.

"Oh, that sounds er … nice. I'll leave you to it. Did you have anything on order at the produce store at all?"

"No, thanks."

CHAPTER ELEVEN

Ismailia to El Arish

May 1917

Billy's head shot up at the sound of a commotion nearby. Riding cantankerous horses all day and then awake on guard duty half the night when his body demanded sleep did nothing for his responses. Lieutenant Burke, the officer on guard duty tonight on the west wing with himself, Carter, Martin, and the one they called Clappers, stood spitting curses into his horse's face, underlining every word with a spiteful slash of his whip.

Slowly Billy figured out what was happening and why. The Lieutenant had fallen off, or maybe been thrown by the most placid horse amongst the two hundred animals they travelled with. The man couldn't ride a rocking horse, in Billy's opinion. How the incompetent scored this job amongst horses was beyond Billy's comprehension. Carter and Martin, the two recruits in the section with Joe and himself, and Clappers, a remount trooper, wandered over.

"Thought he was having a go at you, Billy Boy. Wasn't sure if you were worth saving or not," Carter flashed a wide smile to go with his loud whisper.

"What rider in his right mind treats a horse like that? He'll ruin that mount for some poor sod to ride into battle," Billy ranted softly. He chewed on his bottom lip.

"That old fart shouldn't be allowed within a hundred miles of a horse. He should be locked up in the clink." Clappers added his opinion to the comments.

The glow of an early dawn eased over the horizon with the threat of another hot day. The witnesses said no more. They turned their horses about and guided them back to camp. Their four-hour guard stint was over.

Major Forbes glanced up when he heard the voices of his two lieutenants approaching his tent. He finished recording the latest message received into his log book and stood up. His eyes squinted when he stepped out into the rising sunlight.

After the formalities of saluting, Forbes greeted his officers.

"I was hoping you'd be along; I have the latest report from Headquarters. We are to continue overland all the way to El Arish. Today we will travel to Kantara only. It will be a short trip but it will give you time to have our supplies and rations topped up when we get there." Major Forbes nodded to Lieutenant Burke as he spoke. He then turned towards Lieutenant Baldwin. "It won't hurt the men to have an early day either."

Whipped up by southern winds the desert sands swirled around the legs of the animals; it filled every space with its fine grains. The troopers pulled their hats tight on their heads and knotted neckerchiefs over their mouths and noses. With eyes squinted almost shut, they strained to peer through the hazy dust clouds as they followed Major Forbes the short distance north from Ismailia to the other side of Kantara.

None of the four witnesses forgot the incident of Lieutenant Burke's cruelty to the horse in the early hours of the morning. It remained with them all day as they ate their morning rations of hot tea and army biscuits, while they rode on the wing of the mob of horses, and during the questionable pleasure of consuming their evening ration of bully beef, onion and more army biscuits.

During the day the four spoke intermittently of fitting rewards for such cruelty. It was Billy who came up with the most daring and dangerous plan.

His three friends hesitated before they agreed to assist.

"You do know we'll be set up before a firing squad for this, Billy." Martin grinned his warning.

A sour odour of the sweaty bodies of man and animals hung on the still evening air over the camp just past Kantara. Four young men sat on the ends of their groundsheets. Each man sipped at their hot tea while, speaking in low tones, Billy related what he planned to do during the night.

"The Old Fart …," Billy used Clappers's nickname for Lieutenant Burke, "… always rides the same horse. It's brown with no markings, except of course the tattoo on its hoof. I've never seen Burke check his horse in the morning. In fact, he usually makes some lackey saddle the horse for him."

"Don't I know it; I've been ordered a few times to do that. I've promised myself I'd put a burr under the saddle if he orders me to do it again," Clappers chuckled.

Soft voices continued their sporadic conversation for two hours until the large encampment settled into a hushed quietness.

"Now is as good a time as any to do this if we're going to do it at all." Billy spilt the last of the cold tea from his pannikin into the dry sands. He rose slowly to his feet. "You sure you can find the horse in the dark, Clappers?"

Clappers grunted. Such a question did not deserve anything more.

The four men moved off to their designated tasks. Billy stood within a stone's throw from the Lieutenant's bivouac. Strained snores drifted up from the tightly wrapped body of Lieutenant Burke revealed in the light of a half-moon. Billy soothed the target horse. His trained hands quickly untied the head and hoof ropes from the picket line. At that moment, the Lieutenant snorted. He rolled over onto his back, lifted his head and coughed before settling back over onto his other side.

Billy froze in an uncomfortable half-crouch. He waited, each breath no more than a sip of the night air. Pain, brought on by the awkward position of his body, ripped through his lower back. His ears strained waiting to hear the Lieutenant's breathing steady.

He cursed silently. *Go back to sleep, you bastard.*

The words ran back and forth across his mind. A groan threatened to lift from deep within his gut as the pain now burnt every muscle in his back. It was replaced with a soft sigh as the sleeping man's breathing deepened. Billy held one hand gently over the horse's muzzle to prevent the animal from whickering. The groan almost escaped as he rose from the crouch.

It seemed an age but eventually, Clappers led the replacement mount into the vacant site on the picket line near the Lieutenant. The replacement horse was also a brown horse with no markings. The numbers tattooed on its hoof were different. Martin and Carter stood nearby as cockatoo lookouts. When the lads with the quiet horse returned to the vacancy in the next row of remount horses, the process to secure the animal was reversed.

After their sleepless night twenty-four hours before, Billy, Martin, Carter and Clappers fell into a satisfied sleep.

As the night chill dissipated in the early morning air, Major Forbes finished updating his daily report and placed it in the saddle bag. He heard a shout outside. The major exited his tent just in time to see Lieutenant Burke take a tumble from his horse almost on his very doorstep. Dust erupted around the spluttering displaced rider. The major's lips twitched. But he managed to reclaim control before the officer drew himself to his feet.

"Sir … sir … Major Forbes, I can explain." The man stuttered and stammered. "There is something wrong, this cannot be my usual horse." Burke's head spun about looking for an underling to check the tattoo number on the animal's hoof. His gaze returned to his commanding officer. "Some smart aleck must have switched my horse."

Major Forbes drew in a long breath then sighed slowly. Today was going to be one of those days it seemed. This man tried his patience to the limit. Burke may have been a dab hand as a procurement officer but he had the ability to destroy what should have been the best of days. They were ahead of schedule and the veterinarian reported the horses were in good condition. Forbes ground his teeth and looked the man up and down, concealing his true thoughts.

I'd rather kick you up the arse than pander to such a pampered overgrown schoolboy.

"Lieutenant Burke, what difference does it make what horse you ride? We're here to exercise all the remount horses not stick to favourites. You're supposed to be riding different horses every day to give them all training and exercise."

A vision flashed across the major's mind of the four lads he'd seen hanging about the area at first light when out for a pee. Suspicion flared. His breath caught in his throat as he stamped down on his smile. He admitted to a desire to congratulate the lads but in his position, he must maintain the troopers' respect for the officers. God knows this imbecile commanded little respect.

Forbes sucked in a sharp breath. Warning signals flashed in his mind. As much as it might please him to spill out his inner thoughts to this man, he knew he could be throwing his career down the dunny hole if he did. Burke had powerful friends – perhaps not friends, but certainly a powerful family. Forbes swallowed his irritation and not for the first time thought of how he would rather face a stampeding herd of horses or an enemy machine-gun than tip-toe over the egg-shells of the politics of his job.

"I will endeavour to find out who is responsible, Lieutenant Burke. You do realize we cannot waste time on this. These horses are urgently needed to replace those lost at the two Gaza stunts. They must be at El Arish before General Allenby arrives and he is expected in June." Forbes began to turn towards his tent but changed his mind. He scratched his head as another thought passed through. He looked back at the Lieutenant. "Were you able to get the supplies we needed yesterday evening?"

"Yes, Major, everything we requested is with our supply unit."

"Well, we can get off to Romani then as soon as the men and horses are ready."

When the sun reached its zenith and the riders halted to shift their saddles onto the backs of the second animal they led, they did so at the base of a large sandhill.

In Sergeant Berryman's scout team, it was Rankin who answered Joe's question.

"Royston's Hill – the New Zealand and British Yeomanry had a difficult time here stopping the Ottomans last year. Their army was on its way with heavy weapons to destroy the railhead at Romani." He paused as he lifted his water canteen from the saddle horn. "It was a nasty stunt there for a while. With little to no cover, our fellows eventually overran the enemy artillery and captured five hundred prisoners." The signalman sipped sun-heated water from his canteen. "The Ottoman approached from the desert. They must have had the devil's own job bringing the heavy machinery and artillery with them. By that stage, thanks to the railway through to Romani, our howitzers and field guns were in position before the enemy soldiers even poked their heads over the horizon."

"Is this why Major Forbes has us out on scout duty each day – in case the Ottoman should try again to approach the Suez Canal?"

"They'd be foolish to try. As far as I'm aware, we have them neatly tucked up in the Gaza and Beersheba areas. Although, having said that, don't be surprised if, in a couple of days, you sight the odd German Taube flying above doing a reconnaissance run. Our airmen, or the Brits, usually send them home with their tails between their legs."

Joe dragged out his notebook from inside his shirt. It looked a bit worse for wear with sweat stains on its cover. He began to write his latest entry.

Day 7 – Mid-day break at the base of Royston's Hill. Aim to camp just past Romani this evening.

After a hot and dusty day travelling towards the coast, the remounts were in the process of being settled into their picket lines after watering from the troughs filled by the water pumps on the eastern side of Romani. Major Forbes did not fail to notice the weariness in his men but knew he had a distasteful job to do before they were dismissed. He asked Lieutenant Baldwin to call the troops to order.

After thanking the men for a job well done so far and a reminder, that there was still some way to go to reach their destination, he addressed the issue on his mind.

"We have some pranksters in our midst whose actions had the potential to cause a serious accident to one of our officers." As Forbes drew breath his errant mind drifted off on a tangent for a moment.

Pity Burke wasn't injured. Nothing too serious mind, just enough to keep him back at the Kantara hospital centre. He sighed, took a deep breath, and continued speaking to the troops.

"Would the person or persons responsible for swapping the horses around on Lieutenant Burke step forward?"

Silence rose from the ranks like fetid air. The major did not miss the glances and grins flying about between quite a few on parade.

"There will be no leave at El Arish for anyone if a confession is not forthcoming." Major Forbes did not notice any specific man move. He sensed rather than saw the ruffle through their number like the hint of a movement through a summer garden with the first lift of a soft morning breeze. He imagined the whispering murmurs through the ranks.

"Don't say a word."

"There's nothing to see at El Arish anyway."

"Last I heard there was only smallpox and cholera to be had in El Arish."

"Keep schtum."

Major Forbes did not waste time waiting too long. "I'll be in my tent if anyone has an explanation."

The glow of the small fire at their bivouac site danced in Bluey's ginger hair like flames when Joe returned to his section's bivouac not long after dark. He eased the heavy saddle down on the sand at the top of his sleeping space. Surprise and curiosity filled his gaze when he found the other three of his section, Billy, Carter and Martin sound asleep. These three were usually at a game of cards or off until late, chatting to other recruits they knew.

"The boys left you tea in the pot and your tin of bully beef is near the fire keeping warm. I think you'll find an onion in the coals for you too. And I'm sure they said they'd left a couple of dry biscuits on the end of your groundsheet for you; that's if the small wildlife hasn't run off with it." Bluey delivered the message.

"Thanks, Bluey. Whatcha been up to?" Joe kicked his bully beef tin away from the heat to let it cool off a bit. He found his pannikin and poured tea from the pot. After a sip, he drank deeply.

"Had a couple of good horses to ride today which was a pleasure. I'd hoped to have a game of cards tonight but these three are out to it. I think I'll go up to where the others have a game going. See you later."

After taking his bayonet out and piercing the meat tin with care, Joe looked at the back of the departing horseman.

"Enjoy your cards, Bluey."

As Joe picked at his food, he updated his notes for the day.

End of Day 7- With the remount unit delivering their horses and us recruits to El Arish. Camped east of Romani. Apparently, Romani is a group of oases in a waste of sand dunes.

Joe fired a suspicious glance at his brother. He was not deceived by the innocence of Billy's face in sleep. After years of experience, he knew Billy could look as innocent as a lamb after getting into the most dreadful mischief. Their mother always blamed Joe whatever evidence presented itself. Joe didn't really mind. Billy always provided recompense in the form of a bribe or favour.

Joe shook his head as his thoughts tumbled on. *But this – if he was involved, could mean he might be thrown out of the Light Horse just when he arrived. Silly beggar if he did. He had wanted so much to join up.*

Amidst the rush and thrust of riders hazing and pushing the herd into an orderly gathering, the procession led out from Romani in an easterly direction towards Bir El Abd, a distance of less than twenty miles. Unrest ran through the demeanour of the men like a fidgety breeze on a pond. Quiet laughter at the thought of the audacity of the guilty interspersed with curiosity and admiration for their guts in swapping the lieutenant's horse. If any of the riders held pity for the recipient of the prank, they kept their thoughts to themselves.

Joe moved ahead of the herd with the scouts. He nudged his hat sideways to keep the dawning sun out of his eyes. Beside him rode Sergeant Berryman and the signalman, Rankin. Joe felt a restlessness in the animal he rode this morning. He stroked the horse's neck and spoke soothing words.

"The railway and water pipeline are over there," Rankin waved his left arm. "They only started building both the railway and the pipeline in February last year. Nowadays we'll run almost parallel to them all the way to El Arish." When the sergeant moved ahead, Rankin slipped in on Joe's offside. "With the regular water pump stations all the way, this trip will be a breeze. I did my first trek through here delivering horses to the troops protecting Katia when the Ottoman raided in April last year and again in August when they swarmed down from Bir El Abd onto our men. This led to the battle for Romani. In those days we carried a couple of spearpoint pumps with us to drain the wells and cisterns of the local tribes. The boys turned blue in the face pumping their hearts out in an effort to water the horses we had."

"How far to this El Arish?"

"About eighty miles give or take. Mostly through these sand dunes which exhausts both man and horse very quickly. It will be a short day again. The Major will probably water us at Bir El Abd this afternoon – that's about twenty miles from Romani. I hope you remembered to fill your canteens. The veterinarian, Major Beams, wants to inspect all the horses today." Rankin looked up as the sergeant called him over. He turned his mount and cantered across to where Berryman pointed to the east.

Joe remained on point. His head swivelled in slow arcs from left to right examining the horizons. At regular intervals, he twisted in the saddle to cast his gaze behind. Each time the rising cloud of dust stirred by the hooves of the herd had thickened. Joe smiled at his luck in being out front and not trying to breathe in the midst of that lot.

It was early afternoon when the pumping station at Bir El Abd came into view. With efficiency acquired over days of practice, the horses were watered, secured, groomed and fed. The veterinarian inspection began by mid-afternoon.

Joe found himself sitting alone beside Straps, secured on the picket line. He pulled the notebook from his shirt, gripped the pencil and jotted down his day's note.

End Day 8 – Romani to Bir El Abd: Short day's travel. Vet inspecting all horses after they water.

The dawn's glow on the ninth day of their travels filtered over Bir El Abd now hidden within the dust blowing in on the hot dry winds from the desert. It whistled through the campground bringing a thick haze and collected anything not secured. Occasional slouch hats and ground sheets spun off on the air thick with clouds of sand.

Major Forbes swore when he first stepped outside his tent.

"Blasted khamsins – there'll be horses and men toddling around lost all day." He fought the urge for haste in delivering the remounts and the recruits to the General's camp near El Arish only a day's travel away, but caution tempered his impatience and he decided to remain in the same campsite until the winds died down and the dust settled. He touched his forehead with his forefinger. *Knock on wood, it won't be for more than one day,* he thought. He felt the acid in his gut at the possibility of days stuck here waiting for the sand storms to blow themselves out.

At the sight of Lieutenant Baldwin entering the tent bringing in a puddle of sand as he saluted and removed his hat, Major Forbes grinned.

"Good day out there then, Lieutenant?"

"Damned terrible. It's as thick as your grandma's winter nightie. We're not going anywhere today, I shouldn't think. I can hardly see the nose on my face. If I hadn't worn this neckerchief my lungs would have filled up with blasted sand. Can you drown in sand?"

"You'll be pleased to hear I've decided to stay put today."

"I figured you might. Can you imagine leading this herd through these khamsins as well as playing nursemaid to a mob of recruits at the same time?"

"It doesn't bear thinking about. Was there anything specific you wanted?"

"No, I just came to check if we are staying in situ and if you wanted more reinforcement stakes around this tent."

"Leave it for the moment, I may even drop the tent if the winds get any stronger."

"If you're sure then, I'll go out and get the boys to rig up a few rope lines to reduce the number of new lads getting lost in the storm. They'll need to double-check the picket lines too."

"Thanks – it wouldn't be the first time the horses broke free in a storm, be it sand or rain, and were discovered miles away bunched up against the weather."

It was Baldwin's turn to smile. "Nor would it be the first time the fellows got lost on the way to the dunny. Which reminds me; the canvas partition wall will need to be reinforced. I had the medics check out a bloke who had been knocked unconscious while doing his business when the winds first struck. The force dragged one of the larger stakes at the end of the wall out of the ground while still attached to the canvas. The heavy stake struck the trooper on the head as it flung him from his perch. Thank goodness the canvas formed an air pocket around his head and he was able to breathe because he was there until they found him almost buried in sand this morning."

The Major's glance lifted and a smile tugged at his lips. He visualized the young trooper squatting on a plank across one of the holes dug into the soil for human waste.

"The poor blighter must have got the fright of his life. You're having me on, aren't you?"

"No, seriously – you'll get the medical report later."

"Now I've heard everything."

Both men chuckled at the thought of the trooper explaining his ignominious wounding.

Knowing full well Lieutenant Burke was quite likely to come calling with some petty issue expecting his leader to be confined in his tent during this sand storm, Major Forbes deliberately ventured forth covering his mouth and nose as he went. He paused when the force of the sand and winds first hit him. He made sure to secure the tent ties behind him.

Working his way through the gloom down the long rows of the picket lines, he was pleased to see the horses seemed calm enough with their rear ends into the force of the wind. At the far end of the third row, he came across Sergeant Berryman instructing a group of troopers on living safely in a sand storm such as this.

"If you don't want to disappear and never be seen again, keep within the immediate boundary of this campsite. Later, if things quieten down a bit, we'll have to take the animals to water. In that case, a safety line will be erected from here to the water station, and another coming back. You'll attach yourselves to this line when going in either direction. I cannot stress enough how dangerous these sand storms can be. Only thirty feet away from our boundary and even the best of us can become totally disorientated. You'll find similar guide ropes leading to the latrines.

Major Forbes moved off to reconnoitre his campsite. When his friend the veterinarian, Major David Beams, appeared out of the sandy haze, he smiled.

"Lovely day, Dave? How are the animals? No problems so far?"

"No, Peter, your lads have everything under control." Major Beams paused and stroked his chin. "I was hoping to catch up with you today. Remember you were talking to me about the horse-swapping incident? Well, I did a bit of investigating. I marked both the horses with a hidden mane snip. I marked the quiet horse with one on the left side and the rogue animal on the right side. Blow me down, if last night I didn't find both animals with the snips on the left and right sides."

"We have a smart aleck in our midst."

"There's something else you might find interesting. There's a young bloke here, one of the recruits, who comes and visits the two remount horses involved in that incident morning and night and I've noticed he rides the rogue every day. He's doing a good job too in such a short time. And yesterday, I noticed there were two of the recruit horses hardly ever too far away from him as we travelled. I suspect at least one was allocated to him in Australia."

"You're quite the detective aren't you, Dave? This trooper got a name?"

"Daley, I think. We spoke for a bit late last night." The vet scratched his head. "You know, come to think of it, I bet anything you like that is when he added the extra mane snips to those two horses you were interested in. I never thought of it at the time. You wouldn't think butter would melt in his mouth."

"I had a feeling Trooper Daley might know more than he's letting on."

"Now, I hope you're not going to toss him out on his ear. That lad has a wonderful way with the horses and as I heard on the grapevine, whoever did the horse swap did so because they witnessed the abuse your friend Burke dished out to the horse he usually rides – the quiet one."

"No, Dave, I won't give him the boot. We need more like him but I can't let him get away totally scot-free."

The bayonets attached to the two rifles were stuck into the soil and the rifles butts met in the air above. One groundsheet secured against the rifles protected the two men sitting on a second groundsheet. With his lead pencil, Joe Dawson wrote a few sentences in his notebook on his lap between sweeps of his arm to remove the gathered sand. Billy flipped a coin over and around his fingers. Boredom hung as heavy as the sand in the air around him.

"How long is that letter going to be? I don't know what you have to say. Did you tell Pops about the bloke buried in the dunny this morning? What about the troopers who swapped the Old Fart's horse?"

Joe snapped his head up and gave Billy a long stare.

"Not much point, it would never pass the censors. Anyway, are you sure you don't know more about the horse swap? It sounds very much like one of Pops' old war stories."

Billy looked up to see Joe giving him his look. The glare he produced when Billy was either planning some mischief or had already committed some offence. The glare which Billy always felt could bore a hole through his head. The coin fell to the sand when Joe spoke.

"You did, didn't you – or at least you took part?"

Billy dropped his eyes. "Did what?"

"You swapped those horses on Burke, didn't you?" Joe picked up the notepad and shook the sand from its pages. "Why?" The glare continued. "Who helped you?"

Billy retrieved his coin and slipped it into his pocket.

"Well, he deserved it. We saw him whipping the quiet horse around the head and ears. We thought the fella needed a lesson."

"We – or just you?"

"Well, I thought he needed a lesson."

"You'll be out of the army before you're even in it at this rate." Joe shook his head. He admitted to himself he wasn't totally surprised. Billy loved the horses. Joe glared again sending Billy's gaze downwards. "You'd better not say a word, Billy, or they'll toss you in the clink for the duration of the war."

Billy chuckled. "You should have seen him flying through the air the next morning."

Joe struggled not to enjoy the vision. That officer irritated even his easy-going nature.

Joe shook the sand from his book again and finished jotting down his day's record.

End day 9 – Sand Storm at Bir El Abd: Major remained in Bir El Abd – Can't see the nose on your face. Man injured in the dunny. They have rope lines around the camp so we don't get lost.

Relief shone in the faces of everyone in camp the next morning when the dreadful winds had subsided but for the occasional swirl of a dust devil. Major Forbes had everyone up early and on the track heading in an easterly direction towards El Arish. As he inspected the troops and horses moving out, he took a mental note of the position of Trooper Daley.

During the morning he observed how the young man dismounted and walked beside the horse he rode rubbing the animal's head and ears almost constantly. Even from where he watched on the other side of the mob of horses, he could see Daley's lips moving without a pause. The other horse on Daley's lead rope looked the exact image of the first horse. The trio eased back through the herd as their pace slowed.

Forbes looked up when Dave Beams appeared on his right. "Good day, Dave."

The veterinarian nodded. "And to you. I see you have the young rascal under your eye."

"Yes, I see what you mean. He certainly has a way with the troublesome horses. I presume those two he is with today are the two swapped horses?"

"Certainly, looks like them from here. I'd have to go and check their hoof tattoos to be sure." Dave smiled. "I bet that chap can tell them from a mile away." The veterinarian nodded his head in Billy's direction. "Now I want you to look at those two horses walking on the man's left. See the brown one with a long white strip down its face and the one next to it, the bay, with a blotchy white mark on its nose? Those two are nearly always found together and usually not too far from Daley."

"So, you're saying one of those horses is that recruit's issued mount?"

"I'm willing to bet on it. And I reckon the second horse there belongs to someone within his section too."

At that moment, they watched the recruit lift into the saddle and ease his way forward to his original position. The two horses without leads kept pace with the rider.

The observers shared a smile. The vet changed the subject.

"You'll find in my report how we had two horses down last night after swallowing too much sand with their feed. They ended up with a bit of gripe. We gave them each a ball of clover and our unit boys walked them around for a couple of hours."

"You'll keep an eye on them today, will you?"

"Yes, I'm just on the lookout for them now."

Dave Beams and the Major parted company going off in opposite directions. The Major walked his horse slowly around the moving herd and came up on Billy Daley's off-side.

Billy may have appeared to have no other interest but the horses he worked, but his glances had taken in the Major's approach. Guilt stirred his gut but his belief in the right of his actions kept him calm. He turned in the saddle at the greeting from on his right.

"Good morning, Trooper."

"Morning, Major, sir." Billy's attention returned to his mount as it threw its head up at the sound of a new voice. He murmured quiet words to his horse.

"You seem to have an affinity with troubled horses."

Billy's glance snapped up to watch the Major's eyes more closely. He could not detect any accusation in the man's expression.

"Major, sir, my dad reckons horses and humans are not born bad. He says it's circumstances and treatment which make them bad."

"I'd have to agree with your dad there." The Major paused. "So, what do you think happened to these two you're working on now?"

"Bad handling," Billy's answer almost exploded from his throat. "This one I'm riding now, anyway. The other, I'm not so sure what has upset it; maybe bad breaking-in perhaps."

"You know a bit about breaking-in horses, do you, Trooper?"

"My dad was the best horse-breaker in the whole of north Australia – maybe in all of Australia." Billy was never averse to exaggerating the prowess of his father. "He taught me and my brother … er … my cousin, I mean, how."

Major Forbes tucked the little word slip away into a corner of his mind.

"I'd like you to bring these two horses to me after you're satisfied with them or when we get to El Arish, anyway. I'd be interested in seeing the outcome of your efforts."

"Of course, Major, sir."

"Oh, and there is one other thing, if you notice anyone, and I mean anyone, treating the horses cruelly I'd like to hear about it directly."

Once more Billy's glance shot up to gaze into a pair of piercing blue eyes. His heart rolled over. *Geez, he knows. How'd he find out?* In his relief, Billy's grin could not be contained.

"Yes, sir, Major." He tossed a salute along with his words.

With a brief salute in return, the Major walked his horse in the direction of the leading mounts.

Sergeant Berryman called Joe to his side. He pointed his arm north-east to a smudge on the horizon.

"El Arish." He said nothing for a bit then turned with a smile. "The easiest win of the whole damn war – December 1916. When we were all set for a big stunt, we found the blighters had disappeared out of there and off to the oasis at Magdhaba, twenty-five miles inland. The Ottoman army dug their heels in there. It was our fellow, Major General Chauvel, who sorted them out. Things were a bit touch and go there for a while though. Our horses had been without water for twenty hours and it was late in the day before the Ottoman army's defence began to crumble. It was all over by dark." The sergeant stared off at the horizon for such a long time. Joe thought he had forgotten what he was saying until a bemused look filled the man's eyes. "It was the strangest thing. My cousin in the Anzac Mounted

Division told me recently – he'd got it from one of the Turkish prisoner-of-war chaps. This man told him the Turkish army left El Arish because they had a deep respect for the unique architecture found there and were reluctant to see it destroyed. It makes you stop and think, doesn't it?"

As they moved towards the large army camps within the area of El Arish, Joe found himself considering the enemy in a different light. Were they any different from his own people?

As he wrote up his notebook in the flickering light of the night's fire he pondered again on this thought.

End of Day 10 – Camped in sight of El Arish: The Sarge told me of the Turks leaving El Arish without a fight to protect the architecture. After having it drummed into us to shoot or be shot the thought of the enemy being sensitive to beauty takes some getting used to.

CHAPTER TWELVE

Billabong Downs

May – June 1917

William rubbed his eyes. He dragged his fingers down his face and rested his elbows on the office desk. His head dropped into his hands. He strove to shut out the noise of the doors slamming open and shut in the room next door. For the past three nights, this same racket meant he had achieved little sleep. He jumped to his feet and turned as if to enter the main bedroom where Mabel reigned supreme in recent years. William changed his mind and about turned to stand looking out through the window of his office to the sight of the distant dust where Geoff and Miles were working the new horses. He sighed. Breaking wild colts seemed so much easier than trying to break the back of this overdue paperwork.

With heavy footsteps, he returned to the office chair and drew the account books towards himself. After almost an hour, his head lifted, ears alert. It took William some moments to realize just what had distracted him. Silence – the house was silent. Nips, the young dog, sat up on his haunches. The brown gaze never left William's still and watchful form. Snowy, the old white dog, lay with his eyes shut. He flicked his ear tips.

Where was Mabel? William wondered. *Should he go and ensure she was alright?* He glanced down at the book of figures in front of him feeling no compelling interest there. *No, I'd better go and check up on her. She's like a child these days, more of a worry when you can't hear her.*

He entered the hallway and poked his head around the open door and into her room. Mabel lay sprawled out across the bed. After three days and nights with little or no sleep, her body had succumbed to exhaustion. Soft snuffles whispered up from the tousled head on the pillow. His gaze rested on the sleeping form. A sadness weighed down his heart. Regret washed over him like acid rain. *How did we come to this?* William moved to turn away but the envelopes sticking out of the open drawer of her desk caught his eye. In all the time he had known Mabel, he had never seen what she liked to call her escritoire, unlocked, let alone open.

He tip-toed over to tidy and close Mabel's desk when the address on the top envelope drew his gaze.

THE OFFICER IN CHARGE OF RECRUITMENT

AUSTRALIAN LIGHT HORSE

TOWNSVILLE.

William lifted the envelope to find written on the one beneath a similar but different address.

THE OFFICER IN CHARGE OF RECRUITMENT

AUSTRALIAN LIGHT HORSE

BRISBANE.

William found it difficult to comprehend Mabel's compulsion. It appeared that despite her father's advice, as reported to him by his sister-in-law Fran, Mabel was still doing her best to have Billy brought home.

Guilt caused his fingers to tremble as he lifted the envelopes from the desk. He shut the drawer. *What right have I to touch her mail?* This thought flared uppermost in his mind. Following on its tail, another thought ran through his head to ease his guilty conscience. *Mabel making such a fuss about their son can't be the right thing to do either – not for him, or the family, or the country.* Having nothing clear in his mind on what he was to do with the letters in his hand, he went to the kitchen and poured himself a drink of water. As he sipped the cool drink he looked more closely at the correspondence. The flaps on both envelopes lay open. He withdrew the letter from the first envelope and spread it out on the table. Another rush of guilt held his hand for a moment before he began to read.

The first thing to catch his attention was the standard of the writing. As he remembered, Mabel's hand with a pen always met perfect copybook style. It seemed when writing this letter, her hands trembled to the point where some words were almost illegible.

Dear Sir,
I admire the work you do and am loath to interrupt you with my request. There has been a grave error made in the Australian Light Horse accepting my son William into your number. William is my son and heir and his future rests here at home as the future owner/manager of the family business of The Bank of Queensland Graziers.
There has been no permission granted for his signing up to serve in the war. You can have my second son, Joseph in his place.
I would appreciate it if you could correct this wrong and send my son home.
Yours sincerely
Mrs. Mabel Dawson Daley.

William did not miss the fact Mabel had altered her name to add her maiden name of Dawson. It felt like a kick in the belly. He glanced at the second letter and discovered the wording almost a copy of the first. He stood staring out over the homestead compound not seeing anything at all. In a rush, he folded the papers back into the envelopes and slipped them inside his shirt. His long legs took the back steps three at a time. Nips hung close to William's heels as he strode across the flat to his brother's house.

Fran answered his knock.

"Hello, William, is everything alright?"

"Not really, no, Fran. Is Miles here?"

"No, he hasn't come back from the horse-yards yet."

"Oh, never mind. Sorry to bother you."

"Can I help with something?"

"No thanks, Fran. I had a question but now I think about it, I know what I'll do."

William strode back to his house and up the stairs. His first stop was at the kitchen stove where he slipped the pages from the envelopes and crushed them up before opening the fire-box door and throwing them inside to burn. He tiptoed back to Mabel's room. His head edged around the door. Relief released his pent-up breath at the sight of Mabel still lying on the bed unmoved. William opened the escritoire and removed two blank pages from the ruffled pile inside the drawer. With frequent gazes at Mabel's inert form, he folded a blank page and slipped it inside the first envelope. He repeated the process with the second envelope. On each, he dropped a small blob of pink sealant and using Mabel's silver seal-stamp sitting amongst the pens and pencils he pressed it hard to mark and flatten the sealant. He hoped desperately Mabel might not remember, in her mental confusion of late, having not sealed the envelopes herself. As William slipped these envelopes inside the drawer his hand froze. He recognized the handwriting on the envelope peeping out of Mabel's writing folder. He flashed another glance in the direction of her sleeping body. Reassured, he slipped this communication out. Holding the single-page letter up to the light, he read the words of his daughters written some time ago. Anger flowed like molten lava through his body. But, when he remembered his own guilt in not

140

showing Mabel the letter from her own sons, his temper cooled. Only sadness remained latent in his veins. He folded the paper and slipped it back to where he had found it. He closed the desk without a noise.

His culpability further motivated William's rush down the steps and across to the horse yards. He leant forward on the rails gazing into the pen seeing little but his own actions in swapping Mabel's mail. He jumped when Geoff spoke at his side.

"Miles has done a great job on that pig-eyed horse. I didn't think it was going to be worth anything more than a trip to the glue factory." Geoff looked more closely at his boss. He took in the pallor of his face and the tremble of his hands. "You alright, William? You look like you've just ridden a brumby yourself."

"Nah, I'm fine. It's just that paperwork – it sets my head spinning." William straightened up, lifted his hat off his head and raked his fingers through his hair before he shoved his hat back into place. "Yeah, Miles has always had a fine balance in the saddle. It takes a wily horse to unseat him."

The sound of a gunshot in the distance lifted both men's heads.

"That'll be Gazza. He's gone out to stir up a bit of meat for the dogs."

"I thought that sounded like his old blunderbuss." William smiled.

The two spectators watched as Miles walked the horse towards where they stood at the rail. The animal tried in vain to turn away but Miles nudged him forward then held him in place – if not still at least his front feet shuffled only a step or two one way and then a step or two the other.

William looked up at his brother. "That bag of bones is coming on nicely, Miles."

"This fellow is gonna make you two sit up and eat humble pie; after all the bad-mouthing you have given him." Miles laughed softly.

141

"I'll unsaddle him now. This boy can think about today's lessons until tomorrow."

"Good idea, that sun's getting low on the horizon. Time to call it quits, I reckon," William nodded and turned to walk off but remembered, "Oh, you can tell the ladies I'll be going to town the day after tomorrow if they want to come along. I'll take the papers I was working on this afternoon in to the accountant."

When William stepped onto his verandah, he knew Mabel was awake. He heard her feet shuffling around inside the room. At least the doors weren't slamming. He found one of Fran's lidded saucepans on the kitchen stove. He opened the fire-box door and stirred the coals before adding several more sticks to the fire. After moving the kettle to the heat, he lifted the saucepan lid and breathed in the aroma of Fran's fresh stew and herbs.

William's boots clattered down the steps again as he made his way to the corrugated iron-walled shower room under the house. As he passed the Coolgardie safe, he took out the last two bones from the tray and threw one to Nips, and the other bone to old Snowy. Both waited expectantly near the edge of the steps.

After his shower and wearing only his day trousers, William stepped out of his unlaced boots at the top of the stairs and walked barefoot through to the kitchen. The stew simmered. He pulled it away from the heat. Steam shot out of the kettle through the spout – it rattled the lid. After emptying the teapot of its dregs, over the side of the verandah rail, he added leaves and made a fresh pot of tea. While it steeped, he went and changed into his warm pyjamas. He looked in on Mabel as he passed her room.

"Good afternoon, Mabel, did you rest well?"

Mabel stood still at the foot of her bed staring at the escritoire, a puzzled frown on her face.

"I've made a fresh pot of tea and there's some stew there. Can I get anything for you?" William asked.

"Have you been in my room?" Mabel ignored William's update on the kitchen status.

In turn, William ignored Mabel's question.

"Did I tell you I have to go to town the day after tomorrow to see the accountant? Do you still want to come and do some shopping?"

"William, I asked you if you had been in my room?"

William felt the guilt swirl inside his gut.

"What on earth would I be in here for? You've made it plain enough there is nothing here for me." He spun on his heel and stamped off to the kitchen knowing full well he was avoiding her real question.

CHAPTER THIRTEEN

Stalemate

June – October 1917

Joe squatted on a bent knee in front of the small fire around which sat the quart pots. He felt grubby – he looked grubby. His brown curls lay lank against a scalp thick with dirt and grease. Sand and soil matted the hairs on the chest of his bare torso. Unpolished boots gaped open to reveal the delineation mark of the dirt and reasonably clean skin of his lower legs. Stain marks of unwashed hands covered the sides and rear of his trousers. He sniffed at his armpits.

I'd give a lot for a good bath. I can hardly stand my own smell.

This morning it was his turn to be the commissariat for his section. Billy was off to where the remount horses were picketed to check up on his two favourites and help the remount men in general. Carter and Martin chipped in to feed their own horses plus Billy's and Joe's. They also groomed and watered the animals and disposed of the manure. When a voice sounded behind him, Joe almost fell into his fire as he tried to spin around.

"Hey, Joe, are you the cook today?" Mick McCready laughed. "Is Billy about?"

"No, Mick, he's over checking his clunkers. Can I help you?"

"Nah, I just came to give you the latest news." Mick dropped to his haunches beside Joe. "Major General Chauvel has his men camped further north – south-east of Rafah at a place called Shok es Sufi not too far south of Gaza where the Ottoman army is holed up." Mick drew a pouch of tobacco and papers from his pocket and began to roll a cigarette. "Our boys and the Turkish armies must be staring each other down, along the Ottoman line. It stretches from Gaza on the coast to Beersheba, thirty-one miles inland. They're expecting General Allenby to arrive any day now." Mick stretched out to lift a stick with flame dancing on its end. He put it to the end of his cigarette and drew in deeply.

"Aaah … there's nothing like the first fag of the day." Smoke dribbled out of his nostrils as he sighed. "We have visitors in Major Forbes's tent right now. A couple of officers from Chauvel's administration arrived last night with a message for our Major Forbes. We're to deliver the remounts and you recruits to Chauvel's camp today." The firestick struck the sand near his boot. "Bloody scorpions they're everywhere in this place." Mick flicked the pest into the fire along with his stick.

"How come you know all this, Mick – about the gossip from Chauvel's tent not about scorpions?"

Mick tapped the side of his nose. "Ask no questions you'll get told no lies." He grinned.

"Mick, you've got big ears," Joe spurted laughter. "Anyways, how far is it to this next camp?"

"I think it's about twenty-four or five miles. I've never been past Sheikh Zowaiid myself."

Despite the day's heat, the ripple of excitement fluttered in the belly of each recruit as they trekked on horseback across the miles. From his position as a scout with Sergeant Berryman and the signalman Rankin, Joe kept his eyes peeled knowing, as they bypassed the small township of Sheikh Zowaiid, there was not a great distance between them and the enemy. According to Mick, the pipeline and railway construction ended at Sheikh Zowaiid. The sun hung well above the horizon when the animals and men were watered at an oasis near Rafah before they settled into camp.

It was late that evening when Joe and Billy finished saying their farewells to Mick, Rankin, Clappers and Sergeant Berryman. The Remount Unit were to make an early start tomorrow on their return journey to the Moascar Remount Depot.

"Try to stay out of trouble, Billy." Clappers' handshake went on for some time. Billy's smile was tempered with sadness at saying goodbye to a good friend.

"You too – and don't go swapping the horses around too much." Billy's smile broke through, "Unless it's for Lieutenant Burke." Both men laughed hearty laughs.

Sergeant Berryman looked askance at Mick.

"Don't have a clue what they're on about, Sarge." Innocence glowed in his blue eyes.

Sergeant Berryman rolled his eyes and turned to shake Joe's hand.

"Keep safe, young man, and keep those magic eyes of yours open and your head down."

"Thanks, Sarge, and you too."

All seemed confusing to Joe during their first day camped near Rafah. The Remount Unit handed over their remount horses to a captain in Chauvel's fighting unit who then began to issue mounts to those men who had been without since the first and second failed battles of Gaza in March and April. The recruits, riding their horses issued in Australia, were sent off with a Sergeant Fielding to find their place within the camp spread out in tidy lines across the countryside. The grins on the faces of Joe and Billy as they patted the necks of Straps and Buckles reflected their happiness to be back on board these familiar mounts. They looked up when Sergeant Fielding spoke.

"You recruits will find yourselves mixed with seasoned troops in the hope they'll help you adjust. Just make sure you don't learn any of their bad habits."

Consternation filled the eyes of Joe and Billy at the sound of those words. Their glances met and held. They never anticipated separation.

When eventually they received their allotted section and tent number, Joe and Billy found things were much better than expected. Carter and Martin were removed from their initial section with Billy and Joe but they ended up occupying the second section within the same tent. Two troopers, Gardener and Beatson, part of the Light Horse since Gallipoli, joined Martin and Carter. Another two troopers, Farquharson and Bennet, who were blooded into the Light Horse at the Battle of Romani in August the previous year, made up the other half of Joe and Billy's section.

Billy stomped into the tent after eating a meal of cold stew comprised of unidentified meat accompanied by lots of gravy and a few vegetables at the camp cookhouse. He belched. A rich gas filled his mouth and distorted his face. They may have been short of vegetables but were never short of seasonings. Farquharson and Bennet were not present having gone off searching for a card game. As usual, Joe sat scribbling in his notebook. He looked up into the disgruntled face of his brother.

"What's eating you?"

"We come here to join the war and what have we done since our arrival?" If Joe planned on replying, he was not given the chance. "I'll tell you what – non-stop parade drilling – that's what – for two whole weeks?" Before Joe could think of a comment, Billy continued, "Even Buckles is fed up with it all." Joe threw himself down on his groundsheet. "If I hear the orders: Section-Right, Form-

Troop, or Walk-March, one more time, I'm going to go crazy." While Joe half listened to his brother, he tore at his shirt and began scratching his chest. "And the bloody trenches – how many bloody trenches have I dug so far? I'll be through to China if I dig any more or maybe I'll turn into a bloody wombat."

"I guess it's because we missed out on any further training when we arrived – the parade drilling and things. They need us to catch up on our learning."

"Farquharson tells me, he's heard we're going to get to play with the new Hotchkiss machine-guns which arrived a few months ago. They're to replace the Lewis guns. I'm looking forward to that tomorrow."

Joe was pleased to see the light in Billy's eyes re-ignite.

The gossip ran through the food tent like clouds of sand blown in on the desert winds.

"He's here."

"He's arrived."

"Who's here?"

"The new bloke – the General."

"Allenby – General Allenby."

"Got off the train at El Arish and drove up here in a Rolls Royce car, no less."

"Can't the man ride a horse, then?"

"Oh, he has one of those too. An adjutant bloke came into camp leading it behind him."

"A big grey horse. Its name's Blinkers."

"Where'd you hear that?"

"About – someone who knows someone who knows someone."

"A reliable source then?"

"Absolutely."

Chill of Blame

A week later, Billy joined Joe who was sitting scraping the lice out of the seams of his clothes with the point of his bayonet. Joe flattened each body against the blade of the knife with his fingernail.

Billy threw himself onto the ground beside Joe. He was laughing fit to burst his sides.

"You'd never guess what he's done now."

"Who's done what?"

"The Bull – General Allenby, they're calling him, The Bull. The man never stands in one place for more than a minute at a time. How the devil he manages to have a crap in the morning, I don't know." Billy scratched at the itch on his scalp. "He's been frightening the life out of the boys at the desert outposts – riding that big horse of his. He goes out with a troop of men as escort and does flash inspections."

Joe chuckled at the image Billy had placed inside his head. "The men in the cook tent, the medical stations, supplies, and the air crews will be glad to have him out of their hair for a bit, then."

"And the engineers – I heard them complaining in the food tent yesterday," Billy added before he reported on another piece of news. "Farquharson reckons the signalmen have devised warning messages between themselves – Bull Loose – if the general is heading their way." Billy cracked a nit between his two thumbnails.

"That sounds okay, but I wouldn't think a bloke like Allenby hasn't taken the time to learn basic signalling. He probably knows exactly what the messages are saying."

Billy grinned. "That could be embarrassing."

At their base camp, every day at some time, General Allenby could be seen gazing across the no man's land. It reached thirty miles from the coast towards Beersheba. The width variations ranged from four hundred odd yards to over four thousand yards. The Ottoman army held a line on the other side. The general knew he must destroy their hold in the area if he was to push them further up into Palestine.

Darkness enfolded the troop in its wrappings. A new moon and stars in a dense sky above provided only a limited vision. Lieutenant Smithers led the troop as his eyes scanned the stars in the skies above. At his side, Sergeant Fielding's gaze barely left the face of the compass in his hand. With all the horse bridles padded, the only noise of their passing was in the soft swish, swish, swish of the horses' feet in the sand, which was unlikely to alert the enemy soldiers patrolling their edge of no man's land.

Not a word was spoken by the men on night patrol. When a soft snore from a man sleeping in his saddle broke the quiet, the Lieutenant swung about causing the creaking leathers to issue a louder sound than the sleeping man. A kick in the leg by a fellow section mate brought the guilty party to instant attention.

As far as Joe knew, their mission out into this dry land was two-fold. Behind them, the mules of the Supply Unit carried provisions for delivery to the lonely outpost stations maintained by the infantry along the length of this no man's land. The Lieutenant had been charged with inspecting these posts plus searching a new area on the flanks of Beersheba for previously unknown oases or water wells, serviceable or damaged. Several men from the Engineer Unit, their mules loaded with pipes, ropes, shovels, poles and their treasured spearpoint pumps, all silent within the padding of old sacking around each item, travelled within the escort.

Hidden in the deep wadis by day, the simple bivouac camps did nothing to protect the men from the heat of the summer sun as they attempted to catch up on some sleep when a safe distance lay between them and no man's land.

Chill of Blame

Once the outposts were restocked, the search for old water wells began in earnest. For the remainder of this patrol, the troopers were to assist and protect the engineers as they discovered and repaired old wells.

Not a breath of air cooled the sweat covering the skin of the four lines of troopers. At least the dust raised by the hooves of the horses did not rise any further than their knees. Billy and Joe rode adjacent on the inner two lines while their recent section mates Farquharson and Bennet, rode on the outside lines on either side.

Billy lifted his head when Joe spoke at his side.

"You asleep?"

"Nah, just checking the inside of my eyelids for lice."

"Look around us. I reckon we're somewhere on the southeast flank of Beersheba. This place reminds me a bit of home, don't you think – this undulating brown land riddled with old dried-up water channels?"

"Hmmm," was Billy's only reply.

Farquharson riding on their left went to speak but found his tongue too dry to make a word. He lifted the canteen to his lips and sipped the sun-heated water, swirled it around his mouth and swallowed.

"Have you blokes noticed the changes around our main camp since Allenby arrived?"

Billy dragged his sleeve across his brow before answering, "You'd have to be blind to miss it."

Bennet roused himself from his stupor. "You can bet The Bull is up to something. Every day he has reinforcements arriving."

"And supplies and weapons covered in tarpaulins on the back of those trucks," Farquharson expounded.

Joe turned his head. "How come the Turks have missed their arrival?"

Bennet shook his head slowly.

"Haven't you noticed, young Joe, the sky's full of the Brits' Bristol planes these days? They won't let a German Taube anywhere near our air space."

"Word has it, The Bull's going to have another go at a Gaza stunt in the near future," Farquharson offered. "The boys at the card game were talking last night."

"Maybe not," Billy stirred himself, "from what I hear of his reputation, The Bull's more likely to do the thing least expected."

Neither of the four men noticed the approach of the sergeant until he spoke.

"Unless you fellows want to go offer our General a word of advice, I'd suggest you keep your mouths shut and concentrate on the job at hand."

Before daybreak on the fifth day of this patrol, Billy and Joe watched the engineers reconstructing a damaged well that had been originally built within the walls of a now-apparent wadi. Other than those on guard duty, the troopers took turns digging the hole of the defunct well. Large timber slabs were placed around the hole to reinforce the walls. A winch, secured to another timber pole frame above the hole, provided the leverage to excavate dirt from the old well. The engineers sank pipes to access the water below. As the sun rose, the level of the men's canteens lowered. They hung about the well hoping for a refill but when water eventually became available the medic amongst the group took a sample for testing.

"Stand back, you thirsty lot. Horses will be able to drink this brackish water but you sensitive chappies may not have the stomach for it. I sure don't feel like having to nursemaid a whole troop of you fellows back to the Khan Yunis camp." He shooshed them away with his one empty hand. "Get those supply blokes to set up the canvas troughs and start giving your mounts a drink. I'll let you know when

152

I finish testing this lot." He waved a small lidded container above his head in which the hushed sound of swirling water could be heard by those standing closest. "The Lieutenant says we're heading home in the dark tonight."

"Bloody hell, another one of those secret night marches. What are they planning for us? Do they think we can walk through Gaza and Beersheba in the dead of night and no beggar there will notice us?"

The medic did not identify the speaker but he laughed and moved back to his bivouac to test the water.

Billy turned to his brother. "Come on, Joe, if we're travelling in the starlight later, we won't have the chance to scrounge any bits of timber for our fires. Let's get Buckles and Straps a drink and then gather what firewood we can here in the wadi. It's the most promising place to find anything."

After they had drunk their fill, the two horses followed the pair along the old creek bed nibbling at any scant pickings they found. Joe and Billy recovered any timber visible above or partially buried in the soil. Joe withdrew several lengths of string from his top pocket and tied their treasures in small bundles.

"Joe, when we get back, I want to go talk to that old Arab chap set up outside the camp gates. I hear he sometimes has firewood for sale or trade. If you go early enough, he sometimes has vegetables or some citrus and olive fruits."

"What I could really do with is a loaf of Gran's home-baked bread, steaming hot."

Carter arrived scratching around for his firewood.

"How about we buy a chook between us? The camp tucker is more watered gravy than meat."

Billy laughed, "Have you seen the locals' scrawny poultry? Once you got the feathers off it, you'd turn up nothing but skin and bone. No doubt the feathers weigh more than any meat you'd find."

"Yeah, and look at the old fellow himself. Under all those robes, you'll find nothing but skin and bones on him too." Joe offered his thoughts.

As the sun hung low in the sky, a hushed excitement ran through the troop back at the well. Men were lined up to fill their two canteens before the night march commenced. The medic had approved the water for human consumption.

Their small fires warmed the tins of bully beef and brought the billy pots to the boil. With the onset of evening, little conversation accompanied the scant meals of the weary troopers. Within the hour the food was consumed and the tea slurped down. Every fire was suffocated with dirt and the rubbish was buried. Hushed sounds accompanied the troop's departure on track to their base.

It was only a few weeks later when Joe and Billy found they were on night patrol again – in fact, it seemed their whole squadron and more was going out on a night march. Whispers swirled through the camp along with the sands on the late sea breeze.

"The Bull has something going down. We're about to give the Ottoman something to remember, I'm thinking."

"You can bet the Old Bull has a trick or two up his sleeve."

The mounted troopers, weighed down by enough to live and fight with hanging from their saddles and shoulders, left the sight of their camp, nine miles south of Gaza. They headed in an easterly direction in a state of turmoil. Weariness at the thought of another boring night march was uppermost in their minds, yet, the idea of a chance to give the enemy a bloody nose set them all hoping.

CHAPTER FOURTEEN

Billabong Downs

July 1917

The mid-afternoon sun glinted off the roofs of Charters Towers' houses as the horses pulled the wagon up the last rise and around a stand of thick Chinkie Apple trees. William's stomach churned at the thought of his distasteful appointment later in the afternoon. He swallowed hard and reminded himself, *this is something I have to do for the good of everyone on Billabong Downs.*

After delivering Maggie and her children to the front door of her sister's house, he guided the horses along the main street to where Mabel demanded he let her out at the café several doors down from her favourite dress shop. William glanced over at Fran and Mavis.

"Did you want to get out here too, Fran? I'll leave our things at Mum and Dad's house before my appointment with the accountant?"

Fran did not miss the pleading in William's eyes. She knew William did not want Mabel to run loose in the store even though he had set a limit on her account. Fran thought she saw something else in her brother-in-law's eyes. If pressed for an answer, she may have said "guilt", but why would William be guilty?

"Yes, William, this will be lovely. Mabel, Mavis and I can enjoy what's left of the afternoon browsing through the shops. We'll make our way back to Gran and Pop's place later. A walk through the park after a day sitting on this hard wooden seat for hours will be appreciated."

Fran was right in her speculation of William's guilty conscience. William's appointment with the accountant was not until tomorrow morning. This afternoon he had the pre-arranged meeting with the family doctor.

William could not deny the relief he felt, as he waved the ladies off near Arida's Drapery. It was only ten minutes before he pulled to a stop amidst the groaning of the timber wagon, creaking of the horses' harness and a cloud of dust outside the house his parents had moved into several months after William first brought his wife home to Billabong Downs.

"I thought you'd be in this week or next, being so near to the end of the financial year." Waving a large spanner in his hand, Pop Daley's bald head rimmed by scant snowy hair preceded him out from under his dray.

William leaned over and offered a helping hand. "Is that just maintenance you're up to or something worse?"

"No, just maintenance. Checking all the nuts and bolts." Dust puffs lifted into the air when Pop Daley brushed at his trousers with hands twisted by arthritis and several small skin tears dribbling blood. "Come inside. Your mother will be glad to see you. Is Miles in town with you?"

"No, just me and the ladies, Pop. Maggie and the kids are staying at her sister's place. Fran and Mabel are in the main street sending me broke, no doubt."

Pop laughed, then coughed – a moist rattling cough. He wiped his lips with the sleeve of his shirt.

"Well, come on then. Did you see the accountant?"

"No, … er … I have an appointment later." William felt the acid stir again in his belly at the lie he told his father and at the thought of the actual appointment he did have this afternoon – in less than two hours. He knew the appointment with the family doctor could not be avoided any longer but he felt it a betrayal to discuss Mabel's mental status with anyone, even with the doctor. He was not ready to share his concerns with his father just yet.

"You'll have time to read the latest letter from Joe and Billy. It arrived in this morning's mail."

Steam whistled out of the spout of the kettle on the stove near where the pancakes browned when the two men entered Mary Daley's kitchen.

"I see you brought the wagon today. Are you collecting the monthly supplies this trip, William?" Mary asked.

"Yes, Mum, and if you don't mind, can you put Fran, Mavis and my Mabel up for two nights as well?"

"Of course, son, it will be my pleasure. Just bring their bags in. You and Mabel can use the spare room and I'll put Fran and Mavis in the boys' room. All the beds have clean sheets. The boys remained at the college for football and didn't stay here last weekend." Mary turned back to attend to her pancakes. She also took the opportunity to hide the passing grimace at the thought of Mabel's miserable company. "Now sit down, this won't be a minute," Mary called to her husband who had disappeared into the next room. "Bring William the letter, Pop."

Mr. Daley senior, appeared in the doorway to the kitchen waving the crinkled, stained paper in his hand.

"Sit down, William, and read the news from your boys."

It was the sound of the teapot being placed on the table which stirred William from his reading. The letter was little more than a note really but this time both his sons had contributed. He swallowed down the sour taste of bitterness at having to receive their communication in such a secretive manner. Once more he must make the decision; was Mabel in any fit state to share their letter? He drew

157

some consolation in the hope the appointment later with the family doctor may offer up a better idea of what he should be doing to help his wife. William smoothed the paper out once more and read again the words written with a blunt pencil.

Dear Gran and Pops and Dad,

We left Australia in the care of the Remount Unit – a great lot of fellows who are in the process of delivering over one hundred horses including mules and draught horses to replace those lost in the battles fought by the Australian Light Horse. On the ship, we helped them care for their animals as well as looking after our own allotted mounts.

Caring for the horses took my mind off my seasickness somewhat. Billy hardly got seasick at all but I spent the first three weeks hanging over the ship's rail. I didn't think anyone could be so sick and not die.

Since disembarking the ship, we are still in the care of the Remount boys as their horses and we are heading through the desert to the same destination. We're forbidden to say exactly where we are.

Regards to Cissy and Maud and everyone at home. From Joe.

Below these words was a brief but welcome note written in Billy's scrawled hand.

Gran, Pops and Dad and Cissy and Maud
No matter what this war may dish up, I know I was meant to be a part of the Australian Light Horse. It feels so right for me. Your son and grandson, Billy.

William sighed as he folded the paper slowly, "They seem to be happy with their lot."

"Yes, they do, William. Now, have your tea and pancake while they're hot," Mary urged her son.

After three large pancakes washed down with a drink of tea, William looked up when his father spoke.

"Do you think it safe to let Mabel read this letter?"

William released a rueful smile. "You read my mind. I was just wondering what I should do. I feel drawn between two forces. The boys have not mentioned their mother in this letter either. They must mean it not to be for her eyes. And of course, if Mabel did get to read it and she took offence at not being mentioned, which she is most likely to do, there would be hell to pay." William swirled the dregs in the bottom of his pannikin, deep in thought. "No, I think I must respect the boys' wishes. I do not want to give them a reason not to write to us at all."

Mr. and Mrs. Daley senior both nodded their heads in agreement.

William's stride lengthened as he hurried towards the doctor's surgery. A shout from the inside of a bar drew his attention. He smiled and waved to a fellow stockman in town. William was tempted to have a nip of Dutch courage before this appointment but time was already running out. His pace increased.

On the front step of the surgery, in the arch of fading golden blooms, William drew a deep breath and pushed open the door. Only one of the worn leather-bound seats in the room was occupied. A young mother with her sleeping baby, sat in the corner. Loose tendrils of hair, dark shadows under her eyes and her glance towards him contained a mountain of weariness. The clock on the wall above the receptionist's desk told him he had just made it on time, but he soon discovered he need not have worried because it was another half an hour before he was ushered into the doctor's office. His wait felt twice as long as the clock indicated. During this wait, William shuffled in his seat like a child facing the invading hands of a dentist. He watched the receptionist lead the young mother into the bowels of the building. William made to rise and leave on more than one occasion rather than stay and deal with this meeting and its purpose. His heart rolled over when Doctor Munson appeared at his side.

"Good afternoon, William, please come on through?"

As they filed through a short, dimly lit corridor, William felt again the urge to run. Maybe there was nothing wrong with Mabel. Maybe it was all his fault. Maybe ...

Doctor Munson pushed the heavy polished timber door which opened into a spacious room with the traditional desk and chairs. The late afternoon sunlight filtered through the bushes outside to spread across the polished wooden floor. He extended a hand to indicate an armchair in one corner. The sun-darkened skin on the back of his hands along with thorn scratches and the remnants of ingrained dirt, despite the frequent handwashing required by his profession, revealed a man with a gardening habit. The doctor chose to sit on the second armchair beside William.

"Your mailman dropped your letter off here personally, William. I was sorry to read of Mabel's troubles. Now sit down and tell me everything from the beginning."

The man sat quietly and let William report on Mabel's condition in his own words. At first, William's sentences stumbled from his mouth. It felt as if his tongue did not belong to him – as if it had suddenly grown too large for his mouth. He told of the increasing depth and frequency of Mabel's mood swings, of her weeks of withdrawal from everyday activities, her reaction to Billy's signing up to fight in the war and her obsession with obtaining his release from the contract he had signed. William almost choked as he told of her happiness to offer up her younger son Joe, but not Billy. He hesitated for a moment before going into her lifelong preference for

Billy over all her children, especially Joe. He told of her demands for Joe to protect his brother throughout their lives despite his being the younger of the two and of how Joe was the target for her blame when the boys got into any mischief.

Gradually, William's voice spluttered to an end. Tears glistened in his eyes as he dragged his hands down his face. He kept his gaze on the dancing beams of sunlight through the wind-blown bushes outside.

Doctor Munson sat in silence as he processed all he had been told. Compassion warmed his glance as he turned towards William.

"William, I'm sorry to hear things have been so difficult for you all. I cannot say I'm totally surprised at these revelations. I've only known Mabel since you brought her out to Billabong Downs – what is it – twenty years ago? I do remember her first pregnancy and my concern for her highly-strung mental state at the time. Each of the following pregnancies and births was no different. Yesterday, I delved through my records to find the letter sent by her doctor in Townsville at the time. He had been the family physician for her parents. It appears Mabel has been subject to intermittent flights from rational thought and behaviour even as a young child. In other words, she threw bad-tempered fits when she did not receive the attention she demanded. Most of the time she was the perfect angel, doted on by her parents. Her beauty forgave her many sins."

William nodded his head. He admitted he had done the same thing himself at times.

"Now, William, getting back to her pregnancies – a difficult time for most women with the influx of hormones coursing throughout the body like tidal waves. Each time, Mabel did seem to suffer the resulting mood swings more than most. No doubt, you will have noticed that."

William's rueful smile answered the doctor's unasked question.

"On more than one occasion, at each delivery, I prescribed the occasional sedation, against my better judgement, for the benefit of the unborn child." The doctor stared through the window gathering his thoughts. "It's possible Mabel has reached 'that time of life' too. Some women start earlier in life than others. I see she is over forty years of age so that is a distinct possibility. Based on her medical history, I think there is every chance Mabel will suffer an exacerbation of the usual symptoms and mood swings during this time." Doctor Munson smoothed the deep tracks on his forehead as he glanced at William now leaning forward with his elbows on his knees and his clenched hands blanched white. "I think it would be best if Mabel visited me herself, but as you explained in your letter, this is not likely to happen at this stage. To make any judgement on her condition, I need to know as much as I can about her behaviour." Again Dr. Munson massaged the lines across his forehead. "So, William, I want you to record each and every one of her turns or episodes. Record what triggered the turn as far as you can see and include a description of the turns for me. You can forward these to me by mail."

"Oh God, Doc, I'll feel like a spy."

"Until I can get a better handle on her symptoms, I cannot help Mabel. Once I can achieve this, your life should improve too." The doctor's compassion shone in his eyes. "And please remember, if the opportunity arises, try to convince her to come in for a visit."

William stood. He reached over to shake the doctor's hand.

"Thanks, Doctor, I'll do my best."

It was after sunset when William opened the back door to his parents' house. Wonderful aromas of a roast meal greeted him, but he felt he could not eat a thing. At the sight of Mabel watching him from where she leant against the hallway door leading into the kitchen, his guilty conscience attacked him again. The flush on his cheeks might have been attributed to the heat of the stove but he knew better. It felt to him as if guilt stood out in capital letters across his brow.

"How did you go at the accountant's, William?" Mr. Daley senior asked.

"Er … er … fine – he had a million and one questions. I have to drop back in there in the morning before we go to the cattle sales, Dad.".

"No more questions now, you men. Pull up a seat – this meal is ready to eat and I won't take any blame if you let it go cold." Mary ushered her guests to their places.

William and his father talked business. While Pop Daley ate with gusto, William ate sparingly quite aware of his wife's gaze which never left his face. He felt her suspicion burning into his soul. There was no way she could know of his visit to the doctor this afternoon, was there? Yet his own conscience did nothing to calm the faint tremble in his hands.

Fran encouraged Mabel to tell of the outcome of their visit to the drapery shop. Mabel showed only a hint of a smile as she picked at her food. For a moment, it seemed as if she was not going to speak but then she sat up straighter and took a deep breath.

"William, I chose material and patterns for two dresses. I will visit the dressmaker tomorrow while you are at the saleyards."

William noticed and appreciated the effort Mabel made to maintain good manners in front of the family. His gratitude warmed the smile towards his wife.

"What a good idea, Mabel. Will you go to Mrs. Hubbard, as usual?"

Mabel's face held no warmth as she nodded in the affirmative.

After a more relaxing day for the ladies and the joys of a father and adult son bonding at the cattle sales, the family joined together for a cold meat and salad dinner with plum pudding for sweets. The lights were doused early as the guests planned to rise before daylight to be on their way home.

CHAPTER FIFTEEN

Courageous Ride

31ˢᵗ October 1917

Two regiments of the Australian Light Horse spread out in lines across the eastern slopes – waiting. Exhaustion lined every face. The long night march sweeping out into the desert to approach Beersheba from the southeast took its toll on man and beast alike, particularly when sleeping in the chill of the October desert the previous night. To rest their mounts and relieve them of some of their burdens, the men had dismounted and either sat on the ground with heads draped over their knees or they waited next to their horses. Equine heads hung low. Dry tongues stuck to the roof of the arid mouths of men and horses. Some men dozed, some fidgeted with impatience and discomfort; many prayed.

From the other side of the rise, the crash of heavy bombardment and the clatter of machine-guns were accompanied by regular explosions of hand grenades. As well as this, the uninterrupted crack of rifle fire rose over the crest to fall upon the ears of every man.

Billy shook first one of his water canteens and then the other. A slight smile welcomed the sound of the splash within. He removed the second canteen from about his shoulders, took his hat from his head and turned it upside-down. He poured most of the small amount of fluid into the hat and rubbed the neck of his horse.

"Here, Buckles, it might wet your muzzle at least. It's not much but it's all we have until we get to the water wells inside Beersheba

165

over the hill." The horse slurped and snorted at the fluid inside the hat.

Billy replaced his hat and lifted the canteen to his own lips. He drained the remaining mouthful of water and held it inside his mouth for several moments. After a slow swish around the inside of his cheeks, he let it run down into his gullet. He slung the empty canteen over his shoulder to join the other.

"You do realize, Buckles, this might be our last ride together. I reckon that's a good enough reason to wear our emu plumes. What do you think?" Billy once again removed the hat from his head. Out of his top pocket, he took a brown paper packet holding the emu feather designated for formal dress only and began to attach it to the band on his slouch hat. "There you are, that's more like it."

Buckles nudged his approval almost sending Billy to his knees. Billy looked to his left to where Joe stood leaning against the saddle of his horse. Joe threw him a nod of approval. Billy grinned and then he turned serious.

"If I'm to die here today, Joe, remember what I've always told you. I'm sorry, I know Mum'll blame you but you are not to feel any guilt, because it has nothing to do with you. I will do what I think is right for me; not what Mum thinks I should be doing. It is all me. Promise me you understand what I'm saying. No matter how much blame she lays upon you; you are to remember this. It is my guilt, not yours."

Joe nodded, "Just don't you dare die, brother," he murmured, coughed then spoke louder. "Knee to knee, Billy, like always."

"Knee to knee, Joe."

A whisper ran down the lines like a breath of wind through a forest.

"Commander Grant's up the front. He says to use our bayonets as swords and wishes us the best of luck."

Many comments were made in reply to the words passed down through the troopers. All in a similar vein.

"Bayonets against artillery, machine-guns, grenades and rifles – the man's gotta be mad. It'll be more than luck we'll be wanting."

Horses and their riders cast long shadows as the sun approached the horizon. A ripple of anticipation, excitement and no little amount of fear ran through the men on the hill at the first flag-signal to remount. Line by line they moved off, slowly at first, spreading apart from the men at either side to leave a gap of about fifteen feet between each rider to make them less of a target. Lines began to ease apart leaving three hundred yards between each so the riders coming up behind would get a chance to see and avoid fallen men or horses obscured by the rising dust.

As Billy on Buckles came over the crest, he gasped at the sight of the late afternoon sun reflected like a beacon of white light off the minaret at the pinnacle of the mosque of Beersheba in the distance. It shone out above the haze of dust and smoke heavy with the clamour of weaponry below.

Intermittent sightings through these thickening clouds of dust revealed several miles of open plains with no vegetation for cover between the riders and the town. The men of the Light Horse rode with their rifles hanging down their backs and only their bayonets in their hands against the rows of deeply entrenched and armed enemy. They moved off at a walk-march. This increased into a trot. Soon the pace of the charge increased.

When the hoofbeats thundered into a gallop, the men yelled, they screamed obscenities and laughed wildly. Their defiance declared their bravery. Their voices also tamped down upon the residual slither of fear lurking in the depths of their bowels. Dying sunlight reflected off the sharpened bayonets as the Light Horse galloped at full charge; their throats as dry as the land over which they rode. One hand clenched their bayonet while they guided their horse with the other hand and with their knees. Dust rose thick about them until it was left to the instinct of the horse to guide the rider.

Billy and Joe rode neck and neck, screeching their war cries, and spitting the dust from their dry throats.

Every breath sucked into their starving lungs included gusts of choking dust, the acrid smell of horse sweat blended with their own stale body odour, the sharp bitter smell of explosives and the occasional flurry of the metallic smell of blood.

The Ottoman army in the trenches expected the men of the Light Horse to dismount and fight as they usually did when doing battle. These men defending the trenches before Beersheba stood quietly checking their machine-guns were lined up accordingly. But the Light Horse galloped at full charge down the long gentle slope with no intention of stopping. The Ottoman opened fire with artillery, machine-guns and rifles. They struggled to realign the aim of their weapons. The pace of the charge was too fast for the gunners.

Frequent salvos from field artillery whistled overhead; shrapnel whizzed all around the riders and their horses. The glare from the dying sun reflected in the dust over Beersheba almost blinded the charging troopers. Joe, on Straps, only just evaded a dead horse and a trooper with his arm partly blown off by an exploding shell, lying on the ground beside him. The excitement and thunderous noise became too much for Straps in the maddened rush forward. When the horse's hooves skated down the sides of a deep wadi and Straps scrambled up the other side, Joe felt himself almost dragged from the saddle.

Much of the shrapnel from the Turkish artillery exploded above the lines of horsemen hitting only a few. Due to the pace of the riders, within seconds, the shells burst behind the charging lines of horses.

Chill of Blame

Because of the widely spaced riders, the bombs dropped from the two German planes flying overhead caused little damage.

The Ottoman's machine-guns from the flank went quiet – silenced by British artillery.

Joe and Straps landed smoothly after the first trench. Joe could see nothing but dust around him. He assumed Billy was close by. Within moments the second trench stretched out in front of him. Joe quailed at the sight of the width and depth of the redoubt. A depth exaggerated by several layers of sandbags on the rim of the trench. His first thoughts went to his horse. *Straps must be nearly at the end of his endurance.* With rider, saddle and gear, the horse had carried almost an eighteen stone weight over forty miles with minimum water through the rugged country in two nights. They had suffered a hot, hellish day here waiting without water at all. Straps had galloped flat out over four miles across this plain through a wall of belching lead while negotiating dry creek beds. Joe's heart filled with pride as he felt his horse lift them both into the air. Joe felt the animal stretch his long body to its limit.

As the second trench passed below his horse's tucked-up legs, Joe flinched at the sight of the enemy rifles with fixed bayonets thrust up in their direction. He heard the hand grenades crash and ping above the noise of the machine-guns and rifles.

When Straps' feet thudded back to earth, Joe strained to see through the cloud of dust and smoke. Billy was not to be seen. Fear clenched his chest. *Where's Billy? Surely, he hasn't stopped to enter into hand-to-hand combat. Has he forgotten, we are responsible for going on to Beersheba and saving the water wells and buildings?*

Joe heard a call from his left.

"This way!" He thought the hoarse voice might be that of Farquharson.

A quirky gust of wind cleared the haze for a moment and Joe caught sight of the laneway between two trenches. He yelled to his right.

"This way, Billy, this way." Joe heard the hoofbeats of several horses pounding behind him.

Within only moments they were through the gap. No further trenches lay between the galloping riders and the sight of the Beersheba minaret in front of them. The noise of battle now echoed behind this group of twenty to thirty troopers. The horses, barely under control with the smell of water in their nostrils, raced up the rise towards the town. The men of the Light Horse flew past Ottoman troops fleeing in terror. The enemy threw their rifles down to surrender. There was no holding the horses back.

"Leave them for the next lot," Someone was heard to call.

There was a moment of confusion as horses milled around while their riders decided on where the town entry might be. Two abreast they raced off down a narrow street between buildings ablaze.

Joe heard a voice yell, "Where the hell is the bloody railway and where are those damned wells?"

"That brick building to the East," a hoarse voice strained to be heard. At that moment an explosion and clouds of dust rose into the air from behind the indicated building.

"Looks like they've blown an ammo dump," a Lieutenant within the group shouted as he assumed control and sent half their number to investigate. Joe recognized Lieutenant Smithers from their squadron.

Along with the remainder of the troopers, Joe swung around a group of mud huts on a corner just in time to see a German engineer about to press the plunger on a detonator box set up to blow a large water well to smithereens. The man's hands froze. He never finished the task. The Lieutenant's bullet took him through the face and sent him toppling over backwards. In a flying leap, Lieutenant Smithers left his horse, skidded across the last six feet and tore the wires from the box of death.

Men and horses then charged the water troughs.

"Don't make gutses of yourselves," the Lieutenant yelled. His voice began to fade. "You don't want to kill yourselves or the horses. You can come back for more later."

The town emptied fast. Locals and enemy soldiers hastened to disappear in the direction of the Hebron Road.

In the flickering lights from the burning timbers around them, the men watered their animals. Joe stood back after his first drink searching for a glimpse of his brother.

The horses' hooves pounded beneath him. Billy felt as if he and his horse were isolated within a wall of noise. He had not heard his brother's call. Billy felt Buckles lift at the second trench. He then felt the animal shudder. A piece of shrapnel tore through Buckles' chest. It ripped a channel through that brave heart. Billy knew his mount had been hit, but that was Billy's last thought. A spot of blood appeared in the middle of Billy's forehead. It swelled and overflowed to run down over his nose. Billy's black obsidian eyes, so like his mother's, widened and froze. The piece of hot metal tore out through the rear of Billy's skull removing the slouch hat as it did so. The dislodged emu feather fluttered downwards. Nerveless fingers released their grip on the bayonet; it dropped to the ground. The dead horse beneath him landed from its final jump onto its knees; the crack of broken bones unheard within the sound of battle. Buckles skated forward for a short distance before coming to a stop. The rider's knees remained clamped upon the saddle for several seconds. As if in slow motion, Billy's body sagged forward until his cheek came to rest upon the emu feather snagged in the horse's mane. Billy's lifeless arms and legs draped loosely on either side of Buckles' neck and body. Billy – William – Daley lay still.

When his brother's absence could be ignored no longer, Joe asked the other troopers around him if they had seen Billy. Bloodied mud ran down Sergeant Fielding's thigh. He told Joe how his friend had taken a bullet back at the second trench of the town's defence.

Joe felt as if both back feet of an angry horse slammed into his stomach. His breath caught in his throat. He struggled for air. With the reins of his horse clenched in his hands, Joe turned away and led Straps to a relatively quiet corner formed by the uneven slabs of the rock wall of a town building. He watched, but did not see the men watering themselves and their horses – his raging thirst of moments before forgotten. Straps led Joe back to the well to drink at the trough. It was the gentle hand on his shoulder more than the kind voice of the sergeant that convinced Joe to bend his head and drink.

"You and Daley were pretty close, were you, Dawson?"

Joe gritted his teeth and nodded. The three words he managed to mutter almost choked him.

"We were cousins." Inside his head, he wanted to yell. "Brothers, we were brothers! It's all my fault! I did not look out for him!" Joe dragged the hat from his head and tucked it under the corner of the saddle. He threw water over his filthy brown hair and let it trickle down his face to hide his tears.

"Joe, Joe Dawson!" Farquharson, one of the two other men in the section with Billy and Joe, called above the excited voices of the victors slaking their thirsts. He pulled up to a sliding halt and dropped to the ground. The horse lowered its lips to the water. Farquharson dunked his head and drank thirstily before he turned and spoke to Joe. Max began to relate what he saw of the demise of Billy through the swirling dust clouds at his last jump.

But Joe could not take it in. The words would not register. Regret for the loss of his brother, his best mate, his friend, stole his voice. Guilt for not having taken care of his brother as he had been tasked to do since he could walk, almost suffocated him. He nodded his head. The pallor of his face was unseen beneath the dirt and grime. Joe felt his legs give way beneath him. He sagged. The sergeant's voice brought him back to awareness.

"Watch how much your horse is drinking there, Trooper. You don't want him down with gripe."

Joe and Farquharson pulled their mounts away from the trough and retreated to the quiet corner at the back of the crowd.

"We lost Bennet too, Joe."

Joe nodded his head but his section mate did not think Joe registered what he had been told.

Lieutenant Smithers gathered his squad together and led them off to help with the rounding up of the prisoners of war. In the darkening night, he either did not notice or chose to ignore the absence of Joe who, along with his faithful Straps, wandered off back to the battlefield to search for his brother.

Already the noises of the battlefield faded like the twilight above it. Lanterns of the field ambulance men searching for the wounded flickered their way across the scarred land. Wounded troopers and infantrymen of the Egyptian Expeditionary Forces were collected on sand carts and delivered to the Light Horse Field Ambulance and other Clearance Stations already set up and waiting to treat those who could be treated. Camels with their swaying uncomfortable cacolets delivered some of the wounded and the dead to these aid stations also. Dead bodies did not complain about the rough transport of the camel ambulances.

Within the tents of the Light Horse Field Ambulance, medics worked in the glow of gas lanterns with haste and skill to save as many of the wounded as they could. Blood dripped from the operating table to soak into the dirt below.

With a hand on his horse's reins, Joe stood numb with grief watching men unloading wounded from the sleds and cacolets and wheeling them into the tents to be assessed and treated.

"Mate, you can't stand there, you're in the way," a voice demanded.

"I'm looking for my dead brother."

"Well, you won't find him in the tents. The dead bodies are lying out behind the operating tent." A bloodied hand lifted to point in a vague direction.

Joe led Straps off around the back of the tents until he found the lines of unmoving bodies lying in the partial light. Out of respect, an attempt was made to cover their faces with sacking. Joe froze. It was Straps his horse that nudged him forward. The two wandered up and down the lines while Joe bent to lift the sackcloth over each face.

It was Bennet's body which he found first. Joe drew a sharp breath at the sight of the broken body.

"Sorry, mate." He placed the sacking gently back across his face.

Joe knew before he lifted the cloth when Billy's body lay before him. He knew Billy's body as well as he knew his own. The torso and limbs were undamaged. His brother might have just been asleep. Reluctantly he lifted the sacking. Dried blood traced a line from Billy's forehead to his chin. Joe dragged in a deep breath. He dropped the cloth and struggled to breathe.

"Oh, Billy, my boy, didn't you hear me call you?" Tears welled in Joe's eyes. He took up his brother's cold hand.

"Here, lad," the gentle voice of the Padre brought Joe out of his reverie. "The cooks have hot drinks for everyone."

Being great scroungers, the Billjims, as the men of the Light Horse liked to call themselves, uncovered a huge grain supply the Turkish army kept for their horses. The horses of the Egyptian Expeditionary Forces filled their bellies with food and water. The Billjims found sleeping hens roosting in the trees around the town. These were sacrificed with a quick snap of each neck. After a rough and hasty plucking, they were each cleaned before being thrown upon the cooking fires. Other men sought out the baker shops to find an array of Turkish breads.

The food felt more like sawdust than a hearty meal in Joe's mouth as Farquharson and his previous section mates Carter and Martin encouraged their friend to eat.

Slowly the town quietened as fatigue dragged all but those on guard duty into the arms of sleep.

"What time do you think it is, Carter?" Martin asked.

"Getting on for 2 a.m., I'd be thinking."

"Struth, we've got to get a bit of kip. We're up in two hours for picket duty.

As the glare of the morning sun rose hot upon the weary bodies lying beside their horses, it was discovered that their well had not replenished its water supply. Many went in search of water in the ponds and waterholes left after the rain showers two days before.

CHAPTER SIXTEEN

Billabong Downs

November 1917

William looked up from the diary he kept over the last three months, at the request of Doctor Munson. It was almost time to rewrite his sketchy notes carefully and forward the update to the doctor. After the first report was posted six weeks ago, Mabel's general mood had been almost stable other than the time she exploded and spat on Miles's two boys when home on the August holidays. They had asked her how Billy and Joe liked it with the Light Horse. Mabel chased them around the homestead compound like a deranged harridan. The poor lads were terrified out of their minds. They did not understand. Fran did her best to explain their aunt's condition and warned her sons to keep out of Mabel's sight.

There had been three times when Mabel had wandered off intending to walk into town. On each occasion, she set out in her unwashed clothes without having a bath or dressing in her town clothes. William recalled how this upset him more than the actual action of walking off. Mabel had always been so fastidious in her dress, her bearing and her appearance. It seemed like a stranger lived inside her skin these days.

He wiped the excess ink from the pen nib and laid it on the wooden tray near the inkwells. Firm hands pressed the blotter down upon his work. He put the stopper in the neck of the inkwell. Slowly he closed the hard-covered record book and slid it into the bottom drawer of his desk. He picked up the key hanging from a loop of bootlace tied around his neck. He slipped it over his head and bent to lock the drawer. His long-drawn-out sigh filled the room.

William looked up at the sound of light footsteps on the back stairs. Relief smoothed some of the channels ploughed across his forehead. He lifted the pocket watch from the pouch at his belt. Surprise opened his eyes wide to see the morning so far gone already. Fran and Maggie were here to help Mabel bathe and dress. On the way out to the back verandah to greet them, William glanced in upon his sleeping wife.

"Thank you, Fran. Thank you, Maggie. I have the kettle full of boiling water on the stove for you. I cannot thank you enough. Mabel is in on her bed."

"You're welcome, William, there but for the Grace of God go any of us," Fran smiled.

"Good morning, William, it's no trouble," Maggie added her reassurances.

With much cajoling and encouragement in the form of bribes such as homemade toffees, Fran and Maggie managed to get Mabel into a warm soapy bath. At that point, Maggie went back to her own house to check on her school class while Fran began to clean up the mess in Mabel's kitchen. Not a skerrick of soap had been used in cleaning the table, benches, or stove since the last time Fran completed the chore, three days earlier. She soaped up the scrubbing brush in a bucket of water and bent her back to the chore. In the partitioned-off bathroom on the verandah outside the back door of the kitchen, Mabel lay in the bathtub of warm scented water.

"Are you alright there, Mabel?" Fran called. She did not expect an answer nor did she receive one. Fran emptied the bucket over the railing and poked her head through the bathroom doorway to find Mabel still with her head above water at least.

In the November heat, sweat ran down Fran's face, through her hair and onto her neck. It trickled down between her breasts at the front and along her spine at the back. She lifted her skirt and wiped her face, neck and arms. She smiled at the sound of Maggie's returning footsteps.

"Mabel, here's Maggie come back. It's time to help you out of the bath before you catch a chill in the cooling water." Fran looked up as Maggie rushed into the kitchen with her fingers to her lips.

"What's wrong, Maggie?" she whispered.

At that moment, Fran noticed the pink envelope with the black stripe in her friend's hand.

"Oh, no, is that what I think it is?"

Maggie nodded. "It certainly seems so. We cannot give this to Mabel. She's in no fit state these days to handle what news this might contain."

"No, Maggie, we can't. Here, give it to me and I'll ask Miles to give it to William later."

"What are you two whispering about in there? Stop gossiping and give me a hand here, now."

Fran rolled her eyes at Maggie as she slipped the letter into her deep skirt pocket. The pair went out to help Mabel from the tub.

When they had Mabel dressed and sitting inside her bedroom making a half-hearted effort at brushing her hair, Fran took Maggie aside.

"Has the mailman gone without a cup of tea?"

"No, Gazza has taken him and his dray down to his shed. He'll see Mr. Menkens gets some tea and a slice of the cake I left there yesterday."

"That's good. Mabel would cause merry hell if she spied the mailman around the homestead."

The two friends stood at Mabel's bedroom doorway.

"Can we get you anything before we go, Mabel?" Fran asked.

But Mabel did not answer as she stared deep into the reflection of her mirror.

Maggie and Fran turned and walked along the verandah and down the stairs.

Dusk crept in like a harbinger of bad news as Fran made her way to the horse shed to meet Miles and William returning from the paddocks. She stayed her impatience as they unsaddled and brushed the horses before feeding them some grain and letting them out into the night paddock.

When the brothers returned to her side, she found her speech stuck in her throat. She withdrew the letter from her pocket and handed it to William.

"I am so sorry, William." Fran's words pushed their way out of her mouth. "This arrived with the mailman earlier today."

As William reached forward, his hand froze. His gaze fell upon the official envelope with the black band across the corner. Horror filled his face. His fingers refused to take the letter from Fran's hand.

Seeing the colour of the envelope, Miles reached across and gently took it from his wife's trembling fingers.

"Would you like me to open this and read it for you, William?"

William's mouth opened and shut but the words would not form.

Miles examined the envelope. "It's from the army, William." Miles took the pocket knife from the pouch on his belt and slit the seal. His work-hardened hands struggled to slide the single page out of the packet. His gaze took in the message typed upon the Australian Army's official B104–82 pink page. The words danced across the paper in a blur. Miles dragged in a noisy breath as he made sense of the note. Pain and compassion filled his gaze as he looked up at his older brother.

179

"William," Miles's voice broke, "William, it's Billy. It says that he was killed during a cavalry charge at a place called Beersheba." He gritted his teeth to stop the tears threatening to well in his own eyes. "William, I am so sorry."

William stood unmoving. Thoughts crashed about within his head smashing against the bony walls of his skull. He struggled to make sense of this message and what it meant to himself and what it might mean to his wife. How was Mabel to cope with this disastrous news? William's mind retrieved the memory of his son's wild laughter trailing out behind him like an invisible noisy pennant when he took a new horse to its limits without a hint of fear within his young body. The fearless challenges Billy continually threw out to his brother Joe, and to his cousins, added to the recollections.

As the news of Billy registered, William wondered how his younger son fared in the battle and how Joe might fare at the loss of his closest mate. The pair were inseparable.

"Oh, Miles, what about Joe? What about Dad? We don't know if Joe is alive or not. The pair would have been close together wherever they were. They always stuck together like glue. Joe listed our dad as his next of kin. What if Joe was killed too and Dad has received a similar letter?"

The expression on Miles's face told William this thought had already crossed his mind.

"Perhaps I should dash into Charters Towers tonight," Miles suggested.

"I guess one of us should go." William would have liked to be the one to go. The thought of telling Mabel this news sapped his courage and his self-confidence. "There's no point in rushing in tonight because if that were the case, Dad would already have a similar message – maybe even days ago. Tomorrow morning will be soon enough." Once more William felt his courage slip but he knew this was where his responsibility lay. Mabel needed him too. Who would know what Mabel might get up to once she received this news?

"Give me the message and I'll talk to Mabel now. We may as well find out straight off how she is going to react to this news." William reached over and took the paper and envelope from his brother.

After a quick wash at the pump downstairs, water ran from his hair, his face and his lower arms as far as the bottom of the roll of his sleeves. William dragged his feet, which felt like they were each the weight of a ship's anchor, up the stairs of the house. With a thud, he sat on the stool near the back door and removed his wet and muddied boots. The first port of call was the pantry cupboard inside the kitchen where he pushed bottles aside to claim the rum bottle kept for cooking purposes on the top shelf. He took a long swig before the sharp burn set up a coughing attack. Once his breath returned to normal, he poured a generous dose of the rum into a kitchen cup and returned the bottle to its shelf. He took the cup and walked down the hallway to his wife's bedroom.

Mabel sat in the armchair near the front window. On the small table at her side, a glass lamp with the wick turned low cast a faint light. Her unmanicured fingernails lifted and turned each page of one of several magazines on her lap with regular monotony. William realized she could not have seen the contents of each page; the light was too poor and the speed of page-turning was too fast. Mabel did not look up when William stood at her doorway. He stepped into the room.

"Mabel, I have something I want to talk to you about." He placed the cup of rum on the small table beside the lamp and lifted the correspondence from his top pocket.

Her gaze did not falter when he spoke. Mabel did not move or acknowledge his presence.

William's heart sank further into the heavy lump that was his stomach.

"Mabel, I received a letter from the Australian Light Horse this afternoon." He jumped back a step when Mabel leapt out of her chair scattering magazines across the floor and under the bed.

"Give that to me. That's my letter. It's about time they answered me. I sent my letter off to them months ago." Her scrawny arms stretched out in front of her as she rushed forward. Blood leaked from the scratches made on William's forearm by her chipped fingernails.

William grasped both Mabel's wrists to prevent her from doing any more damage. His eyebrows lifted when he felt the strength within her frail frame.

"Give it to me! Give it to me! That has nothing to do with you!" Mabel bent forward and sunk her teeth into William's forearm.

William cursed and pushed her head away.

"Stop that, woman. Get a hold of yourself. This letter was addressed to me. Now, stop this nonsense and sit quietly in the chair and I'll tell you what it says."

It was as if he had not spoken. Mabel stamped her feet. She screeched. Her teeth clamped open and shut at the empty air like a snapping turtle. William's grip tightened on her arms.

"Stop this at once, you foolish woman. I don't want to hurt you."

The screech and struggle continued until in frustration, William shouted in return.

"Billy's dead. This is the notice of Billy's having been killed in action."

As if a switch had been turned, all the fight left Mabel's body. Wild eyes stared up at William.

"What nonsense are you talking now?"

William's hold on her arms loosened as he spoke.

"The army has sent a notice of our Billy being killed in action at a place called Beersheba."

"What do you mean our Billy? My Billy." Mabel's lips curled in a snarl. The eyeballs rolled in her head until only the whites showed. Slowly her knees gave way and she began to sink to the floor.

William released Mabel's wrists and he swept her up into his arms. Even in the confusion of the moment, his mind registered the featherweight of his wife's body. He lay her gently on the bed as the tears rolled down his cheeks. Tears for his lost son. Tears for his lost wife. Tears for his own heartache. He sat on the floor sobbing until he had no tears left.

In the kitchen of Miles's house, his daughter Mavis snuggled close to her father.

"Why does Auntie Mabel make that dreadful noise?" The child pressed her hands tight against her ears.

Fran turned her back on the dishes in the sink and caught Miles's glance. She raised her eyebrows and smiled a wry smile. She did not offer to save him from the question despite his silent, helpless plea. Miles looked down at his daughter.

"It's not nice, I'll grant you, child, but we must remember, Mabel hasn't been well lately and to have two sons away fighting in a war is a frightening thing even when in the best of health. It's not surprising she's very upset."

"Doug told Mick she was as mad as a cut snake when they were home last holidays." Mavis sat up a little higher, "Is she as mad as a cut snake, Dad?"

Once more, Miles sent out a silent SOS message to his wife. This time Fran hung the tea towel on the nail behind the door and came over to sit on a chair near Miles and Mavis.

"That's not a nice thing to say about anyone, Mavis. You're a big girl now and should know right from wrong and cruel from kind." Fran paused as she gathered her thoughts. "Do you remember when you were ill and had to have your tonsils removed because they were red swollen and very sore? Having an illness in the brain is not a lot different. It is just that, an illness, which needs to be treated."

Mavis sat up higher. Animation stirred her face reflecting the traffic going on inside her ten-year-old head.

"Does that mean they'll have to cut off Auntie Mabel's head to fix her too?"

Surprise, shock, horror and amazement fought for dominance in the shared glances between the parents. Fran noticed the element of amusement glinting in Miles's eyes. Her frown spoke volumes.

"Don't you dare," was her silent demand before she turned to clear things up a little for Mavis.

"No, darling, of course not. The doctors are only beginning to learn how the brain works and how it can go wrong and how it can be fixed."

Mavis's eyes widened. "Did you fix people's brains when you were a nurse? Will you fix Auntie Mabel's brain?"

"Doctor Munson will need to do that, my dear." Fran went back to the sink to finish clearing up for the night.

Mavis sat in silence as all this new information settled inside her head like the leaves falling softly to the ground in autumn. When Mavis next spoke, Fran and Miles again wondered at the process going on inside their daughter's thoughts.

"When will Billy and Joe come home?" She stood up and slipped down off her father's knee. "I'm going to write a letter to Billy and tell him to come home right now. He knows how to fix his mother when she gets into a tizz."

Miles' and Fran's glances clashed mid-stream. Fran shrugged her shoulders and turned her palms upright. As Mavis disappeared into her room, Fran spoke quietly to her husband.

"Miles, we are going to have to explain to her about Billy's death, but I think tomorrow is soon enough. Maggie and I spoke briefly this afternoon. We thought it best to tell the children all together, maybe during their class tomorrow."

Later, with her daughter snuggled under the sheet, Fran went to close her bedroom door.

"Mum, can I sleep in your bed?"

Fran held the sweep of the door as she glanced back at her daughter's tousled head lying on the pillow, seen in the pale moonlight streaming through the window.

"Why on earth would you want to do that, child? We wouldn't all fit on the bed together these days. You are such a big girl now."

"What will I do if Auntie Mabel comes into my room and chops off my head with her carving knife."

Weariness held Fran motionless as she contemplated this strange question. With a sigh, she turned back to sit on Mavis's bed.

"Why on earth would Auntie Mabel want to do that?"

"She might, if she's crazy?"

It did not take too long for Fran to realize her elder boys, now at school in Charters Towers for the final school term of the year, had been telling their younger sister some very strange tales. She sighed a deeper sigh this time. She decided their father could talk to them when they came home for the Christmas Holidays.

'Have your brothers been saying more silly things about your aunt?"

"I can't say; I promised."

Later as the moon crept past their open window, Miles turned to his wife.

"Are you awake, Fran?"

"Yes, dear, it's hard to sleep with all that has happened today. It seems impossible to think of such a live-wire as Billy being dead. Will you go in to tell your parents tomorrow?"

"You've read my mind, as usual, Fran. I'll have to let them know and William has enough on his plate with Mabel. We're worried about Pop as Joe's next of kin. Maybe he was killed at the same time and Pop and Ma will get the notice."

"Surely William and Mabel couldn't be so unlucky."

"It wouldn't be the first time a family has lost two or even more of its sons in war."

"Anyway, will you be going alone?"

"I'll check with Geoff in the morning. If there's nothing needed here, I won't bother with the wagon. I'll ride The Black Devil in."

"Will you see our boys at school and explain to them too?"

"I guess I should. It'll be best coming from us and not from gossip on the wind."

Over in the Bardon house, where the noise filtered into the living room at a lesser volume, Maggie answered the questions from her two eldest children Stewie and Evie, in the best way she knew how using the standard answer for many of the questions they posed relating to their living arrangements.

"It is not our place to make any comment on the way Mr or Mrs. Daley conduct their lives. Mr. William and Mr. Miles are your father's bosses and we must show respect. It is Daley money which puts clothes on your back and food on the table."

It was the younger one, the five-year-old they called Splinter, who silenced everyone when he looked up from the picture book he had been perusing.

"Well, I wish they'd stop putting out good money for spinach; I hate spinach." He slammed the book shut. "And I wouldn't mind a new pair of trousers, I'm sick of wearing all the hand-me-downs."

Maggie dampened the laughter shining in her husband's eyes with a deep frown.

She turned to the children, "Off you go and clean your teeth. It must be bedtime. If you want to stay up a little longer there is a mathematics exercise, I'd like you to have a go at."

Groans and grumbles accompanied the bedtime procession.

"I'll come and tuck you in shortly," Maggie called.

"We want Dad to tuck us in," came the unified reply.

With the children out of sight, Geoff grinned. "They don't trust you not to dump homework on them if you go in there."

Maggie laughed softly until the sad news of the day returned to roost.

"It's terrible news about young Billy. How does any parent cope with that." She ran light fingers down Geoff's cheeks. "Poor Mabel struggles to manage at the best of times these days without that on her plate too."

"Perhaps we should have told the kids about Billy today. Will you and Fran be okay with that tomorrow or do you want me to be there with you? I think Miles will take a trip into town to tell his parents in the morning."

"Young minds want to process the here and now first. And Mabel's ruckus is the here and now." Maggie looked up with her ear cocked. "Hear that? Nothing – it's stopped." A silence lay heavy throughout the homestead compound. Both adults stood listening.

"That's a blessing for both of them," Maggie said before reflecting on their previous conversation. "You are welcome to join us, but we'll manage if you have other things to be getting on with."

"Come on, my beauty, let's go to bed. It will be a day of stress and sorrow tomorrow."

William turned the wick of the office lamp higher. A golden glow leached into the dark shadows. He tossed the rest of today's mail, collected when he was downstairs taking a shower, onto the desk. Since Mabel had commandeered the letters from his daughters several months ago, he had an arrangement with Fran, Maggie and Gazza to ensure any mail delivered by the mailman when William was not home, be placed in a box kept under the house where Mabel never ventured these days.

He struggled to focus his mind on sorting his mail and to shut out the heavy load of sorrow and loss weighing down his heart. Billy was his firstborn. This took nothing away from his love for Joe, his second child. The pair were chalk and cheese in character but they complimented each other. Where one was strong the other was not so well developed and vice versa. They were like twins born twelve months apart and now one half was gone. William's heart ached for Joe. The boy left here a youth but, no doubt, the past ten months have made a man of him. How must he be feeling at the loss of his brother?

Mabel's tortured mind did not rest just because she appeared to be asleep. Her childhood featured prominently in her dreams. The laughter she shared with her parents and her older brothers. She revelled in the attention they lavished upon her. As the only girl and the baby as well, she was never short of devotion from the family.

Like an apparition, William appeared in her life. He could have been a younger replica of her father. He was tall, handsome and strong. With William at her side, she appreciated the same feeling of safety, protection and admiration she enjoyed from her father.

Her love for her first-born Billy never lessened with her recollection of the pain she experienced when he was born. Not like each of the three successive births of Joe, Maud and Cissy. Just looking at them at any time throughout their lives filled her with resentment.

No, Billy was perfect in every way. Even his physical appearance reminded her of her own perfect self. The other children were all so plain, so ordinary – there was not an ounce of flair or charisma in any of them.

Mabel tossed and turned.

In the morning, as William washed the last few dishes, Mabel's words of the previous night bubbled up in his head like the soapy water in the sink.

"My son, not your son."

Leaving the greasy water to cool and clot in the tub, he stormed out onto the verandah. William hoped to be long gone to work before Mabel stirred, but she was standing at the top of the stairs glaring at him her mouth full of further spiteful words. Those words echoed inside his skull at every one of the twenty steps until he was not sure if he really could hear her accusations or whether it was only his memory and imagination repeating past messages.

"You always take everyone else's side but mine. It's always that damn father of yours or that ugly son of yours, Joe. He's a big bully. I wouldn't put it past him to have his brother killed."

William jumped when a plate slapped against the timber palings on the small gate of his house yard. The dog at his heels yelped and snuck off back under the house. Mabel's screech tore down the steps from the kitchen doorway.

It appeared she had awoken with fresh energy to vent her accusations. William was left in no doubt she blamed himself and Joe, along with his father, for Billy's death.

William froze on the spot. He felt the volcano inside his gut bubble to the surface. His brown eyes within a bed of red streaks shone a rich amber as he struggled to control his fury. An overwhelming desire to climb back up the stairs and slap his wife to the floor rushed over him. He took a big breath and turned away. With its tail low and ears lying flat, the dog hustled to the side of its master.

William's stride increased in length and rate. Even the death of a son and definitely not the histrionics of a deranged wife could hold back the work of the property any longer.

The unrelenting heat of the late summer sun burnt Miles's shoulders through his work clothes. Perspiration darkened the shirt on his back. Barbed wire tore at the flesh of his hands. Miles cursed as he repaired the broken fence. It had been three days since the arrival of the pink envelope. Part of his mind focussed on the work at hand as he wound and knotted the barbed wire.

Part of his mind rewound the visit to town to speak with his father. Pop's persistent cough worried Miles even though his mother assured him they had visited Doctor Munson. The man prescribed a cough syrup and a tonic which his father was taking regularly even if not willingly.

Miles growled again as another barbed point ripped its way into his flesh. He drew his hand up to his mouth and sucked on the blood. The pain in his hands was nothing compared to the pain in his heart for his brother William. How does a parent deal with the news of the death of his first-born son killed in a war on the other side of the world? How would William manage with the added weight of his deranged wife screaming blame and abuse – one minute at her husband and the next at her second son still fighting in the foreign deserts? Irrational accusations – neither William nor Joe were in a position to prevent the strike of the hand of fate.

Miles's heart ached for young Joe – a good lad, a strong lad, but one who loved his brother above all else. Miles cursed again as another barb of wire cut a path down the back of his left hand. He dropped his work and sat back on the ground with his head and arms hanging over his knees. The thirsty land sucked up the blood as it dripped from the wound.

He tried to imagine the boy's feelings. Had they been fighting together? Had they been fighting miles away from each other? Had young Joe even received word of his brother's death yet? If so, Miles was in no doubt the lad blamed himself. He always accepted the blame for them both whether blame was called for or not. Thank heavens the boy did not have to listen to the added venom in the accusations of his mother.

He wondered how William and Geoff were doing this morning handling the cow in trouble, calving.

CHAPTER SEVENTEEN

Judean Hills

November – December 1917

Joe lay on the ground. The stench of stale sweat trickled through the layers of sand and grime coating his body. A tremble stirred his limbs as the dream filled his mind, his body, his soul – again and again.

The galloping, galloping, galloping rows and rows of horses
Thundering, thundering, thundering down the slope,
Screeching, screaming, cursing, wailing banshees on horseback,
Ears aching, aching with the drum rolls of the
Pounding, pounding, pounding hoof beats across the land.
Swirling, curling, hurling clouds of dust thrown up from horses' feet
Darkening the late afternoon sun.
Crazy, tormented devils galloping, galloping on to their death.
Thin coats of bravery screened the swelling terror and fear.
The unbroken roar of gunfire; shrapnel exploded all around.
Four miles, three miles, two miles, one mile
Into the trenches running with blood and bone and broken bodies.
Distorted faces with the grimace of the undead.
The tortured rictus grin on the faces of those dead.

Joe jumped to his feet. He paced up and down the lines of the men in camp tossing in their own dreams of horror. He draped himself against his horse seeking comfort in the animal's warmth and understanding of shared experiences. He slept on his feet.

Chill of Blame

His section of four lost two men on the day of the Beersheba campaign. Billy and Bennet did not return. Reorganization followed several days later. Two other men were integrated into the section with Joe Dawson and Max Farquharson – Toby Rawlins and George Turner. The section of Carter, Martin, Gardener and Beatson remained unchanged.

Joe bypassed their bivouac site when he heard the voices of light-hearted greetings. The inevitable had occurred. Billy had been replaced. He spun on his heel and walked off. He wanted no part of greeting his brother's replacement.

His heart felt like a lead weight in his chest as he ambled along the picket line, kicking at the sand, to where Straps crunched the contents of the nose bag. Joe rubbed the animal's coat and lifted each foot to check the hooves. He murmured softly and the animal snickered in sympathy. Tears nestled in Joe's brown eyes.

'Only lost thirty-one men in taking Beersheba,' was the catch cry within the Light Horse Brigade.

Joe wanted to scream every time he heard this being celebrated. *My brother died at Beersheba. It may as well have been every man dead as far as I'm concerned.*

A new moon cast little light over the camp when he returned. He counted the bivouac sites until he reached the one where his section slept. All was quiet. Tomorrow they were in for a long day of travel. The men needed their sleep. Seven bodies lay wrapped in their waterproof sheets like the spokes of a wheel with their feet towards the centre of the group. Joe dropped down upon his sleeping mat and lay on his back with his hands behind his head. Weariness dragged him down but his eyes would not shut. Sorrow and guilt slithered out from where they had lain dormant most of the day. A voice interrupted their progression.

"G'day, mate, sorry we never met earlier. I'm Toby Rawlins. Your second new houseguest is one of the two bodies over. His name is George Turner."

"Joe Daley... er... Dawson." Joe spoke into the darkness and then rolled over onto his opposite side.

Joe remained aloof from his seven fellow bivouac mates – including Carter, Martin, Gardner, Farquharson and Beatson whom he had grown to know quite well over the past months. Rawlins and Turner were virtual strangers – intruders even. Although polite, he did not join the group in any camaraderie. He shared the workload but not his thoughts. Instead of sleep, many of Joe's night hours were spent playing Billy's last day over and over in his mind. Exhaustion greeted him each morning and accompanied him during the days.

Somewhere deep down, Joe recognized why he behaved in such an unfriendly manner. He did not want to become attached to any other human being as he had been with Billy. He did not want to feel responsible for anyone else ever again. It was not the fault of these blokes. No one here understood his close connection with Billy or why. They did not know the pair were brothers – as close as brothers could be. Joe found it too painful to say goodbye. He understood now just how life and death fluttered like fleeting things in all their futures. Death itself held no fear for him. He knew, at this time, he might welcome it with open arms.

After the bully beef tins were buried, the army biscuits chomped to swallowable sizes and the last dregs of the tea leaves poured into the soil, Joe disappeared into the darkness.

"He's an odd cove, isn't he?" Turner asked.

"No, he's not really, when you get to know him," Martin spoke up for Joe. "He's just lost his cousin at Beersheba. He's taking it hard. They were pretty close."

"That was the one you called Billy Daley, wasn't it?" Rawlins asked. "I remember when I first introduced myself to Joe, he called himself Joe Daley."

Farquharson, Carter, Martin, Gardiner and Beatson lifted their heads. Their gazes caught across the flicker of the campfire.

"What?" Rawlins asked.

"Nothing," Carter answered.

"Why are you looking at each other like that?"

The five sat silent for some moments until Carter went on to explain.

"I guess we can tell you both. You won't tell anyone else on pain of death if you do. Swear it." Carter looked up at the other four old hands. "Should I tell them?"

They all nodded. Carter went on speaking, "We reckoned Joe and Billy were brothers. We thought they might have run away to join up. I remember when Martin and I first met the pair of them in the training camp. They were young and rather naïve on their arrival. Many in the army believe brothers won't be allowed in the same units, but we've seen brothers together in other Brigades."

"Anyway, we think that's why they never admitted to being brothers," Martin explained further.

Everyone in the circle remained quiet pondering these thoughts.

In his state of fugue, only occasional incidents clung to his memory. Joe distinctly recalled digging the grave for his brother beside the row of the Light Horse graves at Beersheba. He helped secure the wire netting erected to protect the graves from destruction by stray animals.

For months after Billy's death, Joe's body continued to function by rote. His mind lay within the heavy boulder of pain centered in his chest. Joe thrived on the continual skirmishes encountered as they made their way towards Jerusalem. He fought recklessly – fearlessly. Death meant an end to this excruciating pain of loss and culpability eroding his insides. The discomfort of unending days in the saddle remained almost unnoticed.

He saw the flash of light before the crack of the rifle fire reached his ears. Joe hauled on the reins dragging the horse's head around to the left. All about him other men of the Light Horse employed similar evasive tactics. Their orders were to push the Ottoman army north towards Jerusalem. The Turks ahead were in retreat but they deployed men in rotation to ensure the Light Horse did not have things all their own way.

Blood stained the length of Joe's left sleeve. With a grunt of surprise and pain, he slumped forward scrambling to retain his grasp on the rifle. A bullet slashed a line across his upper back. Blood commenced to colour the back of his shirt. If he had still been facing the enemy head-on, the bullet may have penetrated his chest. Joe pushed himself upright in the saddle and lifted his weapon. The muscles of his arms and shoulders ached with its weight. He aimed for where he last saw the flash of light between two large boulders. It was impossible to know for sure if his bullet found the target. The noise of battle echoed within his head. It was not only a delayed reaction to the near miss which dried his mouth. In recent days, their search for water proved to be a hit-and-miss affair.

"You okay there, Straps?" Joe patted the horse's neck. "Chin up, boy, there are dark clouds in those hills in front of us. We might be lucky with some rain."

In the flickering light of the lantern at the aid station, Joe sat on a stump while the medic cleaned, sutured and bandaged his superficial wounds. The man's eyelashes continually blinked across bloodshot eyes sunk into the wells of deep sockets surrounded by dark shadows. Joe wondered when the man had last slept. After dressing Joe's wounds, the medic issued a word of advice and a replacement shirt, if not new or pressed, at least it was clean.

"Take care, Trooper. Keep your eyes peeled."

The next morning, after a cold autumn night, sleeping on the groundsheet damp from a chilly light rain, Joe collected Straps from the picket lines. He joined the rows of Light Horse as they prepared to sweep up into the Judean Hills. It was Farquharson who offered up his latest piece of gossip gleaned while watering the horses in the pools left on the uneven ground.

"Our regiment has been ordered to relieve a British infantry mob somewhere around here. It will only be overnight."

"One night will be more than enough," Martin offered. "I'd rather the burning summer sun than this freezing sleet."

"Which great leader told us to leave our greatcoats behind when we made the trek to Beersheba?"

"I'm not sure but I hope, whoever it was is freezing his bits off here."

"In all fairness, the extra weight on the horses crossing that desert may have done them in."

What was to have been an overnight relief exercise in the Judean Hills extended into weeks with only their waterproof sheet for protection. Hunched up against the wall of scree, Joe barely noticed the bitter cold and chilling rains. The discomfort was just another torture added to what was already eating away at him. Within the bivouac camps on the bare windblown hills, most areas afforded a little shelter with these walls of loose rock about three feet high. Men struggled with frostbite along with a scant diet of army biscuits and tin bully beef. Joe wore his two pairs of socks together on his feet.

The vision of Pops Daley frequently played in the forefront of Joe's thoughts. He owed it to his grandfather to write and tell him of Billy's death. Pops had written several times since Joe sent that first letter when they left Australia. Joe had sent two off in return but always in Billy's name. He knew full well Pops would recognize his writing. As the darkness of night seeped away to leave the grey skies of dawn, Joe decided to write to his grandfather – the only person, other than Billy, he ever felt able to confide in. He dragged out the tatty notebook from his haversack along with a pencil and his last envelope. He felt the need to explain his guilt for not looking after his brother as he should have. Pops always sent his letters to the name of Billy Daley even though they always started with 'Dear Joe and Billy.' Someone needed to know under what name he was entered on the army payroll. With his hands encased in the remaining pair of Billy's socks, he gripped the lead pencil and wrote.

As he sealed the envelope, it felt like a balm soothing the pain and emptiness within. Joe recalled how his mother's wrath always ended up upon Pops' shoulders even if he was not present or involved in any way with the sins of Billy and himself.

Joe jumped at the touch of a hand on his shoulder. "You want a pannikin of tea?"

"I'd kill for a cuppa, but how did you get a fire going? Any wood, if discovered, must surely be saturated." Joe reached up to take the steaming pannikin from Rawlins' hands.

"A secret shared is not a secret anymore."

Joe looked over to see the men moving around a feeble fire flickering in the harbour of a wonky shelter provided by a waterproof sheet and a natural indent in the wall of scree.

"What the devil is that noise?" Carter was heard to whisper loudly. They had expected the Ottoman army to deliver their calling card sometime during this first clear morning after five weeks of miserable clouds and sleet. "Sounds like someone's gone mad screaming with the pain of the cold and frostbite eating off his toes."

"No, I think it's the screech of some type of new bomb Jacko's got. Tuck your heads in until it explodes."

Farquharson began to laugh. He roared. He could not stop.

"Geez, mate, shut up, will you? You'll have the whole bloody Ottoman army out for our blood," Beatson warned.

Between his bursts of mirth, Farquharson explained, "It's the bagpipes you be hearing – the bloody wonderful, glorious bagpipes. That ain't the bloody Ottoman army out there. It's the bloody mad Scots."

The relief army had arrived in fine form.

Martin edged his mount forward, in beside Joe and Rawlins.

"Thank our lucky stars we're out of those cursed Judean Hills. At least we're getting a bit of sunshine now." An exaggerated shiver shook his shoulders. "Word has it the 10th Light Horse has taken Jerusalem and Bethlehem on the ninth of December while we've been freezing our butts off in the hills. Allenby has left us to mop up after them."

"Well, I for one hope it will be warmer than these damn hills." Rawlins laughed. "I've had enough of cold."

It was George Turner who asked, "It's only a week or two until Christmas. Is Allenby going to be playing Saint Nicholas?"

"All I want is something other than tin bully beef for Christmas dinner, thank you," Farquharson laughed.

"What about a Christmas cake just like my Gran makes, instead of those damn army biscuits. I've broken a few teeth on the bloody things." Rawlins offered his two-bobs worth.

CHAPTER EIGHTEEN

Billabong Downs

November 1917 – January 1918

Fran and Miles sat on the driving seat of the wagon heading in towards Charters Towers. A brown and a grey horse attached by lead ropes to the back of the dray trotted along behind. Their saddles lay in the dray beside where Mavis dozed amongst the hessian bags stacked behind the front seat, near the small Gladstone bag holding her things for a fortnight holiday with her Gran and Pops Daley.

Fran held up her list of chores to be done while in town. She struggled to read the writing between the bumps on the track. She almost dropped her list when she reached out to grab hold of Miles's arm for support at a particularly rough patch in the road.

Miles bent his head and kissed her shoulder. He cast a glance behind him to ensure Mavis was asleep.

"Do you know if Ma was able to collect the presents for the kids last week?"

Both Miles and Fran grunted as the steel-rimmed wooden wheels of the wagon trundled over another pothole.

"Oh, Miles, is there a hole in this track you haven't discovered?" Fran bounced on the wooden seat.

"If it was all smooth going you wouldn't be snuggling into me so much. There'd be no fun in that," he laughed.

She grinned at her spouse before answering his earlier question.

"I have no doubt your mother has Santa's gifts all well disguised and hidden away in your father's shed." It was Fran who turned around to ensure their daughter was still asleep. "There's no reason the shopkeepers wouldn't have everything we ordered. We gave them the list in July."

"I have reservations about having Mabel's parents coming out for Christmas. Remember their last and only visit to the bush? They don't seem to be able to survive for five minutes without all the city's luxuries."

"I think things will be different this time after losing Billy, and now with Mabel losing her grip on the world around her. They have the girls to consider too. Mr. and Mrs. Dawson have become quite attached to Cissy and Maud over the past two years."

"What time did you say we were to pick them up?"

"The train gets in shortly after ten if it's running on time. Tomorrow morning we'll be able to collect the last of our things from the produce store before we need to meet them."

"What about them travelling in this wagon? It's not exactly what they're used to."

"Didn't you read their letter, Miles? Mr. Dawson has arranged to hire a carriage and horses here in town. I can only assume it's from some business connection he has in Charters Towers. They plan to follow us out to Billabong Downs. The owners are happy to let him have the horses stay at our place until they are ready to go back."

Fran returned the shopping list to her handbag bringing out a thick envelope at the same time. "William gave me this letter to deliver to Dr. Munson while we're in town. Did he tell you about that?"

"He did mention he had spoken to the doctor about Mabel's condition. The doctor instructed him to record Mabel's behaviour. Is that what's in the letter?"

"Yes," Fran stared off across the parched country shaded by a thin cover of huge gumtrees under which the kangaroos rested as noon approached. "Thank heavens, there's the creek ahead. I'm looking forward to stretching my legs and a cup of tea."

A flock of white cockatoos lifted into the air when Miles pulled the horses up before the shallows of the stoney crossing. He bucketed water for the horses to drink after which he tied their nosebags, holding a little feed, in place. Fran gathered kindling and leaves to start a small fire. Once the flames settled, she filled the billycan with cool water from the stream and set it to boil.

Mavis stirred in the back of the wagon. She rubbed her eyes and sat up.

"Oh lovely, there's still water in the crossing."

"Don't you go getting dirty, Mavis. Gran and Pop will not want to see you arrive looking like you've never been in a bath." Fran warned.

"No, Mum."

"And bring back some small firewood while you're out exploring."

"Yes, Mum."

"And watch out for snakes around the creek."

"Yes, Mum."

"Can't you say anything but yes, Mum?"

"No, Mum."

Fran rolled her eyes when she looked up to see Miles and their daughter sharing wide grins. She frowned.

"Don't encourage her, Miles." Fran dug into her picnic basket and retrieved a cloth, pannikins and a bundle of sandwiches wrapped in a clean tea towel.

"No, Mum," he laughed.

Mavis raced up to her father and grasped his arm.

"Come on, Dad, let's see if we can find some yabbies."

Chill of Blame

The letter to Dr. Munson was delivered on their way through the town to Miles's parents' house.

"We've made good time today, Fran. It can't be much past two o'clock." Miles reached over and hauled on the brake of the wagon. With a flick of the wrist, he secured the leather strap to hold it in place.

Mavis was over the wooden side in seconds. She raced across the grass to where she was enfolded into her grandparents' arms.

Fran turned to warn her about the dangers of exiting a moving vehicle but shrugged her shoulders instead when she noticed her daughter was safe.

"Come inside, I have the kettle on," Gran Daley called. "Doug and Mick will be back shortly. Pop has sent them to fetch the papers." She released her granddaughter from her arms. "Bring your things in from the wagon, Mavis. I've made up your bed in the sleep-out."

While Mavis ran to do her grandmother's bidding, Miles and his father released the lead ropes on the spare horses and led them down to the stables at the bottom of the garden. Miles asked his father if there had been any further news from Joe.

"Nothing, son. This can only be good news. It means he must still be alive. The army sends reports of woundings as well as death to the next-of-kin and as Joe listed me as his next-of-kin, I'd have news by now if he were either – killed or wounded, I mean."

Miles nodded. "Yes, that'd be so, I guess. But why hasn't he written; do you suppose? He must know we'd be worried."

The hat worn well down on the older man's head hid the sadness deep within the soft brown eyes.

"It'll take Joe time to come to terms with his brother's death I imagine, Miles. They were like Siamese twins, those two. Joe feels things deeply. I've no doubt it will take him some time to accept losing Billy."

As they approached the house, both men looked up at the sound of running footsteps and raucous voices.

"My boys, I presume?" Miles smiled at his father.

Just then Doug and Mick pulled up in a flourish of dust.

The older men swished their arms about to shift the dust from around their faces. Pop Daley coughed.

"Do you two do anything in slow motion?" He grinned.

"Here are your papers, Pops. G'day, Dad, did you bring our horses and the saddles?" the elder boy Doug, the image of his father, asked.

Miles stared at his older son for a moment trying to take in the changes only three months had made. The boy now seemed to tower over his grandfather. It dawned on him Doug was fast becoming a man. A chill ran down Miles's spine. What if this damn war doesn't end soon? Was he to lose a son too, like William? He shook himself.

"Yes, Doug. You and Mick can carry the saddles out of the dray and down to the stables."

Later, after enjoying a light lunch of fresh bread and salted corned meat with the inevitable cup of tea, Gran turned to Mavis.

"Come, child, will you help me clear this lot away?"

Mavis jumped up from the table, "Yes, Gran."

Fran smiled, "If only I could get such instant obedience."

Mavis ran around the table and hugged her mother before returning to work beside her grandmother.

Fran went to rise and join them but Pops reached over and stayed her hand.

"Let Ma enjoy her time with Mavis. Come through onto the verandah." He turned to his grandsons. "You pair can take your horses down to the park for a nibble of green grass."

Bare feet wasted no time in beating a hasty retreat. Helping Gran with the dishes was often their chore when they stayed here during the school terms. As Fran followed her father-in-law out onto the verandah, a sadness settled upon her when she registered the slowing down in a man she loved like her own father. She did not miss the persistent cough that had remained with him since a bad cold last winter. In the cool shade of the green vines growing on a trellis attached to the verandah posts, Pop Daley invited Fran and Miles to sit down.

"Ma said to tell you all the presents are in a well-sealed box in my shed. Don't forget to take them with you in the morning." He thumped the padding on his usual chair before he eased his aging bones into its frame.

"Thanks, Pop, do you need a hand there?" A slight frown formed on Miles's forehead.

"Nah, it's just a few stiff joints. Just old age, nothing to worry about, son. Your turn will come. Now, tell me how are things at home? How's William coping after the loss of Billy?" He wriggled in his seat and then asked, "And how's Mabel handling the news?"

Miles looked over at his wife as if handing the question to her. Fran reached out to touch her father-in-law's hand.

"Pop, it's not all that good. Mabel has retreated into herself even more than when you last saw her. If Maggie and I did not go and check on her each day, she'd never get out of bed, bathe or eat. She screams at William if he tries to do anything for her. She blames him for Billy going off to war. She blames him for Billy's death. She never says a word about Joe, unless it's to berate him too. Maggie and I take turns cooking their meals. That's why Maggie didn't come into town with us, this time. We thought it wise if one of us always stayed home when Mabel was there. We drew straws and Maggie got the short straw today."

Miles took the watch from its pouch on his belt. He looked up.

"Come on then, Fran, we'd best go and get what we can this afternoon, before the shops all shut. We don't want to leave too much to do in the morning and be late to meet the train."

"Are Cissy and Maud coming home for the school holidays?" Pop Daley asked.

"Yes, Pop, and Mabel's parents as well."

Pop Daley's eyebrows reached up to meet the shadow of a hairline of earlier years.

"I don't envy you all that. I remember when they visited Billabong Downs for the first time.

Miles laughed an unfettered laugh.

"Geez yes, remember Mrs. Dawson's shoes? How the hell she ever thought she'd get around the paddocks in those strappy things I'll never know."

Fran smiled as she rebuked her husband.

"Now, Miles, you just leave poor Isabelle Dawson alone. The poor woman had never been past Ross River."

"That may have been so but who in their right mind would have worn shoes designed to grace a ballroom when visiting a working cattle station?" He and Pop Daley began to chuckle in unison.

Fran tried to look serious but her grin revealed her inner thoughts.

"Now I want you both to behave while they are out there for Christmas. It'll be hard for them to accept Billy's death and to see their only daughter reduced to what she has become."

Miles stood; the smile still evident in his sparkling brown eyes.

"Come on, Boss Lady, let's go up the street and annihilate that shopping list you have there. The dray horses will be getting impatient."

Fran followed suit. On their way out of the house, she called back to her mother-in-law.

"Mary, is there anything you want up the street?"

206

"No thanks, dear. We have everything we need here for our tea tonight."

"Bye then. We shouldn't be too long. Bye, Mavis," she called.

After the evening meal, Pop Daley and Miles sat in one corner of the sitting room reading the latest newspapers.

"There's an interesting article in this one here, Miles," Pop's bald head bent over the side of his chair while he riffled through a pile of newspapers on the floor searching for the one that he wanted. "It's a letter from a chap McGregor, he was a Quarter-master at the battle of Beersheba. You'll find it interesting. I've been keeping it for your brother to read when things settle down a bit at home." The arthritic fingers dragged a well-thumbed paper from the pile. "Here it is. Our boys did themselves proud against a very strong opposition after two nights travelling at speed across the desert. It's a wonder we didn't lose a whole lot more of our lads." He handed the roughly folded paper over to Miles to read before digging through his pile of papers once again.

"Aah, here's a second one I thought you might like to see." Pop Daley began rippling through the pages. "Here, this is a copy of another letter from Egypt. It's a letter to a mother who lost her son a few days after the Beersheba stunt – at a place called Tel Khuweilfe only twelve miles from Beersheba."

A third newspaper was also removed from the pile and forwarded to Miles for a read. It had been folded open at a page with several letters from Palestine.

Miles took the newspapers offered. "Thanks, Pop, By the time I finish these and catch up on the cattle sale prices I think I'll be ready for bed."

"Yes, well, you'll be pleased with the cattle sales reports. The prices remain firm. There was a slight rise in some. Anyway, I'll leave you to it. You can take that pile back home with you. William will be wanting to catch up on everything. I'm off to bed myself." Leaning heavily on the arms of his couch chair, Pop stood up. He moved over to where his wife, Fran and Mavis sat with knitting needles clacking furiously. He bent down to kiss his wife with a silent question in his eyes.

"Yes, dear, more socks for the boys at the front. We may be sweltering here but they'll be freezing in Europe and Palestine, from all reports. It will be winter over there now."

The next morning, at the railway station, as Isabelle Dawson stepped down from the train assisted by her husband Bayden's extended hand, Fran was pleased to see durable court shoes on her feet. The dark blue dress worn to just above her ankles was unlikely to show the dust and travel stains. *Maybe Isabelle learnt something on her last visit,* crossed her mind. Fran became caught up with the greetings and hugged her nieces Cissy and Maud tightly.

"You girls have grown, look at you. It will be lovely to see you back on Billabong Downs again."

The girls threw themselves into their Uncle Miles's arms.

"Hello, Uncle Miles, Is Mavis with you?"

"She's staying with Gran and Pop Daley at the moment. They'll bring her out home for Christmas."

Cissy and Maud gravitated towards Doug and Mick where the conversation turned to the pros and cons of their different schools.

A sandy-haired man dressed in dark trousers worn at the knees, unpolished shoes and a dark jerkin approached with his cap in his hand.

"Mr. Dawson, sir?"

Bayden Dawson turned. Realization dawned.

"Oh, are you the man with my carriage?"

"Yes, sir, it's outside. Would you like me to show you which one it is?"

"That will be good." He turned to the others "I won't be long. I'll just go and identify our transport." He turned to his wife. "Isabelle, can I find you a seat? I'll collect our luggage when I return."

"Thank you, Bayden. Miles and Francis will look after me until you come back."

Doug and Mick entertained their younger cousins with their antics on their horses during most of the journey back to Billabong Downs. Mabel's parents travelled sedately in the shaded carriage hauled by a pair of sturdy white horses.

"Bayden must have some influence with whoever owns those horses and the carriage," Miles spoke quietly to Fran sitting up on the driving seat beside him. "There's quite a bit of money in that rig and horse flesh."

"The way Mabel always spoke, when she was talking sense, her father has friends in prominent positions."

Miles stopped the dray near the gate at the bottom of the back stairs of William and Mabel's house. He jumped down to help the girls from the dray but neither felt the need to wait. They were over the side and landed lightly on their feet before the wheels stopped trembling.

William appeared from under the house. A wide smile lit up his face at the sight of his daughters. Together, the girls rushed their father. He gave a solid grunt as they swung into each of his arms, almost lifting him off his feet.

"My little chickens are not so little anymore," he muttered as he stumbled to keep his footing.

"Oh, Daddy, we missed you so much." Maud, the younger, reached up to smother his cheek with kisses.

Cissy now thirteen-years-old held her poise for several more seconds until she too landed kisses upon his face.

"I have missed you too, chickens." William looked up to see his in-laws descending from a classy carriage. He did not miss the look of disdain on Isabelle's face at the sight of his daughters acting in this most unbecoming manner. Silently he felt chuffed to think his girls retained their ability to feel free to be themselves.

He released the pair with soft words of advice, "Your mother's waiting for you on the verandah." He felt the need to give them some warning about the changes they were sure to notice. "Remember, go gently, your mother has not been well lately." He turned to meet his guests.

"Welcome to Billabong Downs, Isabelle," William almost felt the overwhelming need to bow but he restrained himself. He reached his right hand over to his father-in-law. "Welcome, Bayden, please come upstairs, Mabel's sitting out on the verandah."

Before William went to follow the Dawsons up the stairs, Miles spoke to him.

"William, the boys and I will see to the carriage and the unloading. I see Geoff on his way over to give a hand too."

William's nod accompanied his grateful smile before he took the stairs two at a time to rescue whoever needed rescuing on the verandah.

As soon as he reached the top step, William's heart sank at the sight of the look of horror on his girls' faces. They stood back from the chair where their mother sat flicking through a magazine ignoring her visitors. Pity surfaced at the sight of Mabel's parents' expression of surprise and consternation as they gazed upon this frail and listless stranger – their daughter.

"Mabel, your two girls and your parents are here to see you. Aren't you going to say hello?"

Without lifting her eyes, Mabel answered, "They are not Billy, are they? You sent my Billy away."

After some seconds while her audience was held spellbound, the glazed dark eyes lifted and stared directly at her father. Her mouth attempted a smile, but with lips unused to such an exercise for many months the outcome was a pathetic replica.

"Daddy, you're here, have you brought my Billy home?" Sneering eyes turned to William as she went on to explain to her father. "He sent my Billy away and now he won't bring him back."

Bayden Dawson stood stunned. His mind struggled to comprehend the changes in his daughter. He glanced down at his wife and reached for her hand at the sight of the tears running down her cheeks.

William wrapped an arm around each of the girls as they slipped back to stand by his side.

Bayden turned to his son-in-law. "Has she not been told Billy is dead?" He mouthed the words.

"She has been told," William replied.

It was Isabelle who dragged a high-back wooden chair closer and sat at her daughter's side. The tears continued to fall as she took up Mabel's hand.

"My poor baby," she whispered. "Where have you gone?"

William turned the girls around and led them off to the kitchen.

"I think everyone will want a cup of tea about now, don't you agree?"

Relief accompanied the three of them as they went to prepare a tea tray.

As William crawled under his mosquito net to stretch out on his bed on the East verandah outside Mabel's room later that night, his mind wandered through the strange evening after the arrival of the Dawsons. He felt amazed at the way Isabelle turned her hand to assist in the care of Mabel. He admitted he was wrong in thinking she would jump back in the flash carriage and run for her life when she got to see the Mabel of today. Even Mabel's father lent a hand where possible. William felt relieved and pleased that Mabel's parents were happy he had consulted with the doctor and followed up with the recommendations. Most of all though, it was the warm feeling of admiration for his two girls who, once recovered from the shock of seeing this stranger in place of their mother, flitted about to serve up the meal sent over from Maggie and Geoff. They cleaned up after everyone finished eating and later read to their mother after Isabelle had settled her daughter into bed.

For the first time in a long time, he relaxed as he bathed in the moonlight streaming through the verandah blinds.

It was not long after daybreak a week later, when the sound of hoofbeats brought Isabelle to the back steps. Her hand flew to her mouth. Bayden arrived at her side.

"It's alright, Isabelle, the girls have been riding horses since before they could walk."

His presence calmed Isabelle's fears but her sense of righteousness almost overwhelmed her. Isabelle watched the riders, two men and four youngsters; two of whom were her granddaughters, as they galloped out of the homestead compound.

"Oh, Bayden, they are dressed in boys' clothing." A gasp of horror preceded her second exclamation, "Oooh, Bayden they are sitting astride the horses."

"I guess it would be difficult to muster cattle sitting in a side-saddle."

"Muster … muster, you say? Surely the girls are not mustering the cattle?"

"Yes, Isabelle. William, along with our girls and Miles with his sons are going out to round up some cattle. They will be killing a beast today so we'll have fresh meat for our Christmas dinner. You did say last night how you were sick of salted beef stew."

"Oh, good heavens, but it is not the place of young women to be out seeing all that."

"I think on a place like this, everyone has to muck in and do whatever needs to be done." He paused unsure whether to go on or not. He decided it would be good for his wife to see the other side of life for a change. He had mollycoddled her for too long. "They are going to slaughter a pig later also, I understand." He slid his arm around her waist as a precautionary measure, having had previous experiences in softening her falls from fainting attacks.

Shade from the stand of gum trees to the west of Miles's house crept over the roof as Pop Daley hauled on the reins of the horses pulling the dray carrying himself, Gran Daley and Mavis home to Billabong Downs for Christmas.

William's girls burst from their house, only a hundred and fifty yards away, and down the steps. Squeals filled the air. Fran followed the same path in a more sedate manner.

"Mavis, we thought you'd never get here." Cissy and Maud called in unison as they swung up onto the back of the dray before the wheels had completely stopped moving. The girls wobbled as they adjusted their balance.

"Cissy, Maud, how wonderful to see you again." Mavis jumped up lightly and reached out. The girls drew into a wrap of arms.

Mary Daley looked at her husband. "I think we've been forgotten, Pop."

Instantly Cissy and Maud released their cousin and being unable to climb over the mountain of bags and boxes stacked between them and their target, they jumped to the ground and raced to the front of the dray. Nimbly they jumped up via the now-stable wheel spokes. Each hugged their paternal grandparents in delight.

Fran arrived to help Miles's mother from her seat while Pop shuffled his way over to the opposite side. She smiled as her daughter's familiar arms reached up around her neck and Mavis planted a kiss on her cheek.

"Welcome home, Mavis. We've missed you."

"I missed you too, Mum, but I enjoyed my holiday with Gran and Pops."

"Can I help you with your bags, Gran?"

"I'll get them for you, Mum," offered Mavis, "and then can I go with the girls to meet Dad coming back from the paddock?"

"Of course, dear."

Pop Daley stood watching the youngsters as they sped across the compound.

"Ah, if one could only do that again?"

"Well don't you try, old man, I don't want to have to nurse you with a broken hip." Mary Daley turned back to Fran. "Men make the worst patients, as I'm sure you know, dear."

"Now don't be too harsh on Pop, Gran, I've seen some female horrors also."

Pop turned back to the women.

"Mary that's malicious gossip, I'm the perfect patient." He turned his smile onto his daughter-in-law. "Thanks for your support, Fran." The women rolled their eyes.

It was Doug and Mick who approached just as Pop Daley was going to climb up into the dray.

"Leave it, Pops, we'll get the luggage and unharness the horses for you."

A sigh escaped his smiling lips along with a load of relief. The thought of doing both those chores seemed a bit past him today after the long drive.

"Thanks, boys, I'd sure appreciate that. Can you unharness the dray over near the shed? We won't be needing it for the next few days."

Doug jumped into the back of the tray.

"Oh, Pops, Gran has outdone herself. She's got enough gear here to last an army for a year."

Pops grinned at his grandsons. "Well, are you going to tell her that, because I'm sure not?"

"Not on your life," Doug returned.

"Lily liver," Mick teased his brother.

"Okay, hero, you can, but just wait until Pops and I get out of the line of fire," Doug laughed.

It was a sombre group gathered around the trestle tables stretched along Fran's side verandah for Christmas. The sun bobbed in and out of the developing dark clouds. In the heat of the day, coloured paper streamers sagged from the tacks in the timber beams above. All the doors and windows of the kitchen were open in the hope a stray breeze might drag the smoke and steam outside.

"We'll be in for a storm before the end of the day," Pop Daley commented as Miles refilled his glass of ale, "something has to give soon."

Geoff and Maggie, along with their three small children, were away celebrating Christmas in town with Maggie's family. Everyone around the family table missed the sparkle of Billy's presence and the dry humour of his brother Joe – each in their own way. The pair were never far from the thoughts of all those who sat with heads bowed while William recited the Grace. The family gave thanks for all His bountiful gifts and along with William, asked for God's blessing on both his sons – Billy in His care and Joe still at the war.

The teenagers gravitated to the far end of the table. Their conversations alternated from raucous, almost forced laughter, to hushed whispers. William and Mabel's two girls, Cissy and Maud, struggled with the absence of their two brothers at the Christmas table. For Miles and Fran's sons, Doug and Mick and their daughter Mavis, the vacant seats at the gathering were a reminder of all those fighting in a war far from home.

On her way back to the table after a trip to the kitchen, Fran paused in the doorway watching her guests. A light frown creased her brow. Everything looked Christmassy with the streamers, the coloured papers left from opened presents and the red paper flowers in vases on the table. The smell of Christmas flavoured the aromas wafting out from the kitchen: from the crackling of the roasted pork and that of the three sacrificed hens, the basted vegetables and the sweet custards that accompanied the generous servings of plum pudding. Fran still tasted the pleasure of it all upon her tongue along with the stolen mint jelly Christmas lolly in her mouth. Lollies the girls had spent hours cutting to the shape of Christmas trees the previous afternoon. Her arms and her back ached as only Christmas could make them ache. She realized it was the sounds that were wrong. The unrestrained voices were absent. The back-and-forth teasing amongst the younger ones sat flat like stale air. Joke telling did not have the immediate response as usual. It was as if a blanket of constraint weighed down the natural frivolity of a normal Christmas. It leant a dampener upon all of them here.

At first, she wondered if the unusual presence of the Dawsons may have been responsible or maybe the presence of this new Mabel. She admitted she did miss Mabel's wonderful soprano voice filling the rafters above as it had every previous Christmas. She realized that even though these things may have had some influence on the change, she felt it was more. It was the spirits of Billy and Joe sitting like invisible guests upon the shoulders of everyone.

As was usual, Gazza made an appearance for the Christmas lunch but he did not prolong his stay. Too many people made him nervous, especially when there were strangers as Bayden and Isabelle Dawson were to him. Fran did not allow Gazza to leave without a basket of food and a couple of bottles of ale to keep him company.

Mabel never spoke a word during the meal. She nibbled sparingly on the offered food. She drank a glass of lemonade. It was as Fran placed the large teapot on the end of the table beside her matching milk jug and sugar bowls that the celebration was brought to a sudden end when Mabel scraped back her chair and stood. Silence fell along the verandah. The wary gaze of all eyes turned upon her, knowing whatever she was about to say would fall like a thunderclap upon them. William dropped his serviette and made to rise but Mabel's trembling voice nailed him to the spot.

"What's my Billy eating for his Christmas dinner today?"

William and his girls rushed from opposite ends of the table to usher Mabel away.

It was later in William's kitchen, as he and the Dawsons were drinking hot cocoa made with fresh milk when the subject he dreaded was brought out into the open. He was grateful Cissy and Maud were with their mother helping her into bed. The fact that the discussion became disjointed was partly due to the subject itself and partly because of the interruption of frequent claps of thunder from the sky above.

"William, as you know Bayden and I plan to return home the day after Boxing Day. We'll follow your father into town. I think we should take the girls back with us. It will save you a trip to the coast later in the month when they are due back at school. All things considered; it cannot be good for them to see their mother in this state."

William sat in silence as the hot-bladed shaft of pain speared his heart. He did not doubt Isabelle was well-meaning. He watched the tears streaming down her face. The woman was bereft at seeing her daughter's deterioration for herself. Did she blame him for Mabel's condition? He struggled with his conscience. Was his reluctance to let his daughters go a selfish act on his part, or a genuine concern for their well-being? They were all he had left; beside the shadow of the woman he married, lost somewhere within her broken mind.

William cleared his throat. "Thank you, Isabelle," he glanced up at Bayden standing behind his wife's chair, his face beyond expression. "I hear what you're saying, Isabelle, but Mabel is the mother of Cissy and Maud. In these past few days, the girls have proven they love their mother even in this state. There is no doubt their presence has brought Mabel out of herself a little. We have had no screaming tantrums which has to be a good thing. I believe, in the future, the girls might regret not taking every opportunity to share time with their mother when they could have." His long-drawn breath became an extended sigh. "Cissy may not be quite fourteen years old and Maud still only eleven, but they have shown wisdom and understanding beyond their years. I believe they deserve to be consulted on this question themselves."

"Consulted on what exactly, Dad?" Cissy stood with her shoulder propped against the edge of the doorway. Maud peeped out from behind.

Isabelle and Bayden snapped their heads around. William's gaze lifted. He took a moment to recover from his surprise.

"Come in, girls, please. Sit down, if you will?"

William, his girls and Isabelle Dawson spoke on all sides of the suggestion of the girls going back to Townsville either in two days or later, just before the school was due to resume in late January.

"I for one, wish to spend as much time helping my mother as I can." Cissy looked around at her sister. "What about you, Maud? It's up to you what you want to do. If you want to go home with Grandmama and Grandpapa now, you can. I'll join you in a couple of weeks."

Young Maud rushed over to wrap her arms around her father's waist.

"I want to stay and look after you, Daddy – and Mama, too."

William could not speak for some time. His arm fell to Maud's shoulder before his gaze crossed the table.

Cissy walked over to stand on the other side of her father. Their glances met.

"It looks like I get to have a train ride to the coast with my chickens then. I love train rides." He struggled to smile through the threat of tears.

At that moment, the heavens opened. Rain thrummed down upon the tin roof. The flame in the lantern fluttered in the rising wind. William lifted his voice to be heard above the noise.

"I think it is time we all went to bed."

As he lay in bed listening to the rattle of the rain on the roof above, William fought with the doubts burrowing inside his head. Had he done the right thing in letting his girls stay here? The environment could become quite vicious when Mabel took it into her head to turn vindictive. Knowing his sister-in-law was nearby to take them in if the need arose helped ease his conscience.

After the visitors departed, William endeavoured to ensure his girls spent time outside as well as being cooped up with their mother. Geoff Bardon was happy to have them along helping him with checking the stock and mustering cattle onto the fresh green picking resulting from the storm on Christmas night.

Fran appreciated having Cissy's assistance on those occasions when they bathed Mabel together. Fran noted how Cissy's presence did go some way to making Mabel more compliant.

"Auntie Fran, when I finish school, I want to be a nurse." Cissy mused as she poured the buckets of hot water into the bathtub. "Do you think I can be a nurse?"

"There are those who might disagree with me, but I firmly believe nursing is an honourable career." Fran looked directly at her niece. "I think you have all the makings of an excellent nurse."

"I'm going to leave school at the end of this coming year." Excitement flourished in Cissy's smile. "I'll be old enough to become an Assistant Nurse."

"Have you spoken to your father, yet?" Fran's eyes glinted remembering her excitement when she started her nursing career.

Water dripped from his hair and onto the towel draped around his shoulders covering his bare chest. William came out of the shower room under the house wearing only a clean pair of cotton twill trousers. He slipped his feet into the pair of old boots left on the narrow cement path leading from under the house to the back stairs. Dust rose from the handful of dirty clothes as they landed on the bench near the laundry tub next door to the shower room. He retrieved the mail from the box on the ledge above the laundry bench. His fingers flicked through the letters in his hand. He looked twice at the envelope addressed in his father's hand. It had been only a week since they had returned to Charters Towers. Idly his right hand rubbed the towel over his wet hair as he pondered this surprise. With his curiosity aroused, he tossed the damp towel over the wire line taut across the beams above his head and threaded his arms into a faded check shirt. As his feet touched the timber floor of the verandah, he knew something was amiss. The profound silence in the house jangled his nerves.

"Cissy!" he called. "Maud!" He felt his chest tighten. He poked his head through the open kitchen doorway where, at this time of day, the girls were usually preparing the evening meal amidst a combination of laughter and panic. Silence.

He stashed the mail on the ledge above the door and strode off down the hallway towards Mabel's room first. Experience had taught him if something was amiss it was usually generated from Mabel's room. Empty.

Moving faster now, William crossed the room and through the open doorway onto the verandah where he slept in the single bed under the mosquito net. Nothing – not even the old white dog who was usually to be found snoring in the sun. William stretched out over the edge of the railing to investigate the sounds of voices below.

On the old love seat that he had built so many years ago, sat his wife and their two girls. Cissy read quietly from the Jane Austen book she received as a Christmas gift from her grandparents. Maud sat beside her mother holding her hand. The vision held William entranced. How had his daughters managed to bring about this change in their mother?

He recalled thoughts expressed recently by Isabelle when she said, 'I fear Mabel may be getting too much attention. I am not criticizing, William, I confess my own guilt in this when she was a child.'

He pondered on whether there might have been some truth in her words. Was Mabel behaving now because she had the undivided attention of the girls? What was going to happen when they returned to school? He decided it best to enjoy the peace and face what might happen next week when their daughters returned to Townsville. He tidied his clothes and made his way downstairs.

"Daddy, Daddy," Maud dropped her mother's hand and ran to her father, "Cissy is reading her new Jane Austen book to us."

Cissy looked up and smiled. "Look, Mama, Dad's home."

William noticed Mabel's face transform like a theatre stage when the curtain was pulled. Relaxed muscles contracted, black eyebrows descended and her expression darkened as the red lips flat-lined. William presumed the girls had applied makeup earlier.

"Don't talk to him, he stole my Billy. He won't bring Billy home again."

Even though he had witnessed her mood swings on many occasions over the recent twelve months, William was shocked at this sudden change. He looked down to see the tears as they flowed from Maud's eyes and ran down her cheeks. His eldest daughter Cissy, sat unmoving with a finger on the page of the book upon her lap. Her chin wobbled. William's heart felt as if it were breaking.

"Cissy, would you and Maud like to go up and start fixing our evening meal? I'll help your mother up the stairs."

The wailing began as William attempted to help Mabel rise from the seat. It rose in volume as he half-carried her up to her bedroom. The volume dropped some decibels when the bedroom door, crashed shut by her hand, almost hit William in the face.

William retreated to the verandah where he stood at the top of the front steps staring with unseeing eyes over the paddocks where a mob of cattle lay resting in the shade of the tall gum trees. He struggled to regulate his breathing and calm his spirit.

When he went in for his tea, William was pleased to see Cissy had closed the kitchen door which reduced the noise from Mabel's room even further. Maud sat silently with her head bowed over a plate of omelette and toast. Cissy's fork idly stirred the food in front of her with little interest. A plate of eggs thick with vegetables warmed on the edge of the hot stove. Four sausages lay in a bath of gravy in the large frying pan above the fire.

"Why does she say those wicked things, Daddy?"

William fought back his tears as he looked across at his youngest child. Several answers filled his thoughts before he spoke. He took the plate of sausages and egg from Cissy's hand.

"Sit, Cissy," he reached over and took Maud's hand which disappeared within his grasp. "Maud, Cissy, this is a part of your mother's illness. You must never take to heart anything she says at these times. Do you understand, this is not the mother you know."

"Why doesn't the doctor fix her back into my real mother?"

"He is hoping to be able to do this but up to this moment, she hasn't agreed to speak to the doctor. Until she does, there is little he can do." He stood up and moved around the table to kiss each of his girls on the head. "Now eat up, you need your strength to be able to help your mother."

He sat himself down and began to eat forcing himself to pick up his food, shove it in his mouth, chew and swallow while his stomach threatened to reject every morsel.

Quiet settled upon the house by the time the kitchen had been restored to order and the girls retreated to their room. William remembered the mail he'd left on the ledge above the kitchen door

223

earlier. He retrieved this and retired to his office where he lit the lantern on his desk before stretching back in his chair.

Dear William,
A letter from Joe arrived this morning. At the time of his writing, he was safe. He talks of Billy's death. I won't post it on just in case it falls into the wrong hands but will keep it handy for you when you bring the girls back on the way to Townsville.
Love from Ma and your Pop.

As William read, relief eased the remaining tension clamped down upon every muscle within his tall frame. His son Joe was safe. William realized just how uptight he had become with his worry for the lad. He listened to the snuffles drifting out from Mabel's bedroom and promised himself to ensure the girls were involved in outdoor chores tomorrow. *Isabelle may have been correct. Mabel is throwing tantrums like a child when attention is drawn away from her,* were his thoughts as he sifted through the remainder of the mail.

The last days of the holidays flew by. With some reluctance, everyone began to prepare for their return to school. Cissy and Maud were to be accompanied to Grandmama and Grandpapa's house in Townsville by their father. Doug and Mick were to tag along as far as Gran and Pop Daley's place in Charters Towers from where they planned to recommence their attendance at the local school. Maggie Bardon gathered her prepared notes used in her daily classes for her three young children and Fran's youngest, Mavis.

Everyone but Mabel congregated near the loaded dray with William in the driving seat carrying the four students back to their schools. Fran stepped forward out of Miles's arms and assured her brother-in-law she would take care of Mabel while he was away.

224

"I plan to sleep at your house each night. Mavis can look after her father for a few days, I'm sure."

"Thanks, Fran, I appreciate that."

"You're welcome." Fran turned to her departing sons scuffling with their cousins for the best seats in the dray, "Look after your Gran and Pops for us, now."

Hands waved until the travellers were hidden within a cloud of dust.

Doug and Mick were unloaded under the huge fig tree at the front gate of their school.

"You fellows sure you'll be okay here? You don't need me to come sign you in or anything?

"No, Uncle William, we're fine."

From here, the dray wound around the creek and park until the weary driver pulled up at his father's house. Cissy climbed down and William helped Maud pass out their suitcases before the girls ran up to greet their grandparents waiting on the back porch. Later, after they finished eating the hearty meal Gran had cooked, they helped clean up the kitchen before going to their beds.

In the sitting room, Gran Daley's knitting needles clicked a hasty beat in the background while William read the letter from Joe.

Dear Pops and Gran Daley and Dad
December 1917
I guess by now the army has reported the death of our Billy at the Beersheba charge. As usual, Billy was fearless and charged the enemy in full voice. I'm sorry I did not take better care of him. We had been riding side-by-side but then Billy disappeared into the thick dust clouds that lay heavy about us. Even though I blame myself, common sense tells me even if we were still riding knee-to-knee there

was nothing I would have been able to do. The machine-gun took out his horse Buckles and Billy at the same time as they leapt the trench.

Pops I miss him so much. It's like I have lost my right arm. It was good to have someone to confide in, to share gripes with, to laugh with. Now my heart is just a lead weight inside my chest.

I want to say I'm so sorry for the load of blame that our mum is going to lay at your door. No doubt she will save plenty for me too – if I get to return. Please tell Dad I'm sorry for the hell she will be putting him through also. It is nearly twelve months since we left but it seems like I have aged a thousand years in that time. I see so many things much clearer now.

We have the Ottoman on the run. Currently very wet and cold as the Palestine winter settles in.

God Bless you and Gran. Love you both. My love to Dad, Uncle Miles and Auntie Fran and Mrs. Bardon and all the kids of Billabong Downs. I cannot send my love to my mum. I am not sure I have any within me to send. I just pray her spleen is not vented upon the rest of you all.

Regards to Cissy and Maud

You loving grandson – Joe Daley Dawson – in this man's army.

Pop Daley sat quietly allowing his son to absorb what he had read before he interrupted.

"I have written a note in reply saying you would write when you got to see his letter. I have left it unopened in case you want to add a letter of your own."

William remained silent and nodded his head.

"Would you like to see it?"

"Yes, Pop, thanks."

Chill of Blame

The clicking of his mother's knitting needles was the only sound in the room as William opened the folded paper placed into his hand. He read.

Our dear grandson Joe,

We received your letter containing the news of Billy's death. He will be sadly missed BUT I do not want to hear a word of you blaming yourself.

I remember a discussion Billy and I had a few weeks before you both departed. He had a deep understanding of what a soldier at war may have to endure. I knew he had been thinking on the subject for some time. It was not a spur-of-the-moment decision.

Joe, your brother would not want you to be blaming yourself for his death. War is to blame for his death, if anything – and the people responsible for starting a war. No straight-thinking person on Billabong Downs blames you for Billy's death and you are not to do so either.

I can hear you saying. "Mum will blame me for Billy's death."

That may be so, but your mother spent all her life with no thought in her lovely head but presenting herself as beautiful. She lives in a world of make-believe, I'm afraid. She never had a rational thought about the real world in her whole life.

This may sound a bit harsh to be saying to you, her son, but as I see it, this is the case. I think you need to know this too. So, my boy, you stop blaming yourself. Rest assured your gran and I do no such thing. Every morning and night we send up a prayer to bring you home safe and sound.

Gran has just called out to remind me to tell you to keep an eye out for a parcel containing a fruit cake that she made for you. It's on the sideboard setting or drying or whatever it has to do for another five days before she will pack it in a tin and send it on to you. You and

your mates will enjoy that after the hard tack of army biscuits and
bully beef.
Keep your head down, lad,
God bless and keep you safe.

Trembling fingers folded the letter. William took a deep breath before lifting his gaze to his father.

"You were a bit harsh on Mabel, Pop, but I cannot deny what you say is true. Maybe you're right. Joe needs to know no one else will blame him for one single moment."

"Believe me, William, if a soldier has self-blame or other depressing thoughts in his head, he is not going to think clearly when faced with live fire from the enemy in battle."

William nodded. "If you just give me a bit of paper, I'll drop him a line tonight, backing up what you say. Will you add it to yours to post tomorrow?"

"Of course, son."

CHAPTER NINETEEN

Another Year

January – July 1918

During the month of January 1918, Joe, his friends, and his regiment rested outside Jerusalem. There was little to do other than occasional guard duty to protect the road and rail construction undertaken by the engineers and the Egyptian Labour Corps. Their work extended from Jaffa on the coast through to Ludd, which was a quarter of a mile from General Allenby's headquarters near Jerusalem. During the idle hours, they treated their numerous local infections and improved their diet with fruit and vegetables acquired from the district.

Dust sprayed up from Farquharson's feet as he raced into their camp.

"Did you see those two Australian planes going overhead earlier? They're bombing supply boats on the north end of the Dead Sea. The blighters were delivering corn and hay to the Ottoman forces in Amman."

"I'll get them to bomb you if you spray us all with sand again, Farky," Rawlins threatened. "How did you hear this anyway?"

"If you spent more time on kitchen detention washing dishes like I do, you'd get to hear all sorts of bits of info." Farquharson threw himself down on the ground near the three men playing cards. "The cook says, he heard The Bull is planning to take Jericho next and then we're all getting a trip to the Jordon Valley. "I've always wanted to see the Jordon River."

Joe and his fellow troopers mustered several Ottoman garrisons out of the Judean Hills east of Jerusalem, herding them further north. Towards the end of February 1918, Jericho was the next to fall before the will of the Egyptian Expeditionary Force. As spring began to make itself felt three bridgeheads were secured across the Jordon River leading towards the enemy-held towns of Amman and Es Salt.

Dark clouds swept across the wind-blown sky as regiment after regiment of mounted troopers crossed the pontoon bridge over the Jordon River. Envy smouldered in the expression of those men of the Light Horse lined up on either side of the track leading east. Joe wished those heading towards Amman and Es Salt a safe journey, but he wished more that his regiment might be one of those going into battle. Even Straps shuffled his feet in anticipation of heading off to this latest stunt. Straps and Joe quelled their impatience. Their regiment had been charged with ensuring the bridge over the Jordon River remained open for a quick retreat if the need arose.

"We'll be in for a shower of rain by the end of the day," Farquharson whispered. "Those fellows will be heading into heavy rainfall if the clouds are anything to go by."

"I thought it was supposed to be dry weather here now, Max?"

"It goes to show you that the Bull can make his great plans but when it comes down to it, it's the weather in control, not him."

At first, the men welcomed the warmer weather. Their spirits lifted, but as the oppressive heat within the Jordon Valley took hold and their diet once more returned to bully beef and army biscuits, septic sores flourished, flies hung in clouds, mosquitoes skewered every piece of uncovered flesh, scorpions and huge hairy black spiders popped up from everywhere. The men's gripes increased.

During the last day of March 1918, Joe and his friends watched in horror at the sight of the endless line of retreating men of the Light

Horse as they returned across the bridge. Included in the cavalcade of misery struggled the mud-splattered motor ambulances filled with wounded. Some of these vehicles were hauled by harnessed horses. Camel cacolets swayed along behind. Few of the returning mounted men were without a bandaged wound visible somewhere on their body. The procession continued for two days.

While General Allenby's forces reorganized, the bridgeheads were defended on several occasions.

Joe and the other three men in his section lay sheltered amongst the rocks with their backs to the banks on the east side of the Jordon River at the bridgehead where the regiment defended another counter-attack. The Ottoman army fought to regain supremacy over the Jordon River access. A machine-gun had been making a lot of noise to their left. Joe and his friends planned to put it out of action.

Gesturing with his hands, Joe indicated the track he wanted to take. Moving slowly through the rocky outcrop leading to thick bushes growing near the riverside, the four men hunched over almost double. They reduced the distance to where they had last seen and heard the clatter of machine-gun fire aimed at the troops defending the east end of the bridge. When he called a halt again, Joe noticed a wide clear area between where he planned to take his shot and where the enemy in charge of the machine-gun sheltered within their camouflage nearly three hundred yards from the river.

They lay catching their breath.

Rawlins asked in a hushed whisper, "You sure you can take that shot? It's quite a distance? I'm not sure I'm even seeing where the gun is from here."

Farquharson frowned. "Leave him to concentrate. Joe knows what he's doing," he whispered in return.

While the three remained in relatively secure protection near the river bank, Joe lifted his hat from his head and shoved it into his shirt. He felt the heat of the spring sunshine burning his forehead. He stretched out on the ground and began to shuffle along on his belly keeping behind the irregular bumps of the terrain towards a long-fallen trunk of an old dead tree. From within the broken tree limbs, Joe lifted his head ever so slowly to peer in the direction of his target. The heart in his chest pounded, stealing his breath. Will-power alone forced his body to quieten until his lungs sipped in the hot stale air.

Amidst the fronds of bushes camouflaging their machine-gun placement, Joe recognized the different colours of human skin and the material of their shirts. Two enemy soldiers were in the process of reloading weapon belts into the gun. His sharp eyes identified the two sets of white teeth of the machine-gunners as they grinned at each other. He imagined he saw smoke rising from their cigarettes as they sucked tobacco into their lungs.

Slow shallow breaths fluffed small dust puffs near the log where Joe lay for long minutes. He relaxed and became one with the dirt. He cleared his mind and focussed only on his aim, the wind, his trigger finger and what he could see of the faces within the leaves of their camouflage. His finger eased back on the trigger. Joe saw the rose of blood appear on the temple area of the skull of the first soldier on the left. His relief at his success remained under control. The second shot came on the heels of the first, but still, the other soldier had a split second to lift his head. Joe released a relieved sigh on seeing the fountain of blood erupt from the neck of the man on the right. He felt no pleasure in his success other than the knowledge that the threat from this enemy machine-gun nest to the lives of many of his fellow troopers had been removed.

Joe continued to lie unmoving. He waited for two things. Firstly, any evidence of an enemy nearby who may have seen from where the two shots had been fired? Secondly, his body's delayed reaction after killing a human being – a self-awareness developed in the past twelve months of fighting this war. The tremor started in his fingertips. It travelled up his arms and into his chest where it stole his breath and hammered his heart. It rolled down through his guts leaving a swirl of bile in his throat and the taste of nausea in his mouth before it rushed down his legs and exited his body through his toes. In the past twelve months, Joe had learnt there was a big difference between killing wildlife for dog meat on Billabong Downs and killing another human.

His gaze turned to cover all points of the compass before Joe stirred his muscles into life. He began the return journey on his belly towards where Farquharson, Rawlins and Turner remained alert for enemy response.

When off duty between skirmishes against the enemy, men sought any form of entertainment.

"Hey, what you got there, Joe?" Carter called.

Joe stood as still as a stalking waterbird. In his right hand, he held a three-foot length of forked stick. His concentration remained undisturbed until the stick stabbed down to the earth where it was held tight in the soil. Joe's left hand teased an empty syrup tin and a lid from his pocket and placed them on the ground beside the forked end of his stick in which a mottle-skinned snake about two feet in length remained immobilized. Daylight shone through the three small holes punched in the lid using the tip of his bayonet. Joe reached down and took hold of the snake's tail. He lifted the reptile and began to spin the tail back and forth between his thumb and forefinger causing the small body to spin in conjunction with its tail, preventing its futile attempts to bend upwards to bite the hand that held it. Using the forked end of the stick, Joe guided the reptile into the tin and snapped on the lid.

"You still catching those asps for the reward money, Joe? Surely our scientists at the Jerusalem Depot have enough by now. Every other man is out catching the beggars."

"It won't be for too much longer, as I understand. Word has it they're going to stop taking anymore; the laboratory is full up with asp snakes."

The camp hummed with the news from France where the British had suffered the worst defeat of the war. Even Joe stirred from his state of disinterest. Many of the men of the Light Horse were dismounted and transferred to the Western Front in France as replacements. Once again, General Allenby reorganized the remainder of the Light Horse in preparation for a second attack on Es Salt and Amman.

After a miserable month pre-Christmas in the freezing Judean Hills, they now sweltered in the rising temperatures of the Jordon Valley which lay over one thousand feet below sea level and over three thousand feet below the surrounding ranges.

While Joe groomed his mount and relayed all his complaints into the brown ears flicking away the million flies, a young local boy, who helped with feeding the animals, brought a handful of paper notes for him to read. The brown paper had been reused more than once for wrapping. It had been torn into rough squares. The writing on each piece of paper was in a thick nib dipped in a weak solution of ink. The message was the same on each square and the wording left little to the imagination.

"This month flies die – next month men die."

Joe's attention snapped down to the youngster. "Where did you get this, Emre?"

The lad stepped back at the sharp tone of voice from a man he knew to be kind and gentle. A trembling arm pointed further down the line where a crowd had gathered.

Joe saw the fear in the boy's eyes and felt instant regret. He reached down and touched the lad's shoulder.

"Sorry, Emre, thank you for bringing me this note."

Joe finished what he had been doing and went in search of their troop sergeant.

Shouts of excitement and others of despondency rose and fell upon his ears on Joe's return to his section's tent. It was no surprise to find his tent mates gathered around the rusty tin in which they held regular contests to the death between a scorpion and a hairy black spider retrieved from local dark crevices. It was no easy feat to wedge his way to the front row. Money jingled in the upside-down slouch hat held in Rawlins's hand. The man's forest green eyes flashed with excitement as he encouraged the gamblers within the group. Beatson held a stick in his hand to push either of the competitors that might attempt to escape over the rim of the fighting ring.

Joe never felt the need to make a bet but he succumbed to the fascination of watching the wildlife struggle for the upper hand not knowing that win or lose, death, by one means or another, was the outcome for both competitors. When the spider dashed up the stick in Beatson's hand, Joe joined the crowd in explosive laughter at the man's antics to escape its hairy legs on his arms.

Carter, Martin and Farquharson looked up when they heard Joe's laughter. Their glances met across the heads of those sitting, or shoulders of those bent over the fighting ring. Warm smiles flashed. It was good to hear Joe laugh again.

"I wanna make a bet on the spider against the man," someone yelled from the back.

Excitement and not a little anxiety kept Joe and his fellow tent mates awake until late, in their camp outside Jericho. Tomorrow their routine patrol out to the Jordon River was going to be anything but routine. Their regiment was one of many chosen to make the second push against Es Salt. At first light, when he groomed and fed Straps, Joe's head felt heavy upon his shoulders. His body felt hot – hotter than normal in this burning climate. As he rode out with his fellow men in the Light Horse, sluggishness threatened to overtake him. This time it was their turn to take on the Ottoman army. After watching the departure and return of the soldiers from the previous failed attack on Amman and Es Salt four weeks ago, Joe had no intention of being left behind.

The advance towards Es Salt was challenged by the Ottoman army from behind fortified barricades on several fronts. The men of the Light Horse jumped the barricades, spun their horses about and attacked the enemy with rifles and bayonets. Some dismounted and went in hand to hand.

Joe felt himself slipping in the saddle as Straps made the run-up to the jump. Landing in the arms of the defending army seemed inevitable but hardly worried him at all. Straps felt Joe's weight move and shuffled to the near side to balance himself before the jump, securing Joe's seat in the process.

Joe felt Billy at his side as he stood slashing and stabbing with his razor-sharp bayonet. His rifle ran hot with the stream of bullets fired along the line of the defence. The Light Horse worked their way laterally down the line of barricades until they emerged; clear to ride into the town of Es Salt just as dusk descended upon them. Hardly had the first yell of jubilation spread out across the killing fields when they heard the signal for a fighting withdrawal. Astounded expressions questioned what they heard, but training won out as the

Egyptian Expeditionary Force began to answer the command for a fighting retreat.

After the scramble over the hills, it was not until order had been restored within the retreating lines that the whisper spread. Massive reinforcements of the Ottoman army were arriving on the far side of the town of Es Salt.

In their row of four, Farquharson, Rawlins and Turner wedged a reeling Joe in between themselves. Farquharson held his right upper arm and Turner supported the left arm. Rawlins kept in close. The other section of four men in their tent Carter, Martin, Beatson and Gardener ushered in closer also.

"Did you feel that?" Turner asked.

"You mean the way Straps moves under Joe if he sways one way or another?"

"Yes."

"I could do with a horse like that when I ride home from the pub with a skinful. Might save eating dust so much."

Carter called quietly from the next row.

"Where's Joe wounded? Shouldn't we take him off to the Field Ambulance?"

"Hasn't got a scratch on him, but he's as hot as hell."

"You think he's caught the malaria, then?"

"I suspect so. He was looking a bit green when we left this morning – or was that yesterday morning."

Joe vaguely felt the grip on both arms. He heard men talking but not the content of their conversation. He did hear the crack of Billy's whip and his brother's penetrating whistle as they mustered the steers into the home paddock. He heard Billy's voice.

"Come on, Joe, let's take a skinny dip in the waterhole before we go home."

"Our Dad will whip your bare arse if he finds you leaving the cattle unattended, Billy Boy."

"Only five minutes, Brother."

"Okay, five minutes only."

Joe anticipated the cool water but all he felt was hot – the fiery, burning heat of his skin. Had their dad found them swimming and whipped their arses? No, he'd have felt that. He'd be sure to remember that.

Someone supported his head. Joe felt the trickle of water down the back of his throat. He gulped greedily.

"What do you blokes think you're doing squashed up like that? Looks like you're practicing for a night at the picture show with your sweethearts?" The voice of the troop sergeant turned the heads of the two sections of four men each guarding their mate who by now sat drooped in a semi-comatose state in his saddle.

"Joe's got malaria, Sarge," Farquharson explained. "He's not really with us at all."

"Have you been giving him plenty of water?"

"Yes, Sarge, we've given him all we've got. He just gurgles it down."

Sergeant Pritchard unslung the canteen from the front of his saddle.

"Here give him some of this." The sergeant watched as the slumped Trooper Dawson slurped up the last of his water offered. "When we get back make sure you let the medical officers know to have a look at him."

"Yes, Sarge, thanks," Farquharson replied.

Once back at their camp, the men's grumbles settled like the white dust around them. When out travelling on horseback, the dust clouds rose with little encouragement to be sucked up into the soldiers' nostrils and lungs setting off fits of coughing. This became worse as the summer months deepened. Even the flies began to die off in the raging heat but the malarial mosquitoes continued to spread their poison. With the number of patients, work overwhelmed the medics. It was left to fellow soldiers to care for their tent mates.

Joe's temperature raged as he lay on his sleeping mat. He recalled the messages on the brown paper squares. He felt sure he had died and now approached hell's gates. He struggled to search his memory for a glimmer of the battle in which he must have been killed. But the disease consumed his body, distorting any thoughts. Unintelligible gibberish spewed from his mouth along with mind-chilling screams and whispered calls for help.

It was Max Farquharson who nursed Joe Daley Dawson. He fetched a bucket of water and sponged the sweat from the feverish body stripped of all clothes but his short pants. Max held Joe's head and encouraged liquid down his parched throat. For two days and nights, Max tended his fellow trooper. A medic visited every day to ensure both men were still alive and Max had not succumbed to the disease himself. He issued them quinine tablets from his army supply.

Lying in the darkness in a lather of sweat on the third night of Joe's illness, anxiety niggled inside Max's chest. It took him some moments to work out what had woken him – the silence. Healthy snores from the other six men bounced off the canvas roof of their tent, but from young Joe, there was only silence. No ravings and nightmares, no struggles to breathe, only silence. Max dragged his weary body from his mat. His hand rested on Joe's forehead. Max's eyes widened.

"Joe, Joe, can you hear me?" Max whispered at first. When he received no reply, he shook Joe's shoulders and called louder. "Joe, are you awake?"

"I bloody-well am now. What's up? Whatcha want?"

"So, you are alive. You were so quiet I thought you must have died."

"Of course, I'm alive, but if you keep waking me up, I can't guarantee you will be for much longer."

Max chuckled. "Go back to sleep, Grumpy, your fever's gone." He turned and threw himself onto his mat and dropped into a deep slumber himself.

It was Carter who stirred everyone lazing about in the tent late the following morning.

"I hope you've kept Joe alive there, Max," Carter stood at the tent entrance with his arms full of mail and parcels. "It looks like his Gran has sent another cake and there's a letter for him too."

"Max, stir the boy up. He can share his cake around," Rawlins looked up with a grin on his face as he sorted the cards in his game of Patience.

Joe lifted himself onto his elbow. The men in the tent hooted and cheered. Joe slapped his hands over his ears.

"Can the bloody noise." Grime filled the lines in his face. It covered his clothes and body. Lank dirty hair hung down the sides of his face. "Just hold your horses there, you fellows. There'll be no cake happening around here until I can eat it myself. First, I've got to make it to the dunny and then I need a shower, I can't stand my own smell."

CHAPTER TWENTY

Billabong Downs

January – July 1918

Cissy and Maud chose to return to Billabong Downs for the autumn holidays. Their ignorance in their understanding of their mother's condition did not blind them to the awareness of their father's sadness and the extra burden cast upon his shoulders at home.

"Mother, won't you please come out and sit on the verandah with us? Our holidays are almost over and we'll have to go back to school again in a few days," Maud begged. Tears were not too far away as she turned her gaze to Cissy who tidied the toiletries in the drawer near her mother's bed. "Can you talk to her Cissy; she might listen to you?"

"Don't fret, Maud. If Mum wants to stay in her room, we'll only upset her more if we force her outside."

Both girls jumped at the sharp tone in Mabel's voice.

"Get out of my room the pair of you. Don't touch my things. Leave me and Billy here in peace."

Maud's tears overflowed onto her cheeks.

"Billy is not here, Mother, he is dead, remember? He died in the war."

"GET OUT! GET OUT! YOU PAIR OF COWS!" The crescendo of Mabel's voice rose until it seemed even the window in her room rattled. "YOU AREN'T WORTH THE SPIT ON MY BILLY'S BOOTS!"

The magazine in Maud's nerveless fingers slipped to the floor. Cissy threw the hairbrush she had been cleaning onto the bed. She rushed to her sister's side.

"Come away, Maud. There is no reasoning with her when she is like this."

Maud stood stunned. Cissy grabbed her hand and led her out through the nearest doorway – the one which led out into the hallway.

The screams spewing out over the compound lent speed to Fran's racing footsteps. She took the back stairs two at a time. At the sight of her nieces wrapped in each other's arms outside the kitchen, a wave of compassion took her breath away. Fran gasped. She placed her arms around them both. Mabel's screeches from the bedroom seemed to drill through the walls of the house before they crashed down upon them.

"I'm sorry you have to witness this, girls."

"Oh, Auntie Fran, where has my mother gone?" Cissy struggled not to cry. She chewed her bottom lip.

"I hate her," Maud whispered, "I hate her." Maud's voice rose. "She yelled at us. She called us cows. She said we were not worth the spit on Billy's boots."

"Oh, girls, remember what your father and I told you when you were here at Christmas time? Your mother doesn't know what she is saying. You can't take anything, to heart." Fran paused to quell her own emotions. "This is not the mother you knew. Your mother is deep inside the woman you see there. We have to hope she will appear again. Your father is trying to convince her to talk to Doctor Munson. At the moment, she refuses. She believes there is nothing wrong with her."

Cissy tried to speak but no sound passed her lips.

"Your mother is sick, darling. We have to remember that. She must be given a chance to heal. She needs you, but first, you need to protect your own hearts. You go on over to my place and make us a cup of tea. I'll just check Mabel is safe and then I'll join you."

Hoofbeats came to a sudden halt outside the garden gate of Miles's house as the brothers pulled on the reins of their mounts. Intermittent and fading wails from William's house wafted over the two men.

"The girls are here, William," Fran called to his departing back as he spurred the horse towards his own house.

"Thanks, Fran. I'll check on Mabel and then I'll come back." His yell floated back with the dust. Guilt at having allowed the girls to talk him into bringing them home again for the school holidays stirred his gut and tightened his lips – was it selfishness on his part?

When William returned to his brother's home a short time later, his daughters rushed into his arms nearly sweeping him back down the stairs.

"Ooof, you chickens nearly had me over then." He squeezed them tightly. "Sit with me."

He turned to sit on the top step with one arm around Cissy and the other arm holding his youngest tightly. He listened as the girls reported on the afternoon with their mother.

Inside the kitchen, Miles removed two bottles of hops ale from the pantry but hesitated before taking one out to his brother. He turned to his wife.

"Fran, are the girls alright? Mabel didn't hurt them, did she?"

"Only broke their hearts, dear. Mabel's narcissistic airs and cruel tongue are her weapons. I've never known her to be violent." Fran ladled some stew from the large pot on the stove into two smaller pots. "I'll talk to William shortly but I think the girls should not be left alone with her unless there is an adult in the house."

After placing the two drinks on the table, Miles walked over to lift the lid of the larger pot on the stove.

"That smells good. Is the stew in the smaller pots for William and Gazza?

"Yes, dear."

Cissy and Maud returned to the kitchen.

"Daddy asked if we can stay here tonight, Auntie Fran?" Maud hugged her aunt as she posed her question.

"Yes, darling, of course." She smiled across the top of Maud's head to include Cissy in her invitation. "How about we take a walk and leave one of these stew pots in Gazza's shed? When we come back, we'll set up the two stretcher beds in the sleep-out on the verandah."

As Fran and her escort made their way down the stairs on their way to deliver Gazza's meal, she stopped to talk with William sitting sipping from his bottle of ale.

"There's stew for you and Mabel here on the stove, William. The girls are more than welcome to join us here until you get a chance to talk more with Mabel."

When Fran and the girls returned in the faded evening light, a chill could be felt on the light breeze. William's departing back could just be seen as his slow footsteps climbed the back steps to his house. On their arrival in the kitchen, Cissy lit the lantern while Maud set the cutlery and plates on the table. When Miles appeared with fresh clothes and damp hair, Fran was ready to serve their meal.

"Will the boys be long?"

Miles lifted his head with his right ear cocked. "No, I can hear them coming now."

"I'll serve theirs when they come in. It'll be half an hour before they see to the horses and have their shower. In the meantime, we can eat. It feels like an age since I had lunch." Fran pulled her chair under her and sat. "So, Miles, how did the muster go?"

"Yeah, William, Geoff and I sure appreciated having the boys to help. The bullocks for sale are in the north cattle yards. The buyers should be here early tomorrow. We'll need to be sharp in the morning."

"Do you mind if the girls and I ride out later in the day to have a look? Cissy might make a batch of her wonderful jam biscuits and I'll make fresh bread sandwiches with corned meat and pickles for their lunch."

"I'm sure the men will enjoy that."

"What about Mummy?" Maud asked.

"Before we go, we'll take sandwiches over to your mother for her lunch. We'll let Mrs. Bardon know we're going out. She'll keep an eye on things here."

Bellowing stock and clouds of rising dust were more effective than a road sign to guide Fran and the two girls towards the north cattle yards. They pulled up their horses outside the stout wooden railings near where Geoff, Doug and Mick waited inside the yard for instructions from either William or Miles who were talking to the buyers as they assessed the cattle for sale.

Fran watched for ten minutes and then wheeled her horse around heading for the immense fig tree providing shade over a rusty corrugated awning. It covered a rock-edged fireplace straddled by a blackened steel triangle from which a large billycan hung. A roughhewn timber table leaned awkwardly nearby. A metal tank stood at the western corner post of the awning. Maud rode up on her off-side.

"Can I come with you, Auntie Fran? Cissy is staying to watch the men but I got the biscuits from her saddle bag."

245

"Yes of course, dear." Fran dismounted and tied the reins of her horse to the tie-rail in the shade of the tree. "I've got the sandwiches and I do hope the boys checked the tea-making things when they were here yesterday."

Maud slid down from her horse and secured it slowly paying attention to her knot.

Fran made a beeline for the wooden cupboard secreted under the end of the table. She passed out the pannikins, a tin of tea leaves, a tin of brown sugar and several spoons. Maud took each item from her aunt's hands and placed them on the tabletop.

"Will I fill the billy and light the fire, Auntie Fran?"

"Thanks, dear, and call me to help carry it back. It might be a bit heavy for you."

Maud laughed a light-hearted laugh which fell pleasantly upon her aunt's ears.

"I carried the billy full to the top last year when I was here, remember."

"Oh, yes, of course. I had forgotten." It was Maud's proud grin that made Fran's so much wider.

When the men joined them, Fran was pleased to see the laughter in her husband's eyes knowing this was a sure sign of a good sale. Her boys and Geoff Bardon added sandwiches and biscuits to their plates and each filled a pannikin with tea. They retired to the shade of the fig tree.

William called Maud, Cissy and Fran over to meet the two gentlemen who had bought the stock. Fran could not fault the girls' manners in response. They were daughters to be proud of – as would be expected having been in the care of Isabelle and Bayden Dawson in recent years.

While the buyers discussed their business arrangements with William and Miles, Fran with her boys and her nieces mounted their horses and turned for home. As they approached the homestead compound barrier, Fran was left to fend for herself when the younger ones spied their Gran and Pop Daley pulling up in their buggy at Fran's back steps. Her heart lifted as it always did to know Mavis was back home safely. She stood up in the stirrups and waved before turning her mount towards the horse shed. Pop found her there just as she was hanging the curry comb and brush back over the hook on the post.

Fran smiled. "You're early. We were expecting you tomorrow."

"Gran has a special meeting after church on Sunday so we'll need to get back before then. I hope this won't put you out at all."

"Not at all, Pop. You are always more than welcome."

Mabel's moody behaviour was discussed as the pair walked back to Fran's house.

"Are you sure you have enough space for Gran and me if we stay with you, Fran?"

"That will be no problem at all. That house is huge thanks to your forethought. I complain every time I do the housework," Fran laughed.

Pop told her of the latest letter from Joe which he had brought with him for William to read.

"The boy has had a dose of malaria but thank heavens these days they have the Quinine powder to treat it with. He was recovering when he wrote the letter."

"Oh, there's so much to worry about isn't there."

"That's war, Fran, no good things ever come from war." He reached out and patted her arm. He smiled. "Gran couldn't wait to bake another fruit cake and biscuits to send on to him with my reply when I get to write it."

Later when William returned to Miles's house having seen Mabel fed and settled into bed, the sound of chatter and laughter drifted in from the verandah. Doug, Mick, Mavis and their cousins, Cissy and Maud played a game of cards.

"I hope you're not playing Poker out there, Doug?" Fran called.

Miles's head lifted. "Poker? You mean cards' Poker?"

"The very same. The boys have been playing it at school, apparently. Only betting matchsticks, but still …."

Fran's frown at the men chuckling around the table was enough to focus them on the letter Pop held in his hand. As she restored order in her kitchen she listened to William and his father reading the latest news from Joe.

"This is dated May 1918," Pop said as he handed the letter over to William. "It didn't take long to get here this time."

William spread the paper flat and held it towards the lantern light.

Dear Gran, Pops, Dad and everyone at Billabong Downs,

Have recently returned from the Jordon River Valley where I and many others picked up a dose of malaria. The taste of that Quinine stuff is enough to either kill or cure you. It is foul. Well, it cured me and the whisper is we'll be soon heading west towards the coast. Hopefully to the sea and I can drown a few of the lice imbedded in my clothes sucking on my blood. But then whispers have been wrong before.

Hoping all is well there. I guess everyone is busy mustering at this time of the year.

Kindest regards

Did I tell Gran thanks for the last fruit cake?

My mates are all in love with her.

Joe

William sat unmoving when he finished reading. He spoke softly to Fran and Miles.

"I'd like to let the girls read this but we can't take the chance of Mabel getting any wind of Joe writing to us or there will be all hell to pay."

"I think you may be right. It would only take one slipped word to set her off."

CHAPTER TWENTY-ONE

Trek to Damascus

August – October 1918

Like the riffling waves along the canvas of their tents under the breeze of the early morning, excitement rippled through the camp. Wherever the men gathered, gossip rose and fell like the swirls of dust around their feet. On his return from the many pot-washing details in the food tent, Farquharson ensured his section was up to date with the latest whispers.

The Bull was up to his tricks against the enemy again. Under the cover of darkness, troops were being transferred to the west coast while the eastern section gave the appearance of receiving reinforcements. With little resistance, the British aircraft patrolled the skies. The few Taube reconnaissance aircraft of the enemy witnessed only those numbers of troops arriving at the camp with each morning's light. The enemy only saw a few of those who had left the camp under darkness the night before.

Whatever the man was up to, after weeks of repairing the damage to infrastructure such as the hospital and the administration buildings in temperatures of over 120' Fahrenheit, Joe and his friends did not complain when they received the orders to travel from the cesspit of the Jordon Valley, with its spiders, flies, lice, scorpions and malaria to a place called Ludd nearer to the Mediterranean coast. Only a few of the men had escaped the curse of septic sores due to the limited diet, the heat and the dirt.

After feeding and grooming Straps, Joe loaded him up with the saddle and its attached accoutrements. He rubbed his hands over the wide brown rump.

"Well, mate, are you sick of this heat out here, too? Let's hope they're sending us to a place where we'll get a bit of sea breeze."

The horse snickered and turned his head to search Joe's pockets in the hope of a little treat. Joe dragged the dry crust from his top pocket and fed it to his best friend.

In the late afternoon when the bugle sounded, Farquharson raced around the corner of the tent almost taking out the rope ties as he did so. At the picket line, he unhitched his horse while tucking his shirt into his pants. He hopped on one foot after the other to drag on his boots. Holding the reins in his teeth, he pushed his arms through the sleeves of his jacket.

Joe laughed loudly. "Max, one day you're going to be late for your own wedding. What kept you this time?"

"The lineup at the shit house was a mile long. If I'm to die in this place, no matter where I go, the only thing I wish for is to have my own personal dunny. Believe me, that will be heaven."

The pair set their mounts into a canter to catch up with the remainder of their section on the parade ground.

For two nights they travelled west under cover of darkness. By day they sheltered against some low hills near an oasis. Early in the morning of the second day, a sigh escaped the lips of every man within the ranks at the sight of the shady olive groves and the tidy camps already occupied by Light Horse from the 3rd Brigade. Neat avenues stretched as far as one could see within the acres of army tents. Between each row, two lines of shady olive trees sheltered the horses and the men.

"We're about ten miles from the coast." As usual, it was Farquharson who had all the necessary information to relate. "Not close enough for saltwater swimming, but it's better than Jericho."

"It's the best camp we've been in since arriving here. It'll do me." Rawlins gave another deep sigh.

Following the usual drill parade, instructions and directions were issued. After settling their horses, the men wasted little time placing their saddles beside the picket line near their tent before they went to investigate their new home.

The bugle sounded for the mid-day meal and the men were happy to line up at the food tent for better grub than they had seen for a long while.

"Have you seen Farquharson, Joe?" George Turner tapped Joe's shoulder.

"Not since we were talking to those blokes from the 10th Regiment." Joe gave a cheeky grin. "If he's not here scrubbing pots then he can't be putting in more detention time."

But Joe was wrong. Max was indeed doing more detention – at the Casualty Clearance Station. When he returned to the tent late in the afternoon, his section mates wanted to know where he had been and what he had done wrong this time.

"Nothing much. Just the usual. It's that new little upstart, Lieutenant Clay. He's all shine and polish but I wouldn't trust him in a tight spot, I can tell you. We're told we have to salute these officers out of respect when we meet them. Well, it will be a cold day in hell before I salute that weasel." Max grabbed up his pannikin and plate. "The Major gave me a thorough dressing down. He reckoned cleaning pots in the food tent doesn't seem to have helped my memory so he sent me to work with the Egyptian Labour Corps cleaning up at the Casualty Clearance Station." Max bent to exit the tent. He swung around. "The beggar didn't believe a word I said when I told him the sun gleamed off the bloke's shiny brass and it blinded me."

When their laughter settled, Joe struggled to be serious.

"It wouldn't hurt you to throw the blighter a salute, Max. It doesn't mean you have to have any respect for him." Joe could hardly talk for laughing. "They might be able to demand signs of respect but they can't control what you are thinking inside your head." Joe sipped at his pannikin of tea. "And why do you call him 'little' and 'weasel' – the man's well over six feet in height?"

Max shrugged.

"Anyway, Max, how are you going to keep us informed if you're not in the cookhouse to hear all the goings on?" Rawlins wanted to know.

"Huh, the fellows over at the Clearance Station know more about what's happening before our own officers know, I can tell you. The medical folk over there are like a room of gossiping old women at a sewing circle. It's more interesting listening in to them at work than a table of shiny stripes eating their tucker."

The afternoon dampened many spirits as the bugle called their regiment to more ceremonial drilling from horseback. When they were informed by the Major that they were to receive 1908 pattern cavalry swords as part of their weaponry, the complaints dissipated.

"Bayonets and swords – well, I'll be damned," Max grinned at the blokes in his section. "Things are looking up. We could have done with them at Beersheba instead of a pissy little bayonet against all the Ottoman had to offer us that day." He slammed his mouth shut as soon as the words were out. He did not miss the dark shadow looming in Joe Dawson's eyes. Max had forgotten they had lost two of their number, including Billy Daley, at Beersheba. He held his hand up to Joe.

"Sorry, mate."

Joe nodded his acceptance of the apology, but he did not speak. It may have been nearly ten months since the demise of his brother but his loss swam near the surface of his thoughts every minute of every day.

Dawn had not long mounted the horizon when the ceremony began, thus avoiding the worst of the hot summer sun. The eyes of every man on parade gleamed every bit as much as the cavalry sword and its scabbard hanging from each saddle. A rifle bucket was issued with every cavalry sword because, as the men discovered, a rifle across the back impedes a man's ability to fight with the sword. The men were dismissed with the order to reassemble at the parade ground, without their mounts, at 1600 hours for the beginning of their training in the handling of this new weapon – just the men and their swords.

"I could get to like this place," Rawlins commented as he tossed his cards into the centre of the square of sackcloth in disgust. "It's nearly as good as a holiday camp."

"Yeah well, I've never been on one of those, boyo," Farquharson spoke up as he led with a trump card. "You must have had a privileged upbringing."

"Not really, but I used to read a lot of books. Not much except the regimental manual to be read over here."

Joe half listened to the men at the card game as he shuffled through the pages of his notebook looking for a spare page to begin a letter to Pops Daley. He made a mental reminder to acquire a new notebook at the earliest opportunity.

Autumn made itself felt with a chill in the air on the morning of the 18th of September 1918 when they departed Ludd and the camp amongst the olive trees. If they thought they might get a sleep-in they were all in for a big disappointment when the recruit bugler attempted to blow reveille.

"Struth, will someone put a sock in that horn?" George Turner groaned.

"Sounds like our trumpeter had a bad night, last night." Toby Rawlins rolled over.

During the next two days, the regiment travelled north with short rest periods. After a bivouac camp at the Plain of Esdraelon, they were sent to relieve the 3rd Light Horse Brigade which had collected almost nine thousand prisoners during the capture of Jenin. Joe's regiment had the task of delivering five thousand of these prisoners to El Lejjun.

"If we spend our lives here playing nurse-maid to these prisoners too often, we'll never get to give our new swords much of a workout," Turner grumbled.

Joe laughed. "Just think, George, that will be five thousand enemy rifles not spitting out bullets at us further up the track."

After completion of the task, Joe Dawson and his fellow troopers found themselves at the Jordon River once again – near the Sea of Galilee. Nervous excitement travelled down the lines of the Brigade as word spread. At dawn, they were to attack Semakh on the southern end of the Sea of Galilee.

On the 25th of September 1918, darkness still hung heavy around the men of the Light Horse as they approached the town of Semakh – piccaninny dawn only a hint in the sky. The enemy's heavy rifle and machine-gun fire poured out from around the fortified railway station. Joe and his regiment watched as the 11th Regiment charged. Their jealous grumbles turned to grins of anticipation when the charge floundered short of the objective and they were sent to draw fire. On the edge of town, the troopers dismounted and swapped their cavalry swords for their rifles and bayonets. It was Joe's turn to be the horse-holder, having drawn the short straw before the stunt began. Bullets pinged off metal drain pipes and thudded into the timber and adobe walls of the town buildings around his head as Joe swept up the three horses of his section mates and sought shelter not too far from the action. Within an hour, the fierce battle came to a stuttering end. The villagers were first to clear out and the Ottoman army was not too far behind.

Leaving a regiment to garrison Semakh, the Light Horse moved on toward Tiberias. They discovered the enemy in the process of retreating north from this town leaving a substantial supply of stores. Once again, the Light Horse took charge of the prisoners of war.

The Light Horse Brigade began their advance from Tiberias towards Damascus.

After establishing a bridgehead over the Jordon River at Et Min, it was a sober group of men around the bivouac camp that evening when the story of the betrayal by the false surrender flag at Semakh had been dragged out to be rehashed once again. When they heard of the incident where several of the enemy mowed down those men of the Light Horse who advanced to take the surrender, little sleep was had by many of the men despite their weariness.

"Is it just me, or do you blokes feel sick to the stomach of all this killing?" Joe stabbed at the bully beef in the bottom of the tin.

"I know what you're saying," Max Farquharson mumbled around a mouth full of dry biscuit.

Turner poured tea into the pannikins of each man and rested the pot back on the edge of the coals. "That business at Semakh was a cowardly act. Not an honourable action at all. I mean, when we come to war, we expect to fight and die but there has to be some honour involved. That was simply murder."

"It wasn't the Turks, you know," Joe reminded everyone.

"No, so I understand. To wave the white flag and have no intention of surrendering is a hit below the belt." Rawlins mumbled as he removed the tea leaves from his top lip.

"They won't do it again, anyway," Max assured the group.

"That's what I'm saying. So many were killed that may not have needed to die." Joe tossed his can onto the heap of rubbish waiting to be buried.

Eventually, exhaustion dragged the men down into the arms of sleep until the rejuvenated bugler roused them before first light.

From up ahead, sounds of gunfire reached the ears of the men of the 12th Light Horse Regiment. They arrived at Jisr Benat Yakub to discover the Ottoman army fighting a rear-guard action at the Bridge of the Daughters of Jacob. A section of the bridge had been demolished by the enemy. From inside the few buildings on the opposite side of the river and from redoubts dug into the hills behind, rifle and machine-gun fire raked what was left of the bridge and the river banks below.

Fifteen feet below the damaged bridge the brown swirling waters of the ford presented dangerous challenges to the earlier arrivals of the Egyptian Expeditionary Force. These men attempted to find alternative crossings with little success. When the French cavalry, a part of the Egyptian Expeditionary Force, arrived, they dismounted and began firing at the hidden enemy. A regiment had been sent further downstream to search for an alternative crossing.

The gunfire faded as night approached and the men of the Light Horse bit down on their impatience. Joe and his mates sipped hot tea and crunched on their dry biscuits – not short on suggestions for solving the problem. The beams of the three-quarter moon shone brightly upon the gap in the bridge which had to be spanned as soon as possible to allow wheeled vehicles with supplies and motor ambulances to proceed on the road to Damascus.

Not too many soldiers slept before dim lights flickered on the horizon. The noise of the approaching Desert Mounted Corps' bridging lorries brightened everyone's spirits. The Light Horse were happy to provide what protection they could during the five hours it took for the sappers, working in the poor light, to build a patchwork span high upon a timber trestle supported in the rocks below. Cheers rang out in appreciation for their efforts. Slabs of timber replaced the missing road itself. The bridge was passable once again.

They discovered the enemy had moved on under the cover of darkness.

"Geez, you'd want to be saying a few Hail Marys as you go over that," Max Farquharson commented as they stared at the temporary road over which they were to pass. A shiver ran down his body. Was it spurred by the sight of the fragile bridge they were to cross or by the coolness of the early morning air?

It was Toby Rawlins who brought the news to the section this time.

"Max, I don't think you're going to be too pleased but your favourite Lieutenant Clay will be one of the officers within the Divisional Transport mob our squadron is to escort on to Quneitra."

Max froze. His gaze bored into Rawlins's face.

"You gotta be kidding me, right?"

"Sorry, mate, it's true. I just got the news up the line."

"Well, just keep me out of his way. With a bit of luck, he might not make it across that wobbly span in the bridge over there."

Joe smiled quietly. "Now, don't go giving him a push, Max. He's not worth the trouble."

The progress of the transport vehicles over the trestle panel of the bridge was slow. Most of the drivers, and the onlookers, held their breaths as their vehicles crept over the tenuous portion of the bridge.

Once across and moving again, it was not too hard for Joe, George Turner and Toby Rawlins to ensure Max kept out of the sight of Lieutenant Clay.

Later in the day, when they arrived at Quneitra, forty miles from Damascus, the 11th Light Horse Regiment garrisoned the town along with some of the 5th Cavalry Division. They were charged with keeping the peace between the troopers and the locals while protecting the lines of communication North and South.

Planes roared in and out of the local airstrip where the British Bristol fighters now set up a new home. Max Farquharson delivered the news to his section of the airmen's attack on the Damascus aerodrome earlier in the day.

Within hours, the population of the small town of Quneitra had multiplied beyond imagination with the arrival of thousands of troopers and their accompanying units. After a few days, the horses had almost demolished the supply of clover hay. The soldiers of the Light Horse and the townspeople were running low on requisitioned supplies including fresh meat. Everyone watched with relief when provisions brought up from Tiberias were unloaded from the trucks.

Fevers raged throughout the population mostly diagnosed as malaria or pneumonic influenza. The Casualty Clearance stations overflowed with patients. Townspeople swamped the local hospital. The garrison units were hard-pressed to find relief for those on patrols. Their troops succumbed to the diseases too.

When Max strode into their bivouac camp on the morning of the 29th September 1918 his smile heralded the arrival of good news.

"You have news, Max?"

Max's grin widened. "I sure have. We're to get out of this place today. We're on our way to Damascus."

"Where did you hear that? Don't tell me you've been sent to the pot-cleaning sink in the food tent again?" Turner chuckled.

Joe rolled his eyes. "Max, don't tell me you've refused to salute Lieutenant Clay again."

"Nah, I've not even seen the little pipsqueak for days. And no, I wasn't seconded into washing pots and pans again. I was stuck in the shit house and heard it through the canvas wall between the officers and us."

Rawlins was the next of the section to arrive at their bivouac site.

"You should have stayed a bit longer, Max. Yes, we're heading on to Damascus later and it won't be all smooth sailing. There have been reports of the Ottoman rear-guard action near a place called Sa'sa, about twenty miles south of Damascus. There are more on the outskirts of the city."

It was Joe's turn to reveal a news update.

"The Light Horse have taken that damn Es Salt and Amman at last. The blokes were busy down there while we were occupied with Semakh."

"Three cheers for the Light Horse. We always get things done – eventually." Turner lifted his pannikin of tea.

With rations in their haversacks, ammunition pouches full since the arrival of the supply vehicles, their bayonets and sword blades sharpened, and rifles cleaned and loaded, the troopers were pleased to leave Quneitra and move north once again. It was 1500 hours when the advance guard of the 9th Light Horse Regiment, including six machine-guns rolling behind the draught horses, moved off. The 3rd Brigade followed behind. The sun hung low in the sky before Joe and his section received the command to march. The heat of the day dissipated and the cool of evening threatened. They remained alert. When day turned to night, it was the light from a moon, not long past its third quarter, which cast a glow over the countryside as they passed.

At Sa'sa, the enemy chose their position from which to attack the Light Horse with great care. Their artillery threatened the Light Horse from a position strung out across rising ground covered with large boulders. Lights flashed across the evening sky as the enemies' rear guard opened fire upon the advance guard of the 3rd Brigade. Smoke drifted over the landscape.

Seeing the 9th in trouble, the 10th Regiment of the 3rd Brigade attempted to move around the enemy's left flank only to discover it was protected by rough lava formations. The terrain on either side of the road was too rough for the cavalry to advance in the poor light. Meanwhile, the enemy's machine-gun fire swept across their approach.

The pursuit was halted while the machine-guns of the Egyptian Expeditionary Forces were hauled forward and sited. During this time, troops dismounted and made frontal attacks on the enemy's positions along the roadway. They inched forward slowly.

Dawn was not too far away when the enemy position was overtaken and prisoners and weapons captured. Joe and his section arrived to help in the clean-up. In the improved light, Max looked out over the battlefield in awe.

"You have to hand it to these Turks; they know how to pick their attack sites. No way could our mounted troops make any headway through that lot in the dark."

Men slouched in the saddles with heads bowed, some even nodded in sleep, as the faithful horses plodded onwards. Joe and the men in his section could not afford this luxury. Their regiment, the 12th, and the 4th Regiment now rode as the advance guard. The 3rd and 5th Light Horse Brigades had left at dawn travelling to the west of Damascus where they were to cut the lines of retreat west and north.

Ten miles south of Damascus, the Light Horse discovered the Ottoman army's rear-guard infantry entrenched along the Kaukab's volcanic ridge on either side of the main road. Across the Australians' line of advance, a strong row of machine-gun posts waited to deliver their deadly messages.

Patrols were sent to assess the enemy positions while the Egyptian Expeditionary Force delivered a battery of fire of their own from a hillock about one and a half miles from the rear-guard line. The 14th Light Horse Regiment and the French cavalry covered the enemy's flanks. The 3rd Light Horse Brigade covered the rear.

The sun burned hot from the near midday sky. With the 4th Regiment on their left, Joe and his section within the 12th Regiment charged up the slopes. Sunlight flashed off their sword blades. The voices of the men of the Light Horse rang out in defiance above the shelling from the machine-guns and the rattle of the rifle fire. The charge through the difficult terrain commenced at a trot which soon became a gallop.

Straps clattered across the stony ridges. Joe felt his mount slip and shuffle down the gullies before the animal scrambled to seek purchase on the climb up the other side. Every moment, Joe expected to feel the slam of lead into his body or feel his beloved Straps shudder beneath him. But the enemy weapons were now silent – waiting?

"Bloody hell, you bastards, just fire will you," he mumbled. His body clenched against the expected shot.

They arrived at their target to find the enemy fleeing in their thousands – hurtling down the ridges and into the woods. In the distance, the Turkish cavalry galloped furiously up the road to Damascus.

After the battle, Joe's regiment was one of those camped on the outskirts of Kaukab. Having been on patrol for several hours during the night doing guard duty around their prisoners and the captured machine-guns, the four young men huddled up within their small blanket and waterproof sheet. They woke bleary-eyed and grumbling when reveille sounded.

"Someone will have to put a sock in the lad's bugle. He's not showing any sign of improvement." It was Turner who first found the energy to verbalize his displeasure.

Max returned from his early ablutions with news of the goings on while the other three fought to catch just a few extra minutes of shut-eye.

"Our prisoners are to be sent down the line with another regiment later this morning. We're heading towards Damascus."

Toby Rawlins dragged himself into a sitting position where he struggled to find saliva in his mouth to speak.

"When you get home, Max, I do hope you're planning to join your local daily as a news scout. You're a natural."

"Well, it sure won't be any of you three slumber bugs searching for the gossip." Max leant down near his small fire where a blackened billy held water just beginning to bubble. "The water's nearly boiling, if you want a cup of tea. That's the last of our tea leaves. There's barely any colour in it at all. Hopefully, we'll be able to pick up a packet of tea leaves in Damascus."

After a meagre feed of dry biscuits and weak tea, they made their way out to care for the needs of their mounts.

Beyond the carnage of recent battles, the green plains watered by the Pharpar and Abana rivers surrounding Damascus spread out for miles in deep contrast to the rocky harsh terrain and barren deserts they had passed through in recent weeks. On the 1st of October 1918, Joe's regiment walked their horses along the road to Damascus. After passing a small waterway they entered a forest which hid the city. The mosque tower only became visible as they reached the city gates.

The regiment halted just inside the gates of Damascus. Joe, Toby Rawlins and George Turner were happy to sit and doze in their saddles but Max's curiosity flared at the sight of officers from other regiments in deep discussions with their own officers at the front of their line. Using the excuse of the call of nature he dismounted and went seeking other men of the Light Horse who accompanied these officers.

In the shelter of a doorway, he shared a cigarette with a corporal he knew through his times in detention. Whatever the corporal had to share, the pair found it difficult to contain their amusement. Max wasted no time returning to his section and relating the little he had discovered.

"Every man and his dog want to be the first to enter Damascus including, of course, our own Major General Chauvel in lieu of General Allenby, for the British. The French want their two bob's worth and that Brit fellow keeping an eye on the Arabs, that T.E. Lawrence fellow – he had let it be known he and his army want in first." At this point, Max could hardly speak for laughing. "It was those dopey 10th Regiment blokes who were supposed to head out to block the Homs road. They couldn't read their map and got lost. They headed into the town to ask directions. Mind you, they aren't admitting to anything. Their Lieutenant Colonel was dragged into some meeting with the locals and given a surrender to accept. There's a big kerfuffle going on at the moment."

"Oh, oh, look out, we're off again," Rawlins caught their attention.

"Yes, didn't I tell you? We're to patrol the outskirts of Damascus, south of Barada Gorge. There are hundreds of prisoners to go into a concentration camp out that way after we sift out the sick and wounded."

While Major General Chauvel and his administration team organized working parties to repair the meagre electricity supplies within the city, malaria and pneumonic influenza raged through the population and its new arrivals. Troopers cleaned and improved the state of the hospitals and provided cooking facilities. Where possible the weakest of the locals were transferred to homes within the city along with rations and blankets. They were to be cared for by the local doctors.

Joe and his mates found themselves camped near the French Hospital on Aleppo Road. Along with their guard duties, they pitched in to help with the care of their fellow troopers falling like flies, with fever. Their days were long and arduous. Max succumbed to what the doctors diagnosed as influenza; Joe and his section cared for him around the clock. The sides of all the tents were rolled up to allow any breeze to drift in under the canvas roofs.

When Lieutenant Clay arrived as an escort for the medical officer on his rounds, Joe looked up from where he sponged his friend's body with cool water. He attempted to drag himself to his feet. Joe nearly fell to the ground with surprise at the Lieutenant's instructions.

"As you were, Trooper. This is Major Rabatel, the doctor from the French hospital."

Joe immediately recognised Lieutenant Clay with whom Max had locked horns. For whatever reason, Max always refused to salute the man and as a result ended up seeing more of the inside of the cooking pots than the regiment's cook.

Major Rabatel's intelligent grey bloodshot eyes swept around the inside of the tent and his gaze rested again upon Joe kneeling at Max's side. The doctor's grey hair stuck out from under his cap like weeds escaping a garden. Deep lines around his eyes added to the impression of an older man. His long legs unfolded cautiously as he entered the low-roofed tent.

The two officers spoke in French for some moments. Joe watched their every move. Dropping to his knees beside the ill man on the mat, the doctor placed a thermometer under Max's armpit. While the mercury had time to expand under the body heat, the long fine fingers of the medical officer lifted Max's eyelids, felt the glands around his neck and tapped his chest. He poked and prodded Max's abdomen before he placed the earpieces of his stethoscope into his ears. Those fine fingers held the distal end of the stethoscope shifting the round black piece to several areas of Max's chest. After three minutes he removed the thermometer and read the result.

The Major then removed two white pills from a brown bag he had carried into the tent. He lifted the canteen by Max's head and shook it. He spoke to Joe in English.

"This is good. Keep giving him water, Trooper. Now can you lift his shoulders a little and we'll give him these tablets to help reduce the fever."

When Lieutenant Clay knelt on the other side of Max to help him, Joe's mouth opened in surprise. At the same time, George Turner and Toby Rawlins poked their heads inside the tent before they scrambled back out again.

With eyebrows raised, Turner turned to his friend and whispered, "Isn't that Lieutenant Clay, Max's nemesis?"

"The very same, what's he doing here?"

"Maybe he expects Max to salute from his sick bed?"

"Can he be trusted around Max?"

They both eased their heads back under the canvas roof but could find nothing suspicious in the officer's actions in helping the doctor and Joe care for their mate.

Inside the tent, the doctor and the lieutenant stood. The doctor reached over to touch Joe's forehead. Joe pulled his head back in surprise.

"It's alright, son, I just want to check your temperature." When the doctor felt the heat coming off Joe's face he looked up with surprise.

"I think my malaria is coming back, Doctor. I had it twelve months ago when we were in the Jordon Valley."

"What's your name, Trooper?"

"Joe Daley … er … Dawson. Trooper Daley Dawson, sir."

After listening to Joe's chest and asking him further questions, Doctor Rabatel wrote on a small pad in what appeared an illegible scrawl. The Frenchman tore off one page from the pad and began to write on the next page. He removed that page too. The doctor handed the medicine orders to George Turner and issued instructions to the two troopers standing in silence at the tent entrance.

"You're to go to the hospital dispensary tent and tell them to give you these tablets. Do not mix them up. One lot is for Trooper Farquharson and the other will be the quinine tablets for Trooper Dawson." Doctor Rabatel turned to look at Lieutenant Clay who now stood to attention beside the man on the mat on the floor. "At least, I see no evidence of cholera here today. You can let Major General Chauvel know it seems unlikely the disease has reached us from Tiberias."

"Yes, Major, of course."

George and Toby nearly fell over in surprise when the Lieutenant spoke before leaving.

"Will you troopers manage to look after your two sick friends – let me know if you have any trouble." The Lieutenant followed on the doctor's heels.

"He doesn't seem to be a bad cove really – what does Max have against him?" George's gaze followed the officers as they made their way along the row of tents. The trooper then cast his eyes down to study the paper in his hand.

"Who knows, George? Give me that order slip and I'll go and get those tablets for these two. Once Max is better you can ask him then."

On the following day, the heat of the morning sunshine chased the cold of the night from the roof of the tent. The sides were rolled up tidily to allow the occasional breezes to pass over the two sleeping bodies on their mats inside.

Lieutenant Clay stepped into the shade of the tent and stood still, watching the two men for a moment before he spoke.

"You awake, Trooper?"

Joe's eyes snapped open. He struggled to rise.

"As you were, Trooper, no need to get up. How are you feeling today?"

"Lieutenant Clay, sir." Joe's head felt as though it was full of his Gran's dough mixture.

"Where're Turner and Rawlins?"

"Er … oh, they went out on patrol. They were short of men. I'm feeling much better today. I said I'd look after Max. They left me two buckets of water and rations. Max's fever was down this morning when they left."

Joe reached over to touch Max's forehead. "Yeah, he's not hot like he was yesterday, sir."

"I'm glad to hear you're both on the mend; so many others have not been so lucky." The Lieutenant began to drag something out of his pocket. "I brought two lemons for you. If you squeeze them into the billy when it boils and then drink it cool, they'll do wonders for a fever."

"Lemons? How were you able to get them, sir? My Gran always swore by lemon juice if we were ever sick."

"Sometimes it's best not to know."

268

Joe looked up at the man standing tall and slim inside the tent flap. A thought struck him. *Now that's something I'd expect Max to say when he brings us news or other items of interest.* The Lieutenant and Max could not be more unalike. For one thing, Max did not waste time worrying about his dress too much. Joe prevented the grin as it threatened to split his face at the sight of the shine on the man's shoes and as the immaculate state of his dress registered. *How does he do that – out here – with dirt and dust everywhere?*

"Thanks, sir, for the lemons. I'll see Max gets a drink of lemon juice with his midday pills."

"You make sure you get some too. How are you coping with the Quinine tablets? Are the side effects bothering you?"

"Not really, sir, the ringing in the ears makes me a bit dizzy at times but that's better than the other option."

The Lieutenant turned to go but swung his head back. "No need to tell Max I brought the lemons."

"Sir, I'm sure he'll be very grateful." Joe blurted out the next question without really thinking. "Do you know Max from before the army?" Joe dragged in a sharp breath, surprised at his audacity. "Sorry, sir, it's none of my business."

Lieutenant Clay turned back and smiled down at Joe – a pleasant smile.

"Not to worry, Dawson. It's just a family thing. Max is my cousin, well, second cousin, really. You know how these family animosities can get out of hand. It's been going on long before either of us were born. In other circumstances, we might have been friends. Having witnessed all this death and killing in these past few years, family animosity is such a petty issue, best put aside, I think. I'll drop in again later today to see how he is doing. No need to mention what I've told you."

"As you wish, sir."

Elizabeth Rimmington

Joe watched the departing back of Lieutenant Clay as he passed through the lines of tents and leafless tracks swept by the Arab Labour Force every morning. He held the lemons to his nose and sniffed.

"Oh, God, these smell so good."

"So, Brian Clay told you the family secrets?"

Joe jumped when Max spoke from behind him. "I thought you were asleep."

"No, just dozing."

"How are you feeling? I see your fever has settled."

"Yeah, the aches have almost disappeared too. I'm just a bit tired is all. For the first time in days, I feel like a piss."

"With the feeble leading the very feeble, we'll never make it to the latrines. I can help you outside to pee against a tree."

"Thanks, Joe. And when we return, we'll juice those lemons."

"I didn't expect you to have the strength to squeeze a lemon. Can't have you exerting yourself, the Lieutenant will have my guts for garters if I let you do too much."

Max let out a short laugh followed by a dry cough.

Reinforcements arrived in dribs and drabs over the next two weeks and the 12th Regiment returned to almost full strength. Both Joe and Max and their horses Straps and Contrary were becoming restless. They craved a little more action other than the uneventful patrols around the French Hospital site and their own regiment's campsite.

CHAPTER TWENTY-TWO

Billabong Downs

August – October 1918

Fran felt her gut clench. She gazed into the pain-filled eyes of her daughter as she palpated Mavis's right side. Fran's diagnosis was confirmed with Mavis's reaction when she released her hand quickly. The young girl almost jumped off the bed.

"Mummy, that hurt."

"Sorry, darling."

With her earlier years' experience as a nurse, Fran knew having to deal with appendicitis way out here would not be her choice, but she sighed and acknowledged it was better than many other disasters that can befall people living a long distance from a hospital. Her head swirled with the necessary arrangements required to deliver her daughter into Charters Towers without wasting too much time.

Her first port of call was to her friend Maggie's place. While walking across the compound she felt another clench of her gut when she noticed the sun seemed to be rushing towards the horizon. Night threatened.

"Fran, are you alright? You look a bit tense. Has Mabel been playing up again? I haven't heard her all day."

"No, Maggie, it's young Mavis; it looks very much like she has appendicitis. I'd like to get her into town tonight. Can you listen out for Mabel for me?"

"Of course, Fran. Geoff said they were not expecting to get back home tonight."

"Yes, that's what Miles's said this morning. I'll ask Gazza if he'll come with me."

Fran ran all the way over to Gazza's shed. She yelled out as she approached.

"You there, Gazza? It's Fran."

Gazza appeared from around the corner of the shed. He lifted his hat and scratched his head.

"You alright there, Missus?"

"I'm fine but young Mavis needs to go to the hospital tonight. The men won't be back until tomorrow sometime. Will you come with me?"

"Of course, Missus. I'll harness up the dray or should we take the buggy?"

"I think we'd best take the small dray. I can put down a mattress for Mavis to lie on then." Fran turned to rush back to her daughter but she spun around. "We'll need a lantern please, Gazza. It will be dark soon."

"Yes, Missus, of course."

Back at the house, Fran threw a few clothes into a Gladstone bag for Mavis and herself. In the kitchen, she took down her large basket and added a tin of biscuits, a small billy, tea, pannikins and sugar. She filled the small water drum. Heaven forbid they were held up for any reason en route, but over the years she had learnt to expect the unexpected. Two rugs, a pillow and their coats were included. Fran heard Gazza pull the horses to a halt just as she dumped a single mattress at the top of the stairs.

"Can I get that, Missus?"

"Please, Gazza. I'll just get my handbag and shut the windows before I bring Mavis out. We can then be on our way."

Chill of Blame

Fran's heart broke with every whimper that escaped her daughter's lips as the child bounced around on the mattress in the back of the dray. A blanket covered Mavis's curled-up body. Fran sat near her daughter's head holding her hand. The light from the lantern hanging under the dray sent shadows racing back and forth through the trees and over the empty plains as they passed.

"I'll stop up ahead to water the horses, Missus." Gazza hauled on the reins. The dust billowed over the back of the dray. Fran struggled not to cough as she held the blanket lightly over Mavis's head to filter the air for her to breathe.

"Mummy, can I have a drink too?" The whisper rose faintly from the body under the blanket.

"Only a little sip, dear." Fran considered the need to keep her daughter comfortable against the need to reduce the contents of her stomach in case Doctor Munson decided to operate as soon as they arrived in town. As much as she wanted to stop and boil the billy for a long hot cup of tea, she knew time was of the essence. Fran climbed out of the dray to stretch her legs and drink from the running stream. After watering the horses, Gazza threw the buckets up into the dray. Fran climbed back up to her position on the corner of the mattress. They recommenced the journey to Charters Towers.

The horses' hooves clattered along the quiet street as Gazza's knobbly hands on the reins guided them towards the hospital. When he pulled them to a halt, Fran climbed from the dray, again stretching out the kinks in her back. Light from the lantern hanging on the wall at the front entrance revealed the emergency bell. She gave it two sharp clangs. At the familiar sight, viewed through the small panel of glass in the door, of Sister Wainwright's confident stride approaching down the hallway, relief washed over Fran. Relief at knowing her daughter would be in safe hands. An overwhelming urge to burst into

273

tears surprised her. Sister Wainwright had delivered her three children in this hospital.

Much later, Fran's head drooped upon the clean sheet. Her fingers loosened their hold on Mavis's right hand. In the glow of early morning light seeping through the windows, the nurse felt the pulse on the child's other wrist before touching the mother's shoulder.

"Can I get you a cup of tea, Mrs. Daley?"

Fran's head snapped up. She pulled herself upright. Her first glance went to her daughter's face. She smiled to see the absence of the previous lines of pain.

"Thank you, Nurse. Would it be possible to have a second cup for the man who brought us to the hospital? He is sleeping in the dray outside."

"The man called Gazza? He has already had tea and toast, Mrs. Daley. It was his reward for taking the trolley of dirty laundry across to the wash house."

Another smile brightened Fran's face.

"Gazza is always a great help." Silently Fran thanked her lucky stars for Gazza's presence at Billabong Downs. Having to drive the horses and dray into town by herself with her ill daughter was a daunting thought.

A small voice from the ruffled head lying on the white pillow drew Fran's immediate attention.

"Can we go home now, Mum?"

"Good morning, my darling." Fran smoothed back the child's locks. "The doctor took out your appendix when you were asleep, but now you'll have to stay here for a couple of days until the wound heals up." Fran jumped when a male voice spoke at her elbow.

"Fran, if everything goes well, I will have nothing against your taking Mavis home to your mother in-law's place here in town in a day or two. She must remain in town until the stitches come out next week."

"Doctor Munson, goodness me, you must be tired. Have you been up all night?"

"A frequent occurrence, I'm afraid."

"Thank you so much. And yes, of course, Mavis will stay in town with Gran for as long as you want."

"I figured you'd be wanting to get back home with the other Mrs. Daley and your family needing your attention." The doctor reached down and touched Mavis's forehead. He lifted the sheet discreetly and checked the wound dressing. "That all seems good."

"Thank you again, Doctor."

As the door closed behind the doctor, Fran looked down at Mavis who lay with a wide grin and glistening eyes.

"Am I going to stay with Gran and Pops?"

"We'll have to ask Gran and Pop if that suits them. They may have something else they have to do. It will be only until the stitches are removed. Then you can come back home."

"They never have anything better to do than enjoy our company. That's what Gran says."

"Is that so?" Fran smiled.

After a brief stop at Pop and Gran Daley's place to report on Mavis's operation, Fran nodded to Gazza who took up the reins and they began the journey home. She smiled at the recollection of Gran's reaction. Pop Daley was instructed to drop everything he was doing and harness up the buggy. Gran wanted to go and check on her granddaughter immediately.

Fran's head drooped and rocked with the movement of the dray as Gazza clicked his tongue to keep the horses moving. The late winter sun on her back soothed her to sleep. At a particularly deep pot-hole, she woke with a grunt. She rubbed her eyes and dragged her hands down her face.

"You awake, Gazza?"

His grin revealed the gaps between his nicotine-stained teeth.

"Yes, Missus, I ain't tired. I slept in the dray while you were in the hospital last night. I was very comfortable."

"Lucky you. Those hospital chairs are enough to break one's spine when sitting too long."

Fran sighed, a deep sigh when the sight of the homestead appeared through the trees of Lorikeet Creek. As they drove into the compound the sigh turned to a groan at the sound of Mabel's voice screaming for attention.

"Looks like you ain't gonna get much rest today, Missus."

"No, Gazza, I guess not. What do they say, 'No rest for the wicked'?" She smiled. "Would you mind dropping me off at William's house and then leaving my things at the top of my stairs? If the mattress is too heavy, leave it and Miles will take it up later."

Her legs felt like a ton weight as she hauled each foot, one after the other, up the stairs. The siren voice never faltered.

"I AM NOT GOING TO GET INTO THAT BATH WITHOUT FRAN HERE TO HELP!"

The soft murmur of Maggie's patient voice followed but not for long before it was interrupted again.

"MAVIS IS ONLY A CHILD. WHO CARES IF SHE HAS TO GO TO THE HOSPITAL? SHE CAN GO ANOTHER DAY."

Again, the murmured voice.

"YOU ARE ONLY THE HIRED HAND AROUND HERE."

At that point, Fran arrived at Mabel's bedroom door. A tsunami tide of anger, frustration, weariness and impatience almost overwhelmed her. She clamped her teeth down upon her tongue until she tasted blood. She clenched her fists and took deep breaths. With a fixed smile on her lips, she stepped into the bedroom.

"Good afternoon, Mabel." Fran flashed a smile of sympathy and rolled her eyes towards Maggie before she turned back to her sister-in-law. "What have we got here? It's nearly evening and you haven't had your bath?"

"Well, look who it is. Frumpy Fran. WELL, IT'S TOO LATE NOW. SO, I WON'T BE HAVING A BATH TONIGHT."

"You know, Mabel, you're right. It is too late and Maggie and I have plenty to be doing with our own families so you'll just have to miss your bath today. Come on, Maggie, we'll leave Mabel to her own devices."

"GO ON THEN, GO ON. YOU'RE JUST A PAIR OF PEASANT TARTS. WHERE IS MY BILLY? HE'LL HAVE YOU SACKED."

As Maggie and Fran made their way down the stairs, Maggie asked, "How's young Mavis?"

"She'll be fine. Doctor Munson took her appendix out early this morning. Mavis will have to stay in hospital for a few days. Gran will go and visit her each day before she is discharged into Gran's care."

"You must be so relieved."

"I'm sure I am, but to be honest I'm too exhausted to feel anything."

"Geoff and the men are over in the shed. They arrived back a short time ago. You go upstairs and freshen up. I'll go to the shed and tell Miles what has happened, but I'm sure Gazza has already relayed the news." Maggie called back from across the compound. "I'll see Gazza fed tonight. Will you have something there for your supper?"

"Yes thanks, Maggie. There'll be toast and something, I'm sure."

William's lengthening hair dripped water down his forehead as he raised the cutthroat razor. It hid his frown as he peered more closely

277

into the small mirror hanging from the nail in the post inside the shower room under the house. He lifted it aside to sweep another path through the thick layer of soap covering his cheeks. A soft curse exploded through his lips.

"She's driving me bloody grey." He tugged at the locks of almost white hair. A wry chuckle followed the statement. 'Vanity comes before a fall.' Their mother always preached this to Miles and himself as kids. He continued clearing the stubble from his chin.

Dressed in his best work clothes and polished boots, William patted the inside pockets of his dust jacket for his wallet, the mail and his latest report to Doctor Munson. Before passing Mabel's doorway he poked his head inside.

"You're awake then, Mabel?"

A grunt was his only reply.

"How are you feeling today?"

A further grunt landed with a thud on his ears.

"Are you sure you don't want a trip to town? Maybe if you spoke to Doctor Munson, he might be able to give you something for your headaches." William knew better than to mention the term mental breakdown."

"I wouldn't get headaches if I wasn't surrounded by such common people. Why hasn't Billy come home? He understands."

William turned and walked away but his wife's next words followed him down the stairs.

"This place is like a morgue without Billy's smile and laughter. He was always laughing – why can't you laugh?"

"Pity Billy's laughter never caught on with you then," William spoke softly and kept walking.

Before he went over to the shed to harness the horses, he stopped at Miles's back steps.

"Can I get you anything in town, Miles – Fran?"

It was Miles who came to the top of the stairs.

"No thanks, William, just don't forget to bring our daughter back."

Fran called from inside the kitchen, "And don't listen to her excuses why she shouldn't stay until the school holidays."

William laughed. "Yes, Boss."

By the time William arrived at the stables, he found Gazza had the dray ready. William noticed Gazza, dressed in a pair of clean trousers and a wrinkled but clean shirt, leading the team outside. As usual, Gazza's boots remained scuffed and worn.

"Thanks, Gazza, you coming to town too?"

"Yes, Mr. William, bout time I had a day out in the big smoke."

"Isn't this the third time you've been to the Towers in the last twelve months? We can't count the trip to the hospital with Mavis. Have you got a secret woman you're not telling us about?"

A shy grin and red flush crept across Gazza's face behind the snowy beard.

"Come on then, Romeo, we'll need to be smart about it today with those clouds coming in or we'll be paddling home." William stared up at the darkening sky.

At the bottom of High Street, Gazza climbed down from the dray.

William called after him, "I'll pick you up at your favourite pub?"

"Thanks." Gazza walked off patting his pockets as he went.

William turned and made his way to Doctor Munson's surgery where he dropped off his report and collected Miles's medical account for Mavis's surgery.

As William turned to go, the doctor himself beckoned him into his room.

"Good day, William, I figured someone from out there would be in this week to collect young Mavis. How have things been going out on Billabong Downs?"

"Just the same as usual. Bit dry at the moment, but the clouds are building up."

"And your wife?"

"I just left the report with your nurse. Mabel won't even come into town these days. Usually, she'd be nagging for weeks before we'd be making a trip for stores."

Doctor Munson moved to close the door. "I've had a letter from a specialist in Townsville. Apparently, Mabel's parents have asked him to help. He agrees there is nothing we can do unless Mabel wants us to help or if she becomes unmanageable."

"Thanks, Doc. Mabel's intolerable at times but I couldn't, in all honesty, say unmanageable."

After leaving the doctor's surgery, William called into the produce store and left a note listing their requirements, before he made his way to his parent's place.

"Hello, Uncle William," Mavis called from the other side of the garden. "Gran and I are off to take a walk in the park."

William waved to his mother and his niece.

"Come on, son, while your Ma has Mavis otherwise occupied. Another letter came from Joe yesterday." Pop led William in through the back door. He pointed to the kitchen as they passed.

"The kettle should be hot if you want a cup of tea."

"Yes, I'd kill for a cuppa right about now. Do you want a cup?"

"No thanks, we just had one. There are oatmeal biscuits in the tin on the table too."

"Okay, you get the letter out and I'll sort my tea."

When both men were ensconced in the lounge room chairs, William sipped at his hot tea and took a sizeable snap of a biscuit while Pop sorted the letter he wanted, from those within an old shoe box.

"Here we are, this was written in August. They've moved over near the coast to a place called Ludd." William did not miss the tremble in his father's hand as he passed over the paper. "I won't tell you what's in it. You can read it for yourself."

"Is he alright?"

"Yeah, he was fine when he wrote that, anyway."

Dear Pops, Gran, Dad and everyone else at Billabong Downs,
August 1918

Hope this finds everyone well. I guess you're just coming out of your winter. It's still hot as can be here. Can't say I'm looking forward to winter after the last one in the coldest place on earth – well it sure felt like it.

We're not far from the sea now so the breezes when they do arrive are appreciated. Yesterday we received our cavalry swords as part of our uniform. I reckon most of us have grown a few more inches in height with pride.

Straps is looking good with the extra grain rations he has received these past two weeks. I guess I'm looking a bit better too with the improved tucker and regular baths. We have been practising cavalry drilling every day and the exercise is helping build up our bodies again.

No doubt this idle time cannot last and we'll be back into the fray very shortly.

Thinking of you all every day.

Thanks for the cake and biscuits Gran from the blokes in my tent. The biscuits followed us around the country for a bit before I got them.

With love Joe Daley Dawson

"How much longer can this damn war go on for, Pop?"

Elizabeth Rimmington

"From what we are being told, there is some hope for an end in sight."

"Yeah, they said it was only going to last until Christmas back in 1914, and here we are still losing our sons in 1918."

Pop's gaze took in his son's extra lines and greying hair. He reached out and touched his arm.

"Keep strong, lad, your boy needs you to keep strong." He did not miss the shine of tears in the eyes of his firstborn. "I've written a reply. Did you want to add a few words?"

"Yes, Pop, I will, but only a few lines. I need to pick up the supplies and Mavis and I mustn't forget Gazza too. He came in with me this morning. We want to get back tonight"

By the time William added the postscript to Pop Daley's reply for Joe, Gran and Mavis's footsteps could be heard on the back porch. Mavis ran inside to collect her things.

Gran handed a tin of sandwiches and a kiss to her son. "For you to eat on the road. It will be very late before you get home."

"Thanks, Ma."

"Mavis, don't you be doing too much for a while yet, dear," Gran called as she blew kisses to her granddaughter.

"Bye, Gran. Thank you for having me."

Tears accompanied Gran's wave.

CHAPTER TWENTY-THREE

Armistice

October 1918

The smiles lighting up the faces of Joe Daley Dawson and Max Farquharson had not faded in the weeks since their recovery. Following the reports of the number of soldiers wounded and/or killed in action, and those dead from pneumonic influenza or malaria being made public, they were very much aware of their luck in surviving. It felt good to be back in the saddle again with their worldly belongings strapped to, or hanging from every available space. The weight of their ammunition pouches slung across their shoulders, the touch of the rifle bucket and the sight of their cavalry sword in its scabbard behind the riders' left leg provided a welcome sensation. Even the dust stirred up by the horses' hooves failed to dampen their spirits. They were on the Homs Road; wherever that might be, but it was out of the city with all its filth and disease. Joe hummed a tune under his breath.

On the 30th of October 1918, not too far from their destination, the troopers, other than the patrols guarding their number, sat around talking, playing cards, writing home, or singing soft tunes. It seemed a hush fell over the regiment for some moments before the night filled with a rising tide of shouts, laughter, hoots and whistles swirling down the lines.

The Turks have signed the Mudros Armistice. This war is over.

Eleven days later, when his section wallowed in the heat and dust by day and the cooling winds of the nights on the return journey to Damascus, the news whispered through the ranks like a summer rain shower bringing joy to the men's faces furrowed with the dirt-filled lines of exhaustion.

An armistice was signed on the Western Front on the 11th of November 1918.

Joe struggled to understand the conflicting emotions churning around inside him. The idea of an end to killing other human beings and of seeing carpets of the dead everywhere in his nightmares filled him with relief. When he shut his eyes, he almost felt the water pouring over his body in a hot shower with water to spare and his skin clean again with a lather of soap. A sigh escaped his lips as he imagined what it might feel like to lie in a comfortable bed once again. The idea of a settled life and no more travelling appealed enormously.

The colour of his brown eyes deepened in shadow as his thoughts turned to Billabong Downs, the home where he would no longer run and ride with his brother Billy. Long-suppressed guilt slithered like a snake within his guts. He had not protected his brother. Again, the voice of his mother drummed inside his head – it was his duty to care for his older brother. He was the stronger of her boys and therefore he must protect his older sibling. The weight of responsibility dragged at his shoulders in the knowledge he had not only failed his brother and his mother, but he failed himself. What right did he have to be going home without Billy? How was he to face his family if he did?

CHAPTER TWENTY-FOUR

Billabong Downs

November 1918

The heavily censored news began to trickle into the Australian newspapers. The country began to learn of the heavy losses sustained by their soldiers on the western front. Germany gathered momentum in a last effort to overwhelm the British and Allied forces. The family on Billabong Downs feared for the life of young Joe who they believed to be right in the thick of the fighting as the Light Horse Brigade moved north in the Sinai and Palestine areas.

Mabel's failing mind spiralled downwards into a dark abyss. She spent her days, when not walking a track from the front door to the back door, motionless upon her bed. The unceasing mumble of her threats to the army, the enemy forces, her husband, her father-in-law, and her own fighting son became a background hum throughout the house. The distraught William spent his days discovering work that needed attention in the shed.

Fran Daley and Maggie Bardon took turns in caring for Mabel. The two women sat on the front steps of William's house sipping at their cups of weak tea. Summer heat radiated off the bare earth as Christmas bore down upon them.

"I live for the day when we have enough tea leaves to make a decent cuppa; one I can stand the spoon up in, preferably," Maggie set the beverage rocking inside the cup. She lifted her face. Sadness filled her blue eyes. "Fran, I do believe Mabel is only going to get worse."

"All I can say is, thank heavens Mabel's two girls are staying with their grandparents in Townsville and not here to see this deterioration in their mother. William said they will most likely stay there for the Christmas break too."

"I can't agree more. It's not something Cissy and Maud need to see. They're still only young girls." Maggie swirled the cooling liquid around the bottom of her cup. "There are not even enough dregs in this cup to read my future." She raised an arm and pointed her finger northeast to where a thin dust cloud rose on the edge of the horizon. "Fran, I think someone's coming."

They both watched as a single rider appeared through the dust.

"Who is it do you think, Maggie? Your eyes are better than mine."

"I'm not sure – it's not one of our men." Maggie Bardon smoothed her light brown hair and reset a hair clip.

The stranger stopped to open the gate of the night paddock; led his horse through and shut the gate behind him. He remounted without a pause.

"Seems to be in a hurry, I'd say. What do you think, Maggie?"

"I'm thinking it might be Lucky Minky, the mailman's boy. He wears his hat pulled down like that and his damaged shoulder makes him slouch in the saddle."

Fran glanced up at her friend. Anxiety filled both pairs of eyes.

"Oh, saints above, it can't be a telegram can it, Fran? Please, God, don't tell us young Joe has been killed."

As the rider drew closer, a wide grin spread across his face to be seen below the brim of his dusty old hat. He sat up straight to call his message.

"The war is over. It's true. Our boys will be coming home."

Disbelief, buttered with hope, glowed in the ladies' eyes. They hardly dared to think this might be true. Both jumped up when Mabel strode out onto the verandah beside them and yelled at the visitor.

"You can tell them they need not bother coming home. If they can't bring my Billy home alive, they can all remain dead and rotting over there."

The rider's smile disappeared as his jaw dropped leaving his mouth agape.

Fran rushed towards Mabel gathering her up into her arms.

"Hush, Mabel, hush, you have another son to welcome home soon." Fran glanced back. "Maggie, can you take Lucky to your house for a cuppa?"

At that moment, William strode out from the shed with Geoff Bardon at his side. Geoff's daughter Evie lay along the neck of her grey pony as she rode it out from under the shed.

"What's going on?" William asked.

"It's the war; it's over." Lucky reiterated his message.

Tears welled up in the older man's eyes. He struggled to draw breath. Geoff reached over – his grin threatened to split his face. He grabbed his boss's hand and pumped it enthusiastically.

Seven-year-old Evie piped up. "What's happening, Dad?"

"The war is over, Evie. Joe will be coming home."

Not fully comprehending the enormity of the announcement, Evie grinned at the pleasure she saw in her father's eyes.

"Can I go and tell Mister Miles?"

Geoff was tempted to say no, but he knew this youngster of his was quite capable of delivering a message to the workers at the mustering yards.

"Okay, girl, but no galloping. Remember you've got to look after your animal."

"I'll be alright, Dad, I can ride better than both my brothers." She guided the horse into a turn before her legs thumped against the saddle as she encouraged speed.

Pride added to the excitement in Geoff's eyes. He watched the horse move off at a steady trot.

CHAPTER TWENTY-FIVE

Dark Clouds

January – May 1919

One night in a camp where the men of the Light Horse waited to hear the plans for their return to Australia, the singing and laughing fell silent as another piece of news fell upon one set of ears after another. A sourness filled the air like a poisonous miasma in a swampland.

"Because of quarantine regulations and the cost of transport, the horses are to stay behind. They will be sold to the local merchants and farmers."

The veneer of army discipline split like the crack of a ripe watermelon under the cleaver.

Not a horseman among them appreciated this order. Many fell into a well of depression at the thought of their wonderful fighting Walers being left behind.

"Those bastards can't do that to our horses. These animals have suffered enough already."

"They're born fighting horses – not to be used hauling a dusty plough for endless hours in the day."

"Nor are they slaves for use in an overcrowded market, to work unfed until they drop."

"They gave us their lives; are we to treat them like this?"

"Our horses deserve to return home with us."

A single penetrating voice hushed the gathering crowd of soldiers.

"They deserve an honourable death. It's our duty to do the right thing by our faithful mounts."

Joe Dawson's letter from his Pops Daley arrived when Joe was at his lowest ebb. When it seemed the best thing for him to do was to take his mount and himself into the desert and put a bullet through both their heads.

"Joe Dawson!" The gravely voice of the mail deliverer called his name. Joe caught the letter in his grubby hands. He shoved the dirt-marked envelope into his top pocket and carried it around with him for two days before opening it – just before he had to decide on whether to take the last ride out into the desert with his horse.

Our dearest Joe

March 1919

You cannot imagine the excited state of your Gran and your parents, in fact, everyone on Billabong Downs and your other grandparents in Townsville also.

Your sisters, Cissy and Maud, have not stopped talking about your return and all they want to do for you. I swear you'll not have to lift a finger about the place for the rest of your life. Your wish will be their command.

We all carry with pride the memory of Billy who gave his life for his country. We give thanks to our God that we have not lost a second son to this cause also.

Your Uncle Miles and Auntie Fran along with Geoff and Maggie are already in the process of making big plans for your return. Although, if I remember my homecoming after the Boer War, all I wanted to do was crawl into a hole and play Rip-Van-Winkle.

Whatever you do son take care. You have an army of family and friends here waiting anxiously for your safe return.

From your ever-loving and respectful Pops Daley

Chill of Blame

The lone figure trudged through the sands towards the line of tents lost in the setting sun. Tears tracked through the dust on his face. Joe hitched the saddle and reins higher onto his shoulder and adjusted the weight of the rifle on the opposite shoulder.

CHAPTER TWENTY-SIX

Billabong Downs

May 1919

Nobody anticipated the lengthy delays in having their loved ones returned from the battle zones. Fear continued to live in the hearts of every family as the news filtered into the daily papers of the numerous soldiers dying without a bullet being fired. A disease they called the Spanish flu attacked, without favour, soldiers of all armies and populations in all countries. Those at Billabong Downs held their breaths. The sight of every puff of dust rising from the track the mailman used, filled their hearts with an equal measure of hope and dread. Eventually, word reached them. Joe was on the way home.

Miles lifted a hand of acknowledgement towards Geoff who, with his elder son, harnessed the four horses into the wagon. Excitement filled the air along with the chill of the approaching winter dawn. Everyone on Billabong Downs, except Maggie Bardon, who volunteered to stay and care for Mabel, and the old roustabout Gazza who made it clear he was past the long trek into Charters Towers, prepared for the journey to town to meet the late afternoon train carrying the recently demobbed soldiers.

Miles placed his foot on the bottom step of his brother's house and reached over to grab the railing when the screech erupted from inside. Miles froze.

"I'm NOT going to meet any train unless my Billy is coming home."

"Now, Mabel, you know that can never be; Billy's dead. We do have another son remember and Joe will be on the train."

"Why couldn't it be Joe who's dead and rotting in that cursed land over there? I told him not to come home without his brother."

At the bottom of the stairs, Miles did not see the sly and spiteful grin distorting his sister-in-law's lips. All the same, like the blow of an axe between the eyes, shock hit him where he stood, unsure whether to go in or to retreat. His brother's voice hissed, angrier than Miles had ever heard it.

"Mabel, if I thought you ever told Joe that, I would not be responsible for what I might do to you."

"Yes, I did and I don't care if you're going to town to bring your son home, I won't be going with you."

The silence seemed to ooze through the walls and down to where the hesitant Miles stood. Miles shivered at his brother's next words.

"Mabel Daley, I'm giving you this one last warning. Don't you dare tell Joe you blame him for Billy's death – don't you even think of blaming Joe."

"What are you going to do, shoot me?"

A long pause followed.

Outside, Miles swallowed, too caught up in the drama to move off.

William's voice hardened with thick venom.

"If you do, woman, I promise you faithfully, I will have you committed; firstly, to the Reception House in Townsville from where you will be transported to the lunatic asylum at Goodna."

"You wouldn't dare." Doubt trembled in every word.

"I most certainly would dare. Joe has been through hell and back for our country and does not need you to ruin what life he has left. You are a wicked crazy woman with no resemblance to a mother at all."

"Well, I won't be going to town anyway." A door slammed shut.

William's footsteps moved into the kitchen and his final words drifted down to Miles.

"Good, but when we bring Joe home, remember what I promised."

Miles stamped his feet on the step and thudded his way up to the verandah. He called out loudly.

"You coming, William? The Bardons have the wagon ready."

CHAPTER TWENTY-SEVEN

Fork in the Road

May 1919

Now on home soil, Joe lay stretched out on the wooden seat at the farthest end of the Townsville Railway Station. A dodgy electric light flickered on and off on the wall behind him. Joe's head rested upon his haversack. One arm lay hooked over his face securing his slouch hat to his forehead. His second arm cradled his rifle against his body. As usual, it was the whirlpool of his mind that kept sleep at bay. The big question swirled around and around. Should he return home to where his mother was going to blame him for his brother's death, or should he just throw himself and his haversack on a train going in the opposite direction?

A sixth sense developed after months of surviving in enemy territory flicked his eyes open. He peered out from under the brim of his hat. Nothing came into view. He threw his hat aside and rolled over and onto his feet and knees – crouched, searching for the danger, the unloaded rifle at the ready. A young lad jumped back a step and stared – in silence. Spikey blond hair stood upright from his head. A pair of solemn blue eyes scrutinized Joe.

Joe lowered the rifle barrel. "Geez, boyo, you frightened the life out of me."

"Are you a trooper of the 'Stralian Light Horse?"

Joe ran his tongue around the inside of his mouth searching for moisture.

"Yes, I am. Well, I was."

"Then you shouldn't be frightened. Nothing frightens the 'Stralian Light Horse. My dad was a 'Stralian Light Horse." The boy stuck his finger in his nose to remove a lump of snot. "Nothing scares me. I'm gonna be a trooper in the 'Stralian Light Horse when I grow a bit bigger."

Joe rose to his feet and picked up his hat, slapping it against his legs before crunching it down on his head.

"Can I see your Emu feathers?"

Joe removed the hat again from his head and handed it to the boy.

"They're pretty tattered these days, I guess."

Reverence glistened in the lad's eyes as his small fingers stroked the emblem of his dreams. He gave a start at the voice calling from down the platform.

"Tapper, come back here. Leave the poor man in peace."

"That's my mum. She fusses a bit. We're catching the train to Mackay soon. I'd better go."

"Yeah, mum's do that, I believe – fuss a bit."

Joe smiled as he replaced his hat on his head and sat back on the wooden form watching the boy called Tapper return to his large family halfway along the platform.

His head lifted at the sound of the announcement of his train's imminent departure. Joe slung his knapsack over his right shoulder and his rifle over his left shoulder before he joined the lines of people waiting to board the train.

CHAPTER TWENTY- EIGHT

Reception

May 1919

When the screech of the train's whistle announced their arrival, Joe Daley stood. He gathered up his gear and paused. As the wheels came to a grinding halt, he dragged in a deep breath and prepared to climb down from the train along with four other men in uniform. While the grins on the faces of four of the arrivals shone out in the lights of the train station platform and over the Charter's Towers' crowds, including the welcoming committee made up of the official council members and selected pupils from the local school, Joe's face remained sombre.

Joe looked up. He heard his name screamed out from the other end of the platform above the noise of the town band belting out a victory tune.

"Joe, over here."

Pleasure dampened somewhat with hesitancy, filled Joe's expression as he watched his father ploughing his way through the crowd of people. He recognized the figures of his Uncle Miles and Auntie Fran with Mavis, and their sons Mick and Doug. Beside them, the Bardon family waved frantically and squealed as they followed in his father's wake. His mother was absent. He sucked in his disappointment along with the engine smoke trapped against the roof of the platform. At the sight of his father's welcoming grin and the familiar strong arms stretched out towards him, Joe moved forward to greet his dad. Tears ran freely down the cheeks of father and son as they did on many faces amongst the cheering citizens of the town. Joe's body shook as he almost choked on the sobs struggling to escape.

"Dad, I'm sorry, I'm sorry. There was nothing I could do. Billy was lost in the dust. I'm sorry. We ran into a wall of bullets. B-B-Billy…," but Joe could not go on.

"Son, you must not blame yourself. War is a terrible thing." William's arms clenched his son tighter straining to remove the images from his own head as well as those of his surviving son, Common sense told him a lifetime was not going to blot out the memories of the experiences from Joe's mind.

Miles held the Billabong Downs' group back to allow father and son a few brief moments alone before he was overwhelmed. Joe was drawn into their welcome. Everybody talked at once.

With all the friends and families of the returning heroes in full throat, the noise at the train station threatened to lift the platform roof. The heat rising from the crowd of people swamped the cool of the May evening.

"Come on, you lot, let's get back to the wagon." Miles guided them out onto the street. They walked nearly a quarter of a mile to where the patient horses, wearing their now empty nosebags, stood beside the wagon. Moonlight guided their path.

"Did you get to see your sisters in Townsville, Joe?"

"No, Dad, I couldn't face them just yet. I did write a letter though. They'll be out at Billabong Downs for the holidays soon, won't they?"

William nodded. "I don't think we could keep them away, now you're back." Both rode side by side for several moments until William spoke again. "Are you hungry?" he asked his son. "Gran and Pop are beside themselves with eagerness to have you back home again. They have a meal waiting for you at their place. We'll set up camp in their backyard tonight and go home in the morning if that suits you." In the dark, William did not see Joe's head nod nor the moisture on the young man's cheeks.

Miles Daley lay awake in his swag as the moon arched across the night sky. Shock still lay resident within his thoughts; firstly, for the altercation he had overheard before they left the property and then at the sight of the aged young man who had stepped down from the train. Lines creased the face of his nephew not long turned eighteen years of age. A patch of white hair above the right side of his forehead stood out in stark contrast to the boy's remaining dark brown hair.

He felt Fran move in closer to him. Her arm crept across his chest. "You awake, Miles?"

He pulled her tighter into his body.

"Hmmmm. Oh, Fran, what has Joe been through? He looks like he has the weight of the world on his shoulders."

Her whisper fell soft upon his ear.

"All those boys returning tonight have seen and done things no human should ever have to do or witness." Her gentle hand stroked his cheek. "We'll need to let him return to normality in his own time. Perhaps you should have a word with William on our way home and suggest Joe might like to sleep in the men's quarters rather than in the house with Mabel – being as disturbed as she is. There's only Gazza in the quarters now, and he is an experienced man of the world having survived the Boer war himself. He may be able to help Joe adjust back into a world of peace." She lifted onto her elbow. "He is always welcome at our place, but I get the impression it is peace that he craves."

Miles gently squeezed his wife.

"Sometimes I wonder where any of us would be without you, Fran."

After bowls of hot porridge for everyone, the wagon, holding women and children with Geoff Bardon in control of the reins, led off. Evie Bardon sat at her father's side providing a litany of reasons why she should be allowed to hold the reins. The outriders, William, Joe and Miles, rode in close attendance.

On their arrival at Billabong Downs, Joe took up residence in the men's quarters as Fran had suggested. The unpainted split-timber walls of the building bore the scars of thirty years of standing stoic against a harsh climate. Wear and tear of rough ringers during the mustering seasons of many years tracked across the ant-bed floor. A wood stove balanced with one leg propped up on a rock in front of a roughhewn table with a wooden form on either side filled one end of the shed. Eight hessian stretchers built from local timber jutted out from the walls towards the centre of the room. Large rusting nails protruded at assorted angles from the building frame above each bed for the personal use of each occupant. Push-out timber windows lined every available space allowing access to any breeze that may wander by on a summer day. These were closed during the few colder winter months when the lazy westerly winds drove right through a man's body. William led his son into the shed.

"I'm sorry about housing you out here in the men's quarters, Joe. I didn't want to tell you in my letters, but your mother has been deteriorating for quite a few years now. At first, it was only short bouts of mental disturbance, but lately, there are whole days and nights when she lives in a world known only to herself. Sometimes there's little sleep for anyone in the house. You'll need your rest to recuperate. I'm sure you've missed out on a lot of sleep in the past two years yourself. It's thanks to your Auntie Fran and Maggie Bardon that we've managed to keep your mum out of the hospital." William moved over to lean against the door frame staring out to where the dust gusted on a moody wind through the scant trees. "This

300

is why your two sisters have been staying with your mother's family in Townsville most of the year." He removed the grey felt hat bent out of shape after years of wear and tear, from his head and slapped it against his leg. "By the way, Uncle Miles wants you to join his family for meals. Will you let your Auntie Fran know if this is suitable? Gazza eats here and sometimes with the Bardon family."

Joe dropped his knapsack and rifle onto a bed diagonally opposite to where Gazza's jacket hung from the nail above the only other stretcher with a pillow and grey blanket present. He flopped onto the taut hessian covering. He sat with his head bowed staring at his restless hands absorbing the warmth from the wood stove close by. He savoured the familiar aroma of stew containing home-bred beef warming on the edge of the hot plate.

"Did our going away to join up send Mum mad?"

"The local doctor and the Townsville specialist have reviewed her medical history going back to when she was a child. The Townsville bloke thinks she may have had trouble relating to the real world when things did not go all her way even then." William turned to gaze out over the paddocks listening to the rustle of the leaves in the tall gum trees nearby as they swayed in the gentle breeze. He swallowed twice before he felt he could go on speaking. "You and Billy leaving is only one event that has contributed to her confusion over the years."

"She does blame me for Billy's death, doesn't she, Dad?"

"Yes, son, I know. I'm truly sorry. It's all a part of her mental disorder and obsession with Billy. Nobody else does, and I certainly don't. Billy was the elder of you both and he went off to war with his eyes wide open. He should never have allowed you to go with him."

A wry grin only highlighted the strain on Joe's face. "I didn't give him much choice."

"You and Billy were always a body and its shadow and don't think for one minute I didn't know it was you who covered for him, more often than not, when the pair of you got up to any mischief."

Joe sat with his head bowed as he scratched at a loose thread in his uniform. Several times he tried to speak but the words jammed hard against his throat. His father stood quietly giving him time to select his words.

"Dad, common sense tells me I wasn't to blame for Billy's death, but sometimes inside, it eats away at me until I feel I should take responsibility."

William walked over and placed a hand on Joe's shoulder.

"I'm very glad you're safely home, son."

"I know, Dad."

"We were worried sick when we heard of the numbers of soldiers who had survived the years of war and who were then dying like flies with that Spanish Flu. I can't remember your Grandpapa and Grandmama Dawson ever writing so many letters as they have in recent months and not only in concern for their daughter but worrying for you out there in danger."

"A mate of mine had a dose of the flu at Ludd but he got over it okay. We had to bury many mates in those last months."

William reached over and rested his hand on Joe's shoulder.

"Come on now, son, Fran will be serving supper soon. I'll see you there later. I usually help your mother with her meal before I go over and enjoy an ale with your uncle. You'll join us, won't you?"

"Sounds good."

While working in her vegetable garden rescuing what she could before the winter made its presence really felt, Fran jumped at the sound of Joe's quiet voice behind her. Leaning on the shovel handle and holding her back with her spare hand she unwound herself until she stood straight.

"Are you alright there, Auntie Fran? Can I do the shovelling for you?"

"I think I have died and gone to heaven; someone is asking me to hand over the shovel." Her grin triggered the laughter lines at the edges of her hazel eyes. "I won't say no, thanks, Joe." She passed over her shovel and moved aside pointing and explaining what she had been trying to do. They worked in harmony for some time before Fran sat back upon her haunches. Dirt-ingrained hands shoved stray tendrils of hair under her wide-brimmed hat. She wiped the sweat from her face. "Joe, your Uncle Miles will be going into town Thursday of next week to collect Doug and Mick from school for the holidays. Cissy and Maud will have arrived at Gran and Pop's place by then. They'll come in on the Tuesday train with their Grandpapa. Did you want a trip in to meet them?"

Fran did not miss the sudden stillness and tension in her nephew's body. Joe's mouth gaped as he tried to choose the words to say what he wanted without hurting his aunt.

"I'd rather not, if you don't mind, Auntie Fran; unless there is something Miles needs a hand with." He pushed the shovel deep into the earth with his booted foot and rested. "I feel safer out here in the quiet."

"That's quite alright, Joe. It might be the last bit of quiet you get until they return to school in a few weeks after that." Fran walked over to the wire netting fence where half a dozen goats worried the little strands of green grass poking through the gaps. She reached over and scratched the large mother goat behind the ears. Fran turned her attention back to Joe. "Your sisters will sleep at my place, so you will get to see them at meal times. If at any time you want more distance, let me know. I'll send a pot of something over for you to heat up on the stove in the men's quarters."

"Thanks, Auntie Fran."

CHAPTER TWENTY-NINE

Transition

July 1919 – May 1920

Over the following months, Joe and Gazza settled into a comfortable companionship. Neither spoke volumes, but Joe learnt Gazza had difficulty settling back into life after his time fighting in the Boer War; before he ended up here. Joe's father and Uncle Miles took him on – first as a stockman and then when time began to slow Gazza down, he took on the maintenance chores around the homestead.

Christmas 1919 came and went. Fran felt as if she had spent the day in a sauna bath. Sweat coated her skin, it saturated her hair and its odour seemed to rise from the air around her. Cissy and Maud flitted around everywhere. They helped in the kitchen and decorated the table on the verandah. Fran envied their energy.

Their wish to bring Mabel over to share the season's celebrations was denied with a blunt remark from their mother.

"Go away and leave me alone. If Billy does not come and collect me, I will stay right where I am."

Fran refused to let the girls' mother ruin their Christmas. She smiled as she watched Joe cringe under their combined attention. Mavis ensured Joe had ample supplies of the tastiest of morsels.

"Enough," Joe cried as he nearly choked himself laughing. "My stomach's shrunken after years of bully beef and dry biscuits. I can't eat another thing." He turned to peer down the length of the trestle tables searching for reinforcements. "Auntie Fran, rescue me, please?"

Joe remained an enigma for the other youngsters on Billabong Downs. The Bardon boys, Stewie the ten-year-old, and the younger lad they called Splinter, were heard more often than seen. They spent their energies tearing around the homestead compound living out their worlds of exaggeration and wild imaginations, until the middle child Evie, brought them down to earth with either a short sharp delivery of common sense, a more adept physical expertise in most activities, or an echoing cooee few could hope to compete with.

Each evening at the meal tables in his Uncle Miles's house, Joe listened with a sense of affinity to Doug. Joe had been around Doug's age when he and Billy went off to the war. Having recently finished his education, Doug strived to meet the management standards of his father. He entertained everyone as he expounded on the new ideas learnt during his education. Mick, the second lad and the brains of the family, as his mother announced regularly, only returned for the school holiday breaks. Mick was destined for higher things, according to Auntie Fran, but he seemed happy to remain quiet in his brother's shadow listening and observing. Their younger sister Mavis, who now attended the school in Charters Towers, demonstrated frequently the signs of her mother's wisdom. When at home on the holidays she remained by Fran's side learning first-hand how to run an organized household. Joe's sisters remained in Townsville except for the longer holiday breaks when they stayed at Fran and Miles's house.

There were those times when the incoherent screeching of his mother's voice hung over the compound like a witch's curse. It was then that Joe tossed his swag on the back of his horse behind the saddle, tied a quart pot to the saddle bag, cleaned the dust from his rifle and headed out bush to disappear for three or four days. At these times, Joe felt Billy's presence at his side. If he closed his eyes, Joe could see Buckles' unending effort to reach the nosebag of grain Billy always carried tied to the back of his saddle. He heard the horse's snort of disapproval when Billy laughed at his mount. He smelt the sweat and dirt of them both – even sensed Billy's mirth in the air. Joe touched the spurs to his mount at the imagined yell of excitement from Billy.

"Let's ride, brother!"

At the cattle yards, a bellow of insult and discomfort flew up into the dust as the last beast they had castrated and branded struggled up and across the yards to join the other newly made steers. The taste of the dust clung to everyone's mouth. Evie Bardon unhooked the water bag from the rails and handed it to her father with an air of supreme importance. Sweat and dust blended to a muddy consistency on the faces of Geoff and the other three men. William, Miles and young Doug put aside the tools of their trade and walked over to lean against the thick timber rails waiting to quench their thirst in turn.

"There goes Joe again. Mabel must be drumming up a storm at the house," William commented as he wiped the water from his lips and handed the bag to his brother.

Miles looked up in the direction of William's hooked finger. He nodded.

It was Doug who asked, "Uncle William, can I follow Joe to see if he's alright?"

The frown on William's forehead deepened.

"Why shouldn't he be, Doug? Who can blame him for wanting to get away from his mother's screaming accusations? The bush will heal him – eventually."

Doug and his father's gaze connected. Following their conversation after tea the previous evening, Miles knew exactly what was on Doug's mind. Even his son had noticed the increased frequency and lengthening of Joe's disappearances. He and Geoff discussed the very same subject on more than one occasion in recent weeks. If William observed this, he had not mentioned it to his brother or the head stockman. Miles knew his brother well enough to appreciate he just might not want to face any hard questions.

"William, maybe Joe could do with a bit of younger company right about now, do you think?"

William's unguarded look sent a shock wave through Miles. It was obvious his brother also worried about the possibility of Joe's despondency leading him to put an end to his misery and guilt.

"It wouldn't hurt, William," Miles suggested softly.

With gritted teeth, William gave a faint nod.

The three men watched Doug as he saddled up and collected his swag, the makings of tea and left-over damper along with a small billycan from the wagon. A water canteen now hung from the pommel of his saddle. A saddle bag borrowed from William held a halter and a set of hobbles. He patted the rifle in its leather clasp at his knee.

As he rode off, Doug's thoughts gnawed on several conversations overheard between the adults. His father, Geoff and Gazza all seemed to be worried for Joe. He sensed their deepest fear was that Joe might contemplate suicide following the death of Billy and the horrible things he had witnessed in the war. Uncle William said Joe was just coming to terms with the changes in his life.

Within less than an hour, Doug approached the tree line at the point where they had seen Joe disappear. Doug dismounted and squatted on his haunches searching in the dirt to identify the spoor of Joe's mount. Once satisfied, he mounted and nudged his horse forward into a brisk walk through the dry cloying dust wall of summer heat. The sparse shade offered little relief. His eyes dried quickly and he frequently found himself blinking repeatedly searching for moisture beneath his eyelids. The sun hung low in the western sky when the sudden lifting of the horse's ears and the sound of a gravelly voice brought Doug's attention from the trail he followed.

"What do you think you're doing, Doug? Can a man get no peace around here?" Joe stepped out from behind a scrubby bush.

Doug's surprise at the sudden appearance of Joe doubled at the sight of the changes embossed into his cousin's features. Gritted teeth, a down-turned mouth, harsh eyes and deep facial lines remained partly hidden by his sagging slouch hat. Doug's jaw dropped as he struggled to find an answer.

"Er … I just wanted a few days break myself."

"So, you thought you'd follow me?"

"I didn't think you'd mind – thought you might like a bit of company."

A wry grin waved away Joe's expression.

"I've just spent two years living hip and shoulder beside a bloody battalion. Why do you think I'd be wanting company? I just want to be on my own without any responsibility."

"I'm sorry. I'll go back if you want."

"A bit late for that. It'll be night soon. I can't have you getting lost in the dark."

Doug felt his pride battered. "I'll have you know I can follow a trail as good as our Gazza."

The wry grin flashed once again.

"So I've noticed." Joe turned and began to walk away. "Come on then, we'd better find a camp and make a fire."

A three-quarter moon's light shone down upon the two young men sitting on either side of the low fire. The tinkle of a horse bell and an occasional jangle of the hobble chains on their two mounts foraging nearby broke the silence. Doug used his boot to shove a partially burnt log further into the heat. He gave up trying to make conversation with Joe and welcomed the hypnotic effect of the flickering flames. Sometime later the hoot of an owl in a tree quite close to their camp lifted Doug's eyes from his dreaming.

"I'm calling it a night, Joe." He spoke softly and stood to roll out the saddle blanket near the warmth of their fire.

"Goodbye, Doug, sorry I was such poor company."

Doug glanced over at his cousin who had barely said a word since they finished their meal of damper and salted beef nearly two hours before. He stretched out on the blanket with his head resting on his saddle. Doug watched the still figure in the shadows until his heavy eyelids closed and sleep crept in. His last thoughts remained vague in his subconscious. *Joe said goodbye – not goodnight – that was odd.* But sleep dragged him further into oblivion.

Doug could not have said what had woken him. The first thing he noticed was the moon disappearing over the treetops to the west. A faint glow in the sky heralded the promise of an approaching dawn. Fresh flames from a new log on the fire told him Joe must have been awake within the past half hour or so. He raised himself on one elbow expecting to see the form of Joe's body asleep on the other side of the fire, but the area was bare except for the saddle and rolled-up swag. He swung his legs around and sat up. Grubby hands rubbed his eyes as he yawned. The shadows were silent. He strained his ears hoping to hear the clink of the horses' hobble chains nearby. Something small scurried off through the undergrowth. The owl continued its call. Steam from the quart pot of tea sitting at the edge of the heat drifted up in the soft glow of firelight.

Mother Nature stirred Doug into action. He jumped up and stumbled off to the deeper scrub. On his return, Joe had still not appeared. Doug poured tea into his pannikin and sipped at the stewed brew. The morning glow in the east brightened. With the tea in his hand and his head bowed Doug examined the marks in the dirt around the edge of the clearing. It only took a moment to pick out Joe's boot print with the inner side of his right heel worn away.

The tintinnabulation of the small horse bell he had tied around his mount's neck brought his gaze up searching through the bushes to the south. He whistled. The sound of the bell increased as the animal approached. Two horses entered the clearing.

So, Joe hadn't left in the night? Doug thought. He cooeed; a penetrating call. Silence remained his only answer.

A sense of dread rolled over him like black clouds over a rising sea. He pondered again on what it had been that woke him earlier. A thought slid into his consciousness. Was it the memory of a gunshot that hovered behind the dark curtain of his mind?

Has Joe actually shot himself like Geoff suggested he might?

Doug squashed down hard on the tremor where it began in his knees. All the confidence, developed since he turned seventeen and received a working man's wage, suddenly seeped away. Doug shook his head.

Bloody hell, I'm getting as mad as old Mabel.

Doug walked to his horse and rubbed the white blaze, a stark contrast, on the brown nose. The animal nickered. Doug removed the horse bell and tied it to the halter on Joe's horse.

"You'll have to stay around here until I find Joe." He spoke out loud, more as a comfort to himself than an understood piece of information for the horse. Going back to the brown animal with the white blaze, he removed the halter and slid the reins over the long head, settling the bit into place. He fixed the chin strap. Doug bent to remove the hobbles from the gelding's feet before he secured them around the mount's neck. The halter he placed inside his saddle bag. He stood in silence for a moment hoping to hear the approach of Joe's footsteps, but only the breeze rustling the leaves in the trees and the chittering of the black and white willy wagtails dancing through the branches fell upon his ears. He lifted the saddle and slipped it onto the horse's back. In a matter of seconds, the girth strap held firm as Doug swung himself up into the saddle. He moved off through the trees following Joe's trail. After going twenty yards, Doug realized he was headed towards the escarpment above the waterlily creek. It had been a popular campsite with his Uncle William and his father for as long as Doug remembered. When he approached the edge of the ridge, he lifted his head from the trail as a cool breeze, coming off the flats below, brought with it the fresh aroma of the leaves of the eucalypt trees below. He pulled the animal to a halt and breathed in the familiar fragrance.

A reluctance to go on held him back. He shivered and snapped to his horse, "Walk up." The track wound through the grove of chinkie apple bushes and wattle trees and past the fallen black boulder dislodged before his time. Doug's head swung about as he heard the tinkling of the bell on Joe's horse close behind. He paused at the last curve in the path before the large cleared area where he and his cousins and the Bardon children had spent many hours tearing about and disturbing the native wildlife with their squeals of excitement. To his left, a narrow trail led down to the waterhole. Along its length, he passed the several ambush sites used when they had played their cops and robbers or bushranger games. At the bottom of the descent, he paused. His horse began to snort and throw its head up and down as it pawed the ground. Doug felt a shiver run through his body once again. His boot nudged the animal forward. The horse refused to budge. Doug almost came a cropper as it shied sharply when a growl arose out of the thick reeds growing at the water's edge.

"There'll be little breakfast for anyone around here if you insist on clattering about like a goat in your grandma's kitchen."

312

Doug stiffened. He swallowed hard. The bush noises about him appeared to have silenced as his heart thudded against his rib cage. Even though he recognized his cousin's voice immediately, his gut swirled and his hands trembled on the reins. His brain felt like sludge as he struggled to find words.

"… Er … I noticed you were gone … er … figured you'd gone looking for something to eat. I came down for a swim before I thought I might rustle up some tucker. Looks like you beat me to it." Doug worked hard at softening the wobble in his voice.

Joe's slow smile as he emerged from the tall green stems told Doug he did not believe him.

"We could have had duck for breakfast but they all flew off before you were halfway down the trail."

"Sorry."

"That's alright, we won't starve. I've got several nice perch on the bank over there."

"I heard a gunshot." The words were out of Doug's mouth before he realized this might have been better not mentioned.

Joe gave a mirthless chuckle and a sardonic grin. "Did you think I'd topped myself, Dougie?"

Doug stood utterly flummoxed – lost for words.

"It's alright, mate, I have to admit there have been times the thought has appealed to me, especially when Mum's yelling her head off."

"She shouldn't be saying all those things she's been saying. It's not fair."

"Dougie lad, she's been blaming me for everything in the world since I wore nappies. I learnt to ignore it long ago. It drove Billy to distraction too. He didn't fancy being the little angel." Joe laughed. "He learnt to curse real good expressing his disapproval. Now come on, the goanna I shot is over there waiting to be cooked." As they made their way along the bank of the creek, Joe turned back to his younger cousin. "Dougie, I don't think I'll ever be likely to top myself. I've seen too many men die unnecessarily. I was close to dying myself with the malaria. So, no, I'm not ready to die just yet." He smiled a gentle smile.

The sun rode high in the sky when the two young men sipped on their pannikins of tea.

"Joe, you've heard Pops talking about the Strzeleki Stock Route in South Australia, do you know anything about it?"

"Not really, Billy reckoned Pops was in with a cattle duffer down there; a fellow named Henry Redman – no ... no ... – Harry Readford. Billy spent hours in the library at school reading anything he could find in the newspapers about it but I don't know if he learnt much. It was the only reading the lazy beggar ever did at school other than comics." Joe chuckled at his memory.

"Readman was the bloke who took all those cattle from Queensland down to a place in South Australia through the Strzelecki Desert, wasn't he?" A glint of interest sparkled in Doug's eyes.

Joe sat in silence staring into the trees.

"You know, after seeing how the nomad tribes in the Sinai Desert find their way with their stock and camels through the dry sands, probably no worse than our own; I guess it's all been done before." He turned his gaze back to his cousin. "What brought this up?"

"I've been thinking, I'd like to go and see a bit of the country, maybe on a droving trip to somewhere different. Can you imagine the challenges on a trip like that?"

This time Joe laughed out loud. Then, with a cynical face, he recalled his desert memories.

"Yeah, thirst, dust, sand, bully beef, rock-hard biscuits, empty canteens and more thirst."

Silence hung over the fireplace as Joe thought about Doug's ambitions.

"You'd want to know who you were travelling with. An amateur drover leading a group over there would soon have dead bodies everywhere."

"I once heard your dad talking about a friend of his who had been on the Strzelecki route a couple of times. He said they use a lot of camels as well as the horses. I thought if I asked Uncle William, he might put in a good word for me," Doug told Joe.

"Geez, Doug, can you ride a camel? Have you even seen a camel close-up? Ugly beggars, I can tell you … and bad-tempered, more often than not."

"No, but that's the exciting bit isn't it – learning new things?"

A wary look came into Joe's expression.

"I dunno. I can say for sure I never envied those boys riding the camels in the army." Joe stared into the hot coals of their fire.

"I figured they used the camels to carry all the gear and stores," Doug suggested.

"Hmmm, I guess so. I can't imagine them mustering cattle from the back of a camel." Joe looked across at his cousin. "Oh, why not? How about you and I ask him about it when we get back?" Joe offered. "I can't say the idea hasn't got me thinking too. I wouldn't have my mother screeching at me every minute of the day."

"Talking about going back, I thought I'd leave you to your peace and quiet tomorrow morning. I won't say a word about the Strzelecki possibilities until you get back." Doug smiled, the smile of a conspirator.

The early morning sunshine streamed through the window near the kitchen sink. William stood in front of the stove. His thoughts had drifted off to his troubled son while his hand moved the large spoon around and around in the porridge simmering in the small saucepan. Should he have let young Doug go after him? What if Joe did decide to end it all? It would be terrible for his nephew to have to witness such a thing. The boy had only just turned seventeen. Then again, his son was only eighteen but going on eighty, thanks to the bloody war.

He made a decision, *If they don't return by this afternoon, I'll go out and find them.*

The smell of burning food brought him back to the moment in a hurry. Some of the mixture had spilt onto the hot plate and lay sizzled in a blackened dollop.

William had barely stepped inside the open doorway of his wife's bedroom with the tray holding the plate of porridge and a spoon for Mabel's breakfast when she accosted him.

"Why have you sent Billy away again?"

"What are you talking about, woman? How many times do we have to tell you? Billy is dead. He was killed in the war."

William knew as soon as the words left his lips, he was about to regret having said them. He saw it in the widening of her eyes. The lids pushed back until a white edge of the cornea rimmed the perimeter of those black obsidian irises with the glint of fury. He spun around to protect the contents of the tray but it did not stop Mabel's long unkempt nails. Blood oozed through the sleeve of the shirt covering his upper arm and shoulder.

"Don't tell me lies. Don't keep telling me lies. I saw him riding out and he did not come back. You won't let him come to see me. You've driven him away, haven't you."

William drew a long breath.

"Mabel, I can promise you, Billy did not come back from the war. You must have seen Joe. He went out the morning before last. He'll be back in a few days."

"Liar! Don't you think I know my own Billy?" Her voice became a screech.

William walked off back to the kitchen.

"Your breakfast is out here if you want it," he called. After placing the tray on the kitchen table, he left, not even stopping to put on his work boots. He grabbed them up and stormed off down the stairs two at a time.

He idled around in the stables without any direction until he heard hoofbeats. Geoff and Miles were not due back before dark. They were over at the north cattle yards drafting out some young calves. The sun had passed its zenith. A puzzled frown moved slowly across his brow. *Where has the day gone?* When he went to investigate, he recognized Doug riding towards the stables. A wave of fear washed over him. His knees felt weak as if his legs were not going to hold him. All he could think of was, *Where's Joe?*

"G'day Uncle William, Joe's fine. He'll be home in a day or two."

"Thanks, Dougie."

William watched Doug unsaddle and brush his horse. "Where's Dad?" the lad asked.

"They're out at the north yards, Doug. They should be back soon."

"I'll go and see Mum and have a bath, I stink like a camp of bats."

"Okay." William watched Doug walk across the compound towards his home. The relief of hearing Joe was safe, became tempered with the thought that maybe Joe had fooled the younger innocent boy. Maybe he did plan to end everything but did not want to do so in front of his young cousin. Joe had always been a soft soul.

William threw down the leather he had been plaiting and strode out to the night paddock with a bridle in his hands. Several minutes later he and his horse thundered out towards the north yards.

CHAPTER THIRTY

Farewell

June 1920

All but Mabel had congregated at the stables. Even Gran and Pops had arrived with Mavis, Cissy and Maud to see Joe and Doug off on this new adventure. The young men led their horses, two each, one to ride and one with supplies, outside into the early morning dawn. Besides the two canteens of water draped across their shoulders, two other canteens hung from each pack horse.

Miles slipped his hand into his top pocket and removed several banknotes which he passed across into his son's hand.

"Remember, son, if you run short don't go hungry – just send me a wire."

Doug grinned. "I'm supposed to be going to make my way in the world not sponging off my dad."

"Just you remember."

"Thanks, Dad."

Fran and Mavis almost suffocated Doug with hugs and kisses.

"Look after yourself. Don't stay away too long."

William shook Joe's hand as if he did not want to let go. He wrapped an arm around his son's shoulder.

"You will come back, won't you? There are a whole lot of us here who love you." William removed his arm and ceased shaking Joe's hand. "Now are you right for cash? Can I give you a bit to be going on with?"

"No, Dad, the army has paid me."

At that moment, Cissy and Maud almost sent Joe to the ground as they threw themselves at him demanding his attention.

"Joe, you make sure you write."

"Yes, Joe, every week," Maud added emphasis to Cissy's earlier instruction.

Geoff led his family around the group shaking hands and wishing farewell to the adventurers. Ten-year-old Stewie shook hands with Joe and Doug. There'd be no kissing for him. Even though he was going to miss their company, he consoled himself with the knowledge he'd be the oldest boy on Billabong Downs now that Mick had gone off to university in Sydney. He hoped to see a lot more action and hopefully fewer school lessons. A satisfied smile lifted his expression as he recalled his recent day working in the cattle yards with his father and Mr. Miles helping with the gates as they drafted calves.

Joe tossed Doug a messaged nod. "Let's get out of here."

The silent memo was received and in unison, the pair mounted their horses and secured their hold on the pack horse behind.

Both young men looked up at the sound of hoofbeats.

Joe's eyebrows lifted to near his hat brim. He looked at his father. "Someone else leaving home?"

"Don't fret, son, you won't have a stowaway with you. Stewie's gone to open the gate."

Squeals and handwaving followed them until they disappeared out of sight. No one noticed the sour expression on Evie's face. She knew she was a better rider than her brother and should have been sent to open and shut the gate.

William, Geoff, Maggie and their children went to town for supplies. They delivered Mavis to her grandparents in Charters Towers while William escorted his daughters back to the Dawson family to attend school in Townsville.

Miles stamped his feet at the bottom of the stairs to his house. He sat on the bottom step and removed his boots.

"Hello, darling," Fran called from their front garden gate. "It seems so quiet with all the children gone."

"How's your patient over there?" Miles lifted his gaze and nodded towards William and Mabel's house.

"I don't know, Miles, I'm becoming worried. She hasn't spoken a word to me since everyone left three days ago. She mumbles away to herself without stopping. The little she eats would hardly feed a mistletoebird. I can't get near her to bathe her, let alone sponge her. Her hair is like a rat's nest but she won't let me brush it."

"I can't see what you're worrying about. Just enjoy the peace and quiet."

"I'll be glad when William gets back. It's like the calm before a storm."

"I'm expecting everyone back tomorrow. I would suggest, my little peahen, you come upstairs and we make the most of their absence." Fran grinned but a furrow still marked her forehead.

"You're right, oh lord and master, the last one upstairs does the dishes." She laughed out loud as she leant heavily on her husband's shoulders to edge around him and race up the stairs.

Miles and Gazza appeared from the stable at the sound of the horses hauling the wagon as it entered the homestead compound. Fran waved from where she collected the dried washing off the clothesline. Like chickens spilling out of a hen house, the three Bardon siblings hoped to make a quick escape, but Maggie's sharp tone brought her children to heel.

"Each of you children can carry something inside before you disappear, thank you." Maggie's eyes twinkled as she greeted Miles and Gazza who were already helping Geoff unharness the horses.

"Did the girls get off to school without any protests?" Miles asked his brother.

"Your Mavis was no trouble, but my two girls didn't want to leave their mother in the condition she is in. I hope Mabel hasn't given you and Fran any trouble?"

"No, William, we've not heard a peep out of her the whole time you've been away – except for her mumbling all day. Fran was becoming worried."

"That sounds ominous." William climbed up into the wagon and handed boxes and bags of fresh supplies down to his brother. "Any chance she may be improving?"

"Fran thought it might be a calm before a storm."

"She is most likely right. Improvement is a forlorn hope, I guess."

CHAPTER THIRTY-ONE

Mabel

July 1920

The white mosquito net appeared as a ghostlike Indian tepee where it hung from the hook in the rafter of the verandah. The ends, tucked in tightly under the mattress, prevented entry for any insects, snakes or other unwanted sleeping partners. It glowed in the moonlight streaming through the wooden blinds. Dressed in blue, cotton pyjama pants, William slept despite the irritation of perspiration as it trickled from his body. His light snores were accompanied by the snuffles of the old white dog named Snowy, asleep on the mat at the foot of the bed. William grunted at the creak of the timbers of the old house, but he did not stir.

Mabel stood above her husband. Her eyes stretched wide open and her lips pulled back from her teeth in a chilling rictus grin. Like stalks of straw, unkempt hair stood out from her head. With arms raised high, the blade trembled slightly in her clenched hands.

The dog's low growl caused one of William's thick brown eyebrows to lift, but the eye remained shut. A second louder growl opened both eyes. His gaze took in the glint of steel of the raised blade in the moonlight. Before his mind translated what he was looking at, the rush of the dog's body towards the arms holding the large knife triggered his response. The descent of the arms had begun when he threw himself to the far side of the bed just as the dog collapsed onto the mattress dragging the net taut. A spray of warm fluid covered William. He smelt the blood. He tasted it on his lips.

The dog's teeth tore only minor lacerations on Mabel's pale arms. Snowy's defence was a shade too late to prevent the realignment of the blade. The point entered the dog's chest and ripped down to the animal's groin. Mabel lifted the blade and struck again and again in frenzied repetition. Explosive grunts of effort burst forth with the bloodied spittle from her lips. Her banshee wail shattered the quiet night and echoed far and wide throughout the homesteads of Billabong Downs.

William struggled to unwind his feet from the mosquito net. He partially fell to the floor. With one arm he propelled himself forward towards where his wife continued stabbing at the bloodied body of the dog. Coming in behind her, he wrapped his arms around Mabel clamping his fingers over the hands holding the knife. The power within the frail body surprised him. His hands slipped in the blood covering her arms, her hands and her fingers. Mabel almost released herself. He applied more pressure until the thrusts of the knife lessened dribbling away to a stillness. Both husband and wife remained paralysed in time until Mabel began to sag. She fell forward onto the remains of the dog's slashed carcass pulling William along with her. They both lay still with William holding tight to the hands on the knife. The stickiness of blood surrounded him. Its coppery taste filled his mouth and nose.

With the jerky movements of an old man, William began to raise his body dragging the unresponsive Mabel with him. At that moment, he heard a shout from his brother.

"William, is everything alright?"

"Here, on the verandah, I need a hand."

Miles arrived at a run holding a lantern high. "Holy shit, what's going on?"

"Here, Miles, can you take the knife? I'm not game to let her hands go. Mabel might look as if she couldn't hold a full teacup but don't be fooled, she's as strong as a bullock."

The sudden intake of Fran's breath from the open doorway between the bedroom and the verandah as she took in the scene, lifted both the men's heads.

"You'd better not see this, Fran. It's pretty gruesome." Miles attempted to protect his wife as he unwound Mabel's clenched fingers one by one, from the handle of the knife.

Fran swallowed before she answered. Uncertainty flashed across her gaze.

"Rubbish, Miles, you men are going to need a hand to clean Mabel up and settle her down again."

Another shout echoed up the back stairs, "Are you okay there, William?" The head stockman, Geoff Bardon and his wife Maggie had arrived to offer help having been woken by Mabel's wailings.

It was Miles who answered. "Thanks, Geoff, we'll be alright now. Go back to bed and enjoy some sleep."

William stood and lifted the limp body of his wife into his arms. He turned to his brother.

"I'll take her downstairs for a shower with me." He almost stumbled as his body took the weight. "Can you bring down a couple of fresh towels and a clean nighty for her, Fran?"

With Mabel sitting on a wooden chair under the spray of water, a shiver ran down William's body at the sight, within the light of the lantern, of the face of horror staring out from the features of this stranger.

"Close your eyes or they'll sting when I soap up your hair." But the eyes remained open to their full extent and beyond. The lips remained drawn back exposing her gums.

The drain ran blood as he cleaned both their bodies. A knock sounded on the door.

"Here are fresh towels and clothes for you both," Fran called.

William held Mabel's shoulder as he instructed, "Don't move while I get the towels."

His words were wasted. Mabel was past hearing. She was past moving. Her body remained in a catatonic state.

He hurried to dry and dress himself before he struggled to do the same for Mabel which was not easy with her body drooped in the chair and unresponsive to verbal commands.

"Can you walk up the stairs yourself?" But Mabel did not hear or acknowledge his question.

With the blood cleansed from his body, the aftershock crept into William's muscular frame. He felt the trembling within his limbs and a weakness in his spine. He leant heavily against the cool corrugated iron of the shower room wall and breathed deeply. Slowly his strength returned and he lifted his wife into his arms.

"In here, William," Fran called from where she had made up the single bed next to where Mabel usually slept. As William lay Mabel on the clean sheets, Fran explained, "Miles told me what happened. I am sorry, but you will need to tie Mabel's arms and legs to the side of the bed, and that will be easier in the single bed."

Tears stood out on William's eyelashes. "Has it come to this, Fran?" He swallowed the tears of his regret – a noisy swallow through the spasm in his throat.

She bit her lip and nodded her head slowly. "You will not be safe, William, unless we do."

"I know this has to be done, Fran." William held his hands out with the palms upwards in a sign of submission. "Mabel spends most of her days mumbling curses upon Joe and me and the world. She threatens to kill herself. She has refused to take the pills the doctor prescribed. She always refused to believe there was anything wrong with her. You and Maggie should not have to contend with all this extra workload."

Fran moved over to rest a hand on William's shoulder.

"I think we all need a good cup of tea." As if on cue, Miles arrived with a tray upon which stood a steaming teapot, two pannikins, a china cup for Fran, a bowl of sugar, a milk jug and two teaspoons. "Oh, Miles, you are a saint." Fran moved to clear space on the small bedside table. She helped Miles settle the tray and began to pour the tea before she went on with what she had been saying. "William, you must not fret on our account. Maggie and I have known Mabel for more than fifteen years. She wasn't always like this. She has been a good friend until this illness consumed her."

William swallowed. "Thanks, Fran." He turned his head to his brother, "And thank you too, Miles. I'm so proud and grateful that you are my brother." William sucked in a noisy breath and the tears trembled on his eyelids. "She killed my dog. Poor old Snowy – my beautiful dog – after years of faithful service, he ends his life this way."

The three stood sipping their tea struggling to come to terms with the events of the night. It was Fran who broke the dark silence.

"I think Mabel has exhausted herself. Even though her eyes are still wide open and that terrible grin remains on her lips, I'm sure she is asleep and should remain so until morning."

"I thought that when I tucked her in last night." The tears fell. William sobbed for several moments. He dragged the back of his hand across his face and spoke again. "I'm sorry, but I have to face it. Mabel needs professional psychiatric care where she can be watched both day and night. I'm sorry I have not sought this earlier. I kept hoping she would come to terms with the loss of Billy. I've put us all at risk."

"William, I remember you said recently Mabel was mixing Joe up with Billy. Maybe she saw Joe and Doug leaving last week and thinks Billy has gone again."

"Maybe, Fran, maybe. Who knows what goes on inside that head?"

Fran held her tongue on her prediction of the changes this night's events would mean for everyone at Billabong Downs. She collected the tea things and placed them onto the tray.

"Come on, Miles, I'll clean this lot up. Will you finish taking everything down to the rubbish burner and will you bury Snowy? You'd better go on home then and get some sleep. It will be a long day tomorrow, I should think." On her return to the bedroom, she found William slumped in a chair by his wife's side. Mabel lay stretched out with her arms and ankles tied firmly with leather belts to the frame on either side of the bed. Pillowcases had been folded to protect her skin under the straps. Fran stood in the doorway gathering her thoughts before she spoke. "William, you'd best go next door and try to catch a few hours' sleep until morning. I'll rest here in the chair beside her."

"Fran, I can't sleep. I'll sit in the other chair and watch. It may not be safe for you here alone."

Morning found the community, except for Gazza the roustabout, gathered on the verandah of William's house. Maggie Bardon sat in the room with Mabel whose eyelids were now closed and her mouth had returned to normal.

William went to speak but yawned instead.

"Sorry," he held his hand over his mouth. "You are now all aware of the developments in Mabel's condition and I have reached the conclusion that she needs professional care. None of us will be safe in our beds while she is in this state." His face began to dissolve into tears again. He coughed and drew a deep breath. "Miles and I have discussed our next step and we have agreed that he and Fran will accompany me and Mabel to the doctor at Charters Towers." He turned to look at Geoff Bardon and his wife Maggie. "I'll need you to remain here and keep the place running, please Geoff. Thank Heavens Cissy and Maud are in Townsville and haven't had to witness their mother's actions of last night." He looked up again. "I hope young Evie and the boys did not hear the goings on either, Maggie."

"No, William, they have no idea."

"Geoff, will you ask Gazza to drive the wagon into town for us."

"No trouble, Boss, I'll let him know," It was Geoff who answered.

"I imagine us three will be caught up with all the medical goings on at the hospital. It may take days. Gazza can pick up any supplies in town and bring the wagon home." William's mouth opened and closed as if he was loath to say out loud the following sentence. He cleared his throat. "I'll not be at all surprised if they want to send her through to the Reception House for the insane at Townsville. We'll travel with her." He almost choked on his next words. "I'll talk to Cissy and Maud and Mabel's parents when we arrive in Townsville."

Throughout the rough and hot journey lying on the fibre mattress in the back of the wagon, Mabel's eyes remained partially open. Not a word passed her lips. She refused the sips of water offered. The disinfectant tincture Fran had painted on the lacerations along her arms began to run in the sweat. Brown blotches covered her exposed skin. Fran and Miles between them strove to hold the parasol above Mabel's head to keep the burning sun off her face. From his position on the opposite side of his wife, William's head bowed as if under an enormous weight.

Gazza, in the driver's seat, brought the horses to a gentle stop at the hospital gate. William attempted twice to speak. He felt his tongue dry and thick inside his mouth.

"Fran, I think it best if you go in and talk to the doctor. I'll wait here with Miles in case Mabel has another turn."

"Of course, William."

Fran's heart sank a little lower with each footstep as she walked down the corridor to the Sister's Station. Her wait at the desk while the woman delivered a message to Doctor Munson seemed to take forever. When the doctor walked into the room, she struggled to contain the rush of tears threatening to overflow. Fran swallowed several times before she felt able to begin her report. Doctor Munson listened intently.

"Thanks, Fran, I see you haven't forgotten how to deliver a concise and complete report since your nursing days."

"Thank you, Doctor Munson. I feel so guilty. Mabel was my friend and I feel I have let her down."

"You have not done that, girl. You and Maggie Bardon have done a magnificent job over the years as this has developed. I believe the wardsmen and your men have settled Mabel in the one padded locked room we have. We'll be able to keep her here for a few days and see if she improves with sedation. If I find there is nothing left that I can do to help her, I fear she will need to be sent on to the Townsville Reception House for the Insane."

Fran nodded. Exhaustion and sadness rendered her speechless.

Four mornings after leaving Billabong Downs, William, Miles and Fran made up a sober group as they alighted from the train at the Townsville station just as the sun appeared over the horizon. Bayden and Isabelle Dawson were there to meet them. They all watched in silence as a sedated Mabel was removed from the special carriage, with its padded compartment, by two male staff members of the Reception House. She was placed on a mattress inside an ambulance wagon.

"I have a carriage outside. We will go up to the place and see what is happening. I spoke to one of the doctors from there last night." Bayden ushered everyone towards their transport.

It was Isabelle who suggested the family might appreciate a light breakfast and cup of tea first after their long night trip.

"That would be nice, thanks, Isabelle. But I'd like to see Mabel settled in first." William replied.

Fran stepped forward.

"Perhaps we should follow the ambulance out to the Reception House. They will want to ask us questions, no doubt." She turned to William who nodded his acceptance. Fran turned back towards Isabelle Dawson. "Once they have admitted her, the doctors will want to examine her. That will take some time, I'm sure. We could have breakfast then, if that suits you, Isabelle."

"It will be no trouble."

Doctor Elliott Lundy watched the family as they disappeared around the corner on their way out into the sunshine. He turned back to open the observation window into one of several padded cells at the Townsville Reception House for the Insane.

Compassion filled his eyes. He found it hard to believe the woman in front of him had been the sought-after Mabel Dawson – the queen of the debutantes in Townsville over twenty years ago. In those days the stunning young lady with those obsidian eyes and flawless pale skin held his heart in her hands until the bloke from the bush came to town on a whim and stole her away.

He watched this sorry replica of Mabel as she stood facing the padded wall stroking the strong canvas covering. Glazed eyes, now with only a hint of their past exquisiteness, stared at her fingers brushing left to right and back again. He leant away from the window and dropped his gaze to his feet. A ridge separated the deep blue eyes edged with lines developed over years of study, well into most nights, under poor lighting. He was aware William Daley still cared for his once stunning bride. The man refused to make any charges against Mabel for attempted murder knowing to do so meant her incarceration in a filthy cell in the city jail, there to rot. During their interview, the man's emotions overwhelmed him on several occasions as he told of the past three years of his wife's deterioration. Elliott had read it all before in the letters from Doctor Munson.

He lifted his gaze once more towards the patient seen through the small window. The woman dressed in the large white gown now waved her hands in front of her face as if warding off something or someone only she could see. Maybe she was warding off her own unwanted thoughts or visions. Elliott jumped when a low growl began deep within her throat. The volume of noise rose in a crescendo until it sounded very much like a lioness protecting her cub. Urine trickled down Mabel's legs into a puddle at her bare feet. The ammonia smell of urine wafted up to the open viewing window. A shiver ran down Elliott's spine. Mabel threw herself to the floor. Her limbs spread out around her. Her hands and fingers twisted – her ankle joints pulled up in a spasm. She lay still. At that moment, the ward sister interrupted Doctor Lundy's observations.

"Will you be giving the afternoon lecture later, Doctor?"

Elliott shook his head to redirect his thoughts.

"Yes, Sister, I want to talk about the various approaches to the treatment of shell shock and in particular the revolutionary treatment by Arthur Hurst at the hospital in Devon."

"Thanks, Doctor, I'll endeavour to have as many staff as possible attend."

"Oh, Sister, if there is anyone available, this woman will need cleaning up."

"I'll have a nurse and an orderly spare in five minutes."

In his peripheral vision, the movement from the padded room caught his attention. Doctor Lundy turned again towards the viewing panel. Mabel now was on her knees with her two hands clasped over her head as if holding something. Her joined fists pounded down and up and down and up repeatedly onto the padded floor as if stabbing someone. She began to wail. Prolonged screeches filled the room. The words from the reports and from the family made Elliot immediately think his patient might be reliving her attack on her husband. It certainly seemed that way.

Regret and lack of confidence in the ability of the infant science of modern psychiatry to help this caricature of his past love brought tears to the doctor's eyes. He blinked them away.

The woman collapsed into a crumpled and silent heap.

The broken sunbeams pouring through the branches of the trees outside lit the breakfast room where Isabelle and Bayden Dawson and their guests sat quietly while the maid delivered their meals prepared by the cook busy in the kitchen next door.

As they took up their spoons to eat the porridge, the desultory conversation quietened. William stirred his oats with little interest, first one way and then the other. He sipped at the spoon lifted to his lips. His gaze never left the plate but his eyes stared into his soul. When the maid returned with hot servings of bacon and eggs along with a plate holding golden toast, the interruption to his thoughts lifted his gaze and straightened his drooped shoulders.

Fran and Miles struggled to maintain some polite conversation with their hosts and with Cissy and Maud. The sisters sat silent, both with swollen reddened eyes wide with shock.

William managed only one mouthful of egg before his chair scraped on the polished floor as he rose sharply to his feet.

"Sssorry, I need air." He stumbled outside.

Cissy and Maud rose to assist their father. Fran reached across the table and rested her hands on theirs.

"Leave him for a moment, girls. He needs time to process all that has happened."

Once outside, William drew in long, deep and noisy breaths. He brushed at the tears leaking down his face. Of their own volition, his feet took him to the seat beside the rose garden. His eyes did not see the many immature rosebuds – the promise of a glorious spring ahead.

He dropped to the seat where long ago he and Mabel had spent blissful hours courting. A place where once he sat tall, his heart swollen with pride as its thudding beats delivered his love and anticipation to all corners of his body. Today his shoulders drooped. His gaze fell upon his boots. His heart lay heavy in his chest as its feeble beat delivered only sorrow, regret, guilt and blame.

Sometime later Cissy's whisper at his side lifted his head.

"Daddy, can Maud and I sit here with you? We brought you a cup of tea, just how you like it."

William reached his arms out to welcome his girls.

The three sat, each with their thoughts until Maud cleared her throat.

"Daddy, will you write and tell Joe what has happened?"

The quiet sat gently upon their shoulders once again as William pondered his answer.

"No, darling, not just yet. There is nothing he can do for us here, right now. Your brother has earned his peace."

CHAPTER THIRTY-TWO

Birdsville Races

September 1920

In the glow of the pre-dawn, water splashed up around the two men as they bathed in one of the many shallow channels of the Diamantina River. The four horses grazed on the green pickings between the streams. The soft tinkling of the horse bell rose on the still air.

"You sure there's none of that Birdsville Indigo plant we were told to look out for?" Doug turned an anxious gaze towards their mounts.

"Nah, we checked the place out pretty well last night, when we arrived. Anyway, it's time we moved on. It'll be as hot as hell shortly."

The pair climbed out of the stream and dragged their clothes on over their wet skin.

"Do you reckon we'll make Birdsville tonight?"

"As long as you don't mess about with that compass, Doug. You're in charge, remember."

"And if I do mess up … what will happen then?"

"I guess we'll be eating grass with the horses – that's assuming we don't get lost in one of the many deserts out here." Joe grinned as he patted his hip pocket feeling the backup compass. As far as he knew Doug was unaware of its presence.

As they approached their campsite near the red gum trees, a flock of corellas lifted out of the branches in a rush of white feathers and a raucous protest of indignation at having been disturbed. Having travelled nearly two months overland, Joe and Doug had developed a smooth rhythm in packing up their camp and readying for each day's journey.

The men rode in a companionable silence taking in the wide plains broken with occasional stumpy tough growth of bushes around dry gutters gouged out during infrequent wet seasons. Doug called them to a halt. He lifted the sweat-stained hat from his head. Using his sleeve, he wiped the perspiration from his brow.

"That's a tree line out there isn't it, Joe?" He nodded to a dark scud on the far horizon.

"Reckon so."

"Probably water nearby."

"Most likely."

They angled their horses a little to the south-west.

Within the hour a small settlement began to appear. Buildings on either side of a main street were identified. Beneath the trees they had seen earlier, a wide lagoon spread out like an oasis in a barren land. The sound of birds squawking reached their ears as several pelicans circled the area before returning to settle on the calm waters.

What could have been the roar of a crowd of people shouting fell faintly upon their ears.

"What the devil is that, do you reckon, Joe?"

"I'm not sure but look past the town, further along the waterway. Isn't that a mob of people?" Joe pointed

"Maybe," Doug's face lit up, "You're right, it is a mob of people. I can't see exactly what they're up to. I can't see any cattle."

It was half an hour later before the two riders made their way through the main street of Birdsville. Of the few buildings, they recognized the welcome sight of two hotels built of sandstone and with wide shady awnings stretching out to the edge of the dirt road. The only sign of life was a mongrel dog sniffing around the front of a general store. Even the police station appeared unattended.

"There's a post office, Joe. I must post the letter to the folks back home before we go on."

"What day of the week is it? Shouldn't there be kids in the classroom? That looks like a schoolhouse to me." A frown added to the lines as Joe screwed up his eyes against the sunlight.

They hauled in their reins at the sight of a man who galloped into the town on a buckskin horse. He skidded to a halt in front of the shop where a sign, attached to the building's awning by three leather straps, declared this the abode of the "Birdsville Saddlers." The wooden sign squeaked as it swayed gently in the warm breeze channelling down the street. Doug and Joe walked their mounts and the two packhorses to meet the new arrival.

"Is it always this quiet, here?" Joe asked.

"Quiet? You're just in the wrong place, strangers. If you're looking for the races you need to go another mile straight ahead. Towards the Diamantina Crossing." A puff of dust lifted from the man's booted feet as he jumped from his horse. A dirty finger at the end of a long, tanned arm seen below rolled up sleeves of a khaki shirt pointed in the direction from where he had come. The chap dragged a key out of his hip pocket. "If you wait a second, I'll show you where, I've just got to pick up something here." The pointing finger then touched the brim of his hat. "I'm Ned Jackson."

Before Joe or Doug could reply, the man disappeared inside the timber slab shop. He had been telling the truth in what he said. It was indeed only a short time before he reappeared with two new bridles in his hands.

"Come on then, let's go. They can't start the next race until I deliver one of these bridles to Bert Hennessy." The man led off at a trot.

At the mention of the name Bert Hennessy, surprise filled Doug's and Joe's faces. Doug's left eyebrow lifted as he glanced at his cousin. Could this be the man they were looking for? But they rode in silence taking in the scene as they approached what Ned had called the Birdsville Races.

There must have been more than a hundred people, mostly men. The parasols of the few women added colour to the crowd. Joe and Doug both noted the quality of many of the horses tied to a hitching rail set apart from the gathering.

Joe spoke quietly to his cousin.

"Looks like thoroughbred stock over there. They must be the horses for the races."

Doug nodded. But his attention was drawn to the several vehicles he had seen parked behind a sapling-posted awning where ladies toiled at a bench making sandwiches. The aroma from the contents of two large steel pans over a fire near this bark shanty diverted Doug's focus from the two motor cars. His mouth watered. With a long fork held in one hand, the cook transferred slabs of beef onto a dish held in the other hand. A lady stood in the shade of the awning ready to receive the plate of cooked meat for placement on the sandwiches which the ladies were selling at the stall.

"There's a water trough if your horses are looking for a drink. You'll find something more to your liking in the refreshment shed." Ned Jackson pointed to where a group of men, dressed in their best clothes and all with felt hats of one type or another on their heads, gathered in a group around a ramshackle corrugated roof held up by more sapling posts. Great gusts of laughter rose from the crowd at intervals. Doug and Joe walked their horses to the water trough and let them drink before tying them up to one of the many hitching rails. The pair followed Ned, the saddler, on foot, to where several men were gathered around the thoroughbred horses.

"Here you are, Bert, one of these two should suit," the cousins heard Ned say as he handed over the bridles to a tall, snowy-headed man whose broad shoulders and muscles told of years of hard work. The curve of his legs hinted at long periods wrapped around the belly of a horse. Dark blue eyes surrounded by loose tanned facial skin sparkled out from under an overhang of brow. Bert examined both bridles before returning one to Ned.

"How's your rider doing?" Ned asked as Bert placed a new bridle on his horse's head and began to adjust the length of the cheek straps.

"Hmmm, well, there's me next problem. The vet's 'ad a look at me jockey and 'e says the lad's got a broken arm. The fellas are pouring the rum down 'is neck as we speak before the vet'll try to set the bone in 'is arm." Bert looked up as he spoke to Ned. He noticed the two newcomers at his side. "Where'd you drag these two likely lads up from Ned?"

"Oh, Bert meet er … what did you say your names were, lads?"

Joe stepped forward with his hand out.

"Joe Daley and Doug Daley from up Charters Towers way in Queensland."

Bert Hennessy jumped to his feet. The thoroughbred snapped its head back almost dragging the reins out of the man's hand.

"Daley, from Charters Towers? You wouldn't 'appen to know a William Daley out there on a place called Billabong Downs?"

Joe turned to his cousin with a smile.

"Looks like we've got the right Bert Hennessy." He turned back to the man holding the reins of an impressive grey horse in his hand. "William is my father and this," he pointed to Doug at his side, "is my cousin, Doug Daley, son of Miles Daley from up there too."

Bert Hennessy stared into the boys' faces for a long moment.

"Well, there's no mistaking who you are, now I can get a good look at you both. Joe, you are the spitting image of your old man, and Doug, you look so much like your dad did back in the nineties when the three of us knocked about the Northern Territory." He dusted his right hand on the sides of his pants and shook hands with the two young men. "Any chance you can ride a 'orse as good as your father could, Joe?"

"I know my way around a horse. Why?"

"I need a jockey to ride this animal."

Joe paid closer attention to the flighty grey creature. He walked around rubbing it down and lifting its feet, speaking softly all the while. He wiped the animal's face and scratched its forehead.

"Yeah, Mister Hennessy, I'll give your stallion a run."

"Good, that's all set then, I'll just 'ave a word with the chairman of the race club and let 'im know there'll be a change in jockeys."

A small nondescript man with oil dribbling from his brown hair, almost but not quite hidden by a straw hat, jumped forward.

"You can't just do that, Mister Hennessy. This will have to go before the committee."

"You reckon, Simpson?" Bert gave a piercing whistle that lifted all eyes of those within the small hut near the finishing line of the race track. "Hey, Rabbit, is it okay to replace the wounded jockey with this fellow here?"

"No trouble, Bert. Send him over and I'll get his details."

Bert turned back to the Simpson man, "There you are, mate, all sorted with the committee."

The man named Simpson stomped off to check the track before the next race.

"I hope I haven't caused you any trouble, Mister Hennessy." Joe tended.

"Nah, nothing that can't be sorted with a shot of whiskey later. The man's a bit of a pompous arse but he has a magic way with figures and looks after the club's books without a charge."

"So, when is this race, Mister Hennessy?"

Bert Hennessy pulled a fob watch hanging from a chain on his waistcoat.

"Thirty minutes, give or take – and you can cut the Mister business, Bert's me name."

"Is it okay if I take your horse for a bit of a warm-up, Bert? Give us both a chance to get to know each other."

"Go for your life, mate, his name's Smokey." Bert shook his head as if disbelieving his eyesight, "Struth, you're so like your old man."

Joe landed lightly in the saddle soothing the horse with his quiet voice. They trotted off following the straight line of posts that marked out the race track.

"He was in the Australian Light Horse." Pride coloured the words Doug spoke to Bert Hennessy.

Bert looked across at the cousin.

"Now, why doesn't that surprise me." Bert took another look at the man in the saddle of his prize horse. "Can I buy you a drink, Doug?"

"Not just now thanks, Bert, I'm hoping to go and have a closer look at those couple of cars I saw on the way over here."

"I know a bloke who knows a bloke who owns one of those cars. Let me know and I'll get him to take you for a spin."

"Oh, Mister, that would be top-notch."

At the sound of an old cowbell, the crowd rushed from the food and refreshment areas like a bunch of lemmings following the leader – everyone intent on claiming the best site near the finishing post to watch the winners of the final race come in.

In the distance, Simpson strutted around the starting post where eight horses and their riders were lined up behind a large hemp rope lying on the ground across the track. In his hand, he held the starting flag which at a closer glance appeared to be a man's large white handkerchief attached to a length of stick by thick cotton stitches of purple thread.

Bert insisted Joe wore the Hennessy yellow racing shirt over his usual clothes. Beneath him, he felt the grey horse named Smokey shuffle his feet persistently. A tremor ran through the muscled mount. Joe's glance took the measure of his competition. On his immediate right, a small narrow-eyed bloke sat confidently. The red coloured shirt clashed violently with the man's hair. Second, on his right, the fellow wore a dark blue shirt with a large white circle on the chest. The last five riders were seen in a blur as his restless horse stomped his front hoof on the ground. At the end of the line, he did note the green shirt with white stripes near a purple shirt. Between them and himself, he thought he could identify a plain green and a plain white shirt.

Smokey's persistent pawing of the ground upset Mister Simpson.

"Can you not keep that horse under control there?"

Joe ignored the man and kept soothing his restless mount.

When the red shirt spoke, Joe did not at first register what the man said.

"Is that what you are, a Yella one?" He pointed to Joe's shirt.

The comment was relegated to the bin of ignorance along with Simpson's question.

At the other end of the track, marked out in a straight line one mile in length with sapling posts driven into the ground every two hundred and twenty yards apart, in the steward's shelter, the man Bert had called Rabbit was losing patience. The field glasses were pressed hard against his face.

"Flaming hell, Simpson, will you get off the pot? Those horses'll all be worn out before you even let them go." Given the advice was only mumbled, it was only the chuckle of the two men at his side that could be heard.

341

But Simpson did not hear this gee-up. When he was satisfied that no horse was going to have an unfair advantage, he dropped the flag.

And they were away – well not quite.

Smokey threw up his head when the white flag fluttered close to his face. The horse stepped back two paces before Joe regained control. Whether by accident or by design the red-shirted rider and his horse angled straight over to where Joe had planned to be. Smokey's falter prevented the weight of the red-haired rider and his horse from smashing into his off-side.

Joe hauled on the off-side rein and guided Smokey into the spaces made available by that horse and another as well. With his eyes half closed against the dust thrown up by the horses' hooves, Joe followed the dark blue shirt with its white circle forward and through another gap. The horses began to spread out.

At the halfway mark, Joe and Smokey were in the middle of the pack. Joe felt the ripple of muscles beneath him and noted the easy breathing of his mount. He tucked in behind two brown horses, one with its rider in the blue and white shirt and the other with the plain green-shirted rider. Further in front rode two riders – purple shirt and white shirt – by less than twenty yards.

Joe heard the strained breathing of the horse under the blue and white shirt. He eased Smokey to the left and passed two horses. Only the two leaders were out in front of Smokey and beginning to pull away by the time the three-quarter mark flashed by the corner of his eyes. Joe was pleased to feel Smokey in a smooth stride and breathing freely. He nudged him with his heel.

He could have yelled with delight as he felt the animal respond. The race was on. With one hundred yards to go, the three horses were neck and neck. The crowd screamed their encouragement for their favourite horse or jockey or where ever they had their money placed. To Joe, it seemed Smokey lapped up the attention and moved ahead just in time. He had no idea which horse had won but he felt it was between Smokey and the purple shirt.

The people were going wild. Hats and colourful parasols waved about in the air. Joe let Smokey come back to a canter and then a trot at his own pace. He still did not know which horse had won the race as he made his way back to the judges.

Bert struggled through the many well-wishers as he made his way towards his returning horse. Smokey shied left and right at the racket, the people and the damn cowbell ringing out its joy. Joe remained steady in the saddle talking softly as Bert approached.

"Well done, lad, I knew any son of William Daley could take this old escapee from the glue factory on to a win," Bert called as he freed himself from the people at his side. He walked over to rub the animal's face. Smokey recognized the man's smell immediately. The long nose nuzzled into the man's barrel chest seeking the sugar cubes that usually resided in the top right-hand pocket. Bert made sure he was not disappointed.

"So, Mister Hennessy, did we win or not?"

"Smokey won, Joe, by a nose, but an inch is as good as a mile. Come on, they'll be wanting to take photos when you receive the prize."

Joe looked over the tops of the heads to see his cousin standing back from the crowd a grin as wide as all Australia on his face. He raised a lazy salute.

CHAPTER THIRTY-THREE

The Jolly Roger

December 1920

After nearly three months of showing steady but slow improvement, Doctor Elliott Lundy agreed to allow Mabel Daley out for Christmas. Strict conditions were placed on her leave permit. Mabel was to go from the hospital to her parent's house where she was to stay for two nights.

Cissy and Maud helped prepare a room for their mother.

"You really should not be doing those mundane chores. We have a housekeeper and a cleaning lady for that, my girls," their grandmother admonished.

Cissy and Maud shared a knowing smile. Lucky Grandmama did not visit Billabong Downs too often. She would have a seizure if she knew half of what they got up to there.

Excitement filled the air along with the tempting aromas wafting out into the house each time the kitchen door was opened. Every vase had been commandeered for use, filled with numerous flowers from the prolific garden outside. A sprinkling of a few tasteful Christmas decorations hung from elegant holders on display around the house.

Grandpapa was going to collect their father from the railway station before lunch.

"Please can't we go, Grandpapa?" the girls called in unison.

"No, I am sorry, girls. I would have to ask Gordie to change from the sulky to the carriage if we all went. I think your Grandmama has the poor man worn to a frazzle as it is." Bayden Dawson disentangled

344

himself from the arms of his granddaughters. "Besides, I'll be using the sulky when your father and I collect your mother from the Reception House after lunch." Mr. Dawson did not mention he wanted to talk with William in detail about the restrictions the doctor had placed on them all relating to Mabel's leave.

Dark clouds rolled in across the ocean after lunch on Christmas Eve as the horses pulling the sulky clipped clopped along the front driveway between the border edgings of blossoming white and yellow daisies. Bayden Dawson held the reins while William Daley sat beside his wife, in the seat behind.

"Looks like we might get a downpour before Christmas Eve is over." Bayden turned to speak to his daughter and her husband. Mabel sat silent, hunched over in the corner of the seat. She offered no reply.

"I won't bet any money on it either way," William looked up at the sky as if he had only just noticed.

The sulky wheels ground over the gravelled circled entrance at the front of the house, pulling up near the front door at the top of the four wide steps sheltered from the burning sun under a generous awning. The gardener rushed forward to take the reins from Bayden Dawson's hands.

"Good afternoon, Mister Bayden, sir."

"Afternoon, Gordie, can you unharness and feed these two as soon as possible?"

"Right away, sir."

Bayden and William assisted Mabel from the carriage. William swallowed the lump that settled in his throat at the sight of his wife's slow feeble steps reminiscent of someone twice her age. The new arrivals looked up at the sound of shoes sliding to a sudden stop. Cissy and Maud stood at the doorway each with an assorted bunch of flowers. The eyes of both girls opened wide with surprise. Children were not permitted visiting rights at the Reception House and neither had seen their mother over the past three months. Both heads turned with their questioning glances aimed at William.

"Come, my girls, your mother will love your flowers." He and his father-in-law held either elbow as Mabel's slow feet climbed one step at a time until the three stood at the foyer entrance.

Cissy and Maud exchanged glances before they moved forward and offered their bouquets. Mabel went to push on past but paused as if thinking better of it.

"Thank you, girls," she mumbled and moved forward not taking the flowers.

William laid a hand on Cissy's shoulder.

"They are lovely, dear. Can you put them in a vase for the hall table upstairs?"

Isabelle entered the foyer through an open large polished timber doorway. She moved over and bent to kiss her daughter on the cheek. Mabel stood with her head bowed.

"I have made up your old room for you, Mabel, my dear. William is in the room next to you and your father and I will be only across the hallway."

Mabel offered no reply and continued towards the curved staircase leading to the second floor. Isabelle's glance at her husband as they followed Mabel up the staircase overflowed with despair. It was William who attempted to keep the conversation going as they walked slowly upstairs.

"How are your boys, Isabelle, will they be home for Christmas too?"

"No, I am sorry to say. Arthur's ship is on exercises in the North Sea for the next six months. Hopefully, he will get some leave to visit his cousins in Edinburgh during the festive season. John and Peter are still in England, at the London hospital, working all the hours God gives."

Once Mabel's small portmanteau of clothes had been deposited on the chair, she wandered around the room twice, before she turned to her father.

"Will it be alright if I walk in the garden?"

Relief filled the smiles on the faces of her audience.

"How lovely," Isabelle offered.

If anyone amongst them thought it odd that Mabel was more interested in the gardener's old shed, rather than the glorious blooms on display in the manicured gardens, no one said. Mabel walked slowly through the shed with her eyes darting left and right. She reached up and patted the hessian tube legs of the dummy made from a large grain sack filled with cotton rags and tied at the top with a strong twine. About a foot lower down, a second twine pulled in a neck. Paint flecks remained of the once-painted face on the upper bump above the neck.

"Hello, Jolly Roger," Mabel whispered.

The Jolly Roger sat propped up on the top of a cupboard. The words 'Arthur's Stuff. Don't Touch' were scrawled on the cupboard door. After a quick scrutiny of the nearby workbench, Mabel turned towards the doorway.

William could not understand the unease he felt at the sight of the faint smile on Mabel's lips as she turned and made her way out into the garden.

"I think I'd like a rest now, Mama."

"Of course, my dear. I will walk up with you to your room."

Isabelle pulled back the bedspread and helped Mabel make herself comfortable stretched out on her bed. She glowed with pleasure when Mabel spoke.

"Thank you, Mama." Mabel shut her eyes.

After she heard the click of the door latch closing, Mabel's eyes opened. She sat upright and reached over to pull the drawer of the bedside table open. Her hand scrambled around inside until it reappeared with a pencil held tightly in her fingers. The drawer was exposed further as she peered in to search for some paper on which to write her note.

After dinner that evening, the family retired to the music room where Cissy and Maud played the piano and sang several duets. William and Bayden sat engrossed with their game of chess while Isabelle's fine fingers danced her crochet hook around the threads of her tablemat-in-the-making.

Mabel sat back on the chaise longue with her eyes shut.

William's chair creaked as he leant back.

"Bayden, you've done it again. I can count on one hand how many times I've beaten you at this game."

The chess pieces rattled as they were replaced in their box and the set was folded away.

"I guess I get a lot more practice here in town than you do out on the property. I have joined the chess club which helps too."

Isabelle tidied her fancy work away in the basket and turned to her daughter.

"Mabel, I'm going up to bed. Will you come up with me, dear?"

This time it was Mabel's acquiescence which unsettled William's thoughts.

Isabelle, Cissy and Maud settled Mabel into bed. William and Bayden entered her room to say goodnight. As the two men exited, William watched in horror as his father-in-law turned the large key in the lock of the bedroom door.

"A proviso in her home-leave permit," Bayden explained. "It is a terrible thing to do but I am afraid we have no choice." He dropped the key on the small table near the door alongside a vase of Cissy's and Maud's flowers.

In her childhood room with the single bed, dainty furniture, and exquisite doll sitting on the dressing table, Mabel lay with the sheets pulled back and her eyes wide open. A faint moonlight struggled through the intermittent clouds marching across the night sky. She listened to the rustle of the trees in the breeze outside her room. The sound of revellers some distance away drifted into her room through the open narrow ventilator windows set above the large closed and locked windows below. A horse stamped its feet in the stable nearby and a dog howled into the night far away. When the sounds inside the house settled, she remained still and quiet until the clock in the distance chimed one o'clock.

The stick-like legs slipped across the sheet and over the edge of the bed. Mabel pulled herself into a sitting position. She stood upright. The delicate nightdress hanging from bony shoulders draped her body. Her hand reached under her pillow to remove the note she had written during her afternoon nap time. This she placed on top of her pillow.

Without a whisper of noise, she removed the doll from the top of the dressing table, pulled out the stool and climbed up to where the doll had been. From there it was not a difficult climb up onto the top of her clothes cupboard. Her slim body now carried no more, in fact, maybe less, weight than in the years when this journey had been a regular event. Within moments she was through the narrow window and standing on the window ledge. Her hands took hold of the drain pipe attached to the outside wall from the roof above to the garden below. As the weight of her body hung from her arms, Mabel gasped when, in a desperate moment, she thought she might not have the strength to take her weight. Her hands threatened to slip from the drainpipe. Her bare toes scrambled to feel the brackets holding the pipe to the building. Mabel's sigh escaped into the night at their familiar touch. Slowly the descent to the grassy lawn below was made in silence, as it always had been.

Mabel ran over to stand in the shadows of the large thick bushes near the rose beds. She sucked the air into her lungs and rubbed her trembling arms before stepping out towards the garden shed. The door emitted a squeak as she began to pull it open. She stopped, not moving and held her breath, listening with every atom of her body for any sound coming from the house. Even in her frail state, she only just managed to slip through the small gap and into the shed without opening the door any further.

Once more Mabel rested in the darkness to catch her breath. Very little of the scant moonlight outside found its way inside but Mabel knew every inch of this shed. Her feet shuffled over to the bench where her hands found the lantern and matches, she had noted earlier in the afternoon. Once lit, the lantern cast a soft glow over this end of the shed. It was more than enough for her purpose. She opened the wooden latch on her brother Arthur's cupboard. Retrieving the lantern, Mabel searched the shelves. Her hopes were fading when at the back of the bottom shelf she found what she hoped was still there. She dragged out the wooden box filled with ropes of all sizes. Her fingers riffled through the ropes throwing the unwanted ones aside. At the very bottom, she found what she had been looking for. A rope with a hangman's noose at one end and a knotted loop large enough to hold a four-by-four-inch beam at the other end. Altogether the rope including its knots would be no more than four feet in length.

Mabel pushed at the ladder which, as always, rested against the edge of the attic floor above. She pushed until the ladder slid along to rest near the beam which protruded outwards for about one yard in distance. A beam four-by-four inches in size.

A distorted grin lit her face when she reached up and pulled the leg of the hessian bag dummy.

"I won't be needing you this time, Jolly Roger."

Settling the lantern on the bench again, away from anything flammable, Mabel climbed the ladder. She stopped at the rung near the jutting beam and slipped the small loop around the end before pushing it along the timber until it touched the attic floorboards. Mabel hugged the ladder. Her breath came in gasps. She rested for some moments before pulling the hangman's noose over her head. She paused. Usually, it was she or Arthur who had pushed the Jolly Roger, guilty of piracy, murder and plunder, to swing at the end of the noose dangling from the attic floor. Tonight, she was going to have to throw herself outwards and push the ladder away with her feet as she did so. Could she do this?

CHAPTER THIRTY-FOUR

Strzelecki Track

October – December 1920

As the riders came to the top of a bare hill, Bert Hennessy called back to Joe and Doug.

"There it is, Innamincka."

A winding tree line and the narrow band of green pasture promised water ahead. Bert turned in his saddle to watch as the wagon pulled by four horses and loaded with the supplies from Birdsville followed the track to his home. Only the driver and the jockey nursing a painful arm rode in the wagon. The five other men returning from the Birdsville adventure rode their mounts on the wing. The sun, low on the horizon, gleamed orange across the plain.

Bert roared with laughter. Smokey threw his head up.

"I swear even the blinding 'eadaches those boys must still be suffering cannot wipe the smiles off their faces. They made a packet on this 'orse." He reached over and patted Smokey's neck.

Several buildings lined the edge of the track they followed into the settlement. Bert pointed out the station manager's house, a larger residence standing further back from the other buildings. Thick green vines around the verandahs left an impression of a cool retreat.

Joe and Doug followed Bert to a modest building with wide verandah awnings set between two large sheds. Smoke drifted up from a chimney at the back of the house. It wafted off on the hot winds across a forest of stunted trees.

A well-built, handsome woman stood at the doorway of the head stockman's dwelling. Her grey hair drawn tight at the back of her head and her expressionless face warned the newcomers this was not a woman who tolerated any nonsense. She walked out to greet her husband.

"I take it, by that loopy grin on your face, you've had a successful race meeting then, Bert."

"I 'ave, Shirley, I certainly 'ave. Smokey ran a treat," Bert began scratching through his pockets, "and before you ask, 'ere I 'ave my winnings of the day."

"All of it then, Bert?"

"Not counting the bit that I 'ad to lay out for expenses." Bert stood in the stirrups and reached down to place the money in Shirley's open hand. "There's a trophy for you in my swag. Didn't want to lose the polish off it."

"Hmmm," Shirley studied the new arrivals.

"Oh, meet Joe and Doug Daley from Charters Towers," Bert offered.

"Yes, I've been expecting you."

"What are you talking about, woman? I only just run into them in Birdsville."

Shirley's gaze did not leave the faces of Joe and Doug as if sizing up their characters. Her slow smile transformed her face and reassured the young men they passed inspection.

"There's a letter inside, came in the mail with Faiz and his camel team the day before yesterday. It was addressed to a Joe and Doug Daley, c/- Bert Hennessy." Shirley turned to her husband, "Isn't that the name of the men you were droving with in the Northern Territory years ago?"

"Yes, my little sleuth, that was Joe's father William, and Doug's father Miles. They live on Billabong Downs near Charters Towers."

"Pleased to meet you, boys. Now, Bert, you show these chaps where to clean up and bring them into the house for a feed. They can camp on the stretchers out on the verandah." Shirley pointed to the four bare stretchers near where she stood. "You can unload your horses and leave your gear there too, Joe."

Feeling like new men after a shower with running water and soap, Joe and Doug tentatively stood in the doorway of the dining area. They savoured the aroma of a roast meal which sat resting on a large serving plate on the table at the opposite end of where the light of a lamp cast flickering shadows around the room. Heat rose from the variety of vegetables surrounding the beef. Steam drifted up from the simmering gravy in a pan on the stove.

"Come on in then, don't be shy. Find a seat at the table and I'll serve up your meals." Shirley stood behind the table stroking a wet stone down the blade of her carving knife. "I hope you're hungry – there's apple pie and custard to follow."

"How did you know we'd arrive today, Mrs Hennessy?" Doug asked.

It was Bert who spoke up.

"This woman is a witch, Dougie boy. She 'as a glass ball 'idden somewhere but I've not been able to find it as yet, even after thirty years."

Shirley lifted her carving knife and with the flat of the blade, she tapped her husband on the crown of his head before she explained.

"I figured Bert would be home by nightfall today unless they had trouble on the way. Which reminds me, I'll give you your mail now before I forget." Shirley walked over to the ledge above where a washtub sat upside down on a rough-hewn bench. She handed the letter to Joe.

"Thanks, we'll read this later." Joe shoved the letter into his top pocket.

The conversation was slow and intermittent as the men satisfied their hunger. Shirley served up liberal helpings of pie and custard while Bert explained to his spouse.

"The lads were planning on exploring the Strzelecki Track, Shirley."

"Didn't you explain we've no more droving trips planned until next autumn?" She turned to Joe and Doug, "We usually travel with the stock in the cooler months if possible and avoid those months when we are likely to get any rain – if we are going to get any rain at all. Our son, Michael, is away with the drovers and the last herd for this year. They'll be back before Christmas if all goes well."

"Yes, of course, I did woman, but I thought they might like to travel with Faiz on his next trip. If he's here in camp at the moment, he'll be off back to the Ghantown at Farina in a day or so." Bert looked up from his dessert. "You boys know anything about camels?"

Joe grinned. "They stink, they're cranky beggars and they're not the most comfortable ride in the world."

"Of course, you would have encountered them in the Sinai." Bert turned to explain to his wife. "Joe was in the Light Horse in the Sinai and Palestine during the war."

"You'll be familiar with deserts, burning heat and perishing dry then, Joe."

Joe nodded his head – his cheeks bulged. Once he had swallowed his food, he had a question for Bert.

"I didn't realize we had camels still doing mail runs here in Australia, but then I guess it makes sense."

"Faiz and his sons bring the mail and supplies up from the railhead at Hergott Springs, or Marree, as it is known now. It's about three hundred miles southeast of here. Takes about three or four weeks to complete the one-way journey, depending on the conditions. After a rest of three or four days, they return."

Shirley's light hand touched her husband's shoulder.

"He's due to leave the day after tomorrow, Bert. I heard him talking to the boss yesterday."

"There you are then, lads. I'll talk to Faiz in the morning if you want to join him."

"The boys might be sick of travelling, Bert." Shirley turned her attention to Joe and Doug. "If you want to stay here until after Christmas, you're welcome to do so. If you want to go with Faiz there'll be a bed for you at Marree at our daughter's place. Eileen has a shed where she puts up any of our mob going down that way."

"Sleep on that and let me know tomorrow," Bert said as he spooned up the last dregs of the custard on his plate.

As the men relaxed in the sitting room while Shirley cleaned up her kitchen, Bert sucked on an old pipe and sipped on a large pannikin of hot black tea. The not-unpleasant smoke dribbled its way out through the open window behind his head. Joe slipped the letter from his pocket and tore it open with his finger. He removed the two folded sheets of paper within. He handed the one with 'Doug' written on the front, to his cousin. He began to remove the creases from the other with 'Joe' written in his father's familiar hand. Both young men held their letters towards the lamplight and read their mail in silence.

Dear Joe   *28/7/1920*

I do hope you are finding the peace you wanted and deserved while on your journey.

I will post this to my friend Bert Hennessy at Innamincka. I know you took his address with you so hopefully you will get to catch up with the goings on here.

I am sorry to report your mother had a nervous breakdown recently. She is currently in the care of Doctor Lundy in the Townsville Hospital. He seems to think with the right medication and therapy she will return to her old self. I do hope he is right. He did say it could take some months.

Your sisters are both still with the Dawsons and attending school in Townsville. Cissy has been hinting (very loud hints I might add – you know your sister) that she wants to commence nursing training next year.

Maud, with equal determination, keeps saying she wants to come back home and look after me and your mother. Hopefully, I can convince her to stay at school for at least one more year. Can you imagine the upheaval that will fall upon our shoulders with Maud in charge? I might join you on your trip. Only joking.

Your Uncle Miles, Geoff, and I are managing here without any trouble. Geoff's boy Stewie is a big help on occasions when Maggie lets him off his schoolwork.

Your Pops and Gran send their love and will get a letter off to you at some point when we have a more settled address from you.

I have spent some time in Townsville with the Dawsons and of course, they send their love too.

I do hope old Bert isn't telling you any tall tales about Miles and me in the Territory. Don't believe a word he says.

Ha Ha, Your dad.

Keep safe.

Joe sat with his head back and his eyes closed visualizing his home and those he loved.

In the chair opposite him, Doug reread the words his mother wrote.

Dear Doug

Well, my son, if you get this letter, you'll have found your way to Innamincka. A no easy feat I should imagine. Your dad, Geoff and Gazza mustered the eastern paddock this week. They returned yesterday. I will drop you a quick line to add to William's letter for Joe.

Mabel has accepted treatment in the Townsville Hospital and the doctor seems to think she will be okay in a few months.

Your sister Mavis is thriving with her grandparents and loves her schoolwork. Maybe she will follow in Mick's footsteps and want to go on to university. We had a letter (more like a scrappy note - hope you can do better than that) from him about a month ago. He is enjoying his studies and is doing alright in Sydney at my sister's place.

I can hear William downstairs. He is ready to head off on another trip to the Townsville Hospital to see Mabel.

Must close Love from your Mum and the rest of us here at Billabong Downs.

When Joe and Doug looked up, they discovered Bert snoring in his chair. They shared a grin.

"Come on, Doug, I'm beat myself, let's say goodnight to Shirley. I'm ready to hit the hay."

Joe's eyes sprung open. He gazed up at the corrugated iron verandah roof above. Something had disturbed him. He did not move but rolled his eyes in all directions. The pale glow of early morning revealed two brown dogs sitting alert on the bare dirt at the edge of the flooring. Tails thumped on the ground in unison raising small puffs of dust. Two pairs of amber eyes stared at the interlopers.

Slowly he rolled over onto his left side. Two canine heads rolled to the right side of their shoulders. A piercing whistle echoed off the house walls, followed by Bert's call.

"Come on dogs, feed time."

Interest in the strangers dissipated as the pair raced off around to the back of the house, their tongues lolling from the sides of their mouths.

Joe went to speak but only a whisper escaped from his mouth. He swallowed and coughed before trying a second time.

"Doug, you awake?"

"Hmmm, how does one sleep through a whistle like that?"

The stretchers creaked as the pair swung their legs out and dropped their feet onto the floorboards.

Bert's voice full of cheer increased their pace.

"What a slovenly pair. The day's 'alf gone. Come on, Shirley'll be ringing the breakfast bell any minute."

"We've been awake for hours – just waiting to see a bit of life around here ourselves." Doug jammed his hat on his head and tucked the tails of his shirt into his dungarees.

At that moment, the clang of a cowbell announced meal time.

After Joe and Doug devoured the cooked oats followed by pannikins of tea, swallowed to wash down thick slices of freshly baked bread doused in jam, Bert led the newcomers outside. They headed off behind the house, down a worn track, through the low scrub, to a clearing. Here the camels were contained within a large area fenced by trimmed saplings. They snorted and shuffled their long legs raising the dust with their leather-padded broad feet and two thick toenails on the short, webbed protrusions at the front.

"Thought I'd introduce you to Faiz. 'E and his two sons are the cameleers who deliver our mail and goods out here."

Joe and Doug followed Bert to a heavy canvas tent with many colourful designs painted on the walls. Small bells hanging on the edge of the tent flaps jingled softly as the man they learnt was Faiz emerged to greet Bert.

In rough English, Joe and Doug were introduced. They learnt the sons, Tagh and the other with a name which sounded like Saddy were away from their camp training two young camels.

Joe and Doug's concentration drifted to the camp and the camels' enclosure where the large dark eyes of three curious beasts stared back at them. Bert organized with Faiz to have Joe and Doug join the cameleers on their return journey south to Marree.

On their way back to Bert's house, they met Ziggy, a dark-skinned snowy-haired man with accentuated bowed legs who led two goats on short ropes towards the cameleers' camp.

"Those for Faiz and 'is boys, Ziggy?"

"Yeah, Bert, the bossman sent them over."

Bert laughed and turned to his guests. "The manager 'ere looks after Faiz and 'is team, especially when they deliver 'is grog order without the missus knowing." He went on to explain, "I 'ave to go and talk with the boss about some weaner calves. I'll see you two later at lunchtime. Feel free to wander about."

"Thanks, Bert," they replied in unison.

Joe sat on his stretcher bunk sideways with his back against the wall. Doug had his knife out sharpening the pencils aiming the droppings out onto the bare ground. He handed the first pencil to Joe before trimming the lead in the second pencil.

"Here, do you need some paper to write on?" Joe offered as he took up his writing pad.

"No thanks, Mum wouldn't let me out of the house until she stuffed a small writing pad into my duffle bag," Doug grinned.

Joe's neat hand worked its way down the paper, while his tongue held in his teeth helped his concentration.

Doug's scrawl soon covered the page and he finished with large swirls as he signed his name.

360

"Have you got an envelope there?"

"Yes, Doug, but how about we put both letters in the one envelope and save a stamp?"

"Suits me." Doug folded his letter and sailed it across to the other bunk.

Joe tidied up both letters and slipped them into an envelope.

"We'll give these to Bert or Shirley to add to the Innamincka mailbag."

The clang of the cowbell from the back of the house heralded their lunch was ready.

Moonbeams streamed across the floor of the open verandah.

"You awake, Joe?" Doug rolled onto his back and lifted his head onto the palms of his hands.

"How can I be anything but awake with your bed squeaking worse than a hayloft of rats while you toss and turn all night?"

"Sorry, guess I'm just a bit excited about this trip down the Strzelecki Track in the morning. It'll be interesting to see how Faiz works the camels too."

"You planning on learning to be a cameleer, Doug? All I can say is thank goodness we'll be on the horses. Now, lie still and go back to sleep."

The next morning, Joe and Doug ate the breakfast Shirley prepared in the light of the kerosene lamp. Two hessian sugar bags bulging with their contents lay on the end of the table. Each sack contained food supplies including flour, salt, tea, dried meat, dried fruit and tinned food as well as a fresh loaf of bread and a slab of cooked salted beef, all packed by Shirley.

"Can't have you going hungry, boys," she explained. "You did fill your canteens with water, I presume."

Joe and Doug grinned "Yes, Mum."

361

"Get out with you," Her laugh echoed around the kitchen. "Be on your way or Faiz will leave without you."

"I thought we'd just shoot a bit of wildlife to keep us going but with this lot, we'll live like kings," Joe grinned. "Can we pay you for this?"

"No, you will not. It's the least we can do for William's and Miles's boys," Bert announced. "Now, come on, don't muck about, Faiz and his camels like an early start."

"Should we offer to help Faiz or should we pay him for having us along"

"Faiz will be happy for the company. He'd be offended if you offered money. Their work will be light on this return journey." Shirley reassured her departing guests.

A picaninny dawn crept across the plains as Joe and Doug stepped outside. A line of a dozen camels stood sniffing and farting in front of the house. Faiz and Bert stood talking beside the head of the first camel. Two other men walked down the line ensuring everything was as it should be. Just looking at them, Joe guessed they were the sons of Faiz. It would not be possible to make an accurate guess at their ages but they appeared to be about thirty years old. Their faces were covered in thick black beards like their father's. They were each of similar height with slim build and bandy legs.

From the peg, drilled through the nose of each camel, a length of string hung loose. The two men attached long leather leads to each piece of string. Only the lead camel wore a harness draped in faded ribbons. They fussed about with the well-padded wooden framed saddles upon the backs of each camel. Another two young cameleers, with smooth faces not yet with any hint of a beard, followed on the heels of the pair learning the trade. According to Bert, these were also Faiz's sons.

Joe could not recall having seen the pack camels encountered in the Sinai with anything but huge loads on their backs and he had never seen the frames so bare. The heavy loads were attached to lines of strong wooden slats on either side of the saddle. A long leather strap slung around the base of the camel's chest and neck kept the frame from sliding backwards. Another leather strap slung around and under the tail prevented it from sliding forward.

After listening with his ear cocked for a while, Doug heard the jingle of his horse bells. He walked off towards the glow of morning with a bridle in his hand. Joe stacked their belongings on the edge of the verandah ready to load.

As they said their farewells to the Hennessy family, Joe turned to Bert.

"Will we be following the route the cattle usually take? Will there be water for the horses every day? I mean those camels only need to drink once in a couple of days. But I've seen good horses drop for lack of regular water."

"Don't worry, Joe, Faiz will make sure you are on water each night. Over the years, 'e 'as learnt where all the water is to be found. There will be two or three long days of travel to make the next water but it is quite do-able. 'E always carries a spear pump with 'im anyway, in case they get into trouble."

After shaking hands and thanking their hosts, Joe and Doug mounted and moved out at a trot to catch up with the camel train ahead. When they began their day, Faiz and his sons walked, each beside a camel, with Faiz in the lead. After they had stopped for a break in the late morning, Faiz rode in the saddle of the lead camel while the two young lads rode on the second and third camel. The man Faiz named Tagh, led a camel in the middle of the line. Saddy, the other man led the last camel in the train.

"I reckon that last camel must be one of the new camels they're training, Joe. What do you think?"

"Most likely, I guess."

A hot breeze lifted as the day wore on. Dust and sand swirled across the plains as they made their way over the rippling sandhills dotted with mounds of dry spikey spinifex and occasional acacia shrubs. Joe and Doug adjusted their neckerchiefs to cover their mouth and nose. They squinted and pulled their hats low to protect their eyes. Joe felt a sense of déjà vu as the hot sun beat down upon his back. He shivered as the memories of another desert threatened to creep into his head but Doug's frequent questions prevented his mind from slipping back into the past. Whereas in his previous experience in the desert, he struggled to keep alert expecting the enemy to ambush at any time, here there was no such risk. Joe had to retrain himself to relax. He focused his mind on moving forward – to plod on, one step at a time.

The sun hung high in the sky when Joe and Doug watched Faiz halt the camels beside a dry wadi. The five cameleers took their prayer mats from the lead camel's load and lay them with reverence upon the ground within the scant shade of stunted bushes.

"What are they doing?" Doug looked askance at his cousin.

"It is one of their prayer times. They observe five prayer times a day, I believe. If I remember they pray at sunrise, before midday, late afternoon and then at sunset. How many is that?"

"That's only four," Doug raised his eyebrows.

"Oh, and one later at night."

"Wow, what happens if they forget?"

"I'm not too sure, I never thought to ask. We were given a brief instruction on the culture when at the training camp at Holsworth."

After a brief stop, the camel train recommenced the day's journey. The heat pressed down upon the travellers. Conversation was too exhausting to maintain. In his somnolent state, Joe lifted his head in surprise when Doug announced.

"Looks like Faiz plans to make a camp for the night," Doug chuckled as he pointed to where one of Faiz's young lads ran towards them.

"How does he do that with only sandals on his feet? Doesn't the sand burn his skin?"

"Been doing it since a baby, I suppose."

The boy's English was easily understood. Wide black eyes peered out from under the turban on his head and the strands of thick black hair that had escaped from its prison within the cloth.

Joe turned back to his cousin. "This is the one Bert called Charlie. The other boy he called Dadleh."

"Misters, my father say there waterhole over next sandhill. We sleep camels till the sun comes up."

"Thanks, Charlie." Joe turned to speak to Doug. "We'll let Faiz settle his camels before we find a camp. No doubt he has his preferred campsite."

Several stunted trees grew out of the moisture of the small oasis along with some grasses and more acacia shrubs and saltbush. Joe and Doug dismounted and watched as Tagh and Faiz led each camel to drink before they were taken back to where Saddy and the two boys commanded the large animals with the single word, "Hoooosh," drawn out in a long word as the animal lowered itself onto its haunches. The loads and the padded frames were removed from their backs and hobbles were secured in place before the camels were left to rest, graze and sleep at the edge of the tree line. A bell attached to the halter now worn by each camel combined to compose music that tinkled on the breeze drifting through the trees. The lead camel's bell was a larger bell and its tone underlined the musical notes of the other bells. A pair of mistletoe birds darted through the foliage watching all the goings on. The red chest of the male bird matched the darkening colours of the sands they had passed through during the afternoon.

"Not unlike droving cattle, is it?" Doug commented.

"What, you mean with the days, weeks, months of absolute boredom interspersed with moments of utter panic, drama and confusion?"

"Well, I'd prefer no panic or confusion on this trip anyway," Doug smiled.

"I sure hope that is the case. Look, Faiz seems to be settling his lot in on the west side of the water hole. Let's head over to the trees on the other side to make our camp."

After the horses were watered, unsaddled, the hobbles fitted, and their horse bells attached, they also were left to graze and make their own music while Joe fetched timber for the fire. Doug filled their partially empty canteens and filled the billycan with water. He placed it at the edge of his small fire to boil for their tea.

Faiz and the two younger sons approached Joe's camp in the darkness between the disappearance of the sun and the appearance of a partial moon in the sky.

"Misters, you have all you need, yes?"

"Thank you, Faiz, can we offer you some tea, there is plenty here in the billy?" Joe pointed to the brown fluid simmering gently away from the heat of the fading fire.

"Thank you, no thanks, Misters. We all fed and watered."

"How many miles did we come today do you think?" Doug asked.

"Many but not long day, just some many. Same tomorrow and the next tomorrow."

"You sure we can't offer you some tea? We appreciate your allowing us to travel with you, very much, Faiz."

"Thank you, no, I must go and rest. We start early again before the sun you see."

"Good night, Faiz." Joe turned to the young lads. "Goodnight boys, sleep tight, watch the bed bugs don't bite."

Both Charlie and Dadleh gave a burst of laughter and ran off back to the camel camp.

"Good night, Misters. Good the boys laugh. They work hard. Laugh is good."

"Night, Faiz," Joe and Doug spoke in unison.

The following days of that first week produced little change. They often travelled through dry waterbeds gouged out from the overflow of Cooper's Creek, Diamantina River or Strzelecki Creek. Coolabah and red river gum trees sprouted up wherever moisture was to be found. Each night, Faiz brought them to a spring-fed waterhole, or a seepage, or a well. Only one day of that week, they travelled an extra four hours before they came upon the water and made their camp.

Halfway through the second week, they travelled until the moon peeped over the horizon. Having been warned by Faiz it was to be a long stretch until they reached the next water, Joe and Doug collected small pieces of wood for their night campfire wherever they found them during the day. These were tied in bundles and tucked into the load on the packhorses.

As the darkness crept across the landscape stealing the golden glow of sunset, Joe and Doug eased back to follow closely behind the line of camels. Only the music of the camel bells and the swish of their feet through the loose sand provided a guide until the moon rose to reveal the large swaying mounds in front.

Weariness weighed down their progress as they chose a campsite amidst long parallel sand dunes or mounds and ridges of loose sand caused by the wind. They stripped the horses of their loads. Both the horses and the men drank greedily before the hobbles were attached. With dulled enthusiasm, Joe set the fireplace and dragged the tin of wax matches from his pocket. Doug scrounged through the food bags with little interest.

"A tin of anything will do me," Joe offered some help with the decision.

Doug gave a short chuckle. "What, even bully beef?"

Joe's droll smile revealed his disinterest. "Even bully beef, mate."

They lay back on their bedrolls, asleep before the tea had been drained from their pannikins despite the aches and pains in every muscle of their bodies.

It was the agitated tinkling of the horse bells that lifted Joe to his feet in one move. He kicked Doug in the foot.

"The horses, Doug. Wake up."

It was then he heard the dingo call from far across the plains. Joe grabbed the leads, and his rifle resting near the saddle. With Doug now upright if not entirely awake, they followed the sound of the horse bells until they found their mounts huddled together shuffling about in the light of a three-quarter moon. After a short scuffle the leads were attached to the halters and the horses were brought back to the camp where the fire was stoked up to a blaze. The remainder of the night passed without any further disturbance but neither man fell into a deep sleep.

Joe felt dull and listless when he woke the following morning. Reddened eyes told of their restless night.

Faiz led his camels out across the ocean of sand at the break of day. The squeal of a whistling kite filled the sky as it soared on the warm currents above, searching for its breakfast. Joe and Doug scrambled to fall into line. With the mind-numbing sameness of it all, the swaying of his body in the saddle and the unchanging landscape of the sandy desert in all directions, Joe felt himself slipping back into the deserts of the Sinai. Grey clouds swept across the skies. The swoosh, swoosh, swoosh of the horses' hooves in the sand accentuated the hypnotic aura around him. He felt his brother Billy beside him, riding knee to knee. In the sound of the clatter of the billycan not packed tightly, he heard Billy's endless chatter. The creak of the saddle beneath him carried him back to that long, endless, thirsty journey with Billy and the Light Horse on the way to Beersheba. He became oblivious to the darkening clouds over them. The rumble and crack of the thunder when it split the skies above transported Joe into Billy's last charge when they rode into a wall of gunfire, shrapnel, cannon fire and the squeal of the grenades all around. Joe dropped his reins. He threw his hands over his ears to deaden the thundering hoofbeats, the screams of defiance along with the screams of death, all roaring in his head. His gaze turned left and right as he searched through the blinding dust but Billy had disappeared from his side. Joe's heart raced. A shiver ran down the length of his body. It took his breath away. The clouds retreating to the west choked some of the heat from the sinking sun. His horse plodded on. The packhorse behind followed the lead attached to Joe's saddle.

"You alright there, Joe?"

"W-w-what?" Joe's mind fought to focus on the here and now and not on the past. He shook his head and ran his tongue around a dry mouth. "I must have dropped off, a sure sign of old age, I guess."

Doug's smile covered his anxiety. "It won't be long until Faiz calls it a day, I should think."

Whenever possible, Doug joined Charlie and Dadleh as they supervised the one female camel within Faiz's camel train which had a baby camel travelling with her. He never tired of watching the antics of the young animal at the end of the day as it sought the warm milk from the mother's swollen udder.

"They feed baby twenty-four moons," Charlie said with much conviction.

Having spent his life watching calves and foals feeding from their mothers at home, this small head on the long slim neck as it slid unerringly under the mother's belly and between her legs never failed to make Doug laugh.

Changes in the terrain became more noticeable. At first, it was the deep rough gutters as they snaked across the plains before the blue in the distance which suggested higher country. Joe's spirits lifted as the desert gave way to the Flinders ranges. Hills and mountains rose above them on either side of the track Faiz followed. Grass became marginally more plentiful and tall trees greeted them each day. Small birds filled the branches with colour and cheerful calls.

Doug's excitement became infectious.

"Faiz says we're not too many days away from where we turn off to Marree."

Each day they passed other travellers. Some were heading to their homes further up the track while others waved from where they worked on the smaller holdings.

On the last morning of their journey, Joe and Doug were a little slow in stirring. They had only just cinched the girth straps when they heard the grunting sounds of the cameleers' instruction, "Unga, Unga," telling the camels to rise.

A train whistle split the air in the distance. Marree railway station was not too far away.

CHAPTER THIRTY-FIVE

Christmas

December 1920

The ladder crashed back against the cupboard and the bench before falling to the floor with a clatter. Mabel's body swung wildly. Her limbs twitched violently. Gradually the body's contortions ceased and Mabel swayed in a gentle arc with her head at an awkward angle on the thick rope knot, until all movement ceased.

At that moment, a clap of thunder echoed across the township. The skies opened as the torrential rain pelted down upon the tin roof. Like a spectre, Mabel's body, in the white embroidered nightgown, glowed in the pale light of the lantern on the workman's bench.

Upstairs, half asleep and in his rush to get out of bed, William almost fell to the floor when the thunder cracked outside. A lightning strike lit up the room. He struggled upright and straightened his pyjamas before he ran to open the door. William almost collided with Bayden Dawson in the hallway.

"Mabel hates thunderstorms," William explained.

"I know," Bayden picked up the key from the hallway table. Another streak of lightning shone through William's open doorway. "Here, William, open her door while I light the hallway lamp." Bayden passed the key over to William.

William fumbled with the key and the lock for several moments expecting to hear Mabel's screams coming from within. The silence made him even more anxious. At last, William pushed the door back with such force it thumped against the wall. Somewhere in his head he thought, *No one can sleep through this.*

The light from Bayden's lamp sent a glow throughout the room. Both men stood grounded at the sight of the empty bed. William fell to the floor and peered under the bed – nothing, certainly no dust. He pulled open the cupboard doors scattering clothes aside and even throwing shoes out onto the floor as if Mabel might hide underneath them. Both men again stopped and turned in circles searching every corner slowly. Nothing.

"What's that on her pillow?" Bayden lifted the lamp higher and retrieved the folded piece of paper. "Here, William, you'll need to read this, I cannot read without my glasses."

William unfolded the paper and smoothed it out. He held it up closer to the lamplight.

My family,
I cannot live without my Billy.
I cannot face another Christmas without my Billy at the table.
I must find Billy.
Mabel.

"Where has she gone?" William asked.

"How is she gone, is the question," Bayden's face stared blankly. "I haven't been in here since we locked her in earlier, have you?"

"No, Bayden, I have not." William was at a loss. "Isabelle may have felt sorry for her and opened the door."

"Isabelle would never open the door. She knew Mabel would lose her privileges if we did not obey the doctor's instructions."

"I can't imagine Cissy and Maud would do such a thing – at least not without asking one of us. I think they were just as committed as we were in keeping to the rules." William scratched his head. "No, that cannot be. The door was locked when we arrived here." He moved towards the window and peered out without any expectations of seeing evidence of Mabel outside. He froze.

"What's wrong," Bayden asked.

"Bayden do you always keep a light on in the shed at night?"

"No, never."

"I'm sure there is a faint light out there. Turn down the lamp so we can see better."

"You are right, William, there is a light out there."

William felt sick in the stomach. *Why would Mabel be in the shed?* He recalled her insistence on visiting the shed yesterday afternoon. His stomach churned as he remembered her strange smile when she walked back out of the shed and into the garden.

"Bayden are you sure there's no other way out of this room?"

"No, I left the ventilation windows open but they are too high and too narrow for an adult to climb out of. And even if she managed that, it is a long way to jump to the ground."

William walked to the windows and peered out into the darkness. Another flash of lightning lit up the garden. There was no sign of Mabel anywhere to be seen.

"Come on, Bayden, have you got an outside lantern? I want to have a look in the shed."

"Well, keep the noise down or we will have Isabelle and the girls awake and curious."

The storm had eased off to a soft rain shower and it fell lightly upon the two men in pyjamas as they walked across to the back shed.

"The latch has been left open. Gordie would never leave the door unlatched."

William pushed open the door and gasped. "Oh, God, no, Mabel, no."

"What's wrong, what is it, William?" Bayden pushed past into the room. "Oh, my sweet girl." He stumbled to his knees at the sight of his daughter hanging from the beam.

Both men froze – disbelieving what their eyes were seeing. It was William who shook himself and mumbled.

"How long has she accepted Billy is dead? All along, she would not believe it. If I hadn't brought her in for treatment, she might still be alive – she might still have been thinking Billy wasn't dead and she might not have done this."

"William, you did the right thing. Nobody knew this was going to happen. I just hope my girl and Billy find each other wherever they are."

"Come on, Bayden, we can't leave her like this. Help me bring her down at least."

William began to manhandle the ladder upright, leaning it against the attic floor.

"You go up first, Bayden, and lie on the attic floor. Here," William passed him a long-handled hoe, "use this to push the loop off the beam when I take her weight. I'll come up the ladder after you and lift her over."

Working together the men had Mabel down from the noose and lying on two empty feed bags on the shed floor. Bayden found an old carriage rug to throw over her body.

The glow of dawn seeped through the cracks in the slab-walled shed. Bayden walked over and turned the wick of the lantern down until the flame spat and disappeared.

"William, I will take a horse and ride to fetch the doctor. I am not sure of the procedure in things like this. I want to see the doctor first before we call the police." Bayden turned to go but William called him back.

"I'm younger than you, shouldn't it be me finding the doctor?"

"No, William, Cissy and Maud will be up and about soon looking for you and Mabel. I think they will want you to be with them when they find out what has happened to their mother."

"And, Isabelle?"

"She won't surface for two or three hours yet. I will talk to her when I get back."

Christmas Day turned into a nightmare for the Dawson household.

Cissy and Maud appeared to cope with the passing of their mother with little fuss. William worried that they may not have understood exactly what he had told them. It was Cissy and Maud who comforted Isabelle while William and Bayden dealt with the formalities.

Doctor Elliott Lundy arrived first followed closely by the police.

A coroner's wagon arrived and took Mabel's body to the morgue.

Staff were sent home with generous portions of the uneaten Christmas feast and several bottles of Christmas cheer.

William explained to Bayden during the afternoon.

"My father will deliver the news out to Billabong Downs but I can't send a wire to Pop until the Post Office opens. I guess with the Christmas break that won't be until Monday. The chance of getting the news to Joe for at least several months will be next to none, while he and Doug are on their travels."

"Poor Joe, I had not thought about how this would affect him. As if he has not got enough to be blaming himself for – none of which has been his fault, I might add, William."

"Yes, I think I'll write a letter rather than a short wire with the news. It's not as if they can get home in time for a funeral or anything."

"Good idea."

William sat on a seat in the orchard in the dusk of evening, letting his tears fall. He jumped when a small voice whispered beside him.

"Daddy, are you alright?"

He wiped his eyes and looked up into the faces of his two girls. Red blotches marred their cheeks.

"I'm fine, my darlings. How are you?" He edged over to allow them to sit beside him – one on either side. His arms stretched around their shoulders. "Have your Grandmama and your Grandpapa gone to bed yet?"

"They went to their room but I don't think they've gone to bed." Cissy offered.

"Have you had something to eat?" William asked.

"Yes, thanks, and here's a sandwich for you, I made it myself," Maud dragged a wrinkled paper package out of her skirt pocket in which two thick slices of bread slathered with butter and holding large chunks of ham were revealed. "You haven't eaten a thing all day, I watched you."

"Have you now, nosey parker." William chuckled.

He forced himself to eat for his girls' sake, even though the thought of food almost choked him.

"Where will we bury, Mummy?" Maud asked.

"Here in Townsville, I guess. She'll need to be buried as soon as possible."

"After that, can we go home, Dad?" Cissy asked the question.

Maud did not give her father a chance to answer.

"Well, I'm going back there because I'm going to stay at home and look after you now, Dad. I'm nearly fifteen years old and it's time I left school and did something useful."

While William tried to digest his sandwich and this news from his youngest, his elder daughter reached over and took his hand.

"I'll go home for a little while, Dad, but then I'm going nursing. I want to look after sick people who need care."

Soon the three of them wiped fresh tears from their eyes.

The day after Mabel's burial, in a desperate bid to put as much distance from himself and this place of his wife's suicide, William rose early to ensure he and his daughters caught the train to begin their journey home.

The intermittent hiss of the steam and the growl of the train engine surprised William out of his torpid state. He lined up to purchase their tickets. With heads bowed, father and daughters climbed aboard their rail carriage bound for Charters Towers.

Two weeks passed in the sweet pleasure of having his girls close but also in sorrow as they helped in sorting through Mabel's personal belongings. After waving the mailman on his way, William flicked through the letters in his hand. He recognized Joe's neat handwriting on an envelope. He placed the other mail on the second bottom step and sat down beside the heap of envelopes, newspapers and small packets to open his son's letter. Inside he found the two separate folded papers. Again, it was the handwriting that identified his letter without having to even read the words *To Dad from Joe*.

Dear Dad,

We met up with Bert Hennessy at Birdsville. He was there at the races they hold every September. A large crowd gathered for the day and Bert's horse won the cup.

Two days later we accompanied Bert to Innamincka where we met his wife Shirley and the cameleers who bring the mail and supplies up from the railhead at Marree – south of here.

Bert and Shirley were very kind and could not do enough for us. They have asked us back to their place for Christmas but Doug and I haven't made up our minds where we will be then.

Tomorrow, we go with the cameleers south along the Strzelecki stock route to Marree and then we may go on to see the coast or we may travel back north along the Birdsville stock route to Queensland – probably with friends of Faiz the cameleer we met today.

I received your letter which told of Mum being in the Townsville Hospital when we arrived here at Innamincka. I hope she is recovered by now.

Dad, are you managing there alright? Do you need me to return home?

Will have this letter (with Doug's) put into the Innamincka mailbag which will travel with us on the way to Marree.

Best wishes to everyone including the grandparents.

With love to you and Cissy (a nurse-to-be) and to Maud (housekeeper extraordinaire).

(Do I assume there'll be no more dirty boots upstairs when that happens?) from Joe.

30/9/1920

William picked up a rock from near the bottom step and placed it upon the mail. He took up the other sheet of writing paper with the words *To Mum and Dad from Doug.*

He found Fran picking vegetables from her garden near the back of the house.

"Hi, Fran, the letter in the mail with Joe's handwriting also had a letter to you from Doug. I guess the boys are learning to economize on stamps."

"Oh, thank you, William, I did recognize Joe's handwriting. You don't see such neat handwriting in the younger ones these days. I've been hoping Joe may have shamed my Doug into putting pen to paper." Fran reached out to receive the letter and glanced down to absorb the words in the scrawl she recognized, *To Mum and Dad from Doug*. She pulled the paper back to hold against her heart. "I guess they must be safe or you would have said."

"The letters were written on the 30th of September and they were fine then. They're travelling with good people down there so I don't anticipate any trouble."

"They won't have heard about Mabel's passing. Will you be sending a letter to them soon?"

"Yes, I'll have one to send off with the next mailman's visit or whoever goes to town next – whichever comes first. At least I have an idea of where to send it now."

Fran watched William making his way back to his own house before she placed the basket with her pickings on the back steps. She sat and unfolded the paper in her hand.

Dear Dad, Mum and Mavis (and Mick if he is home from University for the Christmas break.)

This has been a tremendous trip. Joe is great to travel with and has taught me so much. We came down through the centre of Queensland and made our way to Birdsville where we arrived just in time for the Birdsville races. Joe rode a horse for Bert Hennessy (Dad will remember him from the Northern Territory) in the cup race and they won.

We travelled with Bert and his men to Innamincka where we met Bert's wife Shirley. We also met a cameleer called Faiz and we will be travelling with him and his camels south down the Strzelecki droving track tomorrow.

We met some of the camels this afternoon. Bit bigger than our horses but they seemed quiet enough.

Sorry to hear Aunt Mabel had to go to the hospital. Hope she will get home for Christmas.

Love to all including that bossy sister of mine and the over-smart brother.

Your son Doug

Today is the 30th of September. 1920.

CHAPTER THIRTY-SIX

Decisions

December 1920 – March 1921

Faiz held the Innamincka mail bag in his hand as the three men stood in front of the Marree Post Office. Weariness and dust clung to their bodies and their clothes.

"After you, Faiz," Joe insisted.

Inside, a small man with grey hair only just reached above the counter. He received the north-eastern mail from Faiz. While they spoke on Faiz's latest journey and the news he had gathered on the way, Joe and Doug perused the many pieces of paper thumb-tacked into the notice board on one side of the room.

"There're a couple of jobs going at the railway workshop here, Joe, if that's of any interest."

"Hmmm, or here's another, going at a place called Cool Water Springs. They want a pair of cattle hands. It's for three months only."

Both their heads spun around when the voice of the postmaster sounded behind them.

"That's for Widow Watson. Her son has taken his wife to live on the coast. The wife has been poorly lately. Widow Watson is getting on in years and it's a bit much for her alone. I can tell you this, she's a fine cook and will provide meals for anyone taking on the job." He returned to his position behind the counter. "Now, is there something I can help you with?"

Joe followed him and explained the purpose of the visit.

"We just wanted to check if there is any mail here in the names of Doug or Joe Daley?"

"Daley, you say; why is that name familiar?" A deep furrow was lost in the wrinkles of the old man's face. "Oh, yes, there was a letter for you some weeks back. I sent it on to Bert Hennessy at Innamincka."

"Yes, thank you. We received that when we stayed with Bert and Shirley before moving down here with Faiz." Joe watched the man stretch his body up onto his toes as he strained to see what was happening outside the doorway. At the man's next words, Joe turned to look also.

"Talk of the devil and here she is."

Joe and Doug watched as a spritely lady of senior years jumped down from the driver's seat of a large wagon pulled by four horses. It was the clothes she wore that caught their attention most of all. Instead of the usual dress of a woman, her navy skirt had been split to encase both her legs separately from thigh to foot. The long sleeves of a man's blue shirt tucked in at the waist were rolled down to cover her arms from shoulder to wrist. A thin cord around her neck held a battered man's wide-brimmed felt hat which hung at the back of her neck, revealing short grey curls. When she spoke, her voice filled the small room with warmth and amusement.

"Any mail today, Toby? I don't know what that boy of mine is doing at the seaside but it's not writing letters to his mother."

Joe glanced up at Doug whose eyes sparkled. Joe's frown flashed a warning. The postmaster walked over to rows of cubby holes along the back wall and reached into one holding envelopes of all sizes. He lifted a blue slip resting on top of the pile and read the handwritten note before he turned to the new arrival.

"There's a large package out the back, Mrs. Watson, I won't be a moment."

Joe and Doug turned to cast their glance back at the notice board again to avoid appearing rude, but they were caught out.

"You boys looking for work?" The warm voice emanated from close behind them. "You know anything about cattle?"

They turned back to face her blue-eyed stare. It was Joe who answered after some seconds.

"Yes, Missus, we are both off a cattle station in North Queensland."

"What brings you down this way?"

Joe turned to Doug for inspiration.

"Just wandering, I guess," he finally replied having received no help from his cousin.

"Where are you staying tonight?"

"Not sure yet, but if that's a hotel I see down the street, we'll see if we can get a bed, bath and feed there."

"My friend runs a boarding house just behind the Post Office. Eileen takes in men from the railway mostly. She runs a clean establishment and provides good solid tucker at a fair rate. Tell her Martha Watson sent you if you're interested."

At that moment, the postmaster arrived with all the mail stacked into a box for Mrs. Watson.

"Thanks, Toby." She turned back to Joe and Doug. "If you are interested in that job, I'll be staying at the house near the first aid centre. You can be waiting for me there at six o'clock in the morning."

The three men watched as Mrs. Watson climbed up into the wagon, took up the reins and released the brake beside the seat. Her voice echoed down the street as she geed up her horses.

"That's one determined lady there," Toby, the postmaster, spoke quietly – more to himself than to the company inside his shop. He jumped when Joe spoke at his side.

"What's her story, then."

"Nothing like the gossip mongers around this place would tell you. She's been left on her own to manage a cattle run. Her husband died eight years ago. The stockman they employed disappeared eighteen months back and shortly after that, her son had to move to the coast for his wife's health. Since then, Martha Watson has worked the place alone and that is a big job by oneself, even for a healthy young man. She has the place on the market and needs a couple of men to help her muster the stock." Toby pointed to the opposite wall. "Here, I'll show you her place, on the map." He reached up on tiptoes and his finger jabbed at a point on the large map, "Cool Water Springs, about thirty-five miles out of town."

After thanking the postmaster for his information, Joe and Doug stepped out into the wide street.

"I think a long cool drink, a feed and a bath, in that order, have been earnt, Dougie boy. Let's pay a few bob and stay at the hotel tonight. We need to talk about our next plan."

Doug grinned and nodded his head. "I'll go along with that."

The sound of a steam engine hissed and rumbled from over at the railway area where the clunking of steel on steel rang out. Stock carriages were being shunted into a siding.

The boys walked across the roadway to their horses waiting in the shade of a bushy gum tree. They untied the reins and led the animals towards the two-storied brick building with the large sign declaring it to be the Great Northern Hotel. While their horses drank from the trough at the back of the building, Joe removed a banknote from the money belt at his waist and slipped it into the pocket of his trousers. He tucked his shirt back into place. After tying the reins to the hitching rail, they walked to the open doorway.

Judging by their dirt-stained clothes, many working men lined the bar. Their voices were a loud hum above the music supplied by the fingers of a man with a large scar distorting the left side of his face. Joe ordered two ales from the barman who walked with a profound limp across to the counter. The man stopped and stared. Joe looked more closely.

"Hey, you're Joe Dawson aren't you, mate?" The bartender asked.

Joe grinned. "Corporal Rankin, isn't it, Remount Unit, 1917. You baby-sat us new arrivals from Alexandria to El Arish."

The man gave Joe a thoughtful look as he poured the drinks.

"First drink is on the house for the men of the Light Horse here," he mentioned as he passed the glasses along the bar.

Joe reached over and they shook hands. "Oh, by the way, it's actually Daley – my surname."

Rankin's eyebrows lifted. "What happened there, then?"

"My brother, Billy Daley and I joined up together. We weren't sure if they'd let brothers into the same unit so I swapped my last name and middle name, and became Dawson. We said we were cousins."

Bill Daley …, wasn't he the fellow who swapped old …, what's 'is name's horse – that mongrel fellow who couldn't ride a horse to save his life.

"Lieutenant Burke." Joe chuckled.

"Yeah, Burke, a right burke, if you ask me. He treated his animals badly." Rankin frowned.

"That was my brother, Billy." Joe turned towards Doug. "Sorry, mate, I'd like you to meet the fellow who first started teaching me how to signal." Joe pointed to the bartender, "Corporal Rankin, I'd like you to meet my real cousin, Doug Daley."

The pair shook hands. The ex-corporal spoke, "You can forget the Corporal, Doug, everyone just calls me Rankin."

"Pleased to meet you, Rankin. I wasn't in the Light Horse so how much do I owe for this drink."

"Nothing, lad. That can be for the one I owe Billy." Rankin's attention switched back to Joe. "I hear Billy copped it in the Beersheba charge."

Joe paused. He swallowed. "Yes, we lost Billy that day, but like always he went in all guns blazing just looking for trouble. I'm sure he took plenty of the enemy before he met his maker."

Rankin noticed Joe's struggle to speak.

"Now tell me, what on earth brings you to this little corner of the world? You were from Queensland, weren't you?" Rankin did not miss the relief in Joe's eyes as the subject changed.

"Just wandering around having a look at the place. Which reminds me, is there a stable or somewhere we can set the four horses up for the night with a feed?"

"Yeah, Fred's Blacksmith houses horses too. He's up past the Post Office."

"Thanks, mate, now as I was saying, we were thinking of getting a couple months' work with a Mrs. Watson on a property called Cool Water Springs. Do you know the place?"

Rankin chuckled. "You're talking about our Widow Watson - the delight of the gossips here in town. They have her down as murdering her old man, who she found dead in his bed one morning (he'd been treated with a bad heart for years), and then her son and daughter-in-law (they left to live on the coast), and a while back, it was the head stockman who disappeared. The body's never been found. If I were putting money on it, I'd say he probably had a bottle of whiskey too many and fell into the deep spring they have out there. Probably sucked into the underground water system. You don't take too much notice of the gossip about here. Gives the old biddies something to be doing while they knit and crochet."

"So, you're saying working out there should be okay, then?"

"I'd say you'd be in clover. Widow Watson cooks good tucker, I believe the men's quarters are quite comfortable, and the labour isn't too strenuous."

"As I understand it, she just wants the place mustered for a pre-sale estimation."

"You'd do it in your sleep. When are you going out there?"

"Sparrow fart in the morning. Any chance of bed and breakfast here?"

"No trouble, we can give you dinner in about half an hour, at mid-day, and then tea tonight at six, if you want, too."

"Does a hot shower go with that?"

"Only if you beat the rush at about five o'clock this afternoon when the men finish over at the rail yards."

"You're on. Now, before we discover this wonderful establishment you have here, we'll just have another drink each and this one is on me, plus one for yourself thanks, mate."

Men at the other end of the bar kept Rankin busy for fifteen minutes. Joe noticed him take a drink to the piano player before he returned to talk some more.

"You see that piano player? I think you'd recognize him if it wasn't for those horrendous scars he got on the ship back to Perth in 1918. That's Sergeant Berryman."

Joe gasped. His head swung to watch the pianist more closely. "What the hell happened?"

"An explosion on board. He went to save one of the men caught in the fire. We only just limped into the harbour. The bloke died and we didn't expect Berryman to make it, but here he is."

"Will he mind if I go talk to him?"

"I think he'd like that very much. He always thought you were a good sport."

"I'll be back in a minute, Doug. Get a feed for me will you, if they come around taking orders?"

Joe walked over to stand behind the musician. He moved to the side where the man's face was not such a shiny, rippled, tortuous scar.

"Hello, Sergeant Berryman, Joe Dawson, but actually, Daley, We met when the remounts led us from Alexandria to El Arish back in 1917."

The man's hands never left the keyboard as the sharp blue gaze held Joe's dark eyes. Suddenly he grinned – a distorted twist of the mouth on the right side.

"Sure, I remember you. You could hit any target as long as it wasn't over the horizon."

Joe laughed, "Not that good, Sarge."

Sergeant Berryman took his hands from the piano and reached out to shake Joe's hand.

While the pair at the piano descended into a deep discussion, Doug nodded to the barman.

"I'll just go and sort out our horses with the blacksmith. Will you order a meal for each of us when they come around looking for takers? Where can I stash our gear?"

Rankin reached behind the counter and handed over a room key on a string attached to a piece of light timber with 'Room 6' painted on it in white.

"Go right, at the top of the stairs."

"Thanks, I shouldn't be too long."

"Don't think you'll have a chance of getting lost," Rankin smiled.

Before dawn, refreshed and ready to seek what the new day had to offer, Joe and Doug paid the blacksmith, saddled up, filled their canteens, loaded their supplies and set off to find the house near the First Aid station and Mrs. Watson.

"That'll be her for sure." Doug pointed to the familiar wagon with the horses already harnessed.

"I see she's added a few things since we last saw her."

A tarpaulin had been stretched tight across a lumpy load within the wagon. Mrs. Watson's voice was heard calling to someone inside the house as they pulled up. Her small frame skipped down the stairs as lightly as anyone half her age.

"Glad to see you, Joe and Doug, wasn't it?"

"Yes, Mrs Watson."

"Call me Martha, thanks. Now, let's be off then before the heat beats us."

Her capable hands set the wagon rolling as she called to each of her horses. Joe noted they were heading northwest out of the town. With impressive skills, she manipulated her team to avoid many of the potholes in a poorly maintained road.

After two and a half hours travelling, Martha Watson turned the wagon left into an even less maintained track.

On a plank of timber almost buried in the sandy soil near the gate, Joe noticed part of the property name in peeling white paint. The 'lcome to Cool W' was all that was visible of the greeting to the property.

"Cool Water Springs," Martha called back to her new employees.

Mounds of tough grasses interspersed with saltbush and low shrubs broke up the arid lands they passed through. Martha's rough hand pointed to an area where the sun above reflected off a small lake of water.

"Cool Water Springs," continued the commentary. "We have four bores to provide water on the place also." Martha sat in silence for ten minutes then continued as if she had only just spoken, "We'll take the horses out tomorrow and I can show them to you. You need to know just where every water supply is in this country."

It had been over a month since Joe and Doug began employment as ringers at Cool Water Springs. To date, they had familiarised themselves with the terrain around them. Temporary repairs to several fences led to stockyard repairs where pens were unusable due to rotten fallen timber posts and rails. Martha showed them the pile of logs delivered some time ago for repairing the stockyards, but they discovered many of these eaten out by termites. After recovering what they could, they searched for any other logs that may fit the purpose, from the limited local timber growing on the property. Joe and Doug then worked to put together a usable set of stockyards.

When this work was completed, Martha planned to muster each paddock separately and record the number of cattle present on the property.

With tucker in their saddle bags and canteens topped up, Martha, Joe and Doug headed out to the north-west paddock first. This was where the older steers were left to fatten, as best they could in this country. Working methodically, the three riders pushed the animals into a corner where water and feed were available. The natural terrain and the fence line provided a funnel into and out of the corner. Martha and Doug sat on their horses at the exit of the funnel while Joe nudged the animals into the entrance pushing them towards the two waiting riders who counted the beasts as they passed. Once they compared the outcome of the count and found their estimates matched, Martha called for a break. She took the pencil from her top pocket and scrawled her findings on a dirty page of her notebook.

It was late when they returned to the homestead. Horses and riders sagged with exhaustion.

"Rest day tomorrow and then we'll go and see what young weaners we can find in the north-east paddock. We'll leave the mothers and their calves until last," Martha informed the two men at her kitchen table where they ate a beef stew with relish.

"You do realize it's the beginning of March tomorrow, don't you, Joe?" Doug lifted the brim of his hat and rubbed the sleeve of his shirt across his face. The pair sat on the log in the shade at the back of their hut cleaning their leather gear. Martha's two black and white collie dogs lay snuggled in behind Joe watching every move the men made.

"I won't argue with you on that subject, Doug. I saw you examining the shapely lady pictured on the calendar inside. I figured you might have taken the time to check the date while your attention was held so near."

"How come I never see ladies like that in real life?"

"I bet she charges a high price, sonny boy. Anyway, what's so important about the first week of March?"

"We've been here almost three months."

Joe scratched his head. "I don't know where that time went. At least we got the muster completed."

"Martha said she'd be back from town today. Hopefully, for her sake, she has received news in her mail of an interested buyer." Doug walked over to drink from the canteen hanging on the corner post. "Have you any idea where you want to go from here?"

Joe indicated with his finger for the canteen. Doug replaced the cork with a thud from his hand and sent the water container in a slow arc to land in his cousin's lap. Joe picked it up and went to remove the cork. He paused as he considered his cousin's question.

"You know, we've been so busy I haven't had time to give it much thought. What about you? Have you got any preferences?"

Both men's heads lifted when the dogs shot off towards the track. They ran around in circles at the front of the house barking fit to burst.

"That must be Martha coming now."

Joe and Doug finished what they were doing and made to follow the dogs. The sound of Martha's urgent calls set their feet running.

As they rounded the side of the house, they found Martha sitting on her seat in the wagon wearing a wide, stupid grin on her face.

"I thought you must be knocking on St. Nick's door when I heard the racket but I find you sitting here like a stunned mullet with a grin a clown could not fit on its face," Joe laughed.

Martha held an envelope up in her hands waving it back and forth.

"Can we take it that's good news?" Doug joined Joe's laughter.

"How can you tell?" Martha giggled. "I have a buyer – walk-in walk-out – for the first price I asked. The cattle will be extra but the buyer doesn't seem to want to quibble."

"Congratulations, Martha," Joe walked over and shook her hand.

Doug followed on Joe's heels. "That is really pleasing for you, Martha, well done."

Martha turned and began shuffling through the bag at her back.

"There's a letter here for you, too." She handed the second envelope over to Joe before releasing the brake as she flicked the reins across the horses' backs. Martha guided them towards the shed.

"We'll unload the supplies and unharness the horses, Martha," Doug called out.

Joe tore at the envelope addressed to Joe Daley c/- Marree Post Office. He was surprised to discover only the one page written in his father's strong hand.

Chill of Blame

Dear Joe

Today is the 30th of December. I am writing this letter while on a train back to Charters Towers.

I am sorry to have to tell you that we buried your mother at the Townsville cemetery yesterday morning. We kept it to a small service although all the Dawson clan from the north were present. It was a lovely service if one can call a funeral lovely. Isabelle had the church filled with your mother's favourite blooms. Her cousin Minnie played the organ.

I did not try to find you with a telegram because you would never have got back in time.

Your two sisters have accompanied me home to Billabong Downs. They send all their love to you and Doug.

All my love

From your father.

Wishing you safe travels.

Joe stood rooted to the spot. His gaze remained on the far horizon – unseeing. He did not notice Doug heading off towards the shed to unload the wagon and unharness the horses. Joe felt that old familiar feeling of guilt dragging him down into a pit of quicksand. He felt the bands of steel contracting around his chest. He struggled to breathe.

If I had been able to keep Billy from going to war, my brother would not have been killed, and my mother would not have become sick and died. Dad and the girls would not have reason to mourn. I should have been able to do something.

It was Billy's voice loud inside his head repeating his well-used warning, which drew Joe back.

"Brother, how many times have I told you? I will always do what I think is right for me; not what my mother thinks I should be doing.

I'm sorry, I know she always blames you, but you are not to feel any guilt because it has nothing to do with you. It is all me. Promise me you understand what I am saying. I don't want to be responsible for you feeling guilty."

Martha opened a small bottle of rum which she had brought back from town with her.

"Celebrating are we, Martha?" Doug asked with a grin.

"I certainly have a lot to celebrate. Cool Water Springs is sold and my son will be here in a week or two to help me pack my things. I would be honoured if you joined me in a drink or three to say thank you for your help and to share my good fortune."

After Martha piled the dishes into the wash tub in the kitchen, she called as she went through to the sitting room.

"Here Joe, Doug, I hope you fellas can sing." Martha stumbled onto a piano stool carved from local timber and stained with polish. She ran her hands across the cover of the keyboard which did little to remove the dust but left well-defined finger and hand prints. She opened the lid at the halfway mark but it clattered back into its usual place.

"Oops, that's getting heavier." Her second attempt proved successful. Joe and Doug shared a grin.

The cousins raised their eyebrows when Martha's fingers ran over the keyboard with obvious skill before she settled into a medley of tunes they all knew well.

Within half an hour the music came to a crashing end.

"Sorry, boys, I'm done in. Good night, I'll see you in the morning." Martha climbed awkwardly from the stool and stumbled off to her room.

Chill of Blame

It was left to Joe and Doug to close the piano lid. They slipped into the kitchen and washed up the dishes from the evening meal. The dishes were left to drain and dry on the table.

As they lay in their bunks, the question asked earlier in the day was bandied about once more.

"We could go to the coast and maybe get work at Port Augusta," Joe suggested.

"If that's what you want to do, I'll go along with that," Doug replied, "but I have to admit I'm not keen on stevedoring work."

"Nah, me either."

"Joe, was there a letter for me this time?"

"No, I'm sorry, mate. Dad wrote it on the train when he was travelling back to Charters Towers from Townsville after Christmas. Mum died and they buried her in Townsville."

"Holy cow, I'm sorry, Joe. I didn't know she was so ill."

"No, nor did I."

A lengthy silence hung like spiderwebs within the small room.

"What do you think they'll be doing at Billabong Downs at the moment?" Doug asked.

"March? Probably getting ready to select the stock for sale."

"You know your father might like to have you home to help with that. He'll be feeling a bit lonely I should think."

"Yeah, I'd been thinking along those lines but I don't want to cut our trip short either if there is still something else that you'd like to do." Joe rolled onto his side facing Doug with his hands under his face. "Cissy planned to go nursing training this year so she is probably in Townsville now, but Maud was mad keen on going back home to look after Dad. He won't be lonely then."

Doug laughed softly. "If I know Maud, Uncle William will be heading bush."

Even Joe found a chuckle. "Most likely."

"So, if we think of nothing else before Martha's son arrives, we're heading home, is that what you're saying?"

"I reckon; if you're agreeable."

CHAPTER THIRTY-SEVEN

Heading North

April – May 1921

It was the ex-Light Horseman Rankin at the Marree Hotel who introduced Joe and Doug to eight drovers heading back to Queensland having delivered two hundred bullocks to the railhead.

There was much laughter and cheers when Joe ran into a mate from the regiment, Max Farquharson, amongst the cattlemen.

"What the hell are you doing here?" they asked in unison.

"You first, Max, I'm glad to see the malaria, Spanish flu and your endless detentions didn't finish you off."

"What the hell am I doing here, you ask? I ask myself that question every morning I open my eyes. Hot, dry, dusty, and not enough water to raise a sweat – I must be mad." Max swallowed deeply from his glass of ale. "You remember Lieutenant Clay, don't you?"

"Your cousin, or something, wasn't he?"

"Yeah, Brian, that's him. He's now running his father's property in the Gulf. It's his stock me and the lads nursed through the centre, down to the markets. We're heading up the Birdsville Stock Route back home tomorrow."

"Can two blokes tag along? We're heading back to my father's place outside the Towers."

"All the more the merrier, as they say."

A hint of sunlight, eased across the plains as eight bleary-eyed drovers saddled up their riding horses and loaded their packhorses ready for the return journey. They were to pick up their remaining horses from a paddock near the blacksmith's shop on their way out of town.

With eyes no less dreary, Joe and Doug restocked their sugar bags and saddle bags with food (at a very reasonable price set by Rankin) and filled their water canteens.

Without cattle to gentle along each day, they made good time but the spare horses as well as the animals they rode still needed the time to forage through country where pasture was often very limited. Everyone was grateful for the bores the government had provided and the occasional waterholes still available in some of the Cooper Creek and Diamantina River overflows.

Each morning, despite the horse-tailer rising before the break of day to recover the horses hobbled out to eat and sleep, the sun was usually well up before the mounts were herded back from their night camps which were often far and wide from the drover's campsite. Within a few days, Joe and Max found their throats quite hoarse from talking and they settled on intermittent bursts of recollections.

Doug spent every day working close with the horse-tailer, named Irish. The Irishman never seemed to tire of the endless questions the young man threw at him and he certainly appreciated the help.

The days ran into each other and Doug lost track of time.

He asked Irish, "It can't be too far to Birdsville now, can it?"

"No, lad, it's just around the corner."

Doug's gaze followed the wide plains to the horizon disappearing in the distance.

"What corner would that be, Irish?"

"You'll see it when we come to it."

Both Doug and Irish turned at the explosion of a loud curse behind them.

Doug gasped at the sight of the long brown snake standing on a very small proportion of its tail with its head swaying towards Joe and his mount. The horse shied away spinning on his hind feet. Joe scrambled to grab the animal's mane, clench his thighs, and hold the reins. His body swayed out towards the snake's head as the horse twirled away. Joe struggled to throw his head back against the centrifugal force.

A rifle shot rang out. The serpent's head disintegrated in front of the stunned audience. The body flew up into the air and over the saltbush from under which it had appeared when disturbed by the foraging horse.

Joe quickly recovered and patted the neck of his mount. He turned to see where the shot had come from. He watched Max return the rifle to its sheath on the saddle.

"You need to be more circumspect when you're making friends there, Joe."

Joe grinned and nodded but said nothing as he struggled to regain his breath, return his heartbeat to a normal rate, and let his tongue search in vain for moisture in his mouth.

The sun rode high in the sky the next day as the welcome sight of the small town of Birdsville appeared in the mirage haze on the horizon.

Today Joe rode his favourite mount – the one named Marble. Joe always claimed he was like a rock of solid marble. His second horse Shoeshine, still irritable after its close encounter with the snake the previous day, had been returned to plodding behind under the weight of supplies.

Joe and Max moved ahead of the herd to select a campsite for the night on the southern side of Cooper Creek.

After the horses were watered and hobbled, the men collected wood and started a fire. The camp cook took only moments to recover his camp oven and mix up a damper mixture. Doug returned from the creek with a large can of water to make the tea.

Max and the cook joined in the discussion on who was going to be first in rotation to visit the Birdsville General Store and order replacements for their supplies. Joe smiled as he watched. He knew he could lay a sure bet on the supplies being least in the minds of the men offering to volunteer for the chore. The Hotel stood like a beacon in their thirsty minds.

Max declared two teams of four men.

"The first team is to be back in camp by four o'clock in the afternoon. The second team's curfew is at dusk, about seven o'clock." Max glared at each man in turn – daring them to argue. "Don't even think of being late or you'll spend our time at Cloncurry on horse duty." He turned around seeking his horse-tailer. "Irish, you take the first run into town. I'm sure Doug will be happy to wait until four."

Max mumbled aside to Joe. "You, Doug and I will be in the late team. I'll need someone to help me dig them out of the pub."

Irish may have had a thumping head when picaninny dawn sent a faint glow of light sneaking across the plain but he was on his way to follow the sounds of his horse bells. Doug followed in silence at his heels. Cook moaned at every step as he prepared the porridge, damper and jam for the men's first meal of the day. A flash of pain crinkled his face at every small clang of a can or pot. Even the metal ladle he lay with silent reverence upon a log.

The drovers continued north through Queensland. They followed the Diamantina River and its tributaries and the Hamilton River and its tributaries. As each day brought the men closer to their homes, smiles flashed often and laughter became more frequent. Max felt the impatience within the souls of his camp every night. They passed McKinlay and eventually pulled up at Julia Creek where the drovers' horses were left to graze on the town common while the men enjoyed cool drinks and showers at one of the two local hotels. Joe and Doug left their four horses in town at the blacksmith's yard.

The hotel rang with the sound of laughter and raucous voices. The following morning the group was to separate. The drovers were heading towards their home station northwest of Cloncurry. Joe and Doug were heading east to Charters Towers. They were in two minds about whether to travel on horseback or to load their horses onto the freight train in the morning.

Max did not look too well when he said farewell to Joe and Doug, neither of whom were heavy drinkers and issued little if any sympathy.

"Oh, well, one thing gives me hope. When you wake with a hangover you know the day can only get better; it can't get any worse." Max cringed at the echoing sound rising from the depths of the kitchen when a pan hit the concrete floor.

"See you, fellas." Joe and Doug shook hands all around.

With a grin on his face, Joe patted Max on the shoulder as he prepared to mount.

"Can I give you a hand up there, mate?"

"While I can stand, I'll get on this nag, my friend." Both men laughed.

With the sun on their backs, the drovers headed off. Joe and Doug watched them until they were lost in the distance.

"So, Dougie," Joe turned to his cousin, "what's it to be, train or hoof?"

"Train, I reckon. We'll try a bit of luxury. I'm looking forward to seeing Billabong Downs again."

A bright sun above failed miserably in warming the cool winter breeze as it whistled along the railway corridor at the Charters

Towers siding. A steam engine huffed and puffed while rail trucks clanged and rattled when they were shunted back and forth at the train driver's will. Eventually, Joe and Doug led their horses back to where their saddles and gear were stacked neatly against the wall of a store shed.

"I think we deserve a cold ale before we head over to Pop's place. It's too late to ride home tonight. Gran and Pop won't mind if we camp with them for the night and leave early in the morning." Joe cinched his girth strap.

"Sounds good to me." Doug swung up into his saddle.

In nearly twelve months, things seemed so different and yet so the same. Doug's head swivelled on his shoulders in an attempt to examine each of the half-dozen cars motoring on the roads. They turned into Gill Street to discover a familiar team of horses harnessed into a just as familiar wagon.

"One of our fathers must be in town, if not both."

"It could be Geoff, Maggie and the kids."

Joe guided his mount towards the nearest hitching rail and dismounted. Hardly had he knotted the reins when he was swept up into what felt like a swirling cyclone. He grunted as his sister wrapped her arms around him. She laughed and squealed as she spun her brother in a circle. Joe caught her around the waist to prevent them both from landing in the dust.

"Very ladylike, Little Sis, is that what they taught you at that fancy school in Townsville?"

Maud Daley stepped back and pinned her gaze on her brother. Happy tears poured down her cheeks.

"Damn propriety, Joe, I'm just so glad to see you and Doug back safely." Maud flipped a wave to her cousin.

Doug burst out laughing. "Yep, I'd say she's from a real ladies' school, Joe."

Maggie Bardon approached from the nearest shop in a more sedate manner.

"Joe and Doug, it's so lovely to see you home again." She moved over to give them both a hug.

"Hello, Mrs. Bardon, it's great to be home. How is Mr. Bardon and the children?"

"Everyone is well, thanks, Joe. Geoff is at the merchandise store and I think you'll find your father in the bank." Her clean but work-worn hands pointed to the imposing building across the street. She looked over at Doug. "I'm sorry, dear, your father didn't come into town today. I bet he would have if he knew you were coming home."

"Thanks, Mrs. Bardon, I'll see him tomorrow. How long will you be in town?"

"We'll be heading back first thing in the morning."

The group all turned at the sound of the hoy from across the street. William Daley's footsteps hastened towards them his face covered in a wide smile. Geoff followed in his wake with a grin no less wide.

William's proffered handshake for his son changed to a bear hug.

"Son, we missed you so much." Both father and son's eyes glinted with moisture. William stepped back to take in the vision of his younger son. "You are looking good, lad. Someone's been looking after you."

Joe and Doug grinned in unison as they turned to greet Geoff with a warm handshake.

"That would be the little old snowy-haired, firecracker called Widow Watson."

"You can tell us all about her later. Come on boys, your Pops will want to hear all you've been up to and you can guarantee Gran will want to smother you in tears." William turned back to Maggie and Maud. "Are you ladies finished spending all my money?"

Maggie turned to Maud and pointed to the shop from which they had both exited.

"Run inside will you, Maud, and collect our parcels? I forgot them in all the excitement of seeing our boys out here."

After leaving Maggie and Geoff at Maggie's sister's house, the Daleys made their way to Pop and Gran Daley's home where the reunion was no less enthusiastic. Even when they were in their beds and the lights had been doused, occasional questions drifted out to the verandah bunks where the returned travellers had settled. Their answers turned to soft grunts declaring a truce.

In their kitchen at Billabong Downs, Miles and Fran lifted their heads from their quiet afternoon tea at the sound of the dogs barking.

"That will be William back," Miles offered.

Fran peeped through the curtains. Miles sat stunned at the sight of his wife tearing off like an excited youngster to meet whoever approached. He drank another swallow of tea before he rose from the kitchen table to see what all the fuss was about. His racing footsteps almost overtook those of his wife when their son pulled up his horse in a cloud of dust.

Fran waved the dust away from her face and rushed over to almost drag her son from the saddle. She drew him into a hug.

"I am so glad to see you home again, Doug." Tears streamed down her face.

"Don't look like it, with all those tears," Doug struggled to laugh as he fought back tears of his own.

Miles held both his wife and his son in a wild embrace.

William handed the reins over to Geoff Bardon and jumped to the ground.

"Thanks, Geoff, we'll be over shortly to unload," William called as Geoff guided the wagon firstly to his own house to drop off his family and then on to the shed.

Leading the two pack horses, Joe rode up to where his father stood with a wide and silly grin on his face. They joined Fran, Miles and Doug in the celebratory reunions.

An exhausted Maud had been sent to bed half an hour earlier but William and Joe sat on the top step in the moonlight. They sipped on the whiskey William had poured for them both.

"Son, I want to tell you something your sisters don't know yet. Maybe when they are older, I'll tell them. For now, only Bayden and Isabelle Dawson and I know. Your mother did not just die of her illness – well not directly – she hung herself. I did not want you to find out by accident. You will need time to reconcile yourself with this."

Joe's head snapped up. "How could she do this in the hospital?"

"It was at Christmas; the doctor had given her a few days' leave to share Christmas with us at her parents' house in Townsville. She had obviously been planning it for a long time. Bayden and I found her on Christmas morning in the shed."

Joe jumped to his feet. His heart pounded inside his chest. He opened his mouth to speak but found he could not. Joe clenched his hands in frustration and anger. Slowly he regained some control. The words rushed forth.

"My God, right up until the end Mum thought of no one, but herself. She always made everyone's life miserable when she couldn't get what she wanted."

"Don't be too harsh on your mother, Joe, although I do understand where you are coming from. She never did treat you fairly."

But Joe had stopped listening. He felt himself sinking into the familiar mire of guilt. He struggled to breathe. His mouth felt as dry as the desert sand. Then, he heard his brother Billy's voice, louder than the pounding inside his skull.

Joe, how many times have I told you? How many times? You are not to let Mum make you feel guilty for anything I do. They are my choices and if required, then my guilt. Do you understand?

Joe sat down again beside his father and wrapped his arm around William's shoulder.

"I'm sorry for your grief, Dad. I refuse to accept any guilt. Billy always berated me about doing that. Billy said he was the only one responsible for whatever he did."

William reached over to hold his son. "I'm glad to hear you say that, Joe. I did not want you to think this was all your fault. Your mother was her own worst enemy because she never let Billy be who he wanted to be. Thank goodness Billy was strong enough to make his own decisions and to live his life how he wanted."

THE END

CHARACTERS Chill of Blame

Billabong Downs

William Daley	Co-owner Billabong Downs
Mabel Daley	Wife of William Daley
Billy, Joe, Cissy, Maud	Children of William & Mabel
Miles Daley	Co-owner Billabong Downs
Fran Daley	Wife of Miles Daley
Mick, Doug, Mavis	Children of Miles & Fran
Geoff Bardon	Head Stockman
Maggie Bardon	Wife of Geoff Bardon
Stewie, Evie, Splinter	Children of Geoff & Maggie
Pop/s Daley	Father of William and Miles
Gran Daley	Wife of Pop/s Daley
Bayden Dawson	Father of Mabel Daley
Isabelle Dawson	Mother of Mabel Daley
Dr. Munson	Doctor Charters Towers
Dr. Elliot Lundy	Doctor Townsville
Gazza	Roustabout
Mr. Menkens & Lucky Minky	Mailman & son

Australian Light Horse Officers

Sgt Sibley (Training Camp)	Corp Linton (Training Camp)
Gen. Allenby	ALH Sinai & Pakistan
Lt. Smithers, Sgt Fielding	ALH Sinai & Pakistan
Sgt Pritchard	ALH Sinai & Pakistan

Lt Brian Clay   Cousin of Max Farquharson
Dr. Rabatel   French Hospital Damascus

ALH Remount Unit
Major Peter Forbes   Major David Beams (Vet)
Lt. Baldwin   Lt. Burke
Sgt Berryman   Sgt Pete Dingle
Mick McCready (Farrier)   Corp Rankin (signalman)
Clappers (nickname)

Section/Tent mates
Carter, Martin, (with Billy & Joe) Section in training
Bluey, Sullivan, Mouse Streak   Tent mates in training

Reorganization Mid. East
Bennet, Max Farquharson (with Joe & Billy)
Beatson, Gardener (with Carter & Martin)
Toby Rawlins, George Turner (with Max and Joe)

NILE DELTA WW1

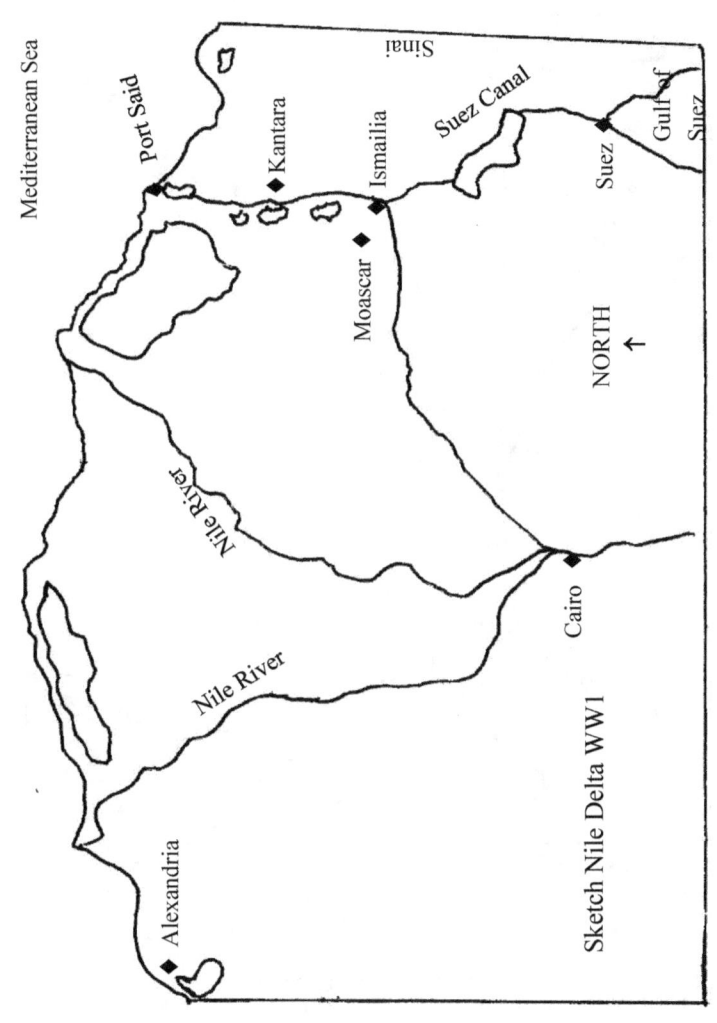

Sketch Nile Delta WW1

SINAI DESERT WW1

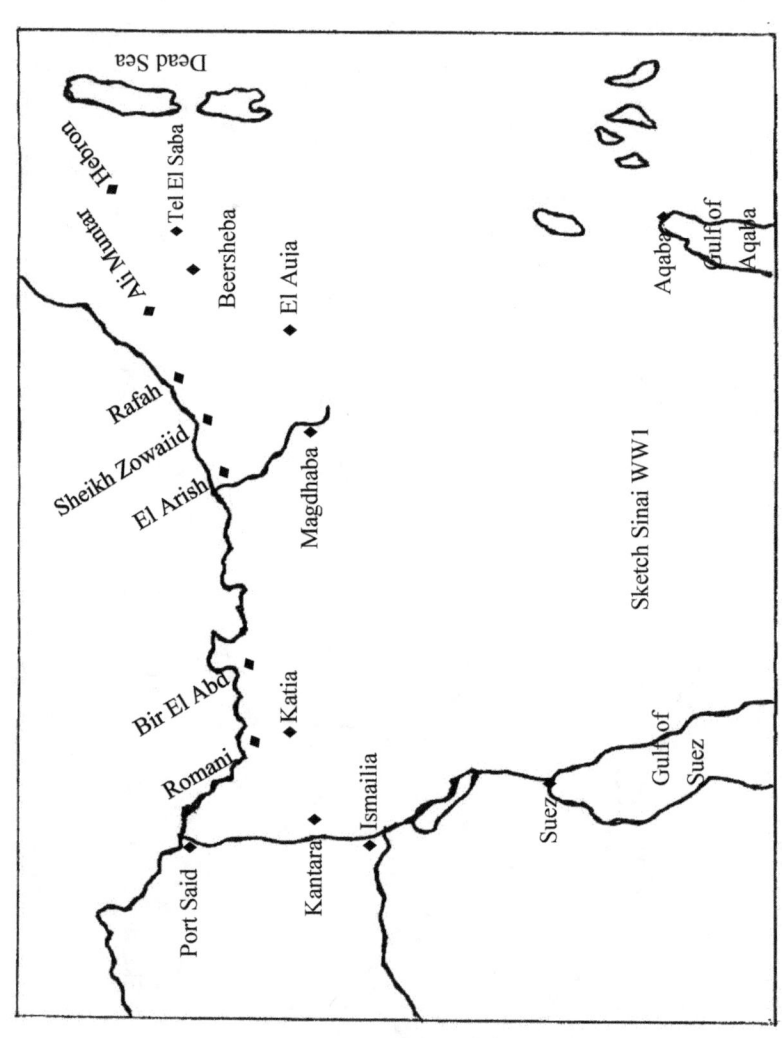

PALESTINE WW1

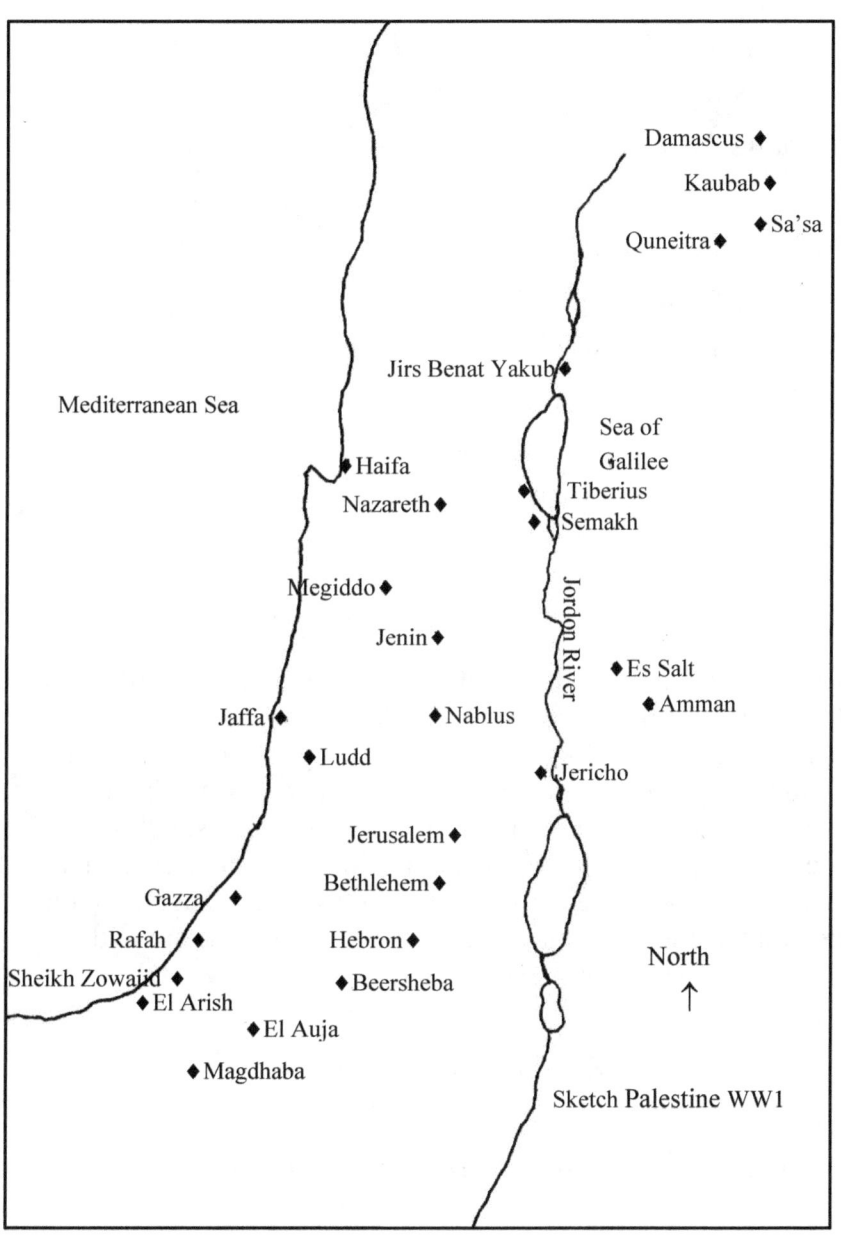

Sketch Palestine WW1

Previous Books by Elizabeth Rimmington:

Trilogy:

Shadow of the Northern Orchid – 2019

Shadows on the Goldfield Track – 2020

Shadows Across Cape York – 2022

Also, by the same author:

Burdekin Heartbeats – 2020

Rhylla's Secret – 2021

Chill of Blame – 2024

Elizabeth Rimmington

Elizabeth is an Australian author living in a rural area of South-East Queensland. Born in North Queensland, Elizabeth retains a deep love for Queensland and the north. During a career in nursing followed by several years driving a taxi cab, Elizabeth has met many and varied people from all walks of life. A storehouse of memories from which to plunder and develop story characters able to infiltrate the reader's heart by osmosis. Their laughter, their heartbreak and their pain will fill the booklover's soul with happiness, tears, fear and empathy.

Visit Elizabeth Rimmington at her website

www.elizabethrimmington.com.au

Find her on Facebook – elizabethrimmington.author

www.ingramcontent.com/pod-product-compliance
Lightning Source LLC
Chambersburg PA
CBHW060816120726
47909CB00006B/1951